Penelope could see guests starting to move. Reaching for those bags of confetti stars and preparing themselves to shower the bride and groom as they went down the aisle together.

She stepped away to move closer, but Rafe's voice stopped her.

"That promise," he asked quietly. "The one you believe in. What is it, exactly?"

Startled, she turned her head. "Security," she responded. "Family. It's the promise of a safe place, I guess. Somewhere you know you'll always be loved."

There was something soft in his eyes now. Something sad?

"You're one of the lucky ones, then."

"Because I believe in marriage?"

"Because you know what it's like to have a family. Parents. You know what it's like to live in that safe place."

And he didn't? Something huge squeezed inside her chest and made her breath come out in a huff. She understood yearning. Her life might look perfect from the outside but she wanted him to know that she understood. That they had a connection here that very few people could have. They might be complete opposites, but in that moment, it felt like they were on opposite sides of the

THE WEDDING PLANNER AND THE CEO

BY
ALISON ROBERTS

Published in Great Britain 2015
by Mills & Boon, an imprint of Harlequin (UK) Limited,
Eton House, 18-24 Paradise Road, Richmond, Surrey, TW9 1SR

© 2015 Alison Roberts

ISBN: 978-0-263-25135-7

23-0515

Harlequin (UK) Limited's policy is to use papers that are natural, renewable and recyclable products and made from wood grown in sustainable forests. The logging and manufacturing processes conform to the legal environmental regulations of the country of origin.

Printed and bound in Spain
by CPI, Barcelona

Alison Roberts is a New Zealander, currently lucky enough to live near a beautiful beach in Auckland. She is also lucky enough to write for Mills & Boon® Medical Romance™ and other lines. A primary schoolteacher in a former life, she is also a qualified paramedic. She loves to travel and dance, drink champagne and spend time with her daughter and her friends.

CHAPTER ONE

'*No?*'

The smile was sympathetic but the head-shake emphasised the negative response and the receptionist's raised eyebrows suggested that Penelope must have known she was dreaming when she thought her request might be considered reasonable.

'There must be *someone* I could speak to?' It was harder to say no face to face than over the phone, which was, after all, why she'd taken time out of her crazy schedule to fight London traffic and come to the company's head office in person.

In desperation?

'There's really no point.' The receptionist's smile faded slightly. 'You might be able to engage a cowboy to let off a few fireworks on a week's notice but to get the kind of show the best company in the country has to offer, you have to book in advance. *Months* in advance.'

'I didn't have months. My bride only decided she wanted fireworks this morning. I'm talking Bridezilla, here, you know?'

There was a wary edge to the receptionist's gaze

now. Was she worried that Penelope might be capable of following her client's example and throwing an epic tantrum?

'I understand completely but I'm sorry, there's still nothing I can do to help. For future reference, you can book online to make an appointment to talk to one of our sales reps.'

'I don't want to talk to a sales rep.' Penelope tapped into the extra height her four-inch heels provided. 'I want to talk to your manager. Or director. Or whoever it is that runs this company.'

The smile vanished completely. 'We have a chief executive officer. All Light on the Night is an international company. An *enormous* international company. We do shows like the Fourth of July on the Brooklyn Bridge in New York. New Year's Eve on the Sydney Harbour Bridge in Australia.' Her tone revealed just how far out of line Penelope had stepped. 'You might very well want to talk to him but there's no way on earth Ralph Edwards would be interested in talking to *you*.'

'Really? Why not?'

The curiosity sounded genuine and it came from a male voice behind Penelope. The effect on the young woman in front of her was astonishing. The receptionist paled visibly and her mouth opened and closed more than once, as if she was trying to recall all the vehement words that had just escaped.

Penelope turned to see a tall man and registered dark hair long enough to look tousled, faded denim jeans and…cowboy boots? One of the sales reps, perhaps?

'She…doesn't have an appointment.' The receptionist was clearly rattled. 'She just walked in and wants to book a show. A *wedding*...'

The man's gaze shifted to Penelope and made her want to smooth the close fit of her skirt over her hips even though she knew perfectly well it couldn't be creased. Or raise a hand to make sure no errant tresses had escaped the French braiding that described a perfect crescent from one side of her forehead to meet the main braid on the back of her head.

'Congratulations.' His voice had a rich, low timbre. It made Penelope think of gravel rolling around in something thick and delicious. Like chocolate.

'Sorry?' Was he congratulating her on her choice of this company?

'On your engagement.'

'Oh...it's not *my* wedding.'

That was a dream too distant to be visible even with a telescope at the moment. And there was no point even picking up a telescope until she knew what it was she was looking for, and how could she know that until she discovered who she really was and what she was capable of? Come to think of it, this was the first step towards that distant dream, wasn't it? The first time she was taking a leap out of any known comfort zone. Doing something *she* wanted— just for herself.

'I'm an event manager,' she said, after the barely perceptible pause. 'It's my client who's getting married.'

'Ah...' The spark of polite interest was fading rapidly. 'You've come to the right place, then. I'm sure Melissa will be able to help you with whatever arrangements you want to make.'

Melissa made a choked sound. 'She wants the show next Saturday, Mr Edwards.'

Mr Edwards? The terribly important CEO of this huge international company wore faded jeans and cowboy boots to work? Penelope was clearly overdressed but she couldn't let it faze her enough to lose this unexpected opportunity.

One that was about to slip away. She saw the look that implied complete understanding and went as far as forgiving the company receptionist for her unprofessional exchange with a potential client. She also saw the body language that suggested this CEO was about to retreat to whatever top-floor executive sanctuary he'd unexpectedly appeared from.

'I'll give her a list of other companies that might be able to help,' Melissa said.

'I don't want another company.' The words burst out with a speed and emphasis that took Penelope by surprise. 'I...I have to have the best and...and you're the best, aren't you?'

Of course they were. The entire wall behind the receptionist's desk was a night sky panorama of exploding fireworks. Pyrotechnic art with a combination of shape and colour that was mind-blowing.

The man's mouth twitched. Maybe he'd been surprised, too. 'We certainly are.' Amusement reached his eyes with a glint. Very dark eyes, Penelope noticed. As black as sin, even. Her pulse skipped and sped up. There was only one thing to do when you found yourself so far out of your depth like this. Aim for the surface and kick hard.

'It might be worth your while to consider it.' She snatched a new gulp of air. 'This is a celebrity wedding. The kind of publicity that can't be bought.' She managed a smile. 'I understand you specialise in huge shows but New Year's Eve and the Fourth of July only happen once a year, don't they? You must need the smaller stuff as well? This could be a win-win situation for both of us.'

An eyebrow quirked this time. Was he intrigued by her audacity? Was that a sigh coming from Melissa's direction?

'You have a managerial board meeting in fifteen minutes, Mr Edwards.'

'Give me ten,' Penelope heard herself saying, her gaze still fixed on him. 'Please?'

She looked like some kind of princess. Power-dressed and perfectly groomed. The spiky heels of her shoes looked like they could double as a lethal weapon and he could imagine that the elegant, leather briefcase she carried might be full of lengthy checklists and legally binding contracts.

She was the epitome of everything Rafe avoided like the plague so why on earth was he ushering her into his office and closing the door behind them? Perhaps he was trying to send a message to the junior staff that even difficult clients needed to be treated with respect. Or maybe there had been something in the way she'd looked when he'd suggested it was her own wedding she'd come here to organise.

A flicker of...astonishment? He'd probably have the

same reaction if someone suggested he was about to walk down the aisle.

Maybe not for the same reasons, though. The kind of people he had in his life were as non-conformist as he was, whereas this woman looked like she'd already have the preferred names picked out for the two perfectly behaved children she would eventually produce. One girl and one boy, of course. She might have them already, tidied away in the care of a nanny somewhere, but a quick glance at her left hand as she walked past him revealed an absence of any rings so maybe it had been embarrassment that it was taking so long rather than astonishment that had registered in that look.

No. More likely it was something about the way she'd said 'please'. That icy self-control with which she held herself had jarred on both occasions with something he'd seen flicker in her face but the flicker that had come with that 'please' had looked like determination born of desperation and he could respect that kind of motivation.

'Take a seat.' He gestured towards an area that had comfortable seating around a low coffee table—an informal meeting space that had a wall of glass on one side to show off the fabulous view of the Wimbledon golf course.

Not that she noticed the gesture. Clearly impressed to the point of being speechless, she was staring at the central feature of the penthouse office. A mirror-like tube of polished steel that was broken in the middle. The layer of stones on the top of the bottom section had flames flickering in a perfect circle.

He liked it that she was so impressed. He'd designed this feature himself and he was proud of it. But he didn't have time for distractions like showing off.

'Ms…?'

'Collins. Penelope Collins.'

'Rafe Edwards.' The handshake was brief but surprisingly firm. This time she noticed his invitation and he watched her seat herself on one of the couches. Right on the edge as if she might need to leap up and flee at any moment. Legs angled but not crossed.

Nice legs. Was that subtle tug on the hem of her skirt because she'd noticed him noticing? Rafe glanced at his watch and then seated himself on the opposite couch. Or rather perched on his favourite spot, with a hip resting on the broad arm of the couch.

'So…a celebrity wedding?'

She nodded. 'You've heard of Clarissa Bingham?'

'Can't say I have.'

'Oh… She's a local Loxbury girl who got famous in a reality TV show. She's marrying a football star. Blake Summers.'

'I've heard of *him*.'

'It's a huge wedding and we were lucky enough to get the best venue available. Loxbury Hall?'

'Yep. Heard of that, too.'

Her surprise was evident in the way she blinked—that rapid sweep of thick, dark eyelashes. He could understand the surprise. Why should he know anything about a small town on the outskirts of the New Forest between here and Southampton? Or an eighteenth-century manor house that had been used as a function venue for the last decade? He wasn't about to tell her that this location did, in fact, give him a rather close connection to this upcoming event.

'It could be the last wedding ever held there because the property's just been sold and nobody knows whether the new owner will carry it on as a business venture.'

'Hmm.' Rafe nodded but his attention was straying. This Penelope Collins might not be remotely his type but any red-blooded male could appreciate that she was beautiful. Classically beautiful with that golden blonde hair and that astonishing porcelain skin. Or maybe not so classical given that her eyes were brown rather than blue. Nice combination, that—blonde hair and brown eyes—and her skin had a sun-kissed glow to it that suggested an excellent spray tan rather than risking damage from the real thing. She was probably no more than five feet three without those killer heels and her drink of choice was probably a gin and tonic. Or maybe a martini with an olive placed perfectly in the centre of the toothpick.

'Sorry…what was that?'

'It's the perfect place for a fireworks show. The terrace off the ballroom looks down at the lake. There'll be six hundred people there and major magazine coverage. I could make sure that your company gets excellent publicity.'

'We tend to get that from our larger events. Or special-effects awards from the movie industry. There are plenty of smaller companies out there that specialise in things like birthday parties or weddings.'

'But I want this to be spectacular. The *best*…'

She did. He could see that in her eyes. He'd had that kind of determination once—the need to get to the top and be the very best, and it hadn't been easy, especially that first time.

'Is this your first wedding?'

Her composure slipped and faint spots of pink appeared on her cheeks. 'I run a very successful catering company so I've been involved in big events for many years. Moving to complete event design and execution *has* been a more recent development.'

'So this *is* your first wedding.'

She didn't like the implied putdown. Something like defiance darkened her eyes and the aura of tension around the rest of her body kicked up a notch.

'The event is running like clockwork so far. Everything's in place for the ceremony and reception. The entertainment, decorations and catering are locked in. Clarissa is thrilled with her dress and the photographers are over the moon by the backdrops the venue offers. We even have the best local band playing live for the dancing. You must have heard of Diversion?'

Rafe's breath came out in an unexpected huff. Another connection? This was getting weird.

'It was all going perfectly until this morning, when Clarissa decided they had to have fireworks to finish the night. She had a complete meltdown when I told her that it was probably impossible to organise at such late notice.'

Rafe had dealt with some meltdowns from clients so he knew how difficult it could be, especially when your reputation might be hanging by a thread. Maybe Penelope was reliving some of the tension and that was what was giving her voice that almost imperceptible wobble. A hint of vulnerability that tugged on something deep in his gut with an equally almost imperceptible 'ping'.

'When it got to the stage that she was threatening to pull the plug on the whole wedding, I said I'd make some enquiries.'

'So you came straight to the top?' The corner of Rafe's mouth lifted. 'Have to say your style is impressive, Ms Collins.'

He'd done the same thing himself more than once.

'I know I'm asking a lot and it probably is impossible but at least I can say I tried and…and maybe you can point me in the direction of an alternative company that might be able to do at least a reasonable job.'

There was a moment's silence as Rafe wondered how to respond. Yes, he could send her hunting for another company but nobody reputable would take this on.

'Have you any idea what's involved with setting up a professional fireworks show?'

She shook her head. She caught her bottom lip between her teeth, too, and the childlike gesture of trepidation was enough to make Rafe wonder just how much of her look was a front. And what was she trying to hide?

'Long-term planning is essential for lots of reasons. We have to have meetings with the client to discuss budgets and the style and timing of the show.'

'The budget won't be an issue.'

'Are you sure? We're talking over a thousand pounds a minute here.'

'I'm sure.' She sounded confident but he'd seen the movement of her throat as she'd swallowed hard.

'The show gets fired to music. That has to be chosen and then edited and correlated to the pyrotechnic effects. The soundtrack has to be cued and programmed into a computer.'

Once upon a time, Rafe had done all these jobs himself. Long, hard nights of getting everything perfect on an impossible schedule. The memories weren't all bad, though. That kind of hard work had got him where he was today.

'The fireworks have to be chosen and sourced. The site has to be mapped and the display layout planned for firing points. There are safety considerations and you have to allow for a fallout range that could be over a hundred metres. You have to get permits. And this all has to happen before you start setting up—fusing all the fireworks together in the correct sequence, putting electric matches in each fuse run, and then testing the whole package to make sure it's going to work.'

'I understand.' There was a stillness about her that suggested she was preparing to admit defeat. 'And you were right. I had no idea how much work was involved. I'm sorry...' She got to her feet. 'It was very kind of you to take the time to explain things.'

The door to the office opened as she finished speaking. Melissa poked her head around the edge.

'They're waiting for you in the boardroom, Mr Edwards.'

Rafe got to his feet, too. Automatically, he held out his hand and Penelope took it. It was a clasp rather than a shake and, for some bizarre reason, Rafe found himself holding her hand for a heartbeat longer than could be considered professional.

Long enough for that odd ping of sensation he'd felt before to return with surprising force. Enough force to be a twist that couldn't be dismissed. A memory of what it was like to be struggling and then come up against a brick wall? Or maybe articulating all the steps of the challenge of delivering a show had reminded him that he'd been able to do all that himself once. Every single job that he now employed experts in the field to do on his behalf.

He could do it again if he wanted. Good grief, he ran one of the biggest pyrotechnic companies in the world—he could do whatever he wanted.

And maybe…he wanted to do *this*.

He had everything he'd always dreamed of now but this wasn't the first time he'd felt that niggle that something was missing. Wasn't the best way to find something to retrace your footsteps? Going back to his roots as a young pyrotechnician would certainly be retracing footsteps that were long gone. Had he dropped something so long ago he'd forgotten what it actually was?

'There is one way I might be able to help,' he found himself saying.

'A personal recommendation to another company?' Hope made her eyes shine. They had a dark outline to their pupils, he noticed. Black on brown. A perfect ring to accentuate them. Striking.

'No. I was thinking more in terms of doing it myself.'

Her breath caught in an audible gasp. 'But…all those things you said…'

'They still stand. Whether or not it's doable would depend on cooperation from your clients with any restrictions, such as what fireworks we happen to have in stock. The site survey and decisions on style and music would have to be done immediately. Tomorrow.'

'I could arrange that.' That breathless excitement in her voice was sweet. 'What time would you be available?'

'It's Saturday. We don't have any major shows happening and I make my own timetable. What time would your clients be available?'

'We'll be on site all day. They have a dance lesson in the morning and we're doing a ceremony rehearsal in the afternoon. Just come anytime that suits. Would you like me to email you a map?'

'That won't be necessary. By coincidence, I'm familiar with the property, which is another point in favour of pulling this off. The site survey wouldn't be an issue.'

The massive image of exploding fireworks was impossible to miss as Penelope left the office but it was more than simply a glorious advertisement now. For a heartbeat, it felt like she was actually *there*—seeing them happen and hearing the bone-shaking impact of the detonations.

Excitement, that was what it was. Ralph Edwards might look like a cowboy but he was going to help her get the biggest break she could ever have. Clarissa's wedding was going to finish with the kind of bang that would have her at the top of any list of desirable wedding planners. On her way to fame and fortune and a lifelong career that couldn't be more perfect for her. She would be completely independent and then she'd be able to decide what else she might need in her life.

Who else, maybe…

Thanks to the traffic, the drive back to Loxbury was going to take well over two hours, which meant she would be up very late tonight, catching up with her schedule. She could use the time sensibly and think ahead about any potential troubleshooting that might be needed.

Or she could think about fireworks instead. The kind of spectacular shapes and colours that would be painted against the darkness of a rural sky but probably seen by every inhabitant of her nearby hometown and have images reproduced in more than one glossy magazine.

As the miles slid by—despite an odd initial resistance—Penelope also found herself thinking about the tousled cowboy she would have to be working with in the coming week to make this happen. He had to be the most unlikely colleague she could have imagined. Someone she would have instinctively avoided like the plague under normal circumstances, even. But if he could help her make this wedding the event that would launch her career, she was up for it.

Couldn't wait to see him again, in fact.

CHAPTER TWO

'No, no, Monsieur Blake. Do not bend over your lady like that, or you will lose your balance and you will both end up on the floor. Step to the side and bend your knee as you dip her. Keep your back *straight*.'

Blake Summers abruptly let go of his bride-to-be but Clarissa caught his arm. 'Don't you dare walk out on me again. How are we ever going to learn this dance if you keep walking away?'

He shook his arm free. 'I can't do it, babe. I told you that. I. Don't. Dance.'

'But this our *wedding* dance.' The tone advertised imminent tears. 'Everyone will be watching. Taking photos.'

'This whole thing is all about the photos, isn't it? I'm up to *here* with it.' Muscles in the young football star's arm bunched as he raised a fist well above head level. 'You know what? If I'd had any idea of how much crap this would all involve I would have thought twice about asking you to marry me.'

'Oh, my God…' Clarissa buried her face in her hands and started sobbing. Penelope let out a long sigh. She felt rather inclined to follow her example.

The dance teacher, Pierre, came towards her with a wonderfully French gesture that described exactly how frustrated he was also becoming.

'It's only a simple dance,' he muttered. 'We've been here for an hour and we have only covered the first twenty seconds of the song. Do you know how long Monsieur Legend's "All of Me" goes for?' He didn't wait for Penelope to respond. 'Five minutes and eight seconds—that's how long. *C'est de la torture.*'

Blake's expression morphed from anger to irritation and finally defeat. 'I'm sorry, babe. I didn't mean it. Really.' He put his arms around Clarissa. 'I just meant we could have eloped or something and got away from all the fuss.'

'You did mean it.' Clarissa struggled enough to escape his embrace. 'You don't want to marry me.' She turned her back on him and hugged herself tightly.

'I do. I love you, babe. All of me, you know, loves all of you.'

Clarissa only sobbed louder. This was Penelope's cue to enter stage left. She walked briskly across the polished wood of the floor and put an arm around her client's shoulders.

'It's okay, hon. We just need to take a break.' She gave a squeeze. 'It's such an emotional time in the final run-up to such a big day. Things can seem a bit overwhelming, can't they?'

Clarissa nodded, sniffing loudly.

'And we've got a whole week to sort this dance out. Just a few moves that you can repeat for the whole song, isn't that right, Pierre?'

Pierre shrugged. 'As you say. Only a few moves.'

Penelope turned her most encouraging smile on the groom-to-be. 'You're up for that, aren't you, Blake? You do know how incredibly sexy it is for a man to be able to dance, even a little bit, don't you?'

'Dancing's for pansies,' Blake muttered.

Penelope's smile dimmed. She could feel a vibe coming from Pierre's direction that suggested she might be about to lose her on-call dance teacher.

'How 'bout this?' she suggested brightly. 'We'll put the music on and Pierre will dance with Clarissa to show you what you'll look like on the night. So you can see how romantic it will be. How gorgeous you'll both look.'

Blake scowled but Clarissa was wiping tears from her face with perfectly French-manicured fingertips. The sideways glance at the undeniably good-looking dance teacher was flirtatious enough for Penelope to be thankful that Blake didn't seem to notice.

'Fine.' He walked towards the tall windows that doubled as doors to the flagged terrace. Penelope joined him as Pierre set the music up and talked to Clarissa.

'Gorgeous view, isn't it?'

'I guess. The lake's okay. I like those dragons that spout water.'

'The whole garden's wonderful. You should have a look around while the weather's this nice. There's even a maze.'

The notes of the romantic song filled the space as Pierre swept Clarissa into his arms and began leading her expertly through the moves. Blake crossed his arms and scowled.

'It's easy for her. She's been doing salsa classes for years. But she expects me to look like *him*? Not going to happen. Not in this lifetime.'

Penelope shook her head and smiled gently. 'I think all she wants is to be moving to the song she's chosen in the arms of the man she loves.'

A sound of something like resignation came from Blake but Penelope could feel the tension lift. Until his head turned and he stiffened again.

'Who's that?' he demanded. 'I told you I didn't want anyone watching this lesson. I feel like enough of an idiot as it is. If that's a photographer, hoping to get a shot of me practising, he can just get the hell out of here.'

Penelope turned her head. The ballroom of Loxbury Hall ran the length of the house between the two main wings. There were probably six huge bedrooms above it upstairs. Quite some distance to recognise a shadowy figure standing in the doorway that led to the reception hall but she knew who it was instantly. From the man's height, perhaps. Or the casual slouch to his stance. That shaft of sensation deep in her belly had to be relief. He'd kept his word.

She could trust him?

'It's Ralph Edwards!' she exclaimed softly. 'I told you he was coming some time today. To discuss your fireworks?'

'Oh…yeah…' Blake's scowl vanished. 'Fireworks are cool.' He brightened. 'Does that mean I don't have to do any more dancing today?'

'Let's see what Pierre's schedule is. We'd have time

for another session later. After the meeting with the florist maybe. Before the rehearsal.'

It was another couple of minutes before the song ended. Clarissa was following Pierre's lead beautifully and Penelope tried to focus, letting her imagination put her client into her wedding dress. To think how it was going to look with the soft lighting of hundreds of candles. The song was a great choice. If Blake could end up learning the moves well enough to look a fraction as good as Pierre, it was going to be a stunning first dance.

Details flashed into her mind, like the best places to put the huge floral arrangements and groups of candles to frame the dance floor. Where the photographers and cameramen could be placed to be inconspicuous but still get great coverage. Whether it was going to work to have the wrist loop to hold the train of Clarissa's dress out of the way. She scribbled a note on the paper clipped to the board she carried with her everywhere on days like this so that none of these details would end up being forgotten.

The dress. Candles. Flowers. There was so much to think about and yet the thing she was most aware of right now was the figure standing at the ballroom doorway, politely waiting for the music to finish before interrupting. Why did his presence make her feel so nervous? Her heart had picked up speed the moment she'd seen him and it hadn't slowed any since. That initial twinge of relief had shattered into butterflies in her stomach now, and they were twisting and dancing rather like Clarissa was.

Not that the feeling was altogether unpleasant. It reminded her of the excitement that strong physical attraction to someone could produce.

Was she physically attracted to Ralph Edwards?

Of course not. The very idea was so ridiculous she knew that wasn't the cause. No. This nervousness was because the fireworks show wasn't a done deal yet and there could be another tantrum from Clarissa to handle if the meeting didn't go well.

It had to go well. Penelope held the clipboard against her chest and clutched it a little more tightly as the music faded.

Rafe was quite content to have a moment or two to observe.

To bask in the glow of satisfaction he'd had from the moment he'd driven through the ornate gates of this historic property.

A property he now owned, for heaven's sake.

Who would have thought that he'd end up with a life like this? Not him, that's for sure. Not back in the day when he'd been one of a busload of disadvantaged small children who'd been brought to Loxbury Hall for a charity Christmas party. He'd seen the kind of kingdom that rich people could have. People with enough money to make their own rules. To have families that stayed together and lived happily ever after.

Yes. This was a dream come true and he was loving every minute of it.

He was loving standing here, too.

This room was stunning. A few weeks ago he'd had to use his imagination to think of what it might be like with music playing and people dancing on the polished floor. Reality was even better. He was too far away to get more than a general impression of the girl who was dancing but he could see enough. A wild cascade of platinum blonde waves. A tight, low-cut top that revealed a cleavage to die for. Enhanced by silicone, of course, but what did that matter? She was a true WAG and Blake Summers was a lucky young man.

What a contrast to Ms Collins—standing there clutching a clipboard and looking as tense as a guitar string about to snap. You'd never get her onto a dance floor as a partner, that's for sure. His buoyant mood slipped a little—kind of reminding him of schooldays when the bell sounded and you had to leave the playground and head back to the classroom.

Never mind. As she'd pointed out herself, this could well be the last time the reception rooms of Loxbury Hall would be used as a public venue and there was a kind of irony in the idea that he could be putting on a fireworks show to mark the end of that era for the house and the start of his own occupation.

Remarkably fitting, really.

Rafe walked towards her as the music faded. Was her look supposed to be more casual, given that it was a weekend? If so, it hadn't worked. Okay, it was a shirt and trousers instead of a skirt but they were tailored and sleek and she still had that complicated rope effect going on in her hair. Did she sleep like that and still not have a hair out of place in the morning?

Maybe she didn't sleep at all. Just plugged herself in to a power point for a while.

Good thing that he was close enough to extend a hand to the young man standing beside Penelope. That way, nobody could guess that his grin was due to private amusement.

'I'm Rafe Edwards,' he said. 'Saw that winning goal you scored on your last match. Good effort.'

'Thanks, man. This is Clarissa. Clarrie, this is Ralph Edwards—the fireworks guy.'

'Rafe, please. I might have Ralph on my birth certificate but it doesn't mean I like it.' His smile widened as Clarissa batted ridiculously enhanced eyelashes at him and then he turned his head.

'Gidday, Penny. How are you?'

'Penelope,' she said tightly. 'I actually like the name on *my* birth certificate.'

Whoa…could she get any more uptight? Rafe turned back to the delicious Clarissa and turned on the charm.

'How 'bout we find somewhere we can get comfortable and have a chat about what I might be able to do for you?'

Clarissa giggled. 'Ooh…yes, *please*…'

'Why don't we go out onto the terrace?' Penelope's tone made the suggestion sound like a reprimand. 'I just need to have a word with Pierre and then I'll join you. I'll organise some refreshment, too. What would you like?'

'Mineral water for me,' Clarissa said. 'Sparkling.'

'A cold beer,' Blake said. 'It's turning into a scorcher of a day.'

'I'm not sure we've got beer in the kitchen at the moment.'

Blake groaned.

'My apologies,' Penelope said. 'I'll make sure it's available next time.' She scribbled something on her clipboard.

'Coffee for me, thanks,' Rafe said. 'Strong and black.'

The look flashed in his direction was grateful. 'That we *can* do. Would you like a coffee, too, Blake?'

'Have to do, I s'pose. At least we're gonna get to talk about something cool. Do we get to choose the kind of fireworks we want?'

'Sure. We need to talk about the music first, though.' Rafe led the way through the French doors to the terrace. 'I'm guessing you want something romantic?'

Music wasn't being discussed when Penelope took the tray of drinks out to the group. Rafe had a laptop open and Blake and Clarissa were avidly watching what was on the screen.

'Ooh…that one. We've got to have that. What's it called?'

'It's a peony. And this one's a chrysanthemum. And this is a golden, hanging willow. It's a forty-five-shot cake so it goes for a while.'

'Nice. I like them loud.' Blake was rubbing his hands together. 'Man, this is going to be epic.'

'With it being your wedding, I was thinking you might want something a bit more romantic.' Rafe tapped his keyboard. 'Look at this for an opening, maybe.'

'OMG.' Clarissa pressed a hand to her open mouth. 'You can do love hearts? For *real*?'

'Sure can. And look at this. Horsetails look a lot like bridal veils, don't you think?'

Clarissa hadn't looked this happy since the first fitting of her wedding dress. Before she'd started to find tiny imperfections that had to be dealt with.

'I want it to be romantic,' she breathed. 'And I've got the perfect song. Whitney Houston's "I Will Always Love You".'

Blake rolled his eyes and shook his head. Rafe lifted an eyebrow. 'Nice, but the tempo could be a bit on the slow side. Maybe a better song to dance to than accompany fireworks?'

'It's soppy,' Blake growled. 'We need something loud. Fun. Wasn't the whole idea to end the night with a bang?'

Clarissa giggled. 'Oh…we will, babes, don't you worry about that.'

Blake grinned. 'You're singing my song already.'

Rafe's appreciative grin faded the moment he caught Penelope's gaze. He took a sip of his coffee.

'What about Meat Loaf?' Blake suggested. '"I'd Do Anything For Love"?'

'Not bad. Good beats to time to effects.'

'No.' Clarissa shook her head firmly.

Penelope was searching wildly for inspiration. 'Bon Jovi? "Livin' On A Prayer"? Or the Troggs? "Wild Thing"?'

'Getting better.' Rafe nodded. The look he gave her this time held a note of surprise. Did he think she wasn't into music or something? 'Let's keep it going. Bon Jovi's a favourite of mine. What about "Always"?'

The words of the song drifted into Penelope's head. Along with an image of it being passionately sung. And even though it was Rafe she was looking at, it was no excuse to let her mind drift to imagining him with wild, rock-god hair. Wearing a tight, black singlet and frayed jeans. Saying he would cry for the woman he loved. Or die for her…

Phew…it was certainly getting hot. She fanned herself with her clipboard and tried to refocus. To push any image of men in frayed jeans and singlets out of her head. So not her type.

She liked designer suits and neat haircuts. The kind of up-and-coming young attorney look, like her last boyfriend who'd not only graduated from law school with honours but was active in a major political party. Disappointing that it had turned out they'd had nothing in common—especially for her grandparents—but she didn't have time for a relationship in her life right now anyway.

She didn't have time to pander to this group's inability to reach an agreement either, but she couldn't think of any way to speed things up and half an hour later they were still no closer to making a definitive choice.

Further away, perhaps, given that both Clarissa and Blake were getting annoyed enough to veto any suggestion the other made and getting steadily snarkier about it. Any moment now it would erupt into a full-blown row and the hint of annoyance in Rafe's body language would turn into disgust and he'd walk away from a job he didn't actually need.

Penelope was increasingly aware that time was running out. They had a meeting with the florist coming up, Pierre was going to return for another dance lesson and there was a rehearsal with the celebrant in the garden at four p.m.

'Did you have anything else you needed to do while you're here?' she asked Rafe.

'A bit of a survey.' He nodded. 'I need to get a feel for the layout and check where I'd position things. I'm thinking a barge on the other side of the lake but I'll be able to get a good view if I go upstairs and—' He stopped abruptly. 'Is that a problem?'

'We're not allowed upstairs,' Clarissa confided. 'Apparently it's one of the biggest rules about using this venue.'

'Is that right?'

It was no surprise that Rafe wasn't impressed by a set of rules and his tone suggested he wouldn't hesitate in breaking them. She could imagine how well it would go down if she forbade the action and she certainly didn't want to get him offside any more than he was already, thanks to the sparring young couple.

If he had to go upstairs in order to be able to do his job, maybe she'd just have to turn a blind eye and hope for the best. At least she could plead ignorance of it actually happening if word got out and she could probably apologise well enough to smooth things over if the owners were upset.

'How long will your survey take?' The words came out more crisply than she'd intended.

'Thirty-nine minutes.' He grinned. 'No, make that forty-one.'

He wasn't the only person getting annoyed here. 'In that case, let's meet back here in forty-five minutes,' Penelope said. 'Blake—take Clarissa to the Loxbury pub and you can get your cold beer and a quick lunch and see if you can agree on a song. This fireworks show isn't going to happen unless we lock that in today. Isn't that right, Ralph?'

His look was deadpan.

'Sorry. Rafe.'

'That's right, Penelope. We're on a deadline that's tight enough to be almost impossible as it is.' He smiled at Clarissa. 'You want your red hearts exploding all over the sky to start the show. What if I told you we could put both your names inside a love heart to finish?'

Clarissa looked like she'd just fallen in love with this new acquaintance. She tugged on Blake's arm with some urgency. 'Come on, babes. We've *got* to find a song.'

'I'll have a think, too,' Penelope called after them. 'I've got my iPod and I need a bit of a walk.'

There was a third-floor level on each of the wings of the house, set back enough to provide an upstairs terraced area. Rafe fancied one of these rooms as his bedroom and that was where he headed. He already knew that he'd have the best view of the lake and garden from that terrace. It took a few minutes to get there. Was he crazy, thinking he could actually live in a place this big?

By himself?

He had plenty of friends, he reminded himself as he stepped over the braided rope on the stairs marking the boundary of public access. The guys in the band would want to make this place party central. And it wasn't as if he'd be here that much. He had his apartments in New York and London and he was looking at getting one in China, given that he spent a lot of time there sourcing fireworks. He'd need staff, too. No way could he manage a house this size. And he'd probably need an entire team of full-time gardeners, he decided as he stepped out onto the bedroom terrace. Just clipping the hedges of that maze would probably keep someone busy for weeks.

In fact, there was someone in there right now. Rafe walked closer to the stone pillars edging the terrace and narrowed his eyes. The figure seemed to know its way through the maze, moving swiftly until it reached the grass circle that marked the centre.

Penelope. Of course it was. Hadn't she said she needed a walk? She stopped for a moment with her head down, fiddling with something in her hand. Her iPod? And then she pressed her fingertips against her ears as though she was listening carefully to whatever music she had chosen.

Rafe should have been scanning the grounds on the far side of the lake and thinking about positioning things like the scissor lift he'd need to hold the frame for the lancework of doing the names in fireworks to end the show. Instead, he found himself watching Penelope.

She was kicking her shoes off, which was probably sensible given that heels would sink into that grass. But then she did something that made Rafe's jaw drop.

Blew whatever it was he'd been thinking of her right out of the water.

She started dancing.

Not just the kind of unconscious jiggle along with the beat either. She was dancing like she thought no one could see her which was probably exactly what she did think, tucked into the centre of that maze with its tall, thick hedges.

Rafe leaned into the corner of the terrace, any thoughts of planning a show escaping irretrievably. His eyes narrowed as he focused on the slim figure moving on her secret stage.

An amused snort escaped him. No wonder she needed to hide herself away. She was rubbish at dancing. Her movements were uncoordinated enough to probably make her a laughing stock on a dance floor.

But then his amusement faded. She was doing something she believed was private and she was doing it with her heart and soul. Maybe she didn't really know how to dance but she was doing more than just hearing that music—she was a part of it with every cell of her body.

Rafe knew that feeling. That ability to lose yourself in sound so completely the rest of the world disappeared. Music could be an anaesthetic that made even the worst kind of pain bearable.

Impossible not to remember wearing headphones and turning the sound level up so loud that nothing else existed. So you couldn't hear the latest row erupting in the new foster home that meant you'd be packed up before long and handed around again like some unwanted parcel.

Impossible not to still feel grateful for that first set of drums he'd been gifted so many years ago. Or the thrill of picking up a saxophone for the first time and starting the journey that meant he could do more than simply listen. That meant he could become a part of that music.

It was another world. One that had saved him from what this one had seemed doomed to become.

And he was getting the same feeling from watching Penelope being uninhibited enough to try and dance.

What was that about?

He'd sensed that what you could see with Penelope Collins wasn't necessarily real, hadn't he? When she'd admitted she knew nothing about setting up a fireworks show. Watching her now made him more sure that she was putting up a front to hide who she really was.

Who was the person that was hiding?

Or maybe the real question here was why did he want to know?

He didn't.

With a jerk, Rafe straightened and forced his gaze sideways towards the lake and the far shore. Was there enough clearance from the trees to put a scissor lift or two on the ground or would the safety margins require a barge on the water? He'd bring one of the lads out here first thing tomorrow and they could use a range finder to get accurate measurements but he could trust his eye for now. And he just happened to have an aerial photograph of the property on his laptop, too. Pulling a notepad and the stub of a pencil from the back pocket of his jeans, he started sketching.

By the time he'd finished what he'd wanted to do he

was five minutes late for the time they'd agreed to meet back on the terrace. Not that it made him hurry down the stairs or anything but he wouldn't have planned to stop before he turned into the ballroom and headed for the terrace. The thought only occurred to him when he saw the iPod lying on the hall table, on top of that clipboard Penelope carried everywhere with her.

If he took a look at what she'd played recently, could he pick what it was that she'd been dancing to? Get some kind of clue to solve the puzzle of who this woman actually was?

Clarissa and Blake were late getting back from lunch and, judging by the looks on their faces, they hadn't managed to agree on the music to accompany their fireworks show.

Which meant that Rafe would most likely pull the plug on doing it at all.

He came through the French doors from the ballroom at the same time as the young couple were climbing the stairs from the garden.

'Did you decide?' Rafe asked.

'We tried,' Clarissa groaned. 'We really did…' Her face brightened. 'But then we thought you're the expert. We'll let you decide.'

Penelope bit back the suggestion she'd been about to make. Throwing ideas around again would only take them back to square one and this was a potentially quick and easy fix.

But Rafe lifted an eyebrow. 'You sure about that? Because I reckon I've found the perfect song.'

'What is it?'

'Doesn't matter,' Blake growled. 'You promised you wouldn't argue this time.'

'Have a listen,' Rafe said, putting his laptop on the table and flipping it open. He tapped rapidly on the keyboard. 'I think you might like it.'

It only took the first two notes for Penelope to recognise the song and it sent a chill down her spine. The very song she'd been about to suggest herself. How spooky was *that*?

'Ohhh…' Clarissa's eyes were huge. 'I *love* this song.'

'Who is that?' Blake was frowning. 'Celine Dion?'

Rafe shook his head. 'This is the original version. Jennifer Rush. She cowrote "The Power of Love" in 1984.'

It was the version that Penelope preferred. The one she had on her iPod. The one she'd been dancing to in her private space in the centre of the maze only half an hour or so ago, when she'd taken that much-needed break.

'It's got some great firing points. Like that…' Rafe's hands prescribed an arc as the crescendo started. 'And we can use the extended version to give us a good length of time. Fade it away to leave your names in the heart hanging over the lake.'

He wasn't looking at Penelope. He didn't even send a triumphant glance in her direction as Clarissa and Blake enthusiastically agreed to the song choice.

Which was probably just as well. Penelope had no idea what her expression might look like but it had to include an element of shock. Surely it had to be more than coincidence and she didn't believe in telepathy but it was impossible not to feel some sort of weird connection happening here. How awful would it be if she looked like Clarissa had when he'd told her he could finish the show by putting their names in a love heart? As though she'd just fallen head over heels in love with the man?

Not that it really mattered. The *pièce de résistance* of the wedding that was going to launch her new career was starting to come together and the choice of song was perfect.

With a lot of hard work and a little bit more luck, this whole wedding was going to be perfect.

CHAPTER THREE

SO FAR, SO GOOD.

They couldn't have wished for a better day weather-wise for what the local media was already billing the wedding of the year. The blue stretch of summer sky was broken only by innocent cotton-wool puffs of cloud and it was warm enough for the skimpy dresses most of the women seemed to be wearing. More importantly, the breeze was gentle enough not to ruin any elaborate hairdos or play havoc with a bridal veil.

The vintage champagne every guest had been offered on arrival was going down a treat and people were now beginning to drift towards the rows of chairs draped with white satin and tied with silver bows. Penelope saw someone open the small gauze bag she'd found on her seat and smile as she showed her partner the confetti that was made up of tiny, glittery silver stars.

How much bigger were those smiles going to be when they were watching the kind of stars that would explode across the sky as the finale to this event? Rafe had arrived as early as Penelope had, driving onto the estate in the chill mist of a breaking dawn. She'd seen him and the technicians he'd brought with him, in their fluorescent vests, working in the field on the far side of the lake at various times over the hectic hours since then. Just orange dots of humanity, really, at this distance, but she was sure it was Rafe who was directing the forklift manoeuvring the pallets from the back of a truck at one point and, much later, the towing of a flat barge to float on the lake.

Because that was the kind of job a boss would do, she told herself. It had nothing to do with that odd tingle of something she had no intention of trying to identify. A tingle that appeared along with that persistent image of the man in frayed jeans and a black singlet she had conjured up. An image that had insisted on haunting her dreams over the last week, leaving her to wake with the odd sensation that something was simply not *fair*...

Heading back inside the house, she popped into the kitchen to check that her team was on top of the catering. Judging by the numerous silver platters of hors d'oeuvres lined up ready for the lull while photographs would be taken after the ceremony, they were right on schedule.

'Any worries, Jack?'

'Apart from an eight-course sit-down dinner for two hundred and supper for six hundred? Nah...it's all good.' The older man's smile was reassuring. 'I've got this side of the gig covered. Go and play with your bride.'

'I do need to do that. But I'll be back later. Keep an apron for me.'

'Are you kidding? That dress is far too fancy to get hidden by any apron.'

'It's not too much, is it?' Penelope glanced down at the dark silver sheath dress she had chosen. A lot of effort had gone into what she hoped would be her signature outfit as she occupied an unusual space in a wedding party that was more than simply hired help but less than invited guest. The dress was demure with its long sleeves and scooped neckline that only showed a hint of cleavage. The skirt was ballet length and fell in soft swirls from thigh level but it did fit like a glove everywhere else and it had a soft sparkle that would probably intensify under artificial or candle light.

Jack grinned. 'You look like the director of the nation's most successful event managing company. Make sure they get some photos of you for one of those flash magazines. Now—stop distracting me. Get out of my kitchen and go and keep our first event ticking. Isn't Princess Clarissa about due for another meltdown?'

'Oh, God, I hope not.' With a worried frown, Penelope headed for a ground-floor room in the west wing that had been set aside for the bride and bridesmaids to get dressed in. A room in the east wing was where the groom and his entourage were waiting. That would be the next stop, to make sure they were in position on time. Penelope checked her watch. Only twenty minutes away. The countdown was on.

She took a deep breath. At least she didn't have to worry about the catering side of things. Jack—her head chef—had worked with her ever since she'd advertised for someone to come on board with a fledgling catering company nearly ten years ago. His own restaurant might have failed despite his talent with food but together they'd built a company to be proud of and it had been his idea for her to take the risky move of taking on event management.

Dreaming about something and even making endless lists of the things that she'd have to keep on top of hadn't really prepared her for the reality of it, though. The catering was only one aspect. Had the celebrant arrived yet? Were the photographers behaving themselves? How were the band going in setting themselves up? She'd seen the truck parked around the back an hour or more ago and people unloading a drum kit and amplifiers but what if they couldn't find enough power points? There was a lighting expert who was coming to supervise the safe positioning and lighting of all those candles and would then be in charge for any spotlighting of key people. He hadn't arrived as far as she knew but they weren't due to meet until after the actual ceremony.

At some point, she would have to find Rafe, too, and make sure that he was happy with his set-up. The fireworks were scheduled to go off at one a.m. to mark the end of the party and there was plenty of security personnel discreetly in place to make sure nobody went into forbidden areas and that everybody left Loxbury Hall when they were supposed to.

It was possible that this was the moment when the tension was at its highest. The moment before the carefully timed show that was going to be the wedding of the year kicked off. With her heart in her mouth, Penelope opened the door of the bride's dressing room. Clarissa—in a froth of white—was standing serenely in the centre of the room with a champagne flute in her hand.

She was surrounded by her six bridesmaids who were in same shade of orange as one of the colours of Blake's football club. One of the girls sent another champagne cork hurtling towards the ceiling with a loud pop and the shriek of happy giggles was deafening. The flash of the camera from the official photographer showed he was capturing every joyous moment.

The hairdresser and make-up artists and their teams were packing up an enormous amount of gear. Hair straighteners, heated rollers and cans of spray went into one set of suitcases. Pots of foundation, dozens of brushes and cards of false eyelashes were heading for another. Penelope smiled at the women.

'I think you deserve to join the celebration. They all look fabulous.' She stepped closer and lowered her voice, although it was hardly necessary as the chatter and laughter as the glasses were being refilled were enough to make any conversation private. 'Any problems?'

Cheryl's smile said it all. 'Bit of a mission to get every one of Clarissa's curls sitting just right but we got there in the end. Thank goodness for industrial-strength hairspray.'

The spirals of platinum blonde hair hung to the bride's waist at the back, easily visible through the sheer mist of an exquisitely embroidered veil. Tresses at the front had been twisted and clipped into a soft frame that supported the tiara holding the veil, as well as offering an anchor for a dozen or more small silver stars. A star made of diamonds sparkled on the perfect spray tan of Clarissa's décolletage—a gift from Blake that had inspired one of the themes for the wedding. Beneath that, the heavily beaded corset bodice of the dress made the most of what had to be close to the top of the bride's assets.

'What d'ya think, Penelope?'

'I think you couldn't look more perfect, Clarrie. It's just as well Blake's got all those groomsmen to hold him up when he sees you walking down the aisle.' She took another quick glance at her watch. 'Five minutes and we'll need you all in position in the reception hall. I'm just going to make sure the boys are out of the building and that those photographs as you come out will be the first glimpse of your dress that the world gets.'

It was Penelope who waited with Clarissa in the main entrance, signalling each pair of bridesmaids when it was their turn to walk out of the huge doorway, down the sweep of wide steps and start the journey along the carpet that led to the raised gazebo where the celebrant was waiting, flanked by the males of the wedding party. Clarissa's song choice of Whitney Houston that had been rejected for the fireworks show was perfect for this entrance but it needed careful timing to make sure the bride arrived beside her groom before the song finished.

Penelope waited until all the heads turned to watch Clarissa take her final position, facing Blake and holding both his hands. Nobody saw her as she quietly made her way to the shade of an ancient oak tree, well away from the audience but close enough to hear the ceremony, thanks to the lapel microphone the celebrant was wearing.

A brief respite from the tension of the day was more than welcome. A private moment to collect her thoughts and remember to breathe.

Except it didn't stay private for long. A figure materialised beside her in the shade. A dark figure. And Penelope forgot to breathe for rather too long.

Had Rafe dressed up for the occasion? He was wearing black jeans today, and a black T-shirt that had a faded image of what was probably an album cover from a forgotten era. The cowboy boots were the same, though, and they were in harmony with a battered, wide-brimmed leather hat that any cowboy would have treasured.

He was dressed for his work and clearly comfortable with being on the hired-help side of the boundary Penelope was balancing on but right now her position in this gathering was unimportant. This short period of time was a limbo where nothing mattered other than the vows the wedding couple were exchanging. This tiny patch of the famous Loxbury Hall gardens was a kind of limbo as well. An island that only she and Rafe were inhabiting.

He was as dark as she was pale. As scruffy as she was groomed. As relaxed as she was tense. Black and white. Total opposites.

It should be making her feel very uncomfortable but it wasn't.

There was a curl of something pleasant stealing through Penelope's body. Try as she might to deny it, the surprise of his company was sprinkled with a condiment that could—quite disturbingly—be delight.

* * *

He'd had something on the tip of his tongue to justify the choice of joining Ms Collins in the shade of this tree. Had it been something about it being the best vantage point to observe the ceremony and that he had the time because everything else that could be a distraction in the background had to be put on hold for the duration? Not that his team had much else to do. Everything was in place and all that was needed between now and about midnight was a rehearsal to check that all the electronic components were in functioning order.

Or maybe it had been something about how well the event was going so far. That it was everything the perfect wedding should be.

No wonder the ability to produce words seemed to have failed him for the moment. This was everything the perfect wedding *shouldn't* be. The epitome of the circus that represented conforming to one of society's expected rules of declaring commitment and faithfulness. A rule that was rarely kept, so why bother with the circus in the first place?

Or perhaps the loss of a conversational opening had something to do with being this close to Penelope?

He'd spotted her discreet position from the edge of the lake where he'd initially positioned himself to be out of sight of the guests. That silvery dress she was wearing shone like a new moon in the dense shade of this ancient tree and…and it was possibly the most stunning dress he'd ever seen. Weird, considering there was no more cleavage to be seen than a tiny, teasing line just where that sun-kissed skin began to swell.

Rafe dragged his gaze away, hopefully before she was aware of his appreciation because the glance had been so swift. Her hair looked different today, too. Softer. She still had those braids shaping the sides of her head but the length of it was loose at the back, falling in a thick ringlet instead of another braid. It was longer than he remembered, almost touching the small of her back in that second, silver skin. What would happen, he found himself wondering, if he buried his fingers in that perfect silky spiral and pulled it apart? Would her whole back get covered with golden waves?

What was more likely to happen was that he would infuriate this would-be queen of event management by messing up her hair. She might not be holding a clipboard right now but the tension was still palpable. She was in control. On top of every moment and ready to troubleshoot any problem with the efficiency of a nuclear blast.

Clarissa's breathlessly excited whisper was being amplified by strategically placed microphones. 'I, Clarissa Grace Bingham, take thee, Blake Robert Summers, to be my lawfully wedded husband. To have and to hold…'

Finally, he found something to say.

'Sounds like she's the happiest girl on earth right now.'

'Of course she is. This is her wedding day. Every girl's dream.'

'Really?' Rafe couldn't help the note of scepticism. 'Does anyone really believe that those vows mean anything these days?'

Uh-oh… Maybe he should have ruffled the spiral of hair down her back instead of dropping some kind of verbal bomb. The look he received made him feel like he'd just told a kid that Santa Claus didn't really exist.

'I believe it,' Penelope said.

She did. He could see it in her eyes. A fierce belief that it meant something. Something important. He couldn't look away. He even found himself leaning a little closer as a soft word of query escaped his lips.

'Why?'

Oh, help… His eyes weren't really as black as sin, were they? The mottled light sifting down through the leaves of the tree was enough to reveal that they were a dark brown, with flecks of gold that made them more like a very deep hazel. And the way he was looking at her…

The eye contact had gone on far too long to be polite but Penelope couldn't break the gaze. It felt physical—almost as though he was holding her in his arms. No… it went deeper than that. He was holding something that wasn't physical. Touching something that was deep inside. The part of her that couldn't be seen.

But Rafe was seeing it and it made her feel… vulnerable?

Nobody had ever looked at her like this. As if they could see that dark, secret part of her. As if the world wouldn't end if the door got opened and light flooded in.

And he wanted to know why she believed in something he clearly had no time for. Marriage. Could he see that she *had* to believe in it? Because there was something about it that held the key to putting things right?

The exchange of vows had been completed on the stage of the gazebo and the applause and raucous whistling told her that the first kiss was happening. The flash of cameras going off was there, like stars in the periphery of her vision, but Penelope still couldn't look away from Rafe's gaze.

'It's about the promise,' she found herself saying softly. 'It's not about the dress or the flowers or…or even the fireworks.'

He raised an eyebrow.

'I don't mean they're not important. That's what weddings are all about. Celebrating the promise.' Penelope drew in a breath. She'd said enough and she should be using the time to make sure the photographers had everything they needed for the next part of the programme. And that Jack was ready to keep the guests entertained with food and wine for as long as it took. 'I can't wait to see the show,' she added with a placating smile. 'I know it'll be fabulous.'

'Oh, it will.' Rafe nodded. 'I'll make sure you get the best spot to watch it, shall I?'

'Won't you be busy? Pushing buttons or something?'

'There's pretty much only one button to push. On my laptop. The rest is automatic.'

'No problems setting up? It is all done?'

'Yes, ma'am.' He tipped his hat. 'We're about to double-check everything and that'll be it until show time.'

'That's great. Thank you so much.' Penelope could see guests starting to move. Reaching for those bags of confetti stars and preparing to shower the bride and groom as they went down the aisle together. She stepped away to move closer but Rafe's voice stopped her.

'That promise,' he said quietly. 'The one you believe in. What is it, exactly?'

Startled, she turned her head. 'Security,' she responded. 'Family. It's the promise of a safe place, I guess. Somewhere you know you'll always be loved.'

There was something soft in his eyes now. Something sad?

'You're one of the lucky ones, then.'

'Because I believe in marriage?'

'Because you know what it's like to have a family. Parents. You know what it's like to live in that safe place.'

And he didn't? Something huge squeezed inside her chest and made her breath come out in a huff. She understood that yearning. Her life might look perfect from the outside but she wanted him to know that she understood. That they had a connection here that very few people could have. They might be complete opposites but in that moment it felt like they were the opposite sides of the same coin.

'I've never had parents. My mother abandoned me as a baby and then died. I have no idea who my father is.' Good grief...why on earth was she telling him this much? She backed off. 'You're right, though. I *was* lucky. My grandparents brought me up. I had everything I could possibly want.'

She saw the change in his eyes. He was backing off, too. Had he thought she understood but now saw her as one of the privileged? One who couldn't possibly have any idea of what it was like not to have that safe place?

Penelope didn't want to lose that tiny thread of connection. She was the one who needed that understanding, wasn't she? Because nobody had ever understood.

'Almost everything,' she added, her voice no more than a sigh. She swallowed past the tightness in her throat. 'Maybe if my parents had believed in marriage they could have looked after each other and things would have been different.' She bit her lip as the admission slipped out. 'Better...'

'You don't know that.' That softness in his gaze had changed. There was a flash of anger there. A world of pain. 'Things could have been worse.' Rafe tugged on the rim of his hat, blocking off his gaze. 'Catch you later,' he muttered as he turned away. 'When it's show time.'

The next hours were a blur. Penelope felt like she needed to be in six places at once to make sure everything was flowing smoothly but the adrenaline of it all kept her going without pause. A reporter from the magazine that had the exclusive, first coverage of the event even asked for a quick interview and photographs.

'You do realise you're going to be inundated with work after this, don't you? Every celebrity who's planning a wedding in the foreseeable future is going to want something this good.'

There was fear to be found hiding in the excitement of how well it was all going.

'We're a boutique company. I'm not ever going to take on more clients than I can personally take care of.'

'You've organised this all yourself?'

'I have a partner who's in charge of the catering today. Come and meet Jack. With dinner over, he should have a minute or two to spare. You could get a great picture of him in his chef's whites in the kitchen. He deserves the publicity as much as I do.'

'Let's get one of you two together.' The journalist made a note on her pad. 'Are you, like, a couple?'

Penelope shook her head as she smiled. 'No. Jack has a family. I'm happily single. Career-woman, through and through, that's me.'

That was certainly the image she wanted to portray, anyway. There was no reason for anybody to ever feel sorry for Penelope Collins.

Not any more.

By midnight, the band had been playing for two hours and the party in the ballroom was still in full swing. The drums pulsed in Penelope's blood and the music was so good it was an effort not to let her body respond. It was just as well she was kept too occupied to do more than make a mental note to download some of Diversion's tracks so she could listen again in private.

People were getting drunk now. Emergency cleaning was needed more than once in the restrooms and an ambulance was discreetly summoned to the service entrance to remove one unconscious young woman. Another one was found sobbing in the garden and it fell to Penelope to sit and listen to the tale of romantic woe and calm the guest enough to rejoin the revelry. Then she escaped to the kitchens for a while and insisted on an apron so she could spend a few minutes helping to prepare the supper that would be served on the terrace, timed to finish as the fireworks started.

And then it would all be over, bar the massive job of clearing up, most of which would happen tomorrow. All the tension and exhaustion of the last weeks and days and hours would be over. What was that going to feel like? Would she crawl home and crash or would she still be buzzing this time tomorrow?

Her head was spinning a little now, which suggested that it might be a good thing if she crashed. Maybe that glass of champagne with Jack a few minutes ago to toast their success had been a bad thing. At least it was quieter in the vast spaces of Loxbury Hall. The dance music was finished and people were crowded onto the terrace, enjoying a last glass or two of champagne, along with the delicious canapés on offer. The bride and groom had gone off to change into their going-away outfits and the vintage car, complete with the rope of old tin cans, was waiting at the back, ready to collect them from the front steps as soon as the fireworks show ended.

It was almost time for those fireworks. Penelope hadn't seen Rafe since that weirdly intense conversation under the tree. She hadn't even thought of him.

No. That wasn't entirely true. That persistent image of him was never far away from the back of her mind. And hadn't it got a bit closer right about the time she'd described herself as 'happily single' to that journalist?

And now he was here again, still wearing that hat, with a laptop bag slung over his shoulder. Right outside the kitchen door, when Penelope had hung up her apron and slipped back into the entrance hall so that she could go and find a place to watch the show.

'Ready?'

Words failed her. She could hear an echo of his voice from that earlier conversation.

I'll make sure you get the best spot to watch...

He'd kept his word. Again. She'd known she could trust him, hadn't she, when he'd turned up for that first meeting here?

Having that trust confirmed, on top of being drawn back into where she'd experienced the feeling that they were somehow connected on a secret level, was a mix so powerful it stole the breath, along with any words, from Penelope's body.

All she could do was nod.

A corner of his mouth lifted. 'Come on, then.'

He held out his hand.

And Penelope took it. His grip was strong. Warm. A connection that was physical. Real, instead of the one that was probably purely only in her own imagination, but if she hadn't already been sideswiped by that visceral force, she would never have taken his hand.

Who in their right mind would start holding hands with a virtual stranger? One who had a 'bad boy' label that was practically a neon sign? What good girl would be so willing to follow him?

Not her. Not in this lifetime. She could almost hear her grandmother's voice. The mantra of her life. Her greatest fear.

'You'll end up just like your mother, if you're not very careful.'

How could it feel so good, then? Kind of like when she knew no one could see her and she could let loose and dance…

No one could see her now. Except Rafe. It was like being in one of her dreams, only she wasn't going to end up feeling that something wasn't fair because she didn't have to wake up any time soon. She had to almost skip a step or two to keep up with his long stride but then she tugged back on the pressure. Silly to feel fear at breaking such a little rule when she was already doing something so out of character but maybe it was symbolic.

'We can't go *upstairs*.'

'We have to. I need to get the best view of the show. I've got people on the ground I can reach by radio if there's any problem but I have to be able to see.' He stepped over the thick red rope. 'It's okay. I'm not really breaking the sacred rules. I've cleared it with the owner.'

He sounded completely convincing. Maybe Penelope just wanted to believe him. Or perhaps the notion of going somewhere forbidden—in his company—was simply too enticing. She could probably blame that glass of champagne for giving in so readily. Or maybe it was because she was letting herself give in to the pulse of something too big to ignore. It might not look like it from the outside, but she was already dancing.

Up the stairs. Along a wide hallway. Past an open door that revealed a luxurious bathroom. Into…a *bedroom*? Yes, there was a four-poster bed that looked about as old as Loxbury Hall itself. It also looked huge and…dear Lord…irresistibly inviting. As if it was the exact destination she'd been hoping this man would lead her to.

Shocked, Penelope jerked her hand free of Rafe's but he didn't seem to notice. He was opening French doors with the ease of knowing exactly where the latches were and then he glanced over his shoulder as they swung open.

'Come on, then. You won't see much in there.'

Out onto the flagged terrace, and the chill of the night air went some way to cooling the heat Penelope could feel in her cheeks. Hopefully, the heat deeper in her body would eventually cool enough to disappear as well.

Rafe checked in with his team by portable radio. Some were as close as it was safe to be to the action, with fire extinguishers available if something went seriously wrong. They would be working alongside him when the show was over, checking for any unexploded shells and then clearing up the rubbish of spent casings and rolling up the miles of cables to pack away with the rest of the gear.

For the next ten minutes, though, there was nothing to do but watch and see how the hard work of the last few days had come together. Rafe set up his laptop, activated the program that synched the music and effects and kept the radio channel open to have the ground team on standby for the countdown. Speakers had been set up along the terrace and the first notes of the song caught everybody's attention.

And then the first shells were fired and the sky filled with expanding, red hearts. The collective gasp from the crowd on the terrace below was loud enough to hear over the music for a split second before the next shell was detonated. The gasp from the woman in the silver dress beside him shouldn't have been loud enough to hear but, suddenly, it was Penelope's reaction that mattered more than anything else.

For the first time in his life in professional pyrotechnics, Rafe found he wasn't watching the sky but he could still gauge exactly what was happening. He could feel the resonance of the explosions in his bones and he could see the colours reflected on Penelope's face. He could see much more than that as well. He could see the amazement, a hint of fear and the sheer thrill of it all. He could feel what it was that had sucked him into this profession so long ago with an intensity that he hadn't realised had become blurred over the years.

And he was loving it.

Penelope had seen fireworks before. Of course she had. She'd always been a little frightened of them. They were so loud. So unpredictable. Too dangerous to really enjoy.

But she felt safer here. She was with the person who was controlling the danger so she could let go of that protective instinct that kept her ready to run in an instant if necessary. She could let herself feel the boom of the explosions in her body instead of bracing herself against them. She could watch the unfurling of those astonishing colours and shapes against the black sky.

She could even watch the new shells hurtling upwards with an anticipation that was pure excitement about what was about to come.

She didn't want it to end. This was the ultimate finale to the biggest thing she had accomplished so far in her life. The wedding was done and dusted and it had been all she had hoped and dreamed it would be. She could let go of all that tension and bask in the satisfaction of hard work paying off.

It had to end, though. The music was beginning to fade. The huge red heart that looked as if it was floating in the middle of the lake came alive with the names of Clarrie and Blake appearing in white inside. The cheering from the crowd below was ecstatic and Penelope felt the same appreciation. Unthinking, she turned to Rafe to thank him but words were not enough in the wake of that emotional roller-coaster.

She stood on tiptoe and threw her arms around his neck.

'That was *amazing*. Thank you *so* much...'

The silver dress felt cool and slippery as his hands went automatically to the hips of the woman pressed against him but he could feel the warmth of her skin beneath the fabric.

This was the last thing Rafe had expected her to do.

He'd been reliving the passion of his job through watching her reaction to the show. Now, with this unexpected touch, he was reliving the excitement of touching a woman as if it were the first time ever. Was this the thing he'd lost? It was a sensation he hadn't even known he'd been pursuing so he couldn't have known it had been missing for so long, but surely it couldn't be real? If he kept on touching her, it would end up being the same as all the others. Or would it?

She drew back and she was smiling. Her eyes were dancing. She looked more alive than Rafe had ever seen her look.

She looked more beautiful than any woman had the right to look.

He had to find out if there was any more to this magic. If he kissed her, would it feel like the first time he'd ever kissed a woman he'd wanted more than his next breath?

He was going to *kiss* her.

Penelope had a single heartbeat to decide what she should do. No. There was no decision that needed to be made, was there? What she should do was pull away from this man. Apologise for being overly effusive in her thanks and turn and walk away.

It wasn't about what she should do. It was about what she *wanted* to do. And whether—for perhaps the first time in her life—she could allow herself to do exactly that. Were the things she had denied herself for ever *really* that bad? How would she know if she never even took a peek?

It was just a kiss but waiting for it to happen was like watching one of those shells hurtle into the darkness, knowing that it would explode and knowing how exciting it would be when it did.

The anticipation was unbearable. She *had* to find

out. Had to open the door to that secret place and step inside.

And the moment his lips touched hers, Penelope knew she was lost. Nothing had ever felt like this. Ever. The softness that spoke of complete control. Gentleness that was a glove covering unimagined, wild abandon.

Not a word was spoken but the look Rafe gave her when they finally stopped kissing asked a question that Penelope didn't want to answer. If she started thinking she would stop feeling and she'd never felt anything like this. It wasn't real—it had to be some weird alchemy of exhaustion and champagne, the thrill of the fireworks and the illicit thrill of an invitation to go somewhere so forbidden—but she knew it would never happen again and she couldn't resist the desire to keep it going just a little longer.

It was bliss. A stolen gift that might never be offered again.

Maybe it wasn't really so astonishing that this woman was capable of such passion. He'd seen her dancing, hadn't he? When she'd thought no one could see her. By a stroke of amazingly good fortune he was sharing that kind of space with her right now. Where nobody could see them. Where whatever got kept hidden so incredibly well was being allowed out to play. Maybe it was true that he wouldn't have chosen a woman like this in a million years but it was happening and he was going to make the most of every second.

Because the magic was still there. Growing stronger with every touch of skin on skin. It was like the first time. Completely new and different and…and just *more*. More than he'd ever discovered. More than he'd ever dreamed he could find.

He took Penelope to paradise and then leapt over the brink to join her. For a long minute then, all he could do was hold her as he fought to catch his breath and wait for his heart to stop pounding. As he tried—and failed—to make sense of the emotions tumbling through his head and heart. Ecstasy and astonishment were mixed with something a lot less pleasant. Bewilderment, perhaps?

A sense of foreboding, even?

What the hell had just happened here?

And what on earth was going to happen next?

CHAPTER FOUR

THE HOUNDS OF HELL were chasing Penelope's car as she drove away from Loxbury Hall.

How awful had that been?

What an absolute, unmitigated train crash.

She'd felt the moment of impact and it had been, undoubtedly, the most shocking sensation of her life. There she'd been, lying in Rafe's arms, floating in a bubble of pure bliss—knowing that there was no place in the world that would ever feel this good.

This safe…

And then she'd heard it. Her grandmother's voice.

'What have you done, Penelope? Oh, dear Lord…it's your mother all over again…you wicked, wicked girl…'

Her worst fear. She'd spent her whole life resisting the temptation to give in to doing bad things and she'd just thrown it all away.

For *sex*… Lust. One of those deadly sins.

Her partner in crime hadn't helped.

'It was only sex, babe.' The look on his face hadn't helped. *'Okay, it was great sex but, hey…it's still no big deal. Don't get weird about it.'*

He had *no* idea how big a deal it was for her.

'It's not as if you have to worry about getting pregnant.'

As if using a condom made it okay. Maybe it did in the world he came from. The world she'd avoided for ever. Sex, drugs and rock 'n' roll.

Her mother's world.

Oh, she'd held it together for a while. Long enough to get her clothes on and retreat from that bedroom with some dignity at least. She'd gone to the downstairs cloakroom, relieved to find that the only people around were the clean-up crew and members of the band, who were still dismantling their sound system. She'd sat in a cubicle for a long time, hoping that the shaking would ease. That the memory of what it had been like in Rafe's arms would fade. Or that she would be able to reassign it as something as horrible as it should be instead of the most incredible experience she'd ever had.

One that she knew she might desperately want to have again.

No-o-o...

She couldn't be that girl. She wouldn't let herself.

Jack had taken one look at her face when she'd gone to the kitchen and simply hugged her.

'It's over, love. You get to go home and get some sleep. I'll finish up here. I've already packed the leftovers into your car. Those kids at the home are going to get a real treat for Sunday lunch this week.' He'd tightened his hug. 'You've done it. Awesome job. You can be very proud of yourself.'

Jack had no idea either, did he?

Somehow, she got home to the small apartment over the commercial kitchen that had been the base for her business for those first years. It was more of a test kitchen now and a back-up for when they needed things they didn't have the time or space to produce in the bigger kitchens that were Jack's domain, but it was full of memories and Penelope loved it with a passion. She transferred the containers of food to the cool room and then slammed the door to the street shut behind her and locked it, hoping to shut those hounds outside. But they followed her upstairs and she could see them circling her bed, waiting to move in for the kill.

One of them had her grandmother's face. Cold and disgusted. With sharp teeth ready to shave slivers of flesh from her bones with every accusation.

One of them had Rafe's face. With eyes that glowed with desire and a lolling tongue that promised pleasures she'd never dreamed of. It stopped and gave her what looked like a grin as she unzipped the silver dress and it felt like it was Rafe's hands that were peeling the fabric from her body all over again.

Where did that heat come from? Coursing through her body like an electric shock that was delicious instead of painful?

Oh, yeah...it was the bad blood. Of course it was. How else could it move so fast and infuse every cell of her body?

Penelope balled the dress and threw it into the corner. So much for it being her trademark wedding outfit. She'd never be able to wear it again.

She'd never be able to sleep if she got into her bed

either. The thought of lying there in the dark with those mental companions was unbearable. Even exhaustion wouldn't be enough protection.

Pyjamas were a good idea, though. Comfortable and comforting. Her current favourites were dark blue, with a pattern of silver moons and stars. A soft pair of knitted booties on her feet and Penelope was already feeling better. All she needed now was a cup of hot chocolate and the best thing about making that was that she could be in her kitchen and that was a comfort zone all of its own.

Or was it?

Encased in the upright, clear holder on the gleaming expanse of the stainless-steel bench was a recipe for cake. Red velvet cake. The cake she'd promised her grandmother she would provide for the dinner party tomorrow night to celebrate Grandad's birthday. No, make that tonight because Sunday had started hours and hours ago.

Before the fireworks. Before she'd blown up the foundations of her life by doing something so reckless she had no idea how to process any possible repercussions.

Easier not to think. To go on autopilot and do what she could do better than anyone. Opening cupboards, Penelope took out bowls and measuring cups and cake tins. She turned an oven on and went to the cool room and then the pantry to collect all the ingredients she would need.

Flour and cocoa. Unsalted butter and eggs and buttermilk. Caster sugar and red paste food colouring. She

could think about the icing later. Cream cheese for between the layers, of course, but the decoration on top
would have to be spectacular to impress her grandmother. Maybe a whole bouquet of the delicate frosted
roses that she was famous for.

It would take hours. Maybe so long she would have
to leave her kitchen and go straight to her Sunday gig
of making lunch for the residents of the Loxbury Children's Home. Another comfort zone.

How good was that?

It wasn't easy to identify the prickle of irritation because it had been a long time since Rafe Edwards had
felt…guilty?

He didn't *do* guilt. He'd learned at a very young age
that it was only justified if you hurt somebody inten-
tionally and that was something else he never did. He
refused to feel guilty for breaking rules that weren't
going to damage anything bar the egos of people who
thought they had the right to control what you did because they were more important. Better educated, or
richer, or simply older.

The snort that escaped as he pulled his jeans back on
was poignant. The age factor hadn't mattered a damn
since he'd been sixteen. Nearly two decades since anyone had been able to make his life unbearable simply
because they were old enough to have authority.

Back then, he'd get angry at being caught rather than
feel guilty about what rule he'd broken. And maybe
there was a smidge of anger to be found right now. Annoyance, for sure. Penelope had wanted it as much as he

had, so why had she looked as if the bottom had fallen out of her world the moment her desire-sated eyes had focused again?

Yep. Annoyance had been why he'd baited her. Why he'd made no attempt to cover himself as he'd lain there with his arms hooked over the pillows behind him. Why he'd tried to dismiss what had happened as nothing important. Had he really said it was no big deal because she hadn't been in danger of getting pregnant?

It had been lucky he'd found that random condom in his pocket. Would either of them have been able to stop what had been happening by the time he'd gone looking? That was a scary thought. Unprotected sex was most certainly one of the rules that Rafe never broke because there was a real risk of someone getting hurt. A kid. Someone so vulnerable it was something he never even wanted to have to think about. Didn't want to have to remember...

Robot woman had returned as she'd scrambled into her clothes. Man, Penelope Collins was uptight. No wonder he'd avoided her type for ever. This aftertaste was unpleasant. A prickle under his skin that didn't feel like it was going to fade any time soon.

He didn't bother straightening the bed before he left the room. He owned the room now. And the bed, seeing as he'd bought the place fully furnished. It was the room he intended on using as his bedroom when he moved in but...dammit...would he ever be able to sleep in there without remembering that astonishing encounter?

And maybe that was where that irritation was coming from. Because he knew it was an encounter he was never going to get the chance to repeat.

Which was crazy because he didn't want to. Why would anybody want to if it left you feeling like this?

It was probably this disturbance to his well-being that made it take a second glance to recognise the man coming out of the ballroom when he got downstairs.

Or maybe it went deeper than that?

More guilt?

This was an old friend. One of the few good mates from the past that he hadn't spent nearly enough time with in recent years because his life had taken him in such a different direction. Such an upward trajectory.

This felt awkward. Was there a chance of being seen as completely out of their league? Too important to hang out with them any more?

But there was relief to be found here, too, being drawn back into a part of his past he would never choose to abandon. A comfort zone like no other, and that was exactly what he needed right now.

And it appeared as if he was welcome, judging by the grin that split the man's face as he caught sight of Rafe.

'Hey, man… What the heck are you doin' here?'

'Scruff. Hey… Good to see you. Here, give me that.' Rafe took one of the huge bags that held part of the drum kit. 'I heard you and the boys. You're still sounding great.'

'Thanks, man. Still missing your sax riffs in some of those covers. Like that one of Adele's. If we'd known you were going to be here we would have hauled you on stage.'

The tone was light but there was a definite under-current there. Rafe hadn't been imagining the barrier he'd inadvertently erected with his neglect. Or maybe it was more to do with how successful he'd become. How rich…

'I was a bit busy. That fireworks show? Put that to-gether myself. Haven't done the hands-on side of the business for years. It was fun.'

'It was awesome.' Scruff dumped the gear he was carrying beside the van parked on the driveway. He leaned against the vehicle to roll a cigarette and when it was done he offered it to Rafe.

'Nah, I'm good. Given it up, finally.'

'For real? Man…' Scruff lit the cigarette and took a long draw, eyeing Rafe over the smoke. The awkward-ness was there again. He was different. Their relation-ship was different. 'Given up all your other vices, too?'

'Nah…' Rafe grinned. 'Some things are too good to give up.'

Like sex.

Scruff's guffaw and slap on the arm was enough to banish the awkwardness. And then other band mem-bers joined them and Scruff's delight in rediscovering a part of Rafe that he recognised was transmitted—unspoken—with no more than a glance.

Rafe was only too happy to take the rebukes of how long it had been. To apologise and tell them all how great it was to see them. Reunion time was just what he needed to banish that prickle.

The one that told him sex was never going to be any-thing like the same again.

Unless it was with Penelope Collins?

The enthusiasm of the other members of Diversion gained momentum as they finished packing their gear into the truck. 'Bout time you got yourself back where you belong. Party tomorrow night... No, make that *tonight*. You up for it?'

'You bet.'

Diversion's lead singer, Matt, grinned. 'We'd better send out some more invites. I can think of a few bods who'll want to see you again.'

Scruff snorted. 'Yeah...like the Twickenham twins.'

The sudden silence let him know that the boys were eyeing each other again. Still wondering how different he might be. It seemed important to diffuse that tension. To get into that comfort zone more wholeheartedly.

'Oh, no...' Rafe shook his head. 'They're still hanging around? Do they still dress up as cowgirls?'

'Sure do.' Scruff gave him a friendly punch on the arm. 'And they're gonna be mighty pleased to see you, cowboy.'

The prickle was fading already. With a bit of luck, normal service was about to be resumed. 'Bring it on. Just tell me where and when.'

The Loxbury Children's Home, otherwise known as Rainbow House, was on the opposite side of the city from Loxbury Hall and its style was just as different as the location. The building had no street appeal, with the haphazard extensions that had taken place over time and maintenance like painting that was well overdue, and the garden was littered with children's toys and a playground that had seen better days.

But it felt like home, and Maggie and Dave, the house parents, welcomed Penelope with the same enthusiasm as they'd done years ago—that very first time she'd turned up with the tentative offer of food left over from a catering event. The same age as her grandparents, Maggie and Dave were the parents Penelope had never had. The house, noisy with children and as messy and lived in as the garden, was so different from where she'd grown up that, for a long time, she'd felt guilty for enjoying it so much.

She'd gone back, though. Again and again. Maggie hadn't discovered for a long time that she actually cooked or baked things when there weren't enough leftovers to justify a weekly drop-off. When she did, she just gave Penelope one of those delicious, squishy hugs that large women seemed to be so good at.

'It's you we need more than free food, pet. Just come. Any time.'

It wasn't enough to just visit. Helping Maggie in the kitchen was the time she loved the best. Cooking Sunday lunch with her favourite person in the world was a joy and what had become a weekly ritual was never broken.

She'd got to know a lot of the children now, too. The home offered respite care to disabled children and temporary accommodation to those in need of foster homes. There were the 'boomerang' kids who sadly bounced between foster homes for one reason or another and some long-term residents that places could never be found for. The home was always full. Of people. And love.

'Oh, my… Is that fillet steak?'

'It is. Jack over-catered for the wedding last night. It came with wilted asparagus and scalloped potatoes but I thought the kids might like chips and maybe peas.'

'Good idea. What a treat. Well, you know where the peeler is. Let's get on with it. Don't you have some special do at your folks' place tonight?'

'Mmm. Grandad's birthday. There's no rush, though. I'm only doing dessert and I've made a cake. I don't need to turn up before seven-thirty.'

Maggie beamed. 'Just as well. The kids have got a play they want to put on for you after lunch. Have to warn you, though, it's a tad tedious.'

'Nothing on how tedious the dinner party's going to be. I'm almost thirty, Maggie, and I still get 'the look' if I use the wrong fork.'

Penelope rinsed a peeled potato under the tap and put it on the chopping board. She reached for another one from the sack and her damp hand came out covered in dirt. With a grimace, she turned the tap back on to clean it. Dusting the particles that had fallen onto her jeans only turned it into a smear but that didn't matter. She'd probably be rolling around on the floor, playing with one of the toddlers, before long. This was the only place she ever wore jeans and it was an illicit pleasure that fitted right in with not worrying about the mess or the noise. She'd just have to make sure she left enough time to shower and change when she went home to collect the cake.

'So, how was the wedding?' Maggie sounded excited. 'Did you know we could see the fireworks from here? A couple of the boys sneaked out to watch them and we didn't have the heart to tell them off for getting out of bed. They were so pretty.'

'Weren't they? I got the best view from upstairs at the hall.'

'Upstairs? I thought that was out of bounds?'

'Hmm. The guy doing the fireworks show had permission, apparently. He needed to be where he could see everything in case there was a problem.'

'And he took you upstairs, too?'

'Mmm.' Penelope concentrated on digging an eye out of the potato she was holding. 'Upstairs' was the least of the places Rafe had taken her last night but, no matter how much she loved and trusted Maggie, she couldn't tell her any of that.

She knew what happened when you did things that disappointed people.

They stopped loving you.

This time, when she picked up a new potato, the mud on her hand got transferred to her face as she stifled a sniff.

'You all right, pet?'

'Mmm.' Penelope forced a smile. 'Bit tired, that's all. It was a big night.'

'Of course it was.' Maggie dampened a corner of a tea towel and used it to wipe the grime off Penelope's cheek. 'Let's get this food on the table. You can have a wee snooze during the play later. It wouldn't go down too well if you fell asleep during dinner, would it? Your folks are going to want to hear all about everything that happened last night. They must be very proud of you. I certainly would be.'

Penelope's misty smile disguised a curl of dread. Imagine what would happen if she told her grandparents absolutely everything? But could she hide it well enough? Her grandmother had always had some kind of sixth sense about her even thinking about something she shouldn't and she'd always been able to weasel out a confession in the end, and a confession like this one would make the world as she knew it simply implode.

Oh, for heaven's sake. She hadn't been a child for a very long time. Wasn't it about time she stopped letting her grandparents make her feel like one?

It was one of the classic saxophone solos of all time. 'Baker Street' by Gerry Raffety. Rafe had first heard this song when he'd been an angry, disillusioned sixteen-year-old and it had touched something in his soul. When he'd learned that it had been released in 1978, the year he was born, the connection had been sealed. It was *his* song and he was going to learn to play the sax for no other reason than to own it completely.

And here he was, twenty years later, and he could close his eyes and play it as though the gleaming, gold instrument was an extension of his body and his voice. A mournful cry that had notes of rebellion and hope. So much a part of him that it didn't matter he hadn't had time to take the sax out of its case for months at a time. It was always there. Waiting for an opportunity that always came when it was needed most.

And, man, he'd needed it tonight, to exorcise that prickle that had refused to go away all day. Even walking the expanse of amazing gardens he could now call his own, as he'd collected the last of the charred cardboard that had enclosed the shells fired last night, hadn't been enough to soothe his soul. Or floating on his personal lake to retrieve the barge. Memories of the fireworks display that had been intended to celebrate his ownership of Loxbury Hall would be inextricably linked to other memories for ever.

Of a woman he'd never expected to meet and would never meet again.

But never mind. He could let it go now. 'Baker Street' had worked its magic again.

'That was awesome, dude.' Scruff had given his all to his drum accompaniment to the song. So had the guitarists and Diversion's keyboard player, Stefan. Now the beer was cold and there was plenty of comfortable old furniture in this disused warehouse that was the band's headquarters for practice and parties.

'As covers go, it's one of the best,' Stefan agreed. 'But it's time we wrote more of our own stuff.'

'Yeah…' Rafe took a long pull of his beer. 'You know what? I've been toying with the idea of setting up a recording company.'

Stefan's beer bottle halted halfway to his mouth. His jaw dropped and his gaze shifted from Rafe to Scruff, who shook his head. Was it his imagination or did the boys take a step further away from him? Okay, so he had more money than he used to have. More money than most people ever dreamed of, but it didn't change who he was, did it? Didn't change how much he loved these guys.

He shrugged, trying to make it less of a big deal. 'I could do with a new direction. Blowing things up is getting a bit old.'

So not true. But there had been a moment today, when memories of the fireworks and of Penelope had seemed so intertwined, that the idea of taking a break from his profession had seemed shockingly appealing.

'Get a whole new direction.' Scruff had recovered enough to grin. 'Join the band again. Come and experience the delights of playing covers at birthday parties and weddings. You too could learn every ABBA song in existence.'

The shout of laughter echoed in the warehouse rafters. He was forgiven for any differences and it felt great. A cute blonde with a cowboy hat on her bouncy curls and a tartan shirt that needed no buttons fastened between an impressive cleavage and the knot above a bare midriff came over to sit beside Rafe on the ancient couch. One of the Twickenham twins. He knew they'd been watching him closely all evening and their shyness had been uncharacteristic enough to make him feel the barriers were still there. Apparently, he'd just broken through the last of them.

'Nothing wrong with ABBA.' She pouted. 'It's great to dance to.'

'Yeah, baby...' Her identical sister came to sit on his other side. Somehow she moved so that his arm fell over her shoulder as if the movement had been intended. And maybe it had been. 'Let's dance...'

Lots of people were dancing already, over by the jukebox that had been the band's pride and joy when they'd discovered it more than a decade ago—when Rafe had been part of the newly formed band. A pall of smoke fog hung under the industrial lights and, judging by what he could smell, Rafe realised he could probably get high even if he didn't do stuff like that any more. The party was getting going and it was likely to still be going when dawn broke.

The thought brought a wave of weariness. Good grief...was he getting too old for this?

'Can't stay too long,' he heard himself saying. 'Got a board meeting first thing tomorrow. We're making a bid for New Year's Eve in London again this year. It's big.'

'Oh...*man*...' Scruff groaned. 'We just find you and you're gonna disappear on us again?'

'No way. I've bought a house around here now.'

'For real?'

'Yeah...' Rafe wiped some foam from above his top lip. 'Given my advancing years, I reckoned it was time to settle down somewhere.' Not that he was going to tell them where the house was yet. That would put him back to square one by intimidating them all with his wealth and success.

The laughter of some of his oldest friends was disquieting. Stefan couldn't stop.

'House first, then a wife and kids, huh?'

Rafe snorted. 'You know me better than that, Stef.'

The twins snuggled closer on both sides. 'You don't wanna do that, Rafey. A wife wouldn't want to play like we can.'

So true. The connotations of a wife brought up images of a controlling female. Someone who made sure she got everything precisely the way she wanted it.

Someone like Penelope Collins?

The soft curves of the twin cleavages that were close enough to touch and inviting enough to delight any man were curiously unappealing right now. There would be no surprises there. It might be nice but it would be old. Jaded, even, knowing that it was possible to feel like sex was brand-new and exciting again.

Rafe sighed. He had to get out of there. The prickle had come back to haunt him.

'You're not the only one with something big coming up,' Scruff said into the silence that fell. 'We're gonna be a headline act at the festival next month.'

'The Loxbury music festival?' Rafe whistled. 'Respect, man.' Then he frowned. 'I thought they'd wound that gig up years ago. Too much competition from the bigger ones like Glastonbury.'

'They did. It's been nearly ten years but this year is the thirtieth anniversary. The powers that be decided it would be a great blast from the past and put little ol' Loxbury back on the map.'

'Sounds fun. You'll get to play some of your own stuff.'

'You could be in on it, mate. You'd love what we're doing these days. Kind of Pink Floyd meets Meatloaf.'

The other band members groaned and a general argument broke out as they tried to define their style.

One of the twins slid her arm around Rafe's neck. 'There's going to be a big spread in one of the music mags. That's Julie over there. She's a journo and she's going to be doing the story. Did you know a girl died at the very first festival?'

'No... Really?'

'That's not true,' the other twin said. 'She collapsed at the festival. She didn't die until a couple of days later. It was a drug overdose.' She raised her voice. 'Isn't that right, Julie?'

'That's not great publicity to rake up before this year's event.'

'There's a much better story.' Julie had come over to perch on the end of the couch. 'There's Baby X.'

'Who the heck is Baby X?'

'The baby that got found under a bush when they were packing up. A little girl. They reckoned she was only a few days old.'

'She'll be nearly thirty now, then.' The twins both shuddered. 'That's old.'

'Not as old as me.' But Rafe was barely listening any more. Penelope's words were echoing in his head.

My mother abandoned me as a baby and then died. I have no idea who my father is.

Holy heck... Was it possible that *she* was Baby X?

The idea that the renewed curiosity of this journalist could expose a personal history that had to be painful was disturbing.

He should warn Penelope. Just in case.

Not his business, he told himself firmly. And that would mean he'd have to see her again and that was the last thing he wanted.

He drained his beer and then stood up, extracting

himself with difficulty from the clutches of the twins. If he was going to believe what he was telling himself, he needed to get a lot more convincing.

He had to get out of there. He wasn't having fun any more.

The resolution to keep an adult poise along with any secrets she might wish to keep lasted all the way to the elegant old house in one of Loxbury's best suburbs. Her shower might have washed away the effects of so many sticky fingers but the glow of the cuddles and laughter was still with her. Her jeans were in the washing machine and she knew her new outfit would meet with approval. A well-fitted skirt, silk blouse and tailored jacket. There were no runs in her tights and she'd even remembered to wear the pearls that had been a twenty-first birthday gift from her grandparents, along with the start-up loan to start her small bakery.

A loan that was about to be paid off in full. Another step to total independence. She was an adult, she reminded herself again as she climbed the steps carefully in her high heels. The same shoes she'd worn the day she'd gone to the office of All Light on the Night. The same shoes that Rafe had tugged off her feet last night shortly after he'd unzipped that silver dress...

Penelope needed to take a deep, steadying breath before she rang the bell. She had a key to the kitchen door but rarely used it. By implicit agreement, being granted admission to the house she'd grown up in was the 'right' thing to do.

As was the kiss on her grandmother's cheek that

barely brushed the skin and, instantly, she was aware of the child still hidden deep inside. Having skinny arms peeled away from their target with a grip strong enough to hurt.

'Don't hug me, Penelope. If there's anything I detest, it's being hugged.'

'How are you, Mother?'

'Fabulous, darling. And you?' She didn't wait for a response. 'Oh, is that the cake? Do let me see. I do hope it's Madeira.'

'Red velvet.'

'Oh…' The sound would have seemed like delighted surprise to somebody who didn't know Louise Collins. Penelope could hear the undertone of disapproval and it took her back instantly to the countless times she had tried so hard to win affection instead of simply acceptance. Why did it still matter? You'd think she would have given up long before this but somehow, beneath everything, she loved her grandmother with the kind of heartfelt bond she'd had as a tiny child, holding her arms up for a cuddle.

It was a relief that the beat of silence was broken by the arrival of another figure in the entranceway. Maybe this was why she'd never been able to let go. Why it still mattered so much.

'Grandad! Happy birthday…' This time the kiss was real and it went with a hug. A retired and well-respected detective inspector with the Loxbury police force, the happiest times of Penelope's childhood had been the rare times alone with her grandfather. Being hugged. Being told that she was loved. Being taken fishing, or on a secret expedition to buy a gift for her grandmother.

The grandmother who'd never allowed the real relationship to be acknowledged aloud.

'For goodness' sake, Penelope. I was only forty-three when you turned up on our doorstep. Far too young to be called a grandmother.'

'I'll take the cake into the kitchen, shall I?'

'Let me have a peek.' Douglas Collins lifted the lid of the box. 'Louise, look at these roses. Aren't they fabulous?'

'Mmm.' Louise closed the box again. 'Don't stay nattering to Rita in the kitchen, Penelope. The champagne's already been poured in the drawing room.'

Rita always made you remember the old adage of 'never trust a thin cook'. Even bigger than Maggie, her hugs were just as good and her praise of the cake meant the most.

'Red velvet? Oh…I can't wait to taste it. Make sure there's some left over.'

'You should get the first piece, Rita. You're the one who taught me to bake in the first place.'

'Never taught you to do them fancy roses. I always said you were a clever girl.'

'I only *felt* clever when I was in here. It's no wonder I ended up being a baker, is it?'

'You're a sight more than that now. How did the wedding go?'

'It was fabulous. As soon as the magazines come out with the pictures, I'll bring some round for you.' The tinkle of a bell sounded from well beyond the kitchen and the glance they exchanged was conspiratorial. Penelope grinned. 'I'll pick a time when the olds are out and we can have a cuppa and a proper natter then.'

'I'd love that, sweet. You go and have them bubbles and enjoy your family time now. Go on…scoot before her ladyship rings that bell again.'

How ironic was it that 'family time' had already been had today. First with Maggie and Dave and then with Rita in the refuge of her childhood.

The messy places that were always warm and smelled of food.

The drawing room should have been overly warm thanks to the unnecessary coals glowing in the enormous fireplace, but somehow the perfection of every precisely placed object and the atmosphere of a formal visit created a chill. Tasting the champagne as they toasted the birthday didn't help either, because it made Penelope remember the taste in her mouth last night, when she'd emerged from the kitchen to take Rafe's hand and let him lead her upstairs.

The spiral of sensation in her belly at the memory couldn't have been less appropriate in this setting. Closing her eyes with a silent prayer, Penelope took another gulp.

'You look tired.' Her grandmother's clipped tones made it sound like she was excusing her lack of manners in drinking too fast. 'I hope you got some rest today instead of playing cook at that orphanage place.'

'Orphanages don't exist any more, Mother. Not like they used to.'

'I know that, Penelope.'

Of course she did. She'd probably gone searching for one as an alternative to doing the right thing and claiming their baby granddaughter.

'Charity work is to be commended, Louise. You know that better than anyone.' That was Grandad in a nutshell. Trying to keep the peace and protect his beloved wife at the same time. He'd always done that. Like the way he'd explained away some of the endless punishments and putdowns meted out by Louise.

She's only trying to keep you safe, sweetheart. We know what it's like to lose a precious little girl.

And now it was her turn to be soothed. 'Good on you, Penelope, if you went and helped when you were tired.'

'I wouldn't call it charity.' Oh, help. Why was she contradicting everything being said? She took another gulp of champagne and found, to her horror, that she'd drained her glass.

'Of course it's charity. Those children are riff-raff that nobody wants. With no-good parents that probably spend all their money on cigarettes and alcohol and have no idea how to set boundaries for themselves, let alone their offspring.'

'Mmm…' Penelope was heading for the ice bucket that held the champagne bottle. 'Bad blood,' she murmured.

'Exactly.'

The long pause was enough for the silent statement that was as familiar as a broken record.

'You can't help having bad blood. You just have to fight against it. Otherwise you know what can happen.'

Yep. Penelope knew.

She'd end up just like her mother.

Funny that the ice bucket was on the occasional table right beside the fireplace. And that family photos were positioned artfully on the top of the mantelpiece. There was Penelope in a stiff, ruffled dress, aged about three, clutching a teddy bear that the photographer had had available in his studio.

A not dissimilar professional portrait of another small girl was to one side of an equally posed portrait of her grandparents' wedding. This girl had the same blonde hair as Penelope but her skin was much paler and her eyes were blue. One of the few pictures of her mother, Charlotte—before she'd gone off the rails so badly.

It wasn't that the Collins blood was bad, of course. Charlotte had been led astray by the person who'd really had it. The unknown father whose genes had overridden her mother's to give Penelope her brown eyes and more olive skin. A permanent reminder to her grandparents of the man who'd destroyed their perfect little family.

Louise Collins rose gracefully to her feet. 'I'll go and let Rita know we're ready for the soup. Come through to the dining room, Penelope.'

'On my way.' Or she would be, when she'd filled her glass again. Heaven knew, she needed some assistance to get through the next hour or so of conversation without causing real trouble. Falling out with her grandmother any more than she had already this evening would only distress Grandad.

The worst thing about it all was that she had just learned what it was like when you lost the fight with the 'bad blood'.

And it was a lot more fun than she was having right now.

CHAPTER FIVE

NEARLY THREE WEEKS.

It should have been plenty of time to put any thoughts of Penelope Collins to bed—so to speak.

No…wrong choice of expression. Rafe Edwards closed his eyes for a moment to try and quell that surge of sensation that was inevitable whenever thoughts of Penelope and beds collided.

Maybe this was a mistake. He eyed the old building in the heart of Loxbury's industrial area with deep suspicion. Why had it even occurred to him that it might be a *good* idea?

Karma?

The amusement that was inherent?

Or was he being pulled along by some cosmic force he couldn't resist?

Fate.

With a dismissive snort, Rafe slammed the door of his four-by-four behind him. He didn't believe in any of that kind of rubbish. You made your own fate unless you were rendered powerless by youth or natural disaster or something. And success was sweet when it was earned.

Perhaps that was why he had grudging respect for Penny.

Oops...*Penelope*.

From the outside they were total opposites but there was a driving force at a deeper level that they both shared. Judging by the magazine and newspaper coverage of that wedding, Penelope was now poised for extraordinary success and she'd earned it. For whatever reason, she was carving her own niche in the world and she was doing it exceptionally well.

Plus...

Rafe rapped on the iron door that was the only entrance the building had to the street. No doubt there was a sparkling commercial kitchen behind the door with a team of loyal employees who could do their jobs with the kind of military precision Ms Collins would demand. Given how late in the day it was, however, it would be disappointing if the door was opened by someone other than the woman he'd come to see.

He wasn't disappointed. It was Penelope who opened the door.

'G'dday...' Rafe let his grin build slowly. 'I think you might owe me a favour.'

Oh...*no*...

She'd assumed it was Jack, who'd said he might drop in the new menus he was working on. She would never have opened the door otherwise. Not when she was wearing her pyjamas and slipper socks, with her hair hanging loose down her back. Funny how she'd never thought it might be a problem, with the only windows facing the street being on the next level where her apartment was.

How stupid was it not to have bothered using the peephole in the door? Not only stupid, but dangerous. It could have been anyone demanding entrance. A drug addict, for instance. Or an axe murderer.

Or…or…*Rafe*…

And he was calling in a favour?

He was still grinning at her. 'I realise you're probably beating off clients after getting so famous.'

'I… Ah…' Yes. Potential bookings were pouring in in the wake of the Bingham-Summers wedding. And part of that success had been down to its glorious finale with the fireworks. And, yes…Rafe had made that happen when he hadn't had the slightest obligation to, so she did owe him a favour.

But what on earth could he want from her?

The thought of what she might *want* him to want from her was enough to make her knees feel distinctly wobbly and that was more than a little disturbing. She'd got past that lapse of character. It had been weeks ago. Her life was back on track. More than back on track. Penelope tried to pretend that she was wearing her suit and high heels. That her hair was immaculate. She straightened her back.

'The thing is, All Light on the Night is booked to blow up a car on a movie set the day after tomorrow but the gig's about to be postponed, which doesn't suit us at all.'

Penelope had no idea where this conversation was going so she simply stared at him. Which was possibly a mistake. Beneath that battered hat she could see the tousled hair that her treacherous fingers remembered burying themselves in and below that there was a glint in those dark eyes that made her think he was finding this amusing. More than that—he was quite confident that she might find it amusing, too. Because he knew what she liked and he was more than able to deliver?

Penelope dragged her gaze away from his eyes. Dropped them to his mouth. Now, that really was a mistake. Staring at his lips, she could almost feel her body softening. Leaning towards him. Hastily, she straightened again.

'Sorry, what was that?'

'The catering company. It went on a forty-eight-hour strike today. Something to do with the union. Your workforce doesn't belong to a union, does it?'

'Um…not that I know of.' They'd started with only herself and Jack. Other employees had come via word of mouth and the company had grown slowly. They were like a family and there'd never been a hint of an industrial dispute.

'So you could take on the job? It's not huge. Just an afternoon and there'd only be a couple of dozen people to cater for, but film crews do like to eat and they like the food to be on tap. Catering for a movie set could be a whole new line of business for you. Could be a win-win situation for both of us, even.'

'In a couple of days?' Initial shock gave way— surprisingly—to a flicker of amusement at the way he was using the exact turn of phrase she'd tried on him in his office that day. Had he remembered that visit in the same kind of detail she had? 'We usually book that kind of job well in advance. *Months* in advance sometimes.' Her lips twitched. 'I could certainly give you a list of other companies that might be able to help.'

Rafe put an elbow up to lean against the doorframe. It pulled the front of his leather jacket further apart and tightened the black T-shirt across his chest. 'But I don't want another company,' he said. 'I have to have the best and…and I suspect that might be *you*.'

Penelope swallowed hard. She knew what was under that T-shirt. That smooth skin with just enough chest hair to make it ultimately masculine. Flat discs of male nipples that tasted like honey…

Taste. Yes. He was talking about food, she reminded herself desperately. *Food*…

'Have…have you got any idea what's involved with setting up a commercial catering event?'

'Nope.' He quirked an eyebrow and tilted his head. He could probably see into the huge kitchen area behind her anyway so did he really have to lean closer like that? Was he waiting for an invitation to come inside and discuss it?

Not going to happen. It was no help trying to channel thoughts of being dressed in something appropriate. She was in her pyjamas, for heaven's sake. At seven-thirty p.m. Any moment now and she might die of embarrassment.

'There's meetings to be had with the client.' Her tone was more clipped than she had intended. 'Menus and budgets and so forth to be discussed.'

'The budget won't be an issue.'

Another turn of phrase she'd used herself that day in his office. When she'd been desperately trying to persuade him to help her. Impossible not to remember that wave of hope when he'd said he might be able to do it himself.

She could do the same for him. Already, a part of her brain was going at full speed. Mini samosas and spring rolls perhaps—with dipping sauces of tamarind and chili. Bite-sized pies. Sandwiches and slices. It wouldn't be that hard. If she put in a few hours in her kitchen tonight, she could get all the planning and a lot of the prep done. She could use the old truck parked out the back that had been her first vehicle for getting catered food to where it was needed.

It might even be fun. A reminder of her first steps to independence and how far she'd come.

'Will you be there?' The query popped out before she could prevent it. What did it matter?

'Oh, yeah…' That wicked grin was back. 'I love blowing things up. Wouldn't miss it. The real question is…' The grin faded and there was something serious about his face now. 'Will *you* be there?'

That flicker of something behind the amusement told her that he wanted her to be there, but was it only about the food?

Penelope couldn't identify the mix of emotions coming at her but it was obvious they were stemming from that place she thought she'd slammed the door on. It would be a struggle to try and contain them and…and maybe it wouldn't be right.

Even her grandmother would tell her that she had an obligation to return a favour.

'Okay.' She tried to make it sound like it wasn't a big deal. 'Give me the details and I'll see what I can do.'

'How 'bout I email them through to you tomorrow?' He tugged on the brim of his hat and she could swear he was smirking as he turned away. 'Don't want to be keeping you up or anything.'

The flood of colour heated her cheeks so much that Penelope had to lean against the cool iron door after she swung it closed. Nobody knew that she liked to wear her pyjamas in the evenings when she wanted to relax. It would have been okay for Jack to find out but... *Rafe*?

Good grief. Penelope tried to think of something to make her feel less humiliated and finally it came to her.

At least he hadn't caught her dancing.

The thought was enough to get her moving. She needed to check supplies in the cold room and the freezers and start making a plan. The way to get over this humiliation was crystal clear. Even if it was only for an afternoon, this was going to be the best damned catering this movie company—and the visiting pyrotechnicians—had ever experienced.

Man, the food was good.

Rafe wasn't the only person on set to keep drifting back to the food truck and the long table set out beside it. Those delicious little triangles of crispy filo pastry filled with potato and peas in a blend of Indian flavours, along with that dark, fruity sauce, were irresistible. Just as well the platter kept getting replenished and he'd arrived just in time to get them at their hottest.

Just in time for Penelope to be putting the platter on the table, in fact.

'Definitely my favourite,' he told her. 'Good job.'

It was more than a good job. She'd not only made it possible for everyone to keep to schedule, there were a lot of people saying they'd never been so well fed on set. His praise brought out a rather endearing shyness in Penelope. She ducked her head and wiped her hands on her apron.

'Samosas are always popular. Try the spring rolls, too, before they run out. These guys sure do like to eat, don't they?'

She wasn't meeting his gaze. Maybe that shyness was left over from the other night when he'd caught her wearing her PJs.

And hadn't that been totally unexpected? About as strange as seeing this uptight woman dancing in the middle of his maze. There were layers to Penelope Collins that just didn't fit. It wasn't the things that were opposite to him that intrigued him. It was the opposites that were in the same person. Did she actually know who she really was herself?

Not that he was going to embarrass her by mentioning the PJs or anything. She'd returned his favour and he was grateful. And that would be the end of it.

'Won't be for much longer. We're all set for the filming and we only get one take.'

'Really? They seem to have been filming the same scene for ages.'

Rafe glanced behind him. They were in a disused quarry and the road had already been used for the sequence of the car rolling off the road.

'That was the hero getting the girl out of the car. I think they've nailed it now. He gets to help her run away from it next and when they hit a certain point is when we blow up the car. My boys are just getting the explosives rigged. It'll look like they're close enough to be in danger but they won't be, of course. All smoke and mirrors but we need the shot of them with the explosion happening behind them and that'll be it for the day.' He glanced upwards. 'Which is just as well. Those thunderclouds are perfect for a dramatic background but nobody wants their expensive camera gear out in the rain.'

'Is it going to be really loud?'

'Hope so. Should be spectacular, too, but you won't see much from here. Want to come where you will be able to get a good view?'

What was he thinking? The flash in her eyes told him she remembered agreeing to that once before and she hadn't forgotten where they'd ended up. The way her pupils dilated suggested that it had been an experience she wouldn't be entirely averse to repeating.

This was supposed to be the end of their association. Favours given and returned but, heaven help him, Rafe felt a distinct stirring of a very similar desire.

'No.' The vigorous shake of her head looked like she was trying to persuade herself. 'I can't. I'm here to do a job.'

'You can just leave it all on the table. Everybody's going to be busy for a while, believe me. Have you ever seen a car being blown up before?'

'N-no…'

'There you go, then. An opportunity missed is an opportunity wasted.'

It was more than a bit of a puzzle why he was trying to persuade her. It was even more of a puzzle why he felt so good when she discarded her apron and followed him to a point well out of shot to one side of the set. He used his radio to check in.

'You all set, Gav? Can you see the point they have to cross before you hit the switch?'

'All good to go, boss.' The radio crackled loudly. 'Reception's a bit crap. …are you?'

'Other side. Raise a flag if you need me.'

'Roger…' The blast of static made him turn the volume down. 'Something to do with the quarry walls, I guess. They won't need me. I don't usually even come to gigs like this any more.'

Oops. Why had he let that slip? Not that Penelope seemed to notice. She was watching the actors being positioned for the take. Make-up artists were touching up the blood and grime the accident and extrication had created. Cameras were being shifted to capture the scene from all angles. The director was near a screen set up for him to watch the take on the camera filming the central action and the guy holding the clipboard moved in front, ready for the command to begin the take.

'Places, please,' someone shouted. 'Picture is up.'

* * *

This was a lot more exciting than Penelope had expected it to be. So many people who seemed to know exactly what they were doing. There were cameras on tripods, others being held, one even on top of a huge ladder that looked rather too close to the car, which must be stuffed full of explosives by now. A sound technician, with his long hair in a ponytail, was wearing headphones and holding a microphone that looked like a fluffy broomstick. The actors were waiting, right beside the car, for the signal to start running.

'That door's going to blow off first,' Rafe said, his tone satisfied. 'With a bit of luck it'll really get some air at about the same time both ends of the car explode.'

'I hope they're far enough away by then.' Penelope kept her voice down, although they were probably far enough away for it not to matter if they talked.

'See where that camera on the tracks is? There's a white mark on the ground well in front of that. When the actors step across that, it's the signal to throw the switch. There's no chance of them getting hit by anything big.' He shielded his eyes with his hand as he stared across the open ground between them and the car. 'There might not be that many rules I regard as sacred but safety is top of the list.'

Penelope's gaze swerved to his face. The anticipation of waiting for a huge explosion was making her feel both scared and excited. The notion that even her safety was important to Rafe did something weird and, for a heartbeat, it felt like she was falling.

But it also felt like she *was* safe.

Rafe was right beside her. He would catch her before she could get hurt.

As if he felt the intensity of her gaze, his head turned and that weird feeling kicked up several notches. A split second before the eye contact could get seriously significant, however, a loud clap of wood on wood and the shout of 'Action' distracted them both.

Game on.

The actors were doing a good job of making it look like a panicked struggle to get away from the crashed vehicle as flames flickered behind them. The girl was only semi-conscious, blood dripping down her face, and the guy was holding her upright and pleading with her to try and go faster.

Penelope could feel Rafe's tension beside her. He had his hand shielding his eyes again and was looking beyond the actors, who were getting closer to the white mark.

The vehement curse that erupted from his lips made her jump.

'What's wrong?'

But Rafe ignored her. He grabbed his radio and pressed the button.

'Gav? Abort…abort… There's a bloody *kid* behind the car.'

The only sound in return was a burst of static. With another curse, Rafe took off, taking a direct line from where they stood to the side towards the car.

The car that was about to explode…

'Oh, my God…' Penelope couldn't breathe. She stood

there, with her hands pressed to her mouth. Should she do something? Run towards the director and shout for help, maybe?

But Rafe was almost at the car now and surely someone had seen what was happening?

Her feet wouldn't move in any case. She'd never felt so scared in her life. With her heart in her mouth she watched Rafe reach the car. He vanished for a moment behind it and then reappeared—a small figure in his arms and half over one shoulder. Incredibly, he seemed to run even faster with his burden. Off to the side and well away from the line the actors had taken.

Were still taking.

In absolute horror, Penelope's gaze swung back to see them cross the white mark and then the first explosion made her cry out with shock. From the corner of her eye she could see the door of the car spiral into the air just the way Rafe had said it would, but she wasn't watching. Another explosion—even louder—and the car was a fireball. Big, black clouds of smoke spread out and she couldn't see Rafe any longer.

Couldn't think about how close he'd been to that explosion and that something terrible had just happened.

She was safe but—dear Lord—she didn't *want* to be safe in that moment. She wanted to be with Rafe. To know that *he* was safe...

And suddenly there he was. Emerging from the cloud of smoke, still well to the side of the set. Still with the child in his arms.

There was no missing what was happening now. All hell broke loose, with people running and shouting, coming towards Penelope from one side as Rafe came from the other. She was right in the middle as they met.

'What the hell's going on?' The director sounded furious. 'What in God's name is that kid doing here? Where'd he come from?'

'He was hiding behind the car.' The director's fury was nothing on what Penelope could hear in Rafe's voice. His face was grimy from the smoke and his features could have been carved out of stone as he put the boy down on his feet.

And Penelope had never seen a man look more compelling. Then her gaze shifted to the boy and she was shocked all over again. She'd seen this child before.

'Billy?' The name escaped in a whisper that no one heard but the boy's gaze flew to meet hers and she could see the terror of a child who knew he was in serious trouble.

A man in a fluorescent vest, holding a radio, looked as white as a sheet.

'Tried to call you to abort firing, Gav,' Rafe snapped. 'Reception was zilch.'

'We had security in place. Nobody got into the quarry without a pass.'

'He was with me.' Penelope cleared her throat as every face swung towards her, including Rafe's. 'In the food truck. I'm sorry...' She turned towards the boy. 'You knew you were supposed to stay inside, didn't you, Billy? What were you *thinking*?'

Billy hung his head and said nothing but Penelope could see the tremor in his shoulders. He was trying very hard not to cry.

Lifting her gaze, she found Rafe glaring at her with an intensity that made her mouth go dry. He knew she was lying.

'He was thinking he might want to get himself killed,' Rafe said quietly. 'He very nearly succeeded.'

'But he didn't.' Penelope gulped in a new breath. 'Thanks to you.'

'I'll have to file an incident report,' the director said, his anger still lacing every word. 'I should call the police. The kid was trespassing.'

'No.' Penelope took a step towards the boy and put her arm around his shoulders. 'Please, don't call the police. I take full responsibility. It's not Billy's fault. It's mine. I should have stayed in the truck with him.'

'You shouldn't have brought him on set in the first place.'

'I know. I'm sorry. But he knew a car was going to get blown up and it was too exciting an opportunity to miss.' She flicked a glance at Rafe. Would he hear the unspoken plea to get him on side by repeating the words he'd used to persuade her?

As if to underline her plea, a distant clap of thunder unrolled itself beneath boiling clouds. And then raindrops began to fall. Heavy and instantly wetting.

The director groaned. 'This is all we need.'

'Shall we start packing up, chief?' someone asked.

There was a moment of hesitation in which it felt like everyone was holding their breath.

'I'll deal with it,' Penelope offered. 'I'll see that Billy gets the punishment he deserves.'

'I think that's *my* call.' Rafe's voice had a dangerous edge. 'Don't you?'

The heat of his glare was too intense to meet but Penelope nodded. So did Billy.

'Fine.' The director held both hands up in surrender. 'It's your safety regulations that got breached. And it was you that brought this flaky caterer on set. You deal with it.' He turned away, making a signal that had the crew racing to start getting equipment out of the rain, but he had a parting shot for Rafe. 'You have no idea how lucky you are that no harm was done. You'd be out of the movie business for good if it had.' He shook his head. 'You're also lucky that your heroics didn't show up on screen or we'd have to be reshooting and you'd be paying for it, mate.'

The last person to leave was Gav.

'I'll pack down and clear the site,' he said. He cast a curious glance at Penelope and Billy. 'Guess you'll be busy for a while.'

The rain was coming down steadily now. The kid was visibly shivering in his inadequate clothing and the look on his face was sullen enough to suggest he was used to getting into trouble.

Rafe saw the way Penelope drew him closer. For a moment the kid resisted but then he slumped as if totally defeated. He wasn't looking at either of the adults beside him but Penelope was looking and she didn't look at all defeated. Her chin was up and she looked ready to go into battle. What was it with this kid? How on earth did Penelope even know his name?

'Want to tell me what this is all about?' Rafe wasn't about to move and any sympathy for how uncomfortable either of these people felt hadn't kicked in yet. 'There's no way this kid was in your truck when you got here.'

'The kid has a name,' Penelope shot back. 'It's Billy.'

'How did you get anywhere near that car, Billy?'

He got no response.

'He didn't know you were going to blow it up. He—'

'Billy's not a puppet,' Rafe snapped. 'Stop talking for him.'

Penelope's mouth opened and closed. She glared at Rafe.

'Billy? Or is your real name William?'

A small sound from Penelope told him that she got the reference to her own name preference. The kid also made a sound.

'What was that?'

'Billy. Only rich kids get called William.'

'And how do you know Penelope?'

'I don't.'

That made sense. Billy looked like a street kid.

Like he'd looked about the same age? Rafe pushed the thought away. He didn't want to go there.

'How does she know your name, then?'

'Dunno.' Billy kicked at the ground with a shoe that had a hole over his big toe.

'I help out at a local children's home.' Penelope's tone was clipped, as if she expected to get reprimanded for speaking again. 'I've met Billy there a couple of times in the last few years when things haven't been so good at home.'

That also made sense. A bit of charity work on the side would fit right in with the image that Ms Collins presented to the world. The image that hid the person she really was?

Rafe stifled an inward sigh. 'So, is that why you sneaked into the quarry? Trying to find a place away from home?'

'I was playing, that's all.' The first direct look Rafe received was one of deep mistrust. 'I saw them doing stuff to the car and I wanted a closer look. You didn't have to come and get me. It was none of your business, man.'

Whoa…did this kid know that he'd almost got killed and didn't care? The anger was still there. In spades.

'You don't get to make decisions like that,' he told Billy. 'Not at your age.'

An echo of something unpleasant rippled through him. People making decisions for him because he was too young. People making rules. Making things worse.

But this was about safety. Keeping a kid alive long enough for him to get old enough to make his own decisions—stupid or otherwise.

'I'm taking you home,' he said. 'I want a word with your parents.'

'No *way*…' Billy ducked under Penelope's arm and took off. If the ground hadn't become slippery already from the rain, he might have made it, but Rafe grabbed him as he got back to his feet. And he held on.

'Fine. If you don't want to go home, we'll go and have a chat to the cops.'

'No.' Penelope looked horrified. 'Don't you think

he's got enough to deal with, without getting more of a police record at his age?'

More of a police record? Good grief.

'I'll take him to Maggie and Dave. They'll know what to do.'

'Who the heck are Maggie and Dave?'

'They run Rainbow House—the children's home. They're the best people I know.'

There was passion in her voice. Something warm and fierce that made Rafe take another look at her face. At her eyes that were huge and...vulnerable?

'And how do you think you're going to get him to this home? In the back of your truck that he could jump out of at the first set of traffic lights?' The tug on his arm confirmed his suspicions so he tightened his grip.

Penelope faced Billy. 'You've got a choice,' she said. 'You can either come with me and see Maggie and Dave or go to the police station. What'll it be?'

Billy spat on the ground to show his disgust. 'You can't make me go anywhere.'

'Wanna bet?' Rafe was ready to move. It was easy to take the kid with him. 'Let's go back to your truck, Penelope. We can call the police from there.'

'No.' Billy kicked Rafe's ankle. He stopped and took hold of the boy's other arm as well, bodily lifting him so that he could see his face.

'That's enough of that, d'you hear me? We're try-ing to *help* you.'

'That's what they all say.' There was a desperation in Billy's voice that was close to a sob as he struggled for freedom. 'And they don't *help*. They just make everything worse...'

Oh, man... This was like looking into some weird mirror that went back through time.

'Not Maggie and Dave...' Penelope had come closer. Close enough to be touching Rafe's shoulder. Was it just the rain or did she have tears running down her cheeks? 'They can help, Billy. I know they can.'

'Then that's where we'll go.'

'*We?*'

'I'm coming with you.' He couldn't help his exasperated tone. 'You can't do this by yourself.'

Which was a damned shame because Rafe could do without a trip to some home for problem kids. Could do without the weird flashbacks, thanks very much. But he'd only get more of them if he left this unresolved, wouldn't he?

And this was supposed to be the end of his association with Penelope Collins. It would be a shame to leave it on such a sour note.

'Let's get going,' he growled, as another clap of thunder sounded overhead. 'Before we all catch pneumonia.'

CHAPTER SIX

IF PENELOPE HAD been a frightened child with a home she was scared to go back to, then Rainbow House was exactly the place she'd want to be. She knew she was doing the right thing here, but the vibes from the two males in the front seat of her little food truck told her they didn't share her conviction.

Penelope was driving and Billy was sandwiched between the two adults to prevent any attempt to escape. A sideways glance as they neared their destination revealed remarkably similar expressions on their faces. It could have been a cute 'father and son' type of moment, except that the expressions were sullen. They were both being forced to do something that ran deeply against the grain. Being punished.

Her heart squeezed and sent out a pang of…what? Sympathy? There was something more than the expressions that was similar. Had Rafe been a kid who had broken every rule in the book to get some attention? He still broke rules—look at the total lack of appreciation for the stated boundaries at Loxbury Hall. Not that he needed to do anything to attract attention now. He was the most gorgeous man she'd ever seen. He was clever and passionate about his work. And he'd just risked his life to save a child.

The memory of the wave of emotion when she'd seen him emerge from the smoke unharmed made her grip the steering-wheel tightly. It gave her an odd prickly sensation behind her eyes, as though she was about to cry—which was disturbing because she had learned not to cry a long time ago.

'Don't cry, for heaven's sake, Penelope. The only difference it makes is that your face gets ugly.'

There was no denying that Rafe Edwards stirred some very strong emotions in her and the fact that he clearly thought she was punishing Billy by taking him to Rainbow House was annoying. Hadn't he been prepared to deliver Billy to the police? He'd soon see that she was right.

His expression certainly changed the moment Dave opened the door and welcomed them in. They must have just finished dinner judging by the rich smell of food. Most of the children were in the playroom, watching television, and the sound of laughter could be heard. Maggie was on the floor in front of the fire, dressing a small baby in a sleep suit. She scooped up the infant and got to her feet in a hurry.

'Oh, my goodness. What's happened? Billy? Oh…' She handed the baby to Dave and enveloped Billy in a hug that was not returned. The boy stood as still as a lamppost.

'This is Rafe Edwards,' Penelope told her. 'He's the

pyrotechnician I told you about—the one who did the fireworks at the wedding?'

'Oh…' Maggie held out her hand. 'Welcome to Rainbow House, Rafe,' she said. 'I'm Maggie. This is Dave. And this is Bianca.' She dropped a kiss on the baby's head. Then it was Penelope's turn to be hugged. 'Good grief, darling. You're soaked. Come upstairs with me while I get baby Bi to bed. We'll find you some dry clothes.' She glanced at Rafe. 'I'm not sure there'd be anything in the chest to fit you, but Dave could find you something.'

'I'm fine.' The sullen expression had given way to… nothing. It was as if the Rafe that Penelope knew had simply vanished. This was a man with no opinion. No charisma. No hint of mischief.

'Stand over by the fire, then, at least. Dave'll get you something hot to drink. Billy? You want to come and find some dry clothes?'

'Nah.' Billy's head didn't move but his glance slid sideways. 'Reckon I'll stand by the fire, too.'

Maggie shared a glance with Penelope, clearly curious about the relationship of the stranger to the boy she knew, but she wasn't going to ask. Not yet. Best let her visitors settle in first. Penelope knew she'd accept them no matter what story had brought them here, and she loved Maggie for the way you became a part of this family simply by walking through the door. When Dave handed her the baby, she was more than happy to take her and cuddle her as she followed Maggie out of the room. Pressing her lips to the downy head was a delicious comfort. It eased the worry of glancing back to see Rafe and Billy both standing like statues in front of the fire.

Rafe had the curious feeling that he'd fallen down one of those rabbit holes in Alice's wonderland.

Had he really thought that Penelope came here occasionally as her contribution to society to read stories to the children or something? She was a part of this family. In this extraordinary house that felt exactly like a *real* home. It even smelt like one. The aroma of something like roast beef made his stomach growl. The heat of the fire was coming through his soaked clothing now, too. A sideways glance showed steam coming off Billy's jeans and the kid had finally stopped shivering. He kind of liked it that Billy had chosen to stay with him, instead of disappearing with the others to find dry clothes. Maybe he felt the connection. Felt like he might have an ally.

Not that Rafe had any qualms about leaving him here, if that was possible. This wasn't like any children's home he'd ever experienced. Hell, it wasn't even like any foster home he'd been dumped in. No point in wondering what kind of difference it might have made if there'd been a place like Rainbow House in his junior orbit. Water under the bridge. A long way under the bridge, and he still didn't want to go swimming in it again. The sooner he got out of here, the better.

Dave had gone to the kitchen and the silence was getting noticeable.

'So you've been here before?'

'Yeah...'

'Not bad, is it?'

'Nah…I guess.'

Dave reappeared with two steaming mugs. 'Soup,' he announced. 'Lucky we always have a pot on the back of the stove.'

Maggie and Penelope appeared by the time he'd taken his first sip and he almost slopped the mug as he did a double-take. What was Penelope wearing?

An ancient pair of trackpants, apparently. And a thick, oversized red woollen jersey that had lumpy white spots all over it. She was still rubbing at her hair with a towel and when she put it down he could see damp ringlets hanging down her back. She had *curly* hair?

She looked so young. Kind of like the way she'd looked in her PJs, only a bit scruffier.

Cute…

The power-dressing princess seemed like a different person. Of course she did. It *was* a different person. Just part of the same, intriguing package that had so many layers of wrapping.

A teenaged girl with improbably blue hair walked through the living room on her way to the kitchen.

'Hey, Billy. How's it going?' She didn't wait for an answer. 'Dave—John's got the remote and he's not sharing.'

A shriek was heard coming from the playroom. Dave shook his head. 'Excuse me for a moment.'

Maggie clucked her tongue as the blue-haired girl came back. 'Charlene, go back and get a spoon. It's bad manners to eat ice cream with your fingers.'

A snort of something like mirth came from Billy

and Penelope caught Rafe's gaze as she came closer to the fire. *This is good*, the glance said. *This is where this kid needs to be.*

She was right. Eventually, there was time to explain why they were here. They were listened to and questions were asked that got right to the heart of the matter.

'You live near the quarry, don't you, Billy? Is that where you go when you need to get away from home?'

Billy shrugged.

'You know it's breaking the law, don't you? The quarry's a dangerous place and that's why there's no public access allowed.'

Another shrug.

'Breaking rules just gets you into trouble, Billy,' Penelope added quietly. 'You *know* that.'

'We'd love to have you back here,' Maggie said, 'And, if you want, Dave'll give Social Services a ring in a minute. Do you think you'd like that to happen?'

The silence was broken by a sniff. Billy scrubbed at his nose, his head still bent so his face couldn't be seen.

'Yeah…I guess.'

'You'd have to follow our rules. Not like last time, okay?'

'Kay.'

'Any knives in your pocket?' Dave's voice was stern.

This time Billy glanced up. Rafe frowned at him.

A pocket knife came out of a back pocket and was handed to Dave.

'Matches?'

The packet of matches that was produced and handed over was too soggy to be a danger but the message was clear. Rules were to be followed and, if they weren't, there would be consequences.

But these were good rules. Rules that kept kids safe. Rafe nodded approvingly.

With a phone call made and permission given to keep Billy at Rainbow House for the time being, the chance to escape finally arrived. Weirdly, Rafe wasn't in a hurry any more. He stayed where he was, as Maggie bundled Penelope's wet clothes into a plastic shopping bag and farewells were made.

Penelope spoke quietly to Billy. 'I'll see you when I'm back on Sunday. Don't tell the others but I'll make a cake that's especially for you. What sort do you like?'

'Chocolate.'

'No problem. And, Billy…?'

'What?'

She was speaking quietly but Rafe could hear every word. 'You don't have to break rules to get people to notice you. It's when you follow the rules that people like you and the more people like you, the more likely you are to get what *you* want.'

What? At least the astonished word didn't get spoken aloud but Rafe had to step away and take a deep breath. Did she really believe that?

Probably. It might explain why this woman was such a complicated mix of contradictory layers. Whose rules was she following? And why did it matter so much that she was liked by whoever was setting those rules? Hadn't she learned by now that what really mattered was whether you liked yourself?

Self-respect. Self-belief.

Obviously not. Man…someone must have done a good job on her self-esteem at some point in her life.

Not his problem. None of what was going on here was his problem and he didn't want to get any more involved. He pulled a phone from his pocket.

'What's the address here?' he asked Dave. 'I'll just call a taxi.'

'No…' Penelope turned away from Billy. 'I can drop you home. It's the least I can do. You saved Billy's *life*…'

A look flashed between Maggie and Dave. A look that suggested she thought there was more going on between him and Penelope than met the eye. Oh, help… Had she heard *all* about the night of the fireworks?

'That's a much better idea,' Maggie said, turning her gaze on Rafe.

He almost grinned. It would be a brave man who went against what this loving but formidable woman thought best.

'Fine.' It came out sounding almost as grudging as Billy had about getting something he was lucky to be offered. He put an apologetic note in his voice. 'I'm a bit out of town, though.'

'No problem.' Penelope stuffed her feet into her damp shoes and picked up the bag of clothing. 'We've still got some samosas in the back if we get hungry.'

Penelope followed the directions to take the main road out of town and then the turn-off towards the New Forest.

'I've been here before. It's the way to Loxbury Hall.'

'Mmm.'

The only sound for a while then was the rough rumble of the old truck and the swish of the windscreen wipers. The heater still worked well, though, and Penelope was starting to feel too warm in Maggie's old jersey. The T-shirt she had on underneath wasn't enough to stop the itch of the thick wool. She couldn't wait to get home and put her own clothes on. Fire up her straighteners and sort out her hair, too.

Good grief…she must look an absolute fright. This was worse than being caught wearing her pyjamas. At least her hair had been smooth and under control.

'What was that for?'

'What?'

'That groan. I did tell you I was out of town a bit.'

Penelope cringed inwardly. And then sighed aloud. 'It's not that. I'm just a bit over you seeing me at my worst, that's all. A girl thing.'

There was another silence and then Rafe spoke quietly.

'Maybe I'm seeing you at your best.'

She tried to figure that out. Couldn't. 'What's that supposed to mean?'

'You do realise you broke the rules, don't you?'

'What rules?'

'The safety regulations that are a legal obligation for anyone who runs a business like mine. I should be filing a "Near Miss" incident report. Billy should have been charged with trespass.'

'And you think that would have helped him? For God's sake, Rafe. He's a kid whose home life stinks.'

'And you stood up for him. You were prepared to break the rules to stand up for him. I'm impressed.'

Impressed? With *her*?

Should she feel this pleased that she'd impressed a pyrotechnician cowboy her grandparents would probably consider riff-raff?

Moot point. The pleasure was irresistible and felt inexplicably genuine. And then he went and spoiled it.

'What were you thinking, telling him that people only like you if you follow all the rules?'

'It's true.'

But she could hear the note of doubt in her voice and this man, sitting beside her, was responsible for that. Rafe didn't automatically follow anybody's rules but he had the kind of charisma that no doubt had women falling at his feet with a single glance. He'd won over a small, troubled boy who had probably never trusted anyone in his short life so far. And even Maggie had fallen for him, judging by the way she'd acted when she'd taken Penelope away to find those dry clothes.

Instead of opening the old chest, she'd sat on the top and fanned her face with her hand, giving her a glance that had made Penelope feel she was in the company of young Charlene instead of the warm-hearted and practical woman who was in charge of Rainbow House.

'I'm not a bit surprised you went upstairs at Loxbury Hall with *him*. I'd have been more than a bit tempted myself.'

'Like' was far too insipid a word to describe how Penelope felt about Rafe but she wasn't going to try and analyse those strong emotions. They were dangerous. The kind of emotions that led to trouble. Shame. Sometimes, even death...

Rafe's voice brought the wild train of her thoughts to a crashing halt.

'Did you follow all the rules today? Do you think I like you less because you didn't?'

She didn't respond. There was a note in his voice that suggested he didn't like her much anyway.

'Turn in here.'

'Are you kidding?' But Penelope slowed as the iron gates of Loxbury Hall came up on the left.

Rafe pulled out his phone, punched in a few numbers and the gates began to swing open.

She jammed on the brakes and they came to a grinding halt.

It was quite hard to get the words out. 'When you said you'd cleared it with the owner about going upstairs, you hadn't actually talked to anyone, had you?'

'Nope.'

'Because you *are* the owner?'

'Yep.'

Oh, no... Penelope let her head drop onto the steering-wheel on top of her hands. Now she felt like a complete idiot. Someone who'd been played like a violin.

'Um...Penny?'

She didn't bother to correct the use of the loathed diminutive. 'Yeah...?'

'Do you think you could get us off the road properly before someone comes along and rear-ends us? Just to the front steps would be grand.'

* * *

The front steps belonged to the property he'd acquired by not following all the rules. He'd got to where he was in life because he'd believed in himself, not because he'd made other people like him.

Billy could do with a message like that.

Not that he wanted to go anywhere near Rainbow House again. It was sorted. This was it. Time to say goodbye to Ms Penelope Collins.

He turned towards her to do exactly that but then he hesitated. Rain beat a steady rhythm on the roof of the truck and it got suddenly heavier. A flash of lightning made Penelope jump and her eyes got even wider at the enormous crack of thunder that came almost instantly.

'The storm's right on top of us. You can't drive in this.' Without thinking, Rafe leaned over and pushed back a stray curl that was stuck to Penelope's cheek. 'Come inside till it blows over.'

She wasn't looking at him. And she shook her head.

He should have left it there but he couldn't. He knew an upset woman when he saw one. Had it been something he'd said? His hand was still close to her face and his fingers slipped under her chin to turn her head towards him. At the same time he was racking his brains to think of what it was that had sent her back into her shell. Revealing that he owned Loxbury Hall? No. That had nothing to do with her. Ah… As soon as Penelope's gaze met his, he knew exactly what it was.

'I still like you,' he murmured. 'Breaking the rules only made me like you more.'

Her lips parted and the tip of her tongue appeared

and then touched her top lip—as though she wanted to say something but had no idea how to respond. The gesture did something very strange to Rafe's gut. The look in her eyes did something to his heart.

She looked lost. *Afraid*, even?

He had to kiss her. Gently. Reassuringly. To communicate something that seemed very important. And, just in case the kiss hadn't got the message across, he spoke quietly, his lips still moving against hers.

'You're beautiful, Penny. Always believe that.'

A complete stillness fell for a heartbeat. There was nothing but the butterfly-wing softness of that contact lingering between their lips. A feeling of connection like nothing Rafe had ever felt in his life.

And then there was a blinding flash of light. A crack of thunder so loud it felt like the van was rocking. Penelope's body jerked and she emitted a stifled shriek.

That did it. Rafe moved without thinking, out of his seat and running to the driver's side of the van. He wrenched open the door and helped Penelope out. He held her against his body and tried to shelter her inside his jacket but even in the short time it took to get across the driveway and up the steps to the front door of his house was enough for them both to be soaked all over again.

Thank goodness for the efficient central heating in this part of the vast old house. But it wasn't enough. Penelope was shivering.

'I could get a fire started.' He was feeling frozen himself.

'Th-that would be n-nice…'

Was the fire already set or would he have to go hunting for kindling and wood?

'It could take a while.' Which wasn't good enough. And then inspiration struck. 'How 'bout a hot bath?'

'Oh...' She looked for all the world as if he'd captured the moon and was offering it to her in his hands. 'I haven't had a bath in...in for ever. I've only g-got a shower at my p-place.'

Rafe felt ten feet tall. With a decisive nod, he walked towards the staircase. 'You'll love my bath,' he said. 'It's well big enough for two people.'

At the foot of the stairs, he had to stop. Why wasn't she following him? Turning his head, he smiled encouragingly and held out his hand.

'You're quite safe. I wasn't actually suggesting that I'm intending to *share* your bath. I just meant that it would be big enough.'

When she took his hand, hers felt like a small block of ice. Weird that it made him feel so warm inside.

As if he was the one who was being given the moon?

CHAPTER SEVEN

HAVING RAFE IN a bathtub with her was crazy.

It also seemed to be the most natural thing in the world.

How had it happened? Penelope had been sitting there, on the closed lid of the toilet, with a big, fluffy towel around her like a shawl while Rafe supervised the filling of the enormous tub. The tap was one of those old-fashioned, wide, single types and the water rushed out with astonishing speed, filling the room with steam. Steam that became very fragrant when Rafe upended a jar of bath salts into the flow. Then he found a bottle of bubble bath and tipped that in as well.

'You may as well use them up,' he said. 'I'm not likely to.'

So the steam smelled gorgeous and the room was warm but Penelope could see that Rafe was shivering.

'You need that bath as much as I do. More... You've been in wet clothes for hours.'

'I'll go and have a shower in another bathroom.' But Rafe had turned his head on his way out and met her gaze and it felt like time had suddenly gone into slow motion. 'Unless...?'

And so here they were. Sitting at either end of this wonderful old, claw-footed bathtub, with Rafe slightly lopsided to avoid the tap and Penelope's legs between his. The bubbles covered her chest enough to be perfectly decent and she kept her knees slightly bent so that her toes didn't touch anything they shouldn't.

For the longest time they simply sat there in silence, soaking up the delicious warmth.

'I've never done this before,' she finally confessed. 'As soon as I got old enough, I wouldn't even let my nanny stay in the bathroom with me.'

'You had a *nanny*?'

Penelope swept some bubbles together with her hands and shaped them into a hill. 'Only because my grandmother didn't want to be a mother again. She'd done it once, she said, and that was enough.'

'I hope it was a nice nanny.'

'She was okay. Rita—our housekeeper—was better. She's the one who taught me to cook and bake, and by the time I was about eight I was spending so much time in the kitchen Mother decided that the nanny was superfluous so they fired her.'

'A housekeeper and a nanny. Your folks must be pretty well off.'

'We only had one main bathroom and my grandparents' room had an en suite that had a shower.' Penelope didn't want to talk about her family any more. Another scoop of bubbles made the hill higher. It wobbled but still provided a kind of wall and it meant she didn't have to look at Rafe directly. 'How many bathrooms have you got?'

'Haven't really counted.' He sounded vaguely discomforted by the query. 'A few, I guess.'

Penelope laughed. 'I'd say so.' Her laughter seemed to diffuse the awkwardness. 'What made you want to live here?'

Rafe tipped his head back to rest on the curved rim of the bath. 'I came here once when I was a kid. To a Christmas party. I thought it was the kind of house that only people with a perfect life could ever live in.'

'Were your parents friends of the owners?'

It was Rafe's turn to laugh. 'Are you kidding? I was one of a busload of what they called "disadvantaged" kids. The ones that went to foster homes because they wanted the extra money but then they'd get found out and the kid would get "rescued" so that somewhere better could be found. Somewhere they wouldn't get so abused.'

Shocked, Penelope slid a little further into the water. Her mind was back under that tree, as Clarissa and Blake's vows had been pledged. Seeing that sadness in Rafe's eyes as he'd told her she was one of the lucky ones.

'You know what it's like to have a family. Parents. You know what it's like to live in that safe place...'

Had he thought that a mansion was that kind of safe place when he'd been a little boy? That it would automatically give him a family and mean he was loved?

Penelope wanted to cry. She wanted to reach back through time and take that little boy into her arms and give him the kind of hug that Maggie would give.

She wanted to scoop him up and take him to Rainbow House—the way they'd taken Billy today.

That explained the hero-worship, didn't it? Had Billy sensed the connection? Somehow realised he was looking at a role model that he could never have guessed could understand what his life was like?

Maybe her thoughts were hanging in a bubble over her head.

'There weren't any places like Rainbow House back in my day,' Rafe said quietly. 'I wish there had been.' Something like a chuckle escaped. 'Maybe then I wouldn't have broken so many rules.'

Penelope's smile felt wobbly. 'Something went right along the way. Look at where you are now. *Who* you are...'

Her foot moved a little and touched Rafe's leg. His hands must have been under the water, hidden by the layer of foam, because his fingers cupped her calf.

'I'm wondering who *you* are,' he said softly. 'Every time I think I have it figured out, you go and do something else that surprises the heck out of me.'

'Like what?'

'Like breaking the rules. Not shopping Billy in to the cops. Going upstairs with me when you thought it wasn't allowed.'

Oh...help. His fingers were moving on her calf. A gentle massage that was sending tendrils of sensation higher up her leg. More were being generated deep in her belly and they were meeting in the middle in a knot that was both painful and delicious.

'Is not dancing in public one of your rules, too?'

'What?' The exclamation was startled.

'I saw you that day. Dancing in the maze. I was up on the balcony.'

Penelope gasped as something clicked into place. 'How did you know what song I was listening to?'

'You left your iPod on the table in the hall. It wasn't rocket science to check what was played most recently.'

'You were *spying* on me.' Penelope pulled her leg away from his touch. She gripped the side of the bath, stood up and climbed out.

Rafe must have climbed out just as fast because he was right there as she wrapped herself in a towel and turned around. Water streamed off his naked body, taking tiny clumps of bubbles with it. He caught her arms.

'Not *spying*,' he said fiercely. 'I was…intrigued.'

The nearness of him was overwhelming. Nearness and nakedness. She could feel the heat coming off his skin. Smell something masculine that cut through the perfume of the bath salts and bubble bath. His hair hung in damp tendrils and his jaw was shadowed by stubble. And the look in his eyes was…

'I still am,' he murmured. 'You intrigue me, Penelope Collins. No…when you get beneath the layers, I think it would be fairer to say you *amaze* me.'

Penelope forgot how to breathe.

She *amazed* him? On a scale of approving of somebody that was too high to be recognisable. Penelope had never amazed anybody in her life. The highest accolade had been her grandad being proud of her. A nod and even a smile from her grandmother.

Rafe had the world at his feet. He ran a huge, successful company. He'd just bought a house that very few people could ever dream of owning. What did he see in her that could possibly amaze him? It was true, though. She could see the truth of it in the way he was looking at her.

Was it possible for bones to actually *melt* for a heartbeat or two? She was still managing to stand but her fingers were losing their grip on the edges of the towel she had clutched in a bunch between her breasts.

Rafe was still dripping wet. His fingers felt damp enough to leave a cool trail as he reached out and traced the outline of her face but coolness turned into enough heat to feel like her skin was being scorched. Across her temple and cheekbone, down the side of her nose and then over her lips, and still they hadn't looked away from each other's eyes. She could feel the dip to trace the bow of her top lip and then his finger seemed to catch on the cushion of her lower lip.

She saw desire ignite in Rafe's eyes and his face came closer. She could feel his breath on her skin. Could feel his mouth hovering over hers—no more than a hair's breadth from touching—but it couldn't be called kissing.

This was something much deeper than kissing. Something that felt spiritual rather than physical. The waiting was agony but it was also the most wonderful thing Penelope had ever felt. The closeness. The knowing what was coming. The feeling of...*safety*? How amazing was that, that she could feel safe when she was so close to something that she knew could explode with all the ferocity and beauty of one of Rafe's fireworks.

The towel slipped from her fingers as his lips finally made contact. This wasn't just one kiss. It was a thousand kisses. Tiny brushes. Fierce bursts of pressure.

He caught her shoulders as her knees threatened to give up the struggle of keeping her upright. He lifted her. Carried her to where they needed to be.

In his bed.

Rafe didn't turn the bedside light off after he'd ripped the duvet back and placed Penelope in his bed. He wanted to see the look in her eyes as he made love to her. To see if he could catch an expression as extraordinary as the way she'd looked when he'd told her that she amazed him.

And he wanted this to be slow. To last as long as he could make it last because—incredibly—it felt like last time, only better. Still as new and exciting as if it had been the first time ever but familiar, too.

Safe…

She smelled like heaven. She *tasted* like heaven and it had nothing to do with all the stuff he'd tipped into that bath.

It was sex but not as he'd ever known it. This was a conversation that went past anything physical. It felt like simply a need to be together.

And even when the passion was spent, it didn't have to end, did it? He could hold her for a while longer. As long as she was willing to stay?

'Oh, Penny…' Rafe drew her more closely to his body, loving the way her head tucked in against his shoulder. 'Sorry.' His words were a murmur that got

buried in her hair. 'Penelope. I forgot how much you
hate that.'

'I don't hate it when you say it.' The husky note in
her voice was full of the lingering contentment of su-
preme satiety.

'It's more you.' Rafe could feel his lips curl into a
smile and it felt odd—as if he'd never smiled quite like
that before. 'It's how I'm going to think of you from
now on.'

'How do you mean?'

'It's like "Penelope" has extra layers of letters that
hide the real stuff. And it sounds kind of…I don't
know…stilted? All professional and polished, anyway.
Like you were when you came into my office that day.
And how you looked in that silver dress at the wedding.'
His breath came out in a soft snort. 'Who knew I'd end
up seeing you wearing your PJs? And trackpants and a
jersey with big fluffy spots on it?'

'Don't remind me.'

He could feel the way her body tensed. He pressed
his lips against her hair and willed her to relax. And it
seemed to work. She sounded amused when she spoke
again.

'I was so embarrassed when you caught me in my
pyjamas. I only do that when I think no one's going to
see me.'

'When you're being Penny instead of Penelope.'

He felt her breasts press against his arms as she
sighed. 'My best friend at school called me Penny for
a while but I made her stop.'

'Why?'

'There were some older kids there who knew more about me than I did. They told me I'd been called Penny because they're not worth anything any more. That nobody wanted me. That my mother had died because even she didn't want me.'

'Kids can be so cruel.' Rafe stroked her hair. 'What did you say?'

'That my name was Penelope and not Penny. And then I told the teacher about them breaking the rules and smoking behind the bike sheds and they got into a whole heap of trouble.'

'Did it make you feel any better?'

'Not really. And then I went home and started asking questions and that got me into a whole heap of trouble. My mother got one of her migraines and had to go to bed for three days and Grandad told me not to talk about it again. It became a new rule.'

'Sounds like you grew up with a lot of rules.'

'Yep.'

'Like what?'

'Oh, the usual ones. Doing what I was told and not talking back, getting good marks in school, not smoking or drinking. Only going out with nice boys that they approved of.'

Rafe snorted again. 'Would they approve of me?'

Penelope sounded like she was smiling but her tone was wry. 'After what we've just been doing? I doubt it very much.'

'Breaking another rule, huh? Lucky me.' He pressed another kiss to her tangled hair. 'Guess I'm a bad influence.'

'More likely it's my bad blood finally coming out. And you know what?' Penelope turned in his arms before he could answer. 'Right now, I don't even care.' She lifted her face and kissed him.

It was true. How could something that felt this right be so wrong, anyway? She waited, in that moment of stillness, to hear the old litany about her turning out just like her mother but, strangely, it didn't come. Maybe it would hit her on the way home, in which case she might as well stay exactly where she was for a bit longer. Maybe she could just go to sleep here in his arms. How perfect would that feel?

But Rafe didn't sound sleepy.

'Bad *blood*? What the heck is that?'

'Oh, you know. A genetic tendency to do bad stuff. Like take drugs or have wild sex with strangers.'

'I'm pretty sure you don't have "bad" blood.' He sounded amused now. 'It was probably one of the rules you grew up with. No bad blood allowed.'

'Pretty much. Nurture had to win over nature. Which is why I was never allowed to ask any questions about my father. That's where I got my bad blood from. He was the one who led my mother astray. Got her into drugs. Got her pregnant at sixteen. Made her run away from home so my grandparents never saw her again. Until she was dead.'

'I don't do drugs,' Rafe said quietly. 'And you're not going to get pregnant if I can help it. I do have a few rules of my own. In my case, nature probably won out over nurture.'

'I'm not sixteen. I get to do what I choose now.' It had been true for a very long time but this was the first time it *felt* true. She was choosing to be here and stay here for a bit longer because…because it felt so good.

'But you wouldn't tell your grandmother.'

'No. Only because it would hurt Grandad so much. He loves her. He loves me, too, but his priority has always been to protect Mother. And I get that. I think their lives got ruined when they lost their daughter. My mother.'

'What was her name?'

She hesitated for a long moment. She never talked about this. She'd never told anyone her mother's name. But this was Rafe and she felt safe. The word still came out as a whisper.

'Charlotte.'

There was a long silence then. Penelope was absorbing how it made things seem more real when you spoke them. How weird it was to have had a mother who'd never existed in reality as far as she was concerned.

Rafe seemed content to leave her in peace. Had he fallen asleep?

No. He must have been thinking about her. About her unusual parentage.

'Have you ever wanted to find out who your father was?'

'I know his name. It was on my birth certificate.'

'What was it?'

'Patrick Murphy. How funny is that?'

'Why funny?'

'They're probably the two most common Irish names there are. Imagine trying to search for him.'

'Have you…imagined, at least?'

'Of course. But maybe it's better not to know anything more.'

'What *do* you know—other than his name?'

'That he played a guitar in a band. Took drugs and got girls pregnant and then left town and never saw them again. Doesn't sound like a very nice person, does he?'

'There are always two sides to every story, darling.'

Darling…nobody had ever called her that before. It sent a weird tingle through Penelope's body. Embarrassingly, it made her want to cry. Or maybe there was more to the prickle behind her eyes than the endearment.

'He didn't want me,' she whispered. 'Any more than my mother did. She *left* me…under a bush. Who does that to their baby?'

'Maybe she had no choice.' Could he hear the imminent tears in her voice? Was that why he was holding her so close? Pressing his cheek against her head as if he could feel her pain? And more…as if he wanted to make it go away.

Nobody could do that. It was ancient history.

'There's something I should tell you. It happened a few weeks ago. The night after we…the night after the wedding here.' The pressure on her head was easing—as if Rafe was creating some distance because he was about to tell her something uncomfortable. 'I went to a party with some old mates. A band I used to be part of. There was a girl there…'

Oh, *no…* Was he about to tell her he was in a relationship with someone? That this was nothing more than a bit on the side? Penelope braced herself for something huge. Something that had the potential to hurt her far more than she had a right to let it.

'She was a journalist. Julie, I think her name was.'

Penelope didn't need to know this. Her muscles were bunching. Getting ready to propel her out of Rafe's bed.

Out of his life.

'Anyway, she's interested in a story. About a baby they called Baby X.'

Penelope went very, very still. There was relief there that he didn't seem to be telling her about a woman who was important in his life but there was fear, too. This was something that was supposed to be hidden. Long forgotten.

'Apparently Baby X was found under a bush. At the Loxbury music festival, nearly thirty years ago.'

There were tears running down Penelope's cheeks. 'That was me,' she whispered. 'It's going to be my thirtieth birthday in a couple of weeks.'

'I'm guessing you wouldn't want someone turning up on your doorstep, asking questions?'

'*No…*' Penelope squeezed her eyes shut. 'Or, even worse, chasing my folks. They'd *hate* that.' She swallowed hard. 'You don't think they'll be able to find out, do you?'

'I don't know. I'm surprised it's been kept such a secret for so long. It's the kind of story people love to know there's a happy ending to.'

'Grandad was pretty high up in the police force back

then. He might have pulled a few strings to have things kept quiet. People knew that my mother had died, of course, and that I was an orphan. But I'm pretty sure no one got told *how* she died or where she was at the time.'

'So there's no way to connect her to Baby X, then. You should be safe.'

But there was a note of doubt in Rafe's voice and Penelope felt it, too. Why hadn't anyone made what seemed like an obvious connection?

More disturbingly, what would happen if they did?

'I should go,' she said. 'Maybe I should have a word with Grandad and warn him.'

'Don't go. Not yet.' Rafe's arms tightened around her. 'It's still raining out there. Why not wait till the morning?'

How good would it be to push that all aside and not worry about it yet? If she stayed here and slept in Rafe's arms, would he make love to her again in the morning?

'Julie's actually coming to see me at the office to-morrow. I've offered to do a fireworks show at the close of the festival as a contribution to the charity they're supporting. I could find out how much she knows already. Whether there's a chance they'll find out who you are. I could try and put her off even, if you'd like. Warn her that she could do some damage to people if she pursued a story that would be better left alone.'

He'd do that? For her?

'Thank you. I'd owe you a big favour if you could do that.'

'You wouldn't owe me anything.' Rafe was smiling. 'I told you, Penny. I like you. I like you a lot.'

'I like you, too.'

She gave herself up to his kiss then, and it was easy to put any other thoughts aside. So easy to sink into the bliss of touching and being touched.

Except that one thought wasn't so easy to dismiss. Again, 'like' was too insipid a word to have used when it came to Rafe.

She felt protected. Chosen. Loved—even if that was only a fantasy on her part.

It was no fantasy in the other direction. God help her, but she was in love with Rafe Edwards. She probably had been ever since he'd chosen the song she'd been dancing to for his fireworks show. Knowing that he had done so after seeing her dancing had shocked her, but now it made it all seem inevitable. How could you not fall in love with a man who'd chosen a song he knew would make you dance?

A man who was amazed by you?

The potential fallout of having her past and her family's shame made public was huge. And frightening.

But it wasn't nearly as big as how she felt about Rafe, so she could still feel safe while she was here. She could catch this moment of a happiness she'd never known existed.

Tomorrow would just have to take care of itself.

CHAPTER EIGHT

PENNY WAS GONE from his bed long before dawn broke. It was a downside of working in the food industry, apparently. If they had a large gig to cater, the kitchens opened for work by four a.m. She didn't go in this early very often now, because her role was changing to event management, but she'd told Jack she wanted to be in charge of this particular event.

It was a special occasion, apparently. Something to do with the Loxbury City Council and her grandfather would be there so she wanted everybody to be impressed.

'And I have to go home first. Can you imagine what people would think if I turned up in track pants and a spotty jersey, with my hair looking like *this*?'

She actually giggled and it was the most delicious sound he'd ever heard. No…that prize had to go to that whimper of pure bliss he'd drawn from her lips not so long ago.

But, yeah…he could imagine. They'd be blown away by seeing a side of their boss they'd never seen before. A glimpse of Penny instead of Penelope.

But she never let people see that side, did she?

Maybe he was the only person who'd ever got this close to her?

That made him feel nervous enough to chase away the possibility of getting back to sleep.

And his bed felt oddly empty after she'd gone anyway, so he shoved back the covers and headed for the shower.

The bath was still full of water from last night. The bubbles had gone, leaving only patches of scum floating on the surface of a faintly green pond. With a grimace, Rafe plunged his arm into the icy-cold water and pulled the plug.

Just like he'd have to pull the plug on whatever was happening between himself and Penny at some point down the track? His nervousness morphed into something less pleasant. He avoided looking in the mirror as he moved to the toilet because he had a feeling he wouldn't like the person he'd see.

Somebody who'd let someone get close and then leave town and never see her again?

The puddle of the towel on the tiled floor was in the way of getting to the shower cubicle. Rafe stooped and picked it up, remembering the way it had slipped from Penny's body as he'd been kissing her last night. He could almost swear a faint scent of her got released from the fabric as he dropped it into the laundry basket. He heard himself groan as he reached into the shower and flicked on the taps.

It wasn't that he was setting out to hurt her. He just didn't do anything long-term. What was the point of making promises that only ended up getting broken? That was when people got really hurt.

She was too vulnerable for him. And her belief that marriage was some sacred promise that made everything perfect was downright scary. She would probably deny it—he'd seen that magazine article where she'd said she was a happily single career-woman—but the truth was she was searching for 'the one.' The man who'd marry her and give her a bunch of babies.

And that man wasn't him.

No way.

Funny how empty his house felt when she'd gone. How empty *he* felt.

Well, that was a no-brainer. How had they completely forgotten to have any dinner last night? A fry-up would fix that. Bacon and eggs and some mushrooms, along with some thick slices of toast and a good slathering of butter.

By the time he'd finished that, he might as well go into work himself. He'd promised a show to remember for the anniversary Loxbury music festival and the pressure was on to get it planned and organised.

It was a weird twist of fate that the original festival had such significance in Penny's life but a seed of something that felt good came in thinking about that connection. He might not be able to give her what she wanted in life but he could do something to protect her right now. To stop other people hurting her.

Yes. By the time Rafe locked the door of his vast, empty house behind him and walked out into the new dawn, he was feeling much better.

He could fix something. Or at least make sure it didn't get any more broken than it already was.

Julie the journalist was young—probably in her early twenties—and she had an enthusiasm that made Rafe feel old and wise in comparison.

She was also cute, trying to look professional in her summery dress and ballet flats, with her hair up in a messy kind of bun.

Compared to Penny in professional mode, she looked like a child playing dress-up. She was a bit of a chatterbox, too, and giggled often enough for it to become annoying. Was she flirting with him?

If so, she had no idea how far off the mark she was. He couldn't be less interested but he kept smiling. He might need her cooperation on something important if the opportunity arose to put her off chasing the Baby X story. No, make that when. He'd make sure that opportunity arose.

There was plenty to show her and talk about before that. Video clips of old shows, for instance.

'This was the Fourth of July in Times Square. A bigger show than the one we're planning for the festival but we'll be using a lot of the same kind of fireworks. And this is a much more recent one.'

'Oh…isn't that the Summers wedding? I've seen that already. Love the hearts. And it's a cool song…' Julie's head was swaying and her hands were moving. He couldn't imagine any inhibitions about dancing in public with this girl. Any moment now she'd probably jump onto his desk and start dancing.

An image of Penny dancing in the maze moved in the back of his mind. Awkward. Endearing…

'That's one of the early challenges, picking the right song for a show. And it's important to get it locked in because that's when the planning really starts. Hitting the right breaks with the right shells. Making it a work of art instead of just a lot of noise and colour.'

'So have you chosen the song for the festival?'

'Mmm. Did that first thing this morning.'

'What is it?'

'I can't tell you that. If word got out, it wouldn't be a surprise and it would lose a lot of its impact.'

'Oh…*please*…?' Julie's eyes were wide as she leaned closer. 'I cross my heart and hope to die promise that I won't tell *anybody*.'

She was desperate to know. And if he gave her what she wanted, would she be more likely to return the favour?

'Okay…but this has to be a secret. Just between us.'

Her nod was solemn. Rafe made his tone just as serious.

'The first festival was held in 1985. The first thing I did was search for all the number-one hits for that year. And then I looked for ones that would work well with fireworks.'

'And…?'

'Strangely enough, Jennifer Rush's "Power of Love" was one of them.' And hadn't that hit him like a brick. How long had he sat there, the list blurring on the screen in front of him, as he relived watching Penny watching his fireworks that night. That first kiss…

'But you've already used that recently, yes?'

'Yeah…then I found another one and remembered something big that happened in 1985. In May. Only a few months before the festival so anyone who was there would remember it very well.'

'Bit before my time.' Julie smiled. 'You'll have to enlighten me.'

'The Bradford stadium fire? Killed a bunch of people and injured a whole lot more. It was a real tragedy.'

Julie frowned. 'Doesn't sound like a good connection to remind people of.'

'That's the thing. A group that called themselves The Crowd released a song to help with the fundraising effort and it's a song that everybody knows. An anthem that's all about exactly that—connection between people and the strength that they can give each other.'

'Wow…so, are you going to tell me what this magic song is?'

'Better than that.' Rafe clicked his mouse. 'Have a listen…'

A few minutes later and Julie was looking misty. 'That's just perfect…' She sniffed. 'I'd love to use it in my story but it'll still make great copy for a follow-up review.'

'There should be lots of great stuff to follow up on. Did you know that they've got a lot of the original artists playing again?'

'And current ones—like Diversion. Are you going to play with them? Matt really wants you to.'

Was there something going on between Diversion's lead singer and Julie? Rafe made a mental note to ask his mate what he thought he was doing when he saw the guys at the pub straight after this. Julie was too young. She'd end up getting hurt.

'I'm thinking about it. It'd be fun but I'll be pretty busy setting up the show.'

Julie folded her notepad and picked up her shoulder-bag. She looked like she was getting ready to leave.

'It can't be just the fireworks you're checking up on for your piece about the festival,' he said casually. 'What else is interesting?'

'Well, there's some debate about what charity is going to benefit from the profits. Last time it was the Last Wish Foundation for terminally sick kids and the time before that it was cancer research, but they want something local this time. It's all about Loxbury.'

'Mmm.' Rafe tried to sound interested instead of impatient. 'What about that other story? The girl who died?'

'Oh…' Julie's face lit up and she let her bag slip off her shoulder to land on the floor again. 'Now, that's *really* interesting. I had to call in a few favours to get any information but I finally tracked it down through someone who had access to old admission data at Loxbury General's A and E department. There were a few girls to choose from that day but only one who was really sick.'

'From a drug overdose?'

'That's the interesting bit. It was a bit of a scandal at the time because everyone assumed it *was* a drug overdose.'

'And it wasn't?'

'No. Apparently there was no trace of drugs. The coroner listed the death as being from natural causes. The poor girl had a brain aneurysm. She got taken off life support a few days after she'd collapsed at the festival.'

Why didn't Penny know that? Why had she been allowed to think that her mother had been some kind of drug addict who'd abandoned her in favour of finding a high? He'd suggested that maybe she'd had no choice other than to leave her baby under a bush. Having a brain haemorrhage certainly came under that category, didn't it? Wouldn't it have caused a dreadful headache or something? Scrambled thoughts enough for the sufferer to not be thinking straight?

'I got lucky.' Julie tapped the side of her nose. 'I got her name. Charlotte Collins. I've been trying to contact her family but do you know how many Collinses there are in Loxbury?'

She didn't wait for him to guess, which was just as well because Rafe was still thinking about Penny. How it might change things if she knew the truth. But, then, why hadn't she already been told? What kind of can of worms might he be opening?

'A hundred and thirty-seven,' Julie continued. 'And this Charlotte might not even have been local.' She paused for a breath. 'Mind you, I did get an odd reaction of this dead silence with one call. And then the phone got slammed down. The number was for a Douglas Collins. He got an OBE for service to the police force and now he's got some important job in the city council. I might follow that up again.'

'Don't you think it would be kind of intrusive to have someone asking about the death of your child?'

'But it was thirty years ago.' Julie looked genuinely surprised. 'I'd think they might like to think that someone remembered her. I might suggest some kind of tribute at the festival even, if I can find out a bit more.'

'I wouldn't.' Rafe summoned all the charm he could muster. 'I'd let the poor girl just rest in peace.'

'Oh...' Julie was holding his gaze. 'Really? But doesn't it strike you as too much of a coincidence that a girl died *and* there was an abandoned baby found? There's got to be a connection, don't you think?'

'Is that why you're chasing the story of the dead girl?'

'It's the only lead I've got. I can't find anything out about the baby. All I've got to go on is that they thought it was a few days old and there was a mention in the news that it had been reunited with family a short time later. Nobody ever said *why* it got left under a bush, though.'

'I guess the family wanted privacy. Maybe that should be respected.'

Julie didn't seem to hear him. 'Do you know how many babies get born in Britain?' She had a habit of asking questions she intended to answer herself. 'One every forty seconds or so. That's a lot of babies. Even if you have an approximate birth date you've got hundreds and hundreds to choose from, but guess what?'

'What?'

'Last night, I found one with the surname of Collins.

Born in London but guess what the mother's name on the birth record is?'

Rafe didn't want to guess. He already knew.

'Charlotte,' Julie whispered. 'But that's just between us, okay? I'll keep your secret about the song and you can keep mine.'

'So you're looking for this daughter now?'

'You bet. But I've got a long way to go. What if she got adopted and has a completely different name now?'

'What if she's adopted and doesn't know about it? You could damage a whole family.'

'She's all grown up now. I'm sure she could cope. She might even like her five minutes of fame.'

Rafe stood up. He couldn't say anything else but he needed to move. He wasn't doing a very good job of putting Julie off the scent, was he? How could he protect Penny?

He really, really wanted to protect her.

Somehow.

'As you said, it's a common name. I suspect you'll find a dead end.'

'No such thing in journalism.' Julie beamed at him. 'It just means there's a new direction to try. And I've got one to go and try right now. Thanks for the interview, Rafe. I'll look forward to seeing the fireworks.'

There might be fireworks of an entirely different kind well before the festival, Rafe mused, leaving his office to get to the pub where his old mates were waiting to have a beer and talk about whether he was going to join the band for a song or two on the day.

As soon as he'd had a beer or two he'd get away. At least he and Penny had exchanged phone numbers now. He could call her and warn her about how close Julie was getting to the truth. Apologise for not being more effective in throwing her off the scent, but how could he when she was so far down the track already? He could do it now, in fact, before he went somewhere noisy. Stopping in the street, he pulled his phone from his pocket. He dialled her number but, as it began to ring, another thought struck him.

Maybe he should also tell her that the truth was not what she believed it to be. But that wasn't something he could tell her over the phone. Cutting the call off, he shoved his mobile back into his pocket. It was a good thing he knew where she lived. A smile tugged at his lips as he pushed his way into a crowded Irish bar. Maybe there was a chance she'd be wearing those PJs again when she opened her door. If he stayed a bit longer at the pub with his mates, the odds of that being the case would only get stronger.

There was a good band playing and the beer was even better. Telling Scruff and Matt and the others that he'd like to get up on stage with them for old times' sake led to a lot of back-slapping and a new round of beer, this time with some whisky shots as well.

'You'll love it, man. Can't wait to tell the Twickenham twins. Bet they'll turn up with their pompoms as well as their cowboy hats. Hey, let's give them a call. They might like a night out, too.'

'I can't stay too long. Somewhere to be soon.'

'You can't leave yet. Band's not bad, eh? For a bunch of oldies.'

Rafe took another glance at the group on stage. 'They're no spring chickens, are they? Best place for Irish music, though. They wouldn't sound half as good at an outdoor gig.'

'Don't let them hear you say that. They'll be playing at the festival. They're one of the original acts that's being brought back.'

Rafe peered at the set of drums. 'What's with the name? The *Paws*?'

'Bit of a laugh, eh? I hear it got picked because it's the nickname of the lead guitarist but it got a lot funnier after the Corrs came along.'

'What kind of a nickname is Paws?' Rafe had another look as a new round of drinks got delivered to their corner. 'His hands look perfectly normal to me.'

'That's not normal. Listen to him—the guy's a genius. Paddy's his real name. Good name for an Irish dude, eh?'

'Don't tell me,' Rafe grinned. 'His surname's Murphy?'

Scruff's jaw dropped. 'You knew all along, didn't you?'

'No.' This time Rafe couldn't take his eyes off the guitarist. Paws. Paddy. Patrick. A Patrick Murphy who played the guitar. Who'd been at the Loxbury music festival thirty years ago? What were the odds?

Maybe Julie was right. Dead ends only led to a new direction. If the truth was going to come out, maybe the best thing he could do for Penny was to make sure that the *whole* truth came out. And this was too much of a coincidence to ignore.

Maybe he'd wait until the band finished for the night. Buy the guy a beer and at least find out if he'd ever known a girl called Charlotte Collins. Get a feel for whether there was any point in going any further.

In the meantime, there were drinks to be had. Conversations to be had along with them.

'Hey, Scruff? What did you do with that old set of drums I gave you way back? The ones I got given before I took up the sax?'

'They're still in the back of my garage. Bit of history, they are.'

'D'you really want to keep them?'

'Hadn't thought about it. Guess I should clean out the garage some time so I can fit my car back into it? Why?'

'Just that I met a kid the other day who looks like he could use a direction in life. A set of drums is a good way to burn up a bit of teenage angst, if nothing else.'

'True. Come and get them any time, man. They were yours in the first place, anyway.'

It was the buzzing in his pocket that finally distracted him from what was turning out to be a very enjoyable evening. He would never have heard his phone ringing but he could feel the vibration. When he saw that Penny was the caller, he pushed his way out of the bar again. Out into the relative peace of an inner-city street at night.

'Penny…hey, babe.'

'How *could* you, Rafe? When you knew how important it was…'

Good grief…was she *crying*?

'I trusted you…and then you go and do *this*…'

Yep. She was crying. Either that or she was so angry it was making her words wobble and her voice so tight he wouldn't have recognised it.

'What are you talking about? What am I supposed to have done?'

'Julie.' The word was an accusation. 'You *told* her.'

'Told her what?' But there was a chill running down his spine. He had a bad feeling about this.'

'About me. About my grandparents. She turned up on their doorstep, asking all sorts of questions… Oh, my God, Rafe… Have you any idea what you've *done*?'

'I didn't tell her anything. She'd already figured it out. I was going to tell you…'

'You really expect me to believe that? You told her and then she turned up and now…and now Grandad's probably going to die…'

'What?'

'They got rid of her but Mother was really upset. Rita called me. By the time I got there, all I could do was call an ambulance.' There was the sound of a broken sob on the other end of the line. 'He's had a heart attack and he's in Intensive Care and they don't know if he's even going to make it and…and this is…this is all… Oh, *God*… Why am I even talking to you about this?'

The call ended abruptly. What had she left unsaid? That it was all his fault?

It wasn't true. It wasn't even fair.

But standing there, in the street, with the echoes of that heartbroken voice louder than the beeping of the terminated call, it felt remarkably like it was, somehow, *his* fault.

CHAPTER NINE

THEY WERE TAKING him away.

Penelope watched the bed being wheeled towards the elevator, flanked by a medical team wearing theatre scrubs, the suddenly frail figure of her beloved grandfather almost hidden by the machines that were keeping him alive.

The elevator doors closed behind the entourage and Penelope pressed her hand against her mouth. Was this going to be the last time she saw him alive? He was the only person in her life she could believe still loved her, even when she messed up and broke a rule. Someone who could see some value in what Rafe called Penny instead of Penelope.

Oh, God…she didn't want to think about Rafe right now. About that shock of betrayal that had felt like a death and only made it so much worse as she'd watched the paramedics fighting to stabilise Grandad before rushing him to hospital.

A sideways glance showed her own fear reflected on her grandmother's face but the instinct to move closer and offer the comfort of a physical touch had to be suppressed.

'I'll take you to our family waiting room.' The nurse beside them was sympathetic. 'Someone will come and find you as soon as we know anything.'

'How long is this procedure going to take?' Louise spoke precisely and it sounded as though she was asking about something as unimportant as having her teeth whitened but Penelope knew it was a front. She'd never seen her grandmother looking so pale and frightened.

Lost, even...

'That depends,' the nurse said. 'If the angioplasty's not successful, they'll take Mr Collins straight into Theatre for a bypass operation. We should know whether that's likely within the next hour or so. Here we are...' She opened the door to a small room that contained couches and chairs, a television and a coffee table with a stack of magazines. 'Help yourself to coffee or tea. Milk's in the fridge. If you get hungry, there's a cafeteria on the ground floor that stays open all night.'

The thought of food was nauseating.

The silence, when the nurse had closed the door behind her, was deafening.

Louise sat stiffly on the edge of one of the chairs, staring at the magazines. Was she going to pick one up and make the lack of conversation more acceptable?

'Can I make you a cup of tea, Mother?'

'No, thank you, Penelope.'

'Coffee?'

'No.'

'A glass of water?'

'*No*... For heaven's sake, just leave me alone.' Her voice rose and shook and then—to Penelope's horror—

her grandmother's shoulders began shaking. She was *crying*?

'I'm sorry,' she heard herself whisper.

What was she apologising for? Telling Rafe her story, which had been passed on to that journalist who'd been the catalyst for this disaster? How *could* he have done that? She'd felt so safe with him. Had trusted him completely. The anger that had fuelled that phone call had evaporated now, though, leaving her feeling simply heartbroken.

Or was she apologising for being the person her grandmother had to share this vigil with? For all the years that her grandparents had had to share their lives with her when they could have been enjoying their retirement together? Was she apologising for having been born at all?

Or was she just sorry this was happening? Sorry for herself and for Mother and most of all for Grandad.

Maybe it was all of those things.

'He's in the right place,' she said softly. 'And he's a fighter. He won't give up.'

Louise pulled tissues from the box beside the magazines. 'You have no idea what you're talking about, Penelope. This is precisely what *could* make him give up. Being reminded...'

Of what? Losing their daughter and getting the booby prize of a grandchild they hadn't wanted? Penelope didn't know what to say.

Louise blew her nose but kept the tissue pressed against her face so her voice sounded muffled. 'He gave up then. He was in the running for the kind of job that would have earned him a knighthood eventually. A seat in parliament, even, where he could have achieved his life's dream of law reform that would have made a real difference on the front line. There were two things Douglas was passionate about. His job. And his daughter.'

'And you.' Penelope sank onto the couch, facing her grandmother. Louise had never talked to her like this and it was faintly alarming. This was breaking a huge rule—talking about the past. Maybe that was why she was crossing a boundary here, too, in saying something so personal. 'He loves you, too, Mother.'

Louise had her eyes closed as she slumped in her chair. 'I gave him Charlotte,' she whispered. 'That was my biggest accomplishment...but I couldn't stop it happening. I tried *so* hard...'

Penelope's mouth was dry. Was Louise really aware of who she was talking to? It felt like she was listening to someone talking to themselves. Someone whose barriers had crumbled under the weight of fear and impending grief.

'What...?' The word opened a door that was supposed to be locked. 'What was happening?'

'The violin lessons. That was what should have been happening.' The huff of breath was incredulous. 'But, no...we found out she'd given up the lessons. It wasn't hard to have her followed and that's how we found out about the boy.'

Penelope's heart seemed to stop and then deliver a painful thump. 'My...father?'

'Patrick.' The name was a curse. 'A long-haired Irish

lout who'd given up his education to be in a band that
played in pubs. He was living in a squat, along with his
band and their friends—the drug dealers.'

'Oh...' She could understand how distressing that
must have been. What if she had a sixteen-year-old
daughter who got in with a bad crowd? A reminder
of the anger she'd felt towards Rafe surfaced but this
time it was directed at the mother she'd never known.
A drug addict. Someone who'd made her parents unhappy and then gone on to abandon her own baby. There
was something to be said for the mantra she'd been
brought up with. Penelope didn't want to end up like
her mother. No way.

'She threatened to run away and live with the boy
if we tried to stop them seeing each other. They were
"in love", she said. They were going to get married
and live happily ever after.' For the first time since
she'd started talking, she opened her eyes and looked
directly at Penelope. 'How ridiculous was that? She
barely knew him.'

Penelope had to look away, a confusing jumble of
emotions vying for prominence. She barely knew Rafe
but there'd been more than one occasion with him when
she'd thought there was nowhere else in the world she'd
ever want to be. A wave of longing pushed up through
the anger. And then there was that hurt again and somewhere in between there was a flash of sympathy for her
mother. A connection born of understanding the power
of that kind of love?

'Douglas was in the final round of interviews for the
new government position. Can you imagine how help-

ful that would have been? How could anyone think that he could contribute to law and order on a national level when he couldn't even keep his own house in order? When his daughter was living in a drug den?'

Penelope was silent. Maybe it could have been a point in his favour. Didn't a lot of people become doctors because they hadn't been able to help a loved one? Have the motivation to help because they understood the suffering that could be caused? Look at the way Rafe had been with Billy. He'd known what that boy was going through and he'd had to step up and help, even when it had clearly been difficult for him. There was something fundamentally good about Rafe Edwards. It was hard to believe he would ever do anything to hurt someone else deliberately. She didn't *want* to believe it but how could she not, when the evidence was right there in front of her?

'It wasn't hard to have the house raided with our police connections. Arrests made.' Louise sounded tired now. 'There wasn't anything that the boy or his band friends could be directly charged with but association was enough. They got warned to get out of town and stay out. *He* was told in no uncertain terms that if he tried to contact Charlotte again, charges could still be laid and they could all find themselves behind bars.'

'So he just left? Even knowing that he was going to be a father?'

Louise fluttered a hand as if it was unimportant. 'I don't imagine he knew. I'm not sure Charlotte knew. Either that or she kept it hidden until it was too late to do anything about it.'

Somehow this was the most shocking thing she'd heard so far in this extraordinary conversation and the words came out in a gasp.

'An abortion, you mean?'

She might not have existed at all and that was a weird thought. She would never have known the satisfaction of being successful, doing something she loved. Or felt the pleasures that creating beautiful food or listening to wonderful music could provide. She would never have danced. She would never have experienced the kind of bliss that Rafe had given her, albeit so briefly.

There was something else she could feel for her mother now. Gratitude at being protected?

'Of course.' The clipped pronouncement was harsh. 'Not that your mother would have cooperated. She became extremely...difficult. She stopped eating. Stopped talking. Your grandfather was beside himself. It was the psychiatrist we took her to who guessed she was pregnant.'

The long silence suggested that the conversation was over as far as Louise was concerned, but Penelope couldn't leave her story there.

'What happened then?'

'I found a boarding school that specialised in dealing with situations like that. She was to stay there and continue her schooling and then the baby would be adopted.'

That baby was *me*. Your grandchild...

But the agonised cry stayed buried. Instead, Penelope swallowed hard and spoke calmly. 'Was Grandad happy about that?'

Louise had her eyes shut again. 'It was a difficult time for all of us but there was no choice. Not if he wanted that promotion.'

A promotion that had clearly never happened.

The silence was even longer this time. Maybe they would hear soon about what was happening with Grandad. No doubt someone would come and talk to them in person but it was an automatic gesture to check her phone. Nothing.

Except a missed call from Rafe.

Hours ago now. Well before she'd called him.

The wash of relief was strong enough to bring the prickle of tears to her eyes. So he had been telling the truth? He had tried to call her? To confess he'd said something he had promised not to and revealed the identity of Baby X?

But why had those questions Julie had been asking had such an effect? Why was it still such a big deal, given that her grandfather had retired so long? This was only getting more confusing.

'How did I end up at the music festival? Do you know?'

Louise shrugged. 'There was a letter that came to the house. From him. Full of ridiculous statements like how he couldn't live without her. That he'd be at the festival and if she felt the same way she could find him there. I didn't forward it, of course, but I presume Charlotte found out somehow. She was in the hospital then, instead of the school, so it was probably wasn't hard to escape.'

Escape... As though she'd been sent to prison. How

hard would it still have been to get away? To take her newborn baby with her?

Penelope felt the ground shifting beneath her feet. She hadn't been abandoned. Her mother could have left her at the hospital but she'd taken her. To the festival. To meet her father?

'We got the call later that day to say she was in the intensive care unit. Right here, in almost the same place as Douglas. How ironic is that? It was obvious she'd recently given birth so we had no choice but to make enquiries about what had happened to the baby. It was your grandfather who insisted on bringing you home. You were the only thing that he cared about after Charlotte died. He gave up on his job and he…he blamed me for sending our daughter away…'

'He still did well. He got an OBE.'

'Hardly a knighthood.'

'He's a well-respected councillor.'

'Not exactly a seat in parliament or a mayoralty, is it? And the passion was never there any more.' Louise was struggling not to cry again. 'I tried to make the best of it. We pulled strings and managed to keep the story out of the papers. I did my best for you but the reminders were always there. And now there's a reporter trying to turn it all into tabloid fodder. Asking questions about why people had been allowed to assume it was a drug overdose when it wasn't. And it's all—'

All what? *Her* fault? Her own fault? What had caused her mother's death if it wasn't a drug overdose? Something that she could have had treated and survived? Had guilt been the poison in her family rather than shame?

The unfinished sentence was an echo of her call to Rafe. And he probably knew that she'd been about to tell him it was all *his* fault. But how could Julie have known it hadn't been a drug overdose? She hadn't told Rafe that because she hadn't known herself.

This was all a huge, horrible mess. And maybe none of it really mattered at the moment, anyway. The door to the room opened quietly to admit the nurse who had brought them here.

'It's all over,' she said. 'And it went very well. Mr Collins is awake now. Would you like to come and see him?'

Louise seemed incapable of getting up from her chair. She had tears streaming down her face. When she looked at Penelope there was an expression she'd never seen before. A plea that could have been for reassurance that she had just heard what she most wanted to hear.

Or could it be—at least partly—a plea for forgiveness?

Penelope held out her hand. 'Let's go,' she said quietly. 'Grandad needs us.'

'So that's about it. The rehearsal starts at five tomorrow. Let's all work together and make this a really family-friendly occasion.'

Rafe glanced at his watch. The meeting of all the key people involved in the organisation and set-up of the Loxbury music festival had filled an impressive section of the town hall. Scruff and Matt were here and he'd noticed Patrick Murphy at the back, no doubt here to find the time his band was expected to turn up for the rehearsal. Surprising how strong the urge still was to seek him out after the meeting and talk to the man who could well be Penelope's father, but he'd already done enough damage as far as she was concerned and he had no desire to get any more involved.

It was over. Or it would be, when he could shake this sense of…what was it? He hadn't done anything wrong in the first place and he hadn't even tried to contact Penny since she'd hung up on him so why did he feel like he was still doing something wrong? Making a monumental mistake of some kind?

'One other thing…' The chairman of the festival committee leaned closer to his microphone. 'We still haven't made a final decision about the charity that will be supported by the festival. If anyone has any more suggestions, they'll need to talk to a committee member tonight.'

Rafe found himself getting to his feet. Raising his arm to signal one of the support crew who'd been providing microphones for the people who'd wanted to ask questions during the briefing.

'I have a suggestion,' he said, taking hold of the mike.

'And you are?'

'Rafe Edwards. My company is providing the fireworks to finish the festival.'

A ripple of interest turned heads in his direction. The chairman was nodding. 'You've made a significant contribution to the event,' he said. 'Thank you.'

The applause was unexpected. Unnecessary. Rafe cleared his throat. 'The message we've been hearing to tonight is that you want this to be a family-friendly event. A mini-festival that isn't a rave for teenagers but something that could become an annual celebration that will bring families together.'

'That's right.'

'So I have a suggestion for the charity that you might like to consider supporting.'

'Yes?'

'The Loxbury Children's Home—Rainbow House—is a facility that this town should be very proud of. It's changing the lives of the most vulnerable citizens we have—our disadvantaged children—and, with more funding and support, it could do even more good for the community.'

A murmur of approval came from the crowd and the chairman was nodding again, after exchanging glances with the other committee members on the stage.

'It's local,' the chairman said. 'And it's about family. It's certainly a good contender.' A nod signalled that the evening's agenda was complete. 'Thanks, everybody. You'll find some refreshments in the foyer. I look forward to seeing you all again on Saturday evening. And, Mr Edwards? Come and see me before you go. I'd like to provide some free passes for the children at Rainbow House to come to the festival.'

Rafe hadn't intended staying to drink tea or eat any of the cake the Loxbury Women's Institute was providing, but there seemed to be a lot of people who wanted to shake his hand and tell him how appreciated the contribution of his fireworks show was and what a good idea he'd had for the charity to be supported.

One of them was Paddy Murphy.

'Kids are everything, aren't they?' He smiled. 'They're the future. Biggest regret of my life was not having any of my own.'

Close up for the first time, there was no doubt in Rafe's mind that this man *was* Penny's father. Those liquid brown eyes were familiar enough to twist something in his chest. About where his heart was. But he had to return the friendly smile. Say something casual.

'I'll probably have the same regret one day.' Oops. That wasn't exactly casual, was it? He shrugged. 'It's a hard road, finding the right woman, I guess.'

'Oh, I found her.' The Irish brogue was as appealing as the sincerity in Paddy's gaze. 'But then I lost her.' He slapped Rafe on the shoulder and turned away but then looked back with a shake of his head. 'Truth be told, *that's* really the biggest regret of my life. Always will be.'

Rafe watched him disappear into the crowd.

And it was right about then that he realised why he couldn't shake that nagging feeling of making some huge mistake.

He knew what that mistake was.

He just didn't have any idea of how to fix it.

CHAPTER TEN

WHAT ON EARTH was she going to do with all these cakes?

Chocolate and banana and carrot and red velvet. All iced and decorated and looking beautiful, and Penelope had no desire to eat a bite of any of them. The baking marathon had been therapy. Something comforting to do while she tried to sort through the emotional roller-coaster of the last couple of days.

She could take one of them in to the hospital for the lovely nurses who were caring for her grandfather so well. Maggie and Dave were always happy to have a cake in the house and her grandmother might like to take one home to help Rita cater for the stream of well-wishers that were turning up at their door. And maybe—the thought came as a gleam of light at the end of a dark tunnel—she could take one to Rafe.

To say sorry. Of course it couldn't make things right again but…it would be something, wouldn't it?

An excuse to see him one last time, anyway.

She chose the chocolate cake for the nurses in the cardiology ward of Loxbury General.

'You didn't need to,' the nurse manager told her. 'It's been a pleasure, caring for your grandad. We'll be sorry to see him go home tomorrow. But thank you…we *love* cake.'

She gave her grandmother the choice of the other cakes.

'Could I take the red velvet? I know your Grandad loved his birthday cake and it *was* rather delicious.'

'Of course. I'm sorry—I didn't think to make a Madeira one.'

'Do you know, I think I'm over Madeira. Such a boring cake, when you come to think of it.'

There was no farewell hug or kiss after handing over the cake but Penelope still felt good. There was something very different about her relationship with her grandmother now. Something that had the promise of getting better. Just like Grandad.

The smile stayed with her as she drove to Rainbow House. How good had it been to sit and hold Grandad's hand in the last few days? To talk to him about things they'd never discussed and even to tell him about that extraordinary conversation with her grandmother.

'She did do her best with you, you know. And she does love you, even if she doesn't let herself admit how much. She got broken by your mother's death, love. We both did. Nobody's perfect, you know. We all make mistakes but what really counts is who's there to hold your hand when it matters.'

'I know.' It was a poignant thought to realise whose hand she would want to be holding hers in a crisis.

Only she'd want more than that, wouldn't she? She'd

want her whole body to be held. So that she could feel the way she had when Rafe had held her.

'Loving people carries such a risk of getting hurt, doesn't it?' There had been an apology in her grandfather's voice as he'd patted her hand. 'Maybe neither of us was as brave as we should have been.'

Penelope's smile wobbled now as she turned into a very familiar street. How brave was she?

Brave enough to take one of those cakes to Rafe's office? To ask that receptionist if there was a chance that the terribly important chief executive officer of All Light on the Night might have the time to see her?

Not that he'd be at work this late in the day.

Maybe it would be better to take the cake to Loxbury Hall? To the place where she had fallen in love with him...

The place where he'd made *her* feel loved...

Phew... Just as well she had a visit to make to Rainbow House first. Some time with Maggie and Dave and the kids was exactly what she needed to centre herself before taking a risk like that.

How awful would it be if he didn't want to see her?

'Cake... And it's not even Sunday.' Maggie's hug was as warm as ever. 'Come in, hon. How's your grandad?'

'Going home tomorrow. His arteries are full of stents and probably better than they've been for a decade or more. Good grief, Maggie...what's that terrible noise?'

A naked, giggling toddler trotted past, with Dave in pursuit. 'I think we have you to thank for that racket.' He shook his head but he was grinning.

Charlene's hair was orange today. She went past with her fingers in her ears.

'I can't stand it,' she groaned. 'Someone tell him to stop.'

'Maggie?'

'Go and see for yourself. Out in the shed.' Maggie looked at the wet footprints on the hall floor. 'I'd better give Dave a hand with the baths.'

Bemused, Penelope put the cake in the kitchen and kept going through the back door to the old shed at the far end of the garden. The noise got steadily louder. A banging and crashing that had to be a set of drums, but they weren't being played by anyone who knew what they were doing.

Sure enough, opening the door and stepping cautiously into the cacophony, she saw it was Billy who was surrounded by the drum set. He was giving it everything he had—an expression of grim determination on his face. And then he stopped and the sudden silence was shocking.

'That was rubbish, wasn't it?'

Penelope opened her mouth to say something reassuring but someone else spoke first.

'Better than my first attempt.'

Rafe… She hadn't seen him in the corner of the dimly lit shed, sitting on a bale of the straw kept to line the bottom of the rabbit's hutch. Billy had his back to her but if Rafe had noticed her entrance he didn't show it. His attention was on the young boy he'd rescued from that imminent explosion.

'You're doing well all round, Billy. Maggie's told me how hard you're trying.'

Maybe she was interrupting something private. Penelope turned. The door was within easy reach. She could slip out as unobtrusively as she'd come in.

'I'm following the rules,' Billy said. 'Like Penny told me to. So that—you know—people'll like me.'

'Penny's an amazing lady,' Rafe said.

The tone of something like awe in his voice captured Penelope so instantly that there was no way she could make her feet move. Was it possible his feelings went further than merely being impressed by her? A smile tugged at her lips but then faded rapidly as Rafe kept talking.

'What she said, though…well, it's absolute rubbish, Billy.'

That stung. Without thinking, Penelope opened her mouth. 'How can you say that?'

Rafe must have seen her come in because he didn't seem nearly as surprised as Billy that she was there. The boy's head jerked around to face her but the shift in Rafe's gaze was calm.

'You've always followed all the rules,' he said. 'How's that worked out for you?'

'Just fine,' Penelope said tightly. What sort of example was Rafe giving Billy by saying this?

She glared at him. He had his cowboy hat on and the brim was shading his face but he was staring back at her just as intently. She could *feel* it.

'Sometimes you haven't followed all the rules. How's *that* working out?'

Oh…maybe he was providing a good example after all. What were those rules she'd broken? The only one she could think of right now was the time she'd gone upstairs at Loxbury Hall when she'd thought it was forbidden. When she'd given herself to Rafe.

She dropped her gaze to try and shield herself from the intensity of that scrutiny. 'Not so good.'

'You sure about that?' The quiet voice held a note of…good grief…*amusement*? As if he knew very well how well it had worked out.

Billy's foot went down on the pedal to thump the bass drum. 'I don't get it,' he growled. 'One minute you're telling me to follow the rules and then you say stuff about *you* guys breaking them. It doesn't make sense.'

Rafe leaned forward on his straw bale, his hands on his knees, giving Billy his full attention again.

'There are a lot of rules that are important to follow, Billy, but people will like you for *who* you are. You just have to show them who that really is and not hide behind stuff.'

'What kind of stuff?'

'Some people try to hide by being perfect and following all the rules.'

Penelope winced.

'And some people try to hide by making out they're tough and they don't care.'

Billy was twisting the drumsticks he still held. 'I *don't* care.'

'Yeah, you do.' The gentle note in Rafe's voice made Penelope catch her breath. 'We *all* care.'

'You don't know anything.' Billy's head was down. The drumsticks were very still.

'I know more than you think. I *was* you once, kid. I was tough. I didn't give a damn and I broke every rule I could and got into trouble all the time. And you know why?'

It took a long time for the reluctant word to emerge. 'Why?'

'Because I didn't *want* to care. Because it was too scary to care. Because that was how you got hurt.'

The long silence then gave the impression that Billy was giving the matter considerable thought but when he spoke he sounded offhand.

'Is it true we're all going to go and see the fireworks tomorrow night?'

Rafe didn't seem to mind the subject being changed. 'You bet.'

'You got us the tickets,' Billy said. He paused. 'And the drums.'

'The tickets are for everybody. The drums are just for you.'

'For real?'

'For real.' Rafe was smiling. 'And you know why I gave them to you?' He didn't wait for a response but he did lower his voice, as though the words were intended only for Billy. He must have known Penelope could hear, though. Without the drums, it was utterly quiet in there.

'Because I care. It's okay to care back, you know. It's quite safe.'

He got to his feet and took a step towards Penelope. But his words had been directed at Billy just then.

Hadn't they? Her stupid heart skipped a beat anyway. A tingle of something as wonderful as hope filling a space around it that had been very empty.

Billy's sideways gaze was suspicious. 'Do you care about her, too?'

The brim of that hat made it impossible to read the expression in Rafe's eyes but she didn't need to. She could hear it in the sound of his voice.

'Oh, yeah...'

Billy made a disgusted sound. 'You gonna get married, then? And have kids?'

'Um... Bit soon to think about anything like that. And I might have to find out how Penny feels first, buddy.'

Billy's tone was accusing now. 'You care, too, don't you?'

Penelope couldn't drag her gaze away from Rafe. 'Oh, yeah...'

The delicious silence as the mutual declaration was absorbed finally got broken by a satisfied grunt from Billy that indicated the matter was settled. 'Can I go and tell the other kids that the drums are just for me?'

'How 'bout telling them that they're going to have the best time ever at the festival tomorrow? And tell Maggie and Dave that you'll help look after the little ones. Fireworks can be a bit scary close up and I'm going to make sure you have the very best place to watch.'

It was still hard to tell if his words were just for Billy or whether he was reminding Penelope of when he'd taken her to the best place to watch his fireworks.

Billy was on his feet now, though—his skinny chest

puffed with pride. 'I can do that.' He put his drumsticks on the stool. 'I'm one of the biggest kids here.'

He had to walk between Rafe and Penelope to get to the door but neither of them seemed to notice because he was below the line of where they were looking—directly at each other.

His steps slowed. And then stopped. The suspense was getting unbearable. Rafe was going to kiss her the moment Billy disappeared and Penelope didn't want to have to wait a second longer.

But Billy turned back. He went back to the stool and picked up the drumsticks. 'I'm gonna need these.'

Rafe grinned. 'Practise on a cushion for a bit. That way you won't drive anyone crazy.'

'I think I might be going crazy,' Penelope murmured, as Billy disappeared through the door of the shed.

'Me, too.' Rafe pushed the door closed. 'Crazy with wanting you.'

But he didn't move any closer. They stood there, for the longest time, simply looking at each other.

'Me, too.' The words escaped Penelope on a sigh. 'I love you, Rafe…'

He held out his hand. Without saying a word, he led her over to the straw bale and sat down beside her. Then he took off his hat and held it in his hands.

Penelope swallowed hard. She'd said it first and he hadn't said it back. He hadn't uttered a single word since she'd spoken.

He could have kissed her instead. That would have been enough. But he hadn't done that either.

She was standing on a precipice here.

Teetering.

Feeling like she might be about to fall to her death.

She'd said she cared.

Not just the way you could care about a lost kid and want to do something to help put him on the right path, even though that kind of caring could be so strong you had to put yourself out there and maybe face stuff that you thought you'd buried a long time ago.

Penelope had gone further. She'd said she *loved* him. She'd just gone right out there and said the scariest thing in the world. Put herself in the place where you could hurt the most.

The weight of how that made him feel had crushed his ability to form words. To form coherent thoughts even, because what he said next could be the most important thing he ever said in his life.

No pressure there…

That weird weight seemed to be too much for his body as well as his brain. He had to sit down, but he wasn't going anywhere without Penny and she seemed happy enough to take his hand and follow along.

But now he had to say something. He heard the little hitch in her breath in the silence. A sound that made him all too aware of how scared she was.

He was scared, too. His hands tightened on his hat, scrunching the felt beneath his fingers.

'You know why I bought Loxbury Hall?' His voice sounded rusty.

From the corner of his eye, he saw Penelope nod. 'You told me. That night—in the bath. You said it was the kind of house that only people who had perfect lives could live in.'

'Yeah… That's what I thought through all those rough years when my life was like Billy's. If you were rich enough, you could make your own rules. Live in a place like that and have a family that stayed together. You called family a safe place once and I guess that's what a huge house that cost a bucket of money represented to me. That safe place. But you know what?'

Her voice was a whisper. 'What?'

'I was wrong. So, so wrong.' The whole hat was twisted in his hands now. It would never be the same. Dropping it, he turned his head to look at Penelope. His empty hands caught hers.

'The safe place isn't a place at all, is it? It's a person.'

Her eyes were huge. Locked on his, and it felt as if something invisible but solid was joining them.

'But it's a place, too. Not a place you can buy. Or even find a map of how to get there. It's the place that you're in when you're with *that* person.'

Her eyes were shining now. With unshed tears? Was he saying something that she understood? That she wanted to hear?

Even if she didn't, it felt right to say it. Maybe so that he could understand it better himself.

'It's a place that only that person can create with you. You can't see it but it's so real that even when you're not together you can still feel safe because you know where that place is.' He had to pause to draw in a slow, steadying breath.

This was it.

The thing he really had to say.

'You're my person, Penny.'

Yep. They had been unshed tears. They were escaping now.

Her voice was the softest whisper but he could hear it as clear as a bell and it felt just as good as if she were shouting it from a rooftop.

'You're my person, too, Rafe. For ever and always.'

CHAPTER ELEVEN

THE WEATHER GODS smiled on Loxbury for the thirtieth anniversary of their first music festival and the lazy, late-summer afternoon morphed into an evening cool enough for people to enjoy dancing but still warm enough for the ice-cream stalls to be doing a brisk business.

The gates had opened at five p.m. and the fireworks show timed for ten p.m. had been widely advertised as something people wouldn't want to miss—an exciting finale to a memorable occasion.

It was a music festival with a difference. Artists who'd been at the original festival were given star billing, of course, but there were many others. New local groups, soloists, dance troupes, a pipe band and even the entire Loxbury symphony orchestra. The appreciative crowd was just as eclectic a mix as the entertainment on offer. Teenagers were out in force, banding together far enough away from parents to be cool, but there were whole families there as well, staking out their picnic spots on the grass with blankets and folding chairs, prams and even wheelchairs.

Between the musical performers, the MC introduced the occasional speaker. At about eight p.m., when the crowd had swelled to record numbers, the person who came out to speak was the mayor of Loxbury, resplendent in his gown and chain.

'What a wonderful event this is,' he said proudly. 'A credit to the countless people who have given up so much of their time both to organise and perform. Thank you, all.'

The cheer that went up from the crowd expressed their appreciation.

'I came to the very first festival,' the mayor continued. 'And I remember how much opposition there was to it even happening. There was even a petition taken to the council to try and prevent it corrupting our young people.'

There was laughter from the crowd now. Penelope caught Maggie's glance and shared a smile. Rainbow House had several rugs on the grass. The younger children had all visited the face-painting booths and even Billy had been persuaded to have his face painted white with a black star around his eye to look like the lead singer of Kiss. Right now, he was sitting with the youngest children, righting the occasional ice-cream cone that threatened to lose its topping.

'I can't see any dangers here,' the mayor smiled. 'Just a heart-warming number of our families having a great time together.'

It was a poignant moment for Penelope. She'd never dreamed of attending such an event in her life because she'd grown up with the belief that terrible things did, in fact, happen at music festivals. She'd considered herself living proof of exactly that.

'I see parents and grandparents,' the mayor continued. 'And I see many of our youngest citizens, who represent the future of Loxbury. Some of you know the story of Baby X—the baby that got found when they were cleaning up after that first festival that we're celebrating again today. That baby got returned to its family but we all know there are some children that aren't always that lucky, and it's my pleasure to tell you that the charity chosen to benefit from this festival is a place that cares for those children. Rainbow House…'

The clapping and cheering were deafening this time but Maggie burst into tears. Dave took her into his arms and Penelope suspected he shed a few tears as well. She had to blink hard herself because she knew what this could mean. The roof getting fixed, along with a dozen other much-needed repairs. All sorts of things that could make life more comfortable and enable these people she loved to keep doing something so wonderful. She might suggest a minibus so that they could transport the children more easily when they had somewhere special to go.

Like the festival today, which had presented a logistical challenge. And the Christmas party that was going to take place this year at Loxbury Hall. It had been a joy planning that with Rafe last night, and she knew it would happen. She was going to talk to Jack this week about the catering they would be doing for it.

The other crazy schemes they'd come up with might need some adjustment. Turning a wing of Loxbury Hall into offices so they could both work at home might be a waste because he'd still want to travel to his big shows. And she might want to go with him. Making the hall and gardens available as a wedding venue again needed thinking about, too. It was very likely to become their home and would they want to share that with strangers—especially when they had their own family to think about?

But how much happiness could it bring? Maggie and Dave had never hesitated to share their home and some of the people cheering so loudly right now were probably those teenagers who had come to find Maggie and Dave from amongst the gathering just to say hello. Young people who had needed shelter at some time in their lives and had a bond that would never fade. They seemed to be heading in this direction again to share the joy of this announcement and her bonus parents were going to be busy giving and receiving hugs for quite some time. She made sure hers was the first.

How lucky had she been to find that bond herself?

How lucky was Billy?

And something else made her feel that she could never become any luckier. After what Rafe had whispered in her ear last night, maybe the next wedding she was going to manage was going to be her own. That would certainly happen at Loxbury Hall. And there was her birthday in a couple of days. Not that she needed any gifts because she had everything she could possibly want in her life now, but a small party would be nice. One that could be an invitation for her grandparents to share her new life in a meaningful way?

The mayor had finished speaking and the MC was introducing one of Loxbury's newer talents. Penelope recognised the group instantly as Diversion—the band that had played at the Bingham wedding. Were Clarissa and Blake here somewhere? If they were, they were probably dancing with the growing number of people in front of the stage. It was starting to get darker and there were glow sticks in abundance as well as headbands that had glowing stars or flashing lights on them.

Billy was on his feet now, jiggling a little on the spot as he listened to the music with his whole body. Penelope could see his hands twitching as if he was holding imaginary drumsticks. But then he stopped to stare at the stage, his black lipstick making his open mouth rather comical.

'Is that…*Rafe*?'

The band was playing a cover of Billy Joel's 'Just the Way You Are'.

Penelope could only nod in response. She'd known that Rafe would be joining the band for this song. He'd told her about it last night, when they'd left the shed in the garden, excused themselves from sharing cake and had gone to the best place in the world to celebrate the declaration of their love—where it had first begun—at Loxbury Hall. The most magnificent place that wasn't as important as the place he'd found with her.

The tears were too close again now. He'd told her what song he was going to be playing. He'd whispered the words as if they'd been written for him to say and it was his voice she could hear now, rather than Diversion's lead singer as he sang that he would take her just the way she was. That he wanted her just the way she was. That he loved her just the way she was.

And each time these lyrics led to a saxophone riff from the black-clad figure in the cowboy hat that had Penelope's total attention. Every bend and sway of his body ignited an all-consuming desire that she knew would never fade. The words were exactly how she felt. This love would never fade either.

The jab of Billy's elbow prevented her from turning into a mushy puddle.

'What's that thing he's playing?'

'A saxophone. He started learning it after he stopped playing on those drums he gave you.'

'That's what I'm gonna do, too.'

'Good idea.' Penelope took a deep breath as the song finished. 'I'll see you later, Billy. I told Rafe I'd meet him after this song to see how it's going with setting up the fireworks.'

'Can I come, too?'

'You promised to help look after the little ones, re-member? You're in the best place to watch and it's not that far away.'

It was just as well there was an acceptable excuse not to take Billy with her. The setting up of the fire-works had been finished by lunchtime today. She was meeting Rafe near the stage simply so that they could be together and she couldn't have kissed him like this if there'd been anyone around to watch.

Couldn't have been held so close and basked in the bliss of all those feelings she'd had during the song that were magnified a thousand times by being pressed

against his body. Being able to touch him—and kiss
him—just like this.

But Rafe wanted to do more than kiss her.

'Come and dance with me.'

'No-o-o… I can't dance.' Penelope could feel the
colour rising in her cheeks. 'You know that. You *saw*
me trying to dance in your maze…'

'Ah, but you weren't dancing with *me*…'

And there they were. Among a hundred people dancing in front of the stage to the music from an Irish band
that had been announced as one of the original festival
artists, and it *was* easy. All she had to do was follow
Rafe's excellent lead. They danced through the entire
set the band played and then they stood and clapped
as the band members took their turns accepting the
applause.

The lead guitarist leaned in to the microphone and
held up his hand to signal a need for silence.

'It's been thirty years since we played here,' he said.
'But my heart has always been in Loxbury.'

He waited for the renewed applause to fade.

'The love of my life was a Loxbury girl.'

Rafe's hand tightened around Penelope's and she felt
an odd stillness pressing in on her. She was still in a
crowd but she felt as conspicuous as if a spotlight had
been turned onto her. Alone.

No, not alone. She had Rafe by her side.

'Who is he?'

'His name's Paddy Murphy.'

'*Patrick* Murphy?'

'I came to that first Loxbury festival hoping to find

her again but I didn't.' Paddy shook his head sadly. 'There's never been anyone else for me but that's just the way things worked out, I guess. Maybe you're out there tonight, Charlie, my darlin'. If you are, I hope you're happy. Here's one more song—just for you...'

People around started dancing again but Penelope was standing as still as a stone. 'Oh, my God...' she whispered.

Rafe led her away from the dancers before anyone could bump into them. Right away from any people. He took them into the area fenced off as the safety margin for the pyrotechnic crew by showing his pass to a security guard. Off to the edge of field that was criss-crossed with wires leading to the scissor lifts.

'Watch your feet. Don't trip...'

The music was fainter now and the people far enough away to be forgotten. Except for one of them.

'He's my father, isn't he?'

'I think he probably is. He looks a lot like you, close up. And he's a really nice person. Special...'

'Did you know about him being here?'

'I knew his name and that his band was going to be playing. And then I met him a couple of nights ago and he told me that losing the woman he loved was the biggest regret of his life.' Rafe drew Penelope close to kiss her. 'That was the moment I realised that I'd be making the biggest mistake of my life if I lost you. That you were the love of *my* life.'

'He doesn't know about what happened to my mother, does he?'

'Apparently not.'

'You know what I think? I think that she brought me here to meet him. That he was the love of *her* life, too.'

'He told me something else, too. That his other huge regret was never having kids of his own.'

Penelope had a lump in her throat the size of a boulder. 'Do you think he'd want to meet me?'

'How could anyone not want to?' Rafe kissed her again. 'To be able to claim a connection to you would make him feel like the luckiest man on earth. No…make that the *second* luckiest man.'

Oh…the way Rafe was looking at her right now. Penelope wanted to be looked at like that for the rest of her life.

'I think I'd like to meet him,' she said softly. 'But it's pretty scary.'

'I'd be with you,' Rafe told her. 'Don't ever be scared. Hang on…'

The buzz of the radio clipped to his belt interrupted him and Penelope listened as he talked to his crew. The countdown to the fireworks was on. The orchestra was in position.

'This is a show to live music,' Rafe told her. 'It's a complicated set-up with manual firing.'

'Don't you need to be there?'

'That's what I train my crew to do. I'm exactly where I need to be.'

'And the orchestra's going to play it?'

'Along with the bagpipes. Can you hear them warming up?'

The drone of sound was getting louder. The lights set up around the field were suddenly shut down, plunging the whole festival into darkness. Glow sticks twinkled like coloured stars in a sea of people that knew something exciting was about to happen. Penelope and Rafe were standing behind the stage, between the main crowd and the firing area. Rafe turned Penelope to face the scissor lifts and stood behind her, holding her in his arms.

An enormous explosion sent a rocket soaring into the night sky and the rain of colour drew an audible cry from thousands of throats. And then the music started, the bagpipes backed up by the orchestra.

'Oh…' She knew this music. Everybody did.

'You'll Never Walk Alone'. An anthem of solidarity.

Penelope had never been this close to fireworks being fired before. The ground reverberated beneath her feet with every rocket. The shapes and colours were mind-blowingly beautiful but flaming shards of cardboard were drifting alarmingly close to where they were standing.

And yet Penelope had never felt safer.

Here, in Rafe's arms.

They would never walk alone. They had each other.

'Wait till you see the lancework at the very end,' Rafe told her. 'It took us a long time to build.'

The intensity of the show built towards its climax. Blindingly colourful. Incredibly loud. How amazing was it to still hear the crowd at the same time? Surely every single person there had to be singing at the tops of their voices to achieve that.

Penelope wasn't singing. Neither was Rafe. She could feel the tension in his body as the final huge display began to fade and something on the highest scissor lift came to life.

The biggest red love heart ever. And inside that was a round shape with something square inside that. Chains and a crown on the top. It was a coin. An old-fashioned penny. It even had the words 'One Penny' curving under the top.

'For you,' Rafe whispered. 'For my Penny.'

It was too much. Something private but it was there for the whole world to see. Penny. The person she really was. The person she'd tried to hide until Rafe had come into her life. Her smile wobbled precariously.

'A penny's not worth much these days.'

'You couldn't be more wrong. My Penny's worth more than my life.'

Rafe turned her in his arms so that he could kiss her. Slowly. So tenderly she thought her heart might break, but it didn't matter if it did because she knew that Rafe would simply put the pieces back together again.

Every time.

* * * * *

Cameron couldn't breathe, couldn't think, couldn't form a damn thought with Megan's curvy body pressed against his.

This was his best friend, yet with the way she was all but spilling out of her barely there black dress, his thoughts weren't very friend-like at the moment.

Hadn't he just pep-talked himself into trying to keep his thoughts out of the gutter?

"Wh-what are you doing here?" she asked.

Why was her voice all breathy and sultry?

Cameron dropped his hands, took a step back, but that didn't help his hormones settle down. Now he was able to see just how hot she looked wearing that second-skin dress that hit her upper thigh at a very indecent level.

Jealousy ripped through him. "Where the hell are you going like that?"

The St. Johns of Stonerock:
Three rebellious brothers come home to stay

FROM BEST FRIEND
TO BRIDE

BY
JULES BENNETT

Published in Great Britain 2015
by Mills & Boon, an imprint of Harlequin (UK) Limited,
Eton House, 18-24 Paradise Road, Richmond, Surrey, TW9 1SR

© 2015 Jules Bennett

ISBN: 978-0-263-25135-7

23-0515

Harlequin (UK) Limited's policy is to use papers that are natural, renewable and recyclable products and made from wood grown in sustainable forests. The logging and manufacturing processes conform to the legal environmental regulations of the country of origin.

Printed and bound in Spain
by CPI, Barcelona

Award-winning author **Jules Bennett** is no stranger to romance—she met her husband when she was only fourteen. After dating through high school, the two married. He encouraged her to chase her dream of becoming an author. Jules has now published nearly thirty novels. She and her husband are living their own happily-ever-after while raising two girls. Jules loves to hear from readers through her website, www.julesbennett.com, her Facebook fan page or on Twitter.

There's nothing like spending all of your days with your best friend. This book is dedicated to not only my best friend, but my real-life hero. Love you, Michael, and I love our very own happily ever after.

Chapter One

"You know how to please a man."

Megan Richards desperately wished those words coming from her best friend's kissable lips had been said in a different context. Alas, Cameron St. John was only referring to the medium-well steak she had grilled, and not a bedroom romp.

One day she would shock them both when she declared her desire, her need for the man she'd known since kindergarten, when he'd pulled her pigtails and she'd retaliated by taking her safety scissors to his mullet. A mutual respect was instantly born, and they'd been friends since—sans pigtails and mullet.

"I figured you'd been eating enough take-out junk and needed some real food," she told him, watching in admiration as he picked up their dinner plates and started loading her dishwasher.

Oh, yeah. His mama had raised him right, and Megan didn't think there was a sexier sight than a domestic man...especially one with muscles that flexed so beautifully with each movement.

Since his back was turned, she soaked up the view. The man came by his rippled beauty honestly, with hours dedicated to rigorous workouts. She worked out, too—just last night she'd exercised with a box of cookies—which would be the main reason his body was so perfectly toned while hers was so perfectly dimpled and shapely.

Cameron closed the dishwasher door and gave the countertop a swift swipe with the cloth before turning to face her. With his hands resting on either side of his narrow hips, he might have looked all laid-back and casual, but the man positively reeked of alpha sexiness. His impressive height and broad shoulders never failed to send a sucker punch straight to her active hormones.

Too bad he was married to his job as chief of police in Stonerock, Tennessee. Besides, she was too afraid to lose him as a friend to really open up and let years of emotions come pouring out. Well, that and Cameron and his family had been the only true stability she'd known since her parents were killed in a car accident during a snowstorm when they'd been traveling up north to visit friends. Megan couldn't risk damaging the bond she had with Cam.

Oh, and he'd made it perfectly clear on more than one occasion that he wouldn't get into a committed relationship. Not as long as he was in law enforcement, thanks to an incident involving his partner when they'd been rookies.

Yup, he didn't do relationships; just like he didn't do healthy food.

"I don't eat junk," he defended himself.

Megan tipped her head, quirking a brow.

"I'll have you know that Burger-rama is real food, and they know my order without me even repeating it." Cameron crossed his arms over his wide chest and offered her that lady-killer smile.

Laughing, Megan came to her feet. "I rest my case."

With a quick glance at his watch, Cameron pushed off the counter and sighed. "I better get going. I need to rest before heading out tonight."

She had no clue what he was working on; she rarely did. He was pretty adamant about keeping his work absent from their conversations. He'd tell the occasional funny drunken-fight story, but when it came to a serious investigative case, he was pretty tight-lipped.

Whatever he was working on must be major, seeing as how he'd been heading out to work at midnight several nights a week—not something a chief normally did. The new lines between his brows and the dark circles beneath his eyes spoke volumes about his new schedule.

"You're working yourself to death. You know that, right? Between all the crazy hours and the junk food. You can't be getting enough sleep."

One corner of his mouth tipped up in a smile. That cocky, charming grin always had the same heart-gripping impact. How many women had been mesmerized by that beautiful, sexy smile?

"I'll be fine," he assured her, pulling her into a friendly hug. "This case should wrap up soon, and I'll be back to somewhat normal hours, complete with sleep. The junk food remains, though."

Two out of three wasn't too bad. Besides, normal for him meant ten-hour days instead of twelve or fourteen. Reminding him of his father's bypass surgery last year would do no good. The St. John men were a stubborn bunch. She should know; she'd been the family sidekick since grade school.

Megan kept her mouth shut and wrapped her arms around his waist as she slowly inhaled his familiar scent. Closing her eyes, she wished for so much. She wished Cam would wake up and see how deeply she cared for him, she wished her brother would straighten his life out and she wished she knew what to do about the out-of-town job offer she'd just received.

None of those things were going to happen right now, so she held on tight and enjoyed the moment of being enveloped by the man she'd loved for years. If friendship was all they were destined for, then she'd treasure what she had and not dwell on the unattainable.

Cameron eased back, resting his firm hands on her shoulders. "You okay? You seem tense."

Really? Because she'd pretty much melted into his embrace. The cop in him always managed to pick up every little detail around him, yet the man in him was totally oblivious to the vibes she sent out. It would be so much easier if he just magically knew how she felt and took that giant first step so she didn't have to. The passive-aggressive thing was never her style, but in this instance she really wished he'd just read her mind.

"I'm fine," she assured him, offering a grin. "Just a lot on my mind lately."

Wasn't that an understatement?

His dark brows drew together as those signature bright blue St. John eyes studied her. "What can I do to help?"

Oh, if he only knew. One day.

"Nothing." She reached up, patted his stubbled jaw and stepped back to avoid further temptation. "Go rest so you can head out and save Stonerock from all the bad guys."

The muscle in his jaw jumped. "I'm working on it."

"I hope you're careful," she added, always worried she'd get a phone call from one of his brothers or his parents telling her the worst. Because Cameron would put his life on the line for anybody. He just wouldn't put his heart on the line.

He laughed. "Yes, Mom, I'm careful."

Swatting him on his hard pec, Megan narrowed her eyes. "I have to ask. You make me worry."

"Nothing to worry about," he assured her, with a friendly kiss on her forehead. "I'm good at my job."

"You're so humble, too."

With a shrug, he pulled his keys from his pocket. "Eli and Nora's baby is being christened tomorrow. You're still planning on coming, right?"

"Are you going to make it?"

Cameron nodded and headed toward the back door. He always came and went via her back door. He never knocked, just used a key when it was locked and made himself at home.

"I'll make it," he told her, his hand resting on the antique knob. "I may even have time to run home and nap and shower for the occasion."

"How about I pick you up?" she offered.

He lived in her neighborhood, and they tended to ride together when they went anywhere. They were pretty much like an old married couple, you know, just without the sex and shared living quarters.

"Be there at nine." His finger tapped on the doorknob. "Lock up behind me."

Rolling her eyes, she gave him a mock salute as he left. The worry was definitely a two-way street.

Now that she was alone with her thoughts, she had to face the unknowns that circled around in her mind. This job offer had come out of nowhere.

Was it a sign that she needed to move on? She'd been in Stonerock nearly her entire life; she was still single and had nothing holding her back.

Except Cameron.

After scrubbing her sink and table, Megan was still no closer to making a decision. She loved being a therapist at the local counseling center; she loved her patients and truly felt as if she was making an impact in their lives.

The new job would be in Memphis, nearly two hours away. The new facility would offer her a chance at helping more people, even taking charity cases, which would allow her to comfort and guide people she never could've reached otherwise.

How could she say no?

As she sank onto the chair at her kitchen table, she thought of her brother. He was an adult, but he'd never been able to take care of himself. The questionable decisions he made kept snowballing into more bad decisions—each one seemingly worse than the last. He always counted on her as a crutch to fall back on. What would happen to him if she left? Would he finally man up and take control of his life? See just how dependent he'd become and actually want to change?

More to the point: What would happen with Cameron? Before she made the decision, she would have to seriously consider gathering up the courage to tell him the secret she kept in the pit of her soul.

This job was a catalyst for pushing her in that direction. She needed to move on one way or another... though she'd rather move on with him. Either way, she'd know if years of wanting and dreaming had been for naught.

She'd wanted a relationship with him since they'd graduated high school, but the timing to reveal her feelings had never been right. Between her parents' deaths, his deployment and Megan always putting her life on hold to help her brother, she just had never found an opening.

Cameron was the only solid foundation in her life. What happened if she told him how much she loved him and it ruined their friendship? Could she take that risk?

He'd told her he'd never consider being in a committed relationship. He'd shared the story of the night his partner had died and how he'd had to witness the widow's complete breakdown. Cam had told her he'd never put anyone through that.

Still, she had to let him know how she felt. She couldn't go through life playing the what-if game forever, and he deserved to know. By not giving him a chance to make a decision, she could be missing out on the best thing that had ever happened to her.

Megan folded her arms across the table and rested her head on them. She really had no choice...not if she wanted to live her life without regrets.

Some risks were worth taking. She knew without a doubt if Cameron wanted to take things beyond friendship, the joy would be totally worth the bundle of nerves that had taken up residence in her stomach.

Cameron had managed about a three-hour nap before the christening. He'd also showered and shaved for the occasion. His mother would be so proud.

He'd just finished adjusting his navy tie when his front door opened and closed. Heels clicked on the hardwood floor, growing louder as Megan approached the hallway. He assumed the visitor was Megan, unless one of his brothers had opted to don stilettos today.

He knew of Megan's love for breakneck shoes when she wasn't wearing her cowgirl boots. Didn't matter to him if she was barefoot. Cameron had fought his attraction to Megan for a few years now. At first he'd thought the temptation would go away. No such luck. Being a cop's wife, even in a small town, wasn't something he'd put on anyone he cared about. He couldn't handle knowing he'd put the worry and stress of being a cop's wife on Megan, so he pulled up every bit of his self-control to block his true feelings.

Unfortunately, Cameron had never wanted to avoid his best friend as much as he did right this moment. Dread filled his stomach as he recalled the things he'd witnessed last night while monitoring the drugstore parking lot. The events that had unfolded on his watch put a whole new spin on this case…and quite possibly his relationship with Megan. No, not quite possibly. Without a doubt the new developments would shatter their perfect bond.

Her brother had gotten involved with the wrong crowd—a crowd Cameron was about to take down.

She deserved to be happy, deserved to live free from her brother's illegal activities, and Cameron would do anything and everything to keep Megan safe.

Although he was torn about whether or not she should find out, he was obligated to his job first, which meant he had to keep every bit of this operation to himself. She would be hurt and angry when she discovered what her brother was doing, and even more so when she realized Cameron had hidden the truth from her.

"You wearing pants?" she called out.

With a chuckle, Cameron shoved his wallet and phone into his back pocket. "Pants are a requirement?"

When he stepped into the hall, he stopped short. *Damn*. Megan had always been beautiful, and she always presented herself as classy and polished for work, but this morning she looked even more amazing than usual. There went that twist to his heart, the one that confirmed she was the most perfect woman for him. But he couldn't let her in, wouldn't subject her to his chaotic schedule, his stress from the job. Because if he was stressed, he knew she'd want to take some on herself to relieve him of any burden. He'd signed up for this career...Megan hadn't.

With her fitted red dress, a slim black belt accentuating her small waist and rounded hips and her dark hair down around her shoulders, she stole his breath— something that rarely happened with any woman. Always Megan. Everything was always centered around Megan. She was special.

Which was why he shouldn't be looking at her as if she were a woman he'd met at a bar and wanted to bring home for the night. Not that he remembered what that was like. He hadn't been in a bar for personal recreation in so long, never mind bringing a woman back to his bed.

Megan deserved to be treasured, to be loved and come first in any man's life. Unfortunately he could only offer two of the three.

Cameron had always figured one of his brothers would scoop Megan up, and the thought had crippled him each time the image crept through his mind. Thankfully, both Eli and Drake had found the loves of their lives. Cameron was thrilled for them, but love wasn't for all the St. John boys. Cameron barely had time to catch any sleep, let alone devote to a relationship.

"Should I go back home and change?" she asked,

raising a brow with a smirk on her face. "You're staring at me."

"No, no." He adjusted his jacket, hating the confining garment and feeling somewhat naked without his shoulder holster. "You're just looking exceptionally beautiful this morning."

"You mean my old paint-stained tank and tattered shorts I had on yesterday didn't make me look beautiful?" She fluttered her eyelids in a mocking manner he found ridiculously attractive.

He loved that no matter what life threw at her, she always found a way to be a bit snarky. Why hadn't some guy come along and swept her off her feet? Any man would be lucky to have her. She grilled an amazing steak, she was always there for him no matter what, she joked and she even drank beer with him.

If she married someone who loved her and treated her the way she deserved to be treated, Cameron might be able to get this notion that he was worthy of her out of his head. Because he sure as hell knew that was false. He wanted to see her happy with that family she'd always wanted. But she wasn't even dating anybody. Still, he couldn't tell her his feelings because there wasn't a happy ending if he chose that path. Telling Megan would only cause an awkward, uncomfortable wedge between them, and hurting her in any way would destroy him.

As she stood in his hallway, looking like a classy pinup model with all her curves, Cameron cursed himself for allowing his thoughts to travel where they had no business going. Her curves weren't new, but when the two of them got together she never dressed like this.

It was the dress. That perfectly molded dress. He was used to seeing her in professional work clothes or old tees and shorts. If he was looking at her in a way that stirred him, how would other men be looking at her today? They were attending a church service, for crying out loud, and he was standing here fighting off an ever-growing attraction to his best friend. There was so much wrong with this situation he didn't even know where to start.

"I'm ready." He moved into the foyer, careful not to touch her as he passed, and retrieved his keys from the side table.

After he'd locked up behind them, Cameron followed her down the stone path toward her black SUV parked in his drive. They'd barely gotten their seat belts fastened before her cell chimed. Casting a quick glance down to where it rested on the console, Cameron spotted Evan's name on the screen. More anxiety filled his stomach, but he kept his mouth shut. Now was not the time to expose him. He'd actually made a point to not come between Megan and her brother. Their issues went way beyond those of regular siblings. He might not be able to tell Megan what had happened last night, but Cameron would throw himself in front of her to protect her from anyone...including Evan. Family loyalty meant everything to him; unfortunately, her brother was only loyal to himself.

Megan's bright green eyes darted up to his as she sighed. "I'm sorry."

Wasn't that the story of her life? Always apologizing for her brother, always coming to his defense? Megan was never fully able to live her own life the way she wanted because she'd had to play mom, dad, sister and therapist to the ungrateful punk for years.

She snatched her cell on the second ring. "Hello."

Cameron couldn't make out what Evan was saying, only the rumble of a male voice filtered through the SUV. Not that Cameron needed to know what Evan was saying. The man only called his sister to ask for money, use her car or some other random favor.

Megan's head fell against the back of her seat as she gripped the phone with one hand and her steering wheel with the other. "I can't, Evan—I'm busy right now."

Cameron resisted the urge to pull the phone from her hand and tell Evan to grow a set and quit using his sister as plan A. The man, and he used the term loosely, had never held a job that Cameron was aware of…or at least not a legal one. Evan had been a troublemaker in school, getting kicked out of two before he even started junior high. Megan's parents had moved the family to the next town as a result of Evan's troubles, causing Cameron and Megan to lose touch for a year. Thankfully Megan had transferred back and their relationship had picked up right where they'd left off—with them goofing off and her hanging at his house with him and his brothers.

Unfortunately, switching schools had only made Evan angrier, resulting in his behavior growing more reckless. Now, as an adult, he had made no strides to clean himself up. Actually, after what Cameron had witnessed last night, he knew Evan was even worse than he'd thought. The man was straight up running drugs. And there was no way in hell Megan knew the trouble her brother was in.

No wonder Megan adored Cameron's family so much. They were all she had in the form of a loving, solid foundation.

"I'm sorry, Evan," she went on, her tone exhausted. "That's not something I can do right now. If you can wait until this afternoon, then I can help. Otherwise, I don't know what to tell you."

The more Megan argued, defending herself, the more Cameron felt his blood pressure soar. He was thankful that even though he and his brothers had been hellions in school, they'd never crossed the line into illegal activity. They'd been standard cocky teens. There just happened to be three of them with that arrogant attitude, and when one had done something, the others had jumped on board.

"No, Evan, I—"

Cameron refused to let this go on another second. He pried the phone from her hand and ended the call without a word. Megan jerked toward him, but Cameron clutched the device in his hand, holding it by his shoulder as a silent sign he wasn't giving in.

Her deep red lips parted in protest before her shoulders sank and her hands fell to her lap. Megan's head drooped. With all her hair tucked back, he could see every emotion that slid over her face, even though he could only see her profile. Her eyes closed, she bit her lip and her chin trembled. She looked positively defeated.

That right there was why Cameron loathed Evan Richards. The man constantly deflated the life out of fun-loving, bubbly Megan. Moments ago, when she'd stood in Cameron's hallway, she'd been sassy, confident and vibrant...everything he loved. What he didn't love was how quickly one person could bring her down. Evan was nothing but a bully, always seeking his own selfish desires and not giving a damn who he hurt along the way.

"Don't you dare feel bad," he scolded, maybe harsher than he should have. "That's exactly what he wants, Meg. He plays that guilt card with you because he knows you'll give him anything he wants."

"I know," she mumbled. Smoothing her hands down her fitted skirt, she let out a sigh and turned to face him. "I'm trying, really. It's way past time he stood on his own two feet. It's just so hard..."

She shook her head and reached for the keys in the ignition. After sliding his hand over her slender arm, Cameron gripped her hand.

"That's what he's counting on." Cameron gave her a gentle squeeze as he softened his tone. She wasn't a perp; she was his friend. "He continually plays the poor sibling, expecting you to ride to his rescue. He's the one who made this mess of his life."

Cameron seriously doubted she knew just how much of a mess Evan was in. There was no way he could protect her from the end result. The helpless feeling in the pit of Cameron's stomach nearly made him sick.

Tears brimming in her eyes, she held his gaze. "You think I don't know how much Evan has screwed up? That he doesn't use me on a daily basis? You don't know what I go through, Cameron. You have the picture-perfect family. I have no parents and a brother who'd just as soon wipe out my bank account as spend five minutes talking with me on how to straighten his life out, how to help him. I'm praying maybe one of these times he comes to me, he'll be there for more. I'm praying he'll let me help him, that he'll be ready to turn his life around. So if I have to get stepped on along the way, it's worth it."

The last sentence came out on a choked sob. Well, hell. Now he was the one feeling guilty. He never wanted to make her cry, make her feel as if his life was better than hers.

After placing her phone back on the console, Cameron reached across and wrapped his arms around her the best he could, considering their positions.

"I'm sorry." Her silky hair tickled his cheek, and her familiar floral scent reminded him she was nearly everything to him and he'd die before he'd hurt her. "I don't mean to be hard on you. I just hate seeing what he does to you."

Megan's hands slid up his torso between his jacket and his shirt, coming to rest against his chest. "What I deserve and what I'll have are two different things."

Easing back, Cameron studied her face. "You deserve everything you've ever wanted."

A sad smile spread across her face as she reached a

hand up and cupped his freshly shaven jaw. "All I've ever wanted may not want me back."

What?

Before he could question her further, her hand fell away and she started the vehicle. Whatever secret longing she kept locked deep inside was obviously something she'd all but given up on. Cameron refused to let Megan give up on any dream or goal she had.

He vowed that once this major case was over, he'd find a way to make her happy, living the life she desired and deserved. It would be worth everything to him. For years he'd seen her always put her needs behind everyone else's. And while he may not be the man to settle into her life intimately, he would do everything in his power to make sure her dreams were fulfilled.

Chapter Two

"I'm so glad you could make it."

Bev St. John hugged Cameron after the christening service, then looped her arm through his as they walked back up the wide aisle of Santa Monica Church.

"You don't know how much this means to me to have all my boys here for my first grandbaby's milestone," Bev said, her wide smile spreading across her face.

Straight ahead, near the tall double doors, Nora and Eli stood with Megan. Megan held his infant niece, who was just over a year old. Cameron's heart filled. The glow on Megan's face as she placed a kiss on top of Amber's curly blond head solidified the fact he couldn't be the man for her. She would be an amazing, loving, selfless mother. Just not to his kids.

Cameron's dad, Mac, approached and looked over Megan's shoulder, smiling down at his granddaughter. Cameron didn't know where Megan would be if it weren't for his family. She'd taken to them even before her parents had died suddenly, but she'd really leaned on them during that difficult time. Even as strong as Megan was, she'd been so blindsided by the shock of losing both parents, and then taking over the care of her younger brother when she'd barely gotten out of high school herself. "I'm so glad Megan could make it." His mother's soft tone pulled him back. "I just love that girl."

Over the years his mother had made it no secret she wouldn't mind Megan being part of the family—in the legal, choosing-china-patterns type of way. Of course now that Eli and Drake were taken, his mom would just have to settle for Megan being a friend and the daughter she'd never had.

Cameron steered them toward the little grouping, and Megan glanced up, caught his eye and smiled. Yeah, there was that invisible pull once again that threatened to wrap around his neck and strangle him.

He wanted her. Wanted her so much sometimes he physically hurt. But she deserved more.

The memory of the darkest time in his life took over. His partner had taken a bullet meant for Cameron. On his last breath, his partner had made Cameron promise to make sure his wife knew he loved her.

That moment changed everything. Letting a woman into his life, letting her get close enough to be devastated like his partner's wife had been, was not something he'd ever take a chance with. If he entered into a deeper relationship with Megan and something happened to him, it would kill her. Besides, worrying about her while he was trying to do his job was a sure way for him to get hurt. He needed to concentrate, needed to keep Megan out of his mind.

If he could only figure out how the hell to do that.

"Megan, you look beautiful, as always." His mom leaned forward and kissed Megan's cheek. "Thanks for being here today."

"I wouldn't miss it."

"Are you and Megan coming to eat with us after?" Eli asked Cameron. "We're heading to that new Italian place just outside of town."

Cameron started to agree, but Megan chimed in. "I have to get home, but if you want to go, go ahead."

Oh, no. If she was going home to wait on her freeloading brother to show, Cameron would be right there with her. No way would Evan try to pull her into this latest mess. Hell no.

"I need to head out, too," Cameron stated. Work was always beckoning, so he knew everyone would just assume that's why he needed to go. "And she's my ride."

Cameron and Megan said their goodbyes and stepped out of the church. The bright sun hit them as they descended the concrete steps. Cameron pulled his glasses from his jacket pocket and slid them on to block the brightness. A headache from lack of sleep and plenty of worry had settled in, and the fiery glare was making it worse.

"Skipping out?"

Cameron turned to see his other brother, Drake. Right at his side was his fiancée, Marly, and Marly's daughter, Willow.

"Megan and I need to head out," he told Drake.

"You look pretty," Willow said, standing beside Megan and looking up at her as if she were looking at a movie star. "I like your hair."

The free-spirited little six-year-old had on her beloved cowgirl boots, as usual, and was sporting a new grin, sans two teeth.

Megan bent down and slid her hand through Willow's long ponytail. "I love yours, too. I used to wear my hair just like this when I was your age. You have good taste."

"I was going to call you," Marly told Megan. "Nora and I were hoping for a girls' night sometime soon. You interested?"

Megan smiled and nodded. "Sounds good. Just let me know when."

More goodbyes were said, and finally Megan and Cameron were settled back in her SUV and headed toward their neighborhood.

"That was a beautiful service," she commented after a bit. "Thanks for inviting me."

"You're family." Cameron tried to hold back the yawn but couldn't. Damn, he was getting too old to pull all-nighters. "You belong here, too."

"You know, one day you may actually replace me with a girlfriend or a wife. I doubt she'll understand if I'm still hanging around your family."

Cameron snorted, shifted in his seat and rested his

elbow on the console. "For one thing, you could never be replaced. For another, I think you know my stance on committed relationships and marriage."

"Your reasons may be valid, but they can't be your crutch for life."

"It's not a crutch," he muttered in defense.

Megan threw him a glance and a smile as she pulled onto their road. "You never know when the right woman will come along and claim you."

The only woman he'd ever allow to "claim" him was sitting right next to him, but he'd never do that to her. He'd seen firsthand what being a cop could do to even the strongest of marriages. Even though he and Megan had a bond that rivaled the toughest relationships, he wouldn't put that kind of strain on something, or someone, so important.

She was part of his life in the deepest way he could allow and he'd just have to be satisfied with that. The fact she would likely marry one day was something he couldn't even think about right now. If he thought of Megan with another man, Cameron would likely lose that wall of control he'd built up.

Megan put on her signal to turn into his drive.

"I'm going to your house," he told her.

Totally ignoring him, she pulled up to his garage. After throwing her SUV in Park, she turned to face him, her green eyes studying his face. "You need to go in and get more sleep."

She was preaching to the choir. Unfortunately, even if he went in, he wouldn't be able to just close down and relax. Besides, he wanted to make sure Evan didn't show up and try to pour on more guilt or ask for any favors.

"I'll be fine," she assured him, patting his leg as if he were some toddler. "I know what you're doing, but don't worry. I've handled Evan long enough."

Cameron slid his hand over hers and squeezed. "And that's the problem. You shouldn't have to deal with a grown man whose behavior is that of an out-of-control teen."

Megan tilted her head, and her hair spilled over her shoulder; the strands tickled his arm on the console. "I deal with you, don't I?"

He couldn't help but smile. "You only keep me around to set your mousetraps in the winter."

"True." With a smile, she turned her hand over in his and squeezed. "Seriously. Go sleep."

Stroking his thumb along the backs of her smooth fingers, Cameron stared into those eyes that were too often full of worry—eyes that had captivated him on more occasions than he could count.

"I'm a guy and a cop. I can't help but want to take care of you."

Drawing in a shaky breath, she offered a sweet smile, one he'd witnessed for years and never grew tired of seeing. Megan's genuine, contagious smile that came from within, that lit up a room...that's what kept him going.

"I love you for that," she told him. "But really, you need to take care of yourself, and I'm going to make sure you do. Now go."

Stubborn woman. She wouldn't pull out of this

driveway until his butt was out of her car. *Fine*. He was just as stubborn, but he knew how to play the game. He knew his Megan better than anyone else did. She would always put herself out to make others comfortable, to keep those around her happy. But Cameron wasn't about to let her fall down his priority list. She was, and always had been, at the top. Just like family.

"All right," he conceded. "You will call me if you need anything."

It wasn't a question, but she nodded anyway as she leaned over to kiss his cheek. "Go on, Chief. You can't protect the town if you're dead on your feet."

"Yes, Mommy."

Cameron tugged on the handle and stepped from the SUV. Turning to rest his arm on the open door, he peered back inside. "You know, tough love is a good thing."

"Yeah." Megan sighed, and her shoulders fell slightly. "It's just easy to say and harder to do."

Cameron hated how torn she was between loyalty and forgiveness. He, too, was torn between loyalties right now. Megan had been his everything for so long. Yet he couldn't protect her, couldn't even warn her of the evils hovering so close to her life.

Tapping the top of her car, he stepped back. "I'll call you later."

As he made his way up to his porch, Cameron knew he wouldn't be sleeping. Too much was on his mind, and it all involved work and Megan. She always seemed to be the center of his thoughts. Unfortunately, this scenario had nothing to do with his desires.

Yet Megan's odd declaration earlier alluding to something or someone she wanted still weighed heavily on his mind, too. They shared everything…at least all the personal stuff. What was she keeping from him?

Granted, he'd been holding back his own feelings for so long, but he didn't think she reciprocated those emotions. Or did she? That would put a whole new spin on things and add another layer of worry to his already stressful life. Damn it, why couldn't he just have those friend feelings or that brotherly bond? When had he taken that turn into wanting more?

Cameron waited until Megan headed down the narrow road toward her own house before he turned in the opposite direction and took off for a much-needed walk around their neighborhood. He needed to clear his head and figure out how best to approach this delicate situation with Evan.

Cameron also needed to figure out how to get the image of Megan in that classy yet sexy-as-hell red dress out of his mind. No other woman could shoot for polished and timeless and come off as a siren. Megan's beauty had always been special, but today she'd taken it to a whole new level. The more time passed, the deeper his feelings went. There was nothing he could do; he'd tried denying it, tried ignoring it. Unfortunately, Megan had embedded herself so deeply into his life that he had no clue how to function with all of these lies.

Yeah, a walk was definitely what he needed to get his head on straight because losing himself in his thoughts where Megan was concerned was only throwing fuel on the proverbial fire. Too often when they were close together in a car, on her sofa watching a movie, he'd fought not to kiss her, not to touch her. The struggle he battled with himself was a daily occurrence, but he'd sacrifice anything, even his desires and his sanity, to keep her happy and safe.

Lust, love or anything other than a simple friendship had no room in the well-secured bond they'd honed and perfected since childhood.

So focusing on this case from hell that had just taken a turn for the worse was the only thing he had time to dwell on. Because in the end, no matter his feelings for Megan, she would hate him for standing by and watching her brother make mistake after mistake, for waiting to take down him and his criminal friends. But Cameron didn't have a choice. His job had to come before his feelings for Megan.

Clothes were strewn around her room, hanging over the treadmill, draped across her bed, adorning the floor mirror in the corner. Pretty much every stationary object had taken a hit from the purging of her closet.

Megan tugged on the black tank-style dress that used to be her favorite. When she gave a pull to cover her rear end, it pulled the scoop neck down. When she tried to pull the material up over her breasts, her butt nearly popped out.

Damn that new Ben & Jerry's flavor. Ice cream was her weakness, and now she'd discovered something else to feed her addiction…and her thighs.

So here she was, going through her closet because she needed to de-clutter. Nobody needed this many clothes, and she'd gained a few pounds, so why keep all this stuff? If she ended up losing the extra weight, she deserved a shopping spree, anyway. And if she opted to take that new job in Memphis, she would want to start fresh. That meant getting rid of this too-tight, hoochie-mama-looking dress.

Besides, reorganizing her overflowing closet was a great stress reliever and a good way to keep her mind off Cameron.

With a laugh, she fingered through the pile of too-small clothes on her bed. Like Cameron was ever off her mind. She'd nearly slipped up and bared her soul to him earlier when he'd declared he wanted her to have all she'd ever desired. Could the man be so blind that he couldn't see she desired him? Did he pay no attention to the fact she rarely dated and when she did it was only one date because nobody could ever compare with Cam?

She knew why he didn't go out with women. He was married to his job. But he'd never questioned her on why her social life was nonexistent.

Or perhaps she was the blind one. Maybe she wasn't ready to face the fact that he truly didn't want anyone in his life, and even if he did, she would only be a friend to him.

Though he had given her a visual sampling when he'd first seen her before the christening. That was a good sign...right? Or maybe he'd just had indigestion from all the garbage he ate the night before. Who knew?

Groaning, she started to attempt to get out of the

body-hugging dress when she heard her back door open and close. Jerking around, she tried to listen to the footsteps.

Evan? Cameron? Either way she was clearly not dressed for company.

"You wearing pants?"

A slight sigh of relief swept through her as she laughed at Cameron echoing her earlier question to him. Her body was half hanging out, but extra pounds or not, men usually just saw skin and got excited. Could this work to her advantage? Maybe being a bit more out there, literally, would get Cameron to wake up.

"Actually, no," she called back, then stepped into the hall to tell him she'd be right out.

As soon as she left her room, she ran into Cameron's solid chest. Firm, strong hands immediately came up and gripped her shoulders. Her breasts, already spilling out of her dress, pressed against his hard pecs. Megan sucked in a breath, unable to think of anything but how nicely they molded together in all the perfectly delicious ways.

The way his eyes widened, his nostrils flared and his fingertips bit into her bare skin told her he wasn't so unaffected by her femininity.

Game on.

Chapter Three

Holy—

Cameron couldn't breathe, couldn't think, couldn't form a damn thought with Megan's curvy body pressed against his. This was his best friend, yet with the way her breasts were all but spilling out of her barely-there black dress, his thoughts weren't very friend-like at the moment.

Hadn't he just pep-talked himself into trying to keep his thoughts out of the gutter?

"Wh-what are you doing here?" she asked.

Why was her voice all breathy and sultry?

Cameron dropped his hands and took a step back, but that didn't help his hormones settle down. Now he was able to see just how hot she looked wearing that second-skin dress that hit her upper thigh at a very indecent level and scooped low enough to show off her breasts.

Jealousy ripped through him. "Where the hell are you going like that?"

She flinched. Maybe he'd sounded a tad gruff, but seriously? Every visual that came to mind involved a bedroom.

Megan lifted her chin defiantly as she crossed her arms, doing nothing to help her cause of breast spillage. "For your information, I'm cleaning my closet and trying things on. Now, why are you here and not home asleep?"

He was starting to question that himself. "I couldn't sleep."

Not that he'd tried, but she didn't need to know that. He glanced into her room and laughed. Megan always had everything in its place, but something tragic had transpired with her clothes. He wasn't dumb enough to make a comment because he was pretty sure that some rage had been unleashed in that room.

"Not a word," she growled, as if daring him to comment on the chaos. "Let me change real quick."

Before she turned away, the back door opened and closed. Cameron nearly groaned. Nobody else would just walk in other than him or Evan.

Megan let out a sigh. "Be nice," she whispered. "I'll go change."

Cameron turned away just as Evan rounded the hall corner. His disheveled hair and black eye were so predictable. He looked like a deadbeat who'd obviously been on the wrong end of one of his "friends'" fists.

Cameron wouldn't allow him to come in here and make Megan feel like crap.

"Am I interrupting something?" Evan asked, his narrowed eyes darting between Cameron and Megan.

Cameron wanted to tell the guy yes, but he didn't figure Evan would leave and the lie would only make Megan upset. No matter what, he was treading a fine line because if this weren't Megan's only living relative, Cameron wouldn't think twice about hauling his butt in if for nothing else than to shake him up a bit.

Megan stepped into her room and came out seconds later tying a robe around her waist. At least she was covered now. Cameron didn't like that judgmental glance that Evan had thrown at them. Even if Cameron and Megan had been doing something intimate, that wouldn't have been Evan's business…or anyone else's for that matter.

"What happened?" Megan asked, stepping toward her brother.

Evan waved a hand, his eyes still moving between Cameron and Megan. "Nothing for you to worry about."

Cameron knew those blow-off comments hurt Megan. The woman obviously cared for her brother, and Evan didn't even acknowledge the fact.

"I do worry," she told him with a softer tone.

Cameron maintained his place between the two siblings. No way was he budging. When it became clear that Evan wasn't going to offer any more feedback over his recent fight, Megan sighed.

"What do you need, Evan?" Megan asked as she took a step back, landing her next to Cameron.

Good. Cameron wanted her to feel safer with him there. The silent gesture clearly showed who she trusted, who she felt more comfortable with. The primal part of Cameron liked to think her easing closer to him showed whose side she was on, as well.

"I need to talk to you," Evan told her, then shifted his eyes to Cameron.

"Go ahead," Cameron replied, resting his hands on his hips and in absolutely no hurry to budge.

"Alone."

Megan moved down the hall, squaring her shoulders. "I'm not giving you money," she informed him as she got closer. "If you want to visit with me, that's fine."

Evan raked a hand through his hair, then threw another glance at Cameron and back to Megan. Cameron didn't move, didn't even consider giving them privacy because he wanted Megan to know he was here for support. He wouldn't chime in, wouldn't say a word unless he saw she couldn't be strong. But he had faith in her. He knew she was getting tired of her brother only coming around for money.

Evan leaned down, whispered something to Megan and gripped her arm. Cameron went on full alert.

"No, Evan," Megan said softly, shaking her head. "I don't have it to give. I'm sorry."

"You're not sorry," he spat as he released her with a forced shove. "I don't need that much."

Megan stumbled back a step, but caught herself as she crossed her arms and tipped her chin. "I have obligations, too, Evan. I can't always give you money because you get into trouble."

Evan's focus darted over Megan's shoulder, and Cameron merely narrowed his eyes, silently daring Evan to cross the line. The arm incident was more than enough to have Cameron ready to smash his face, but Megan wouldn't like Cameron interfering. Plus as an officer of the law, Cameron couldn't just go around punching all the people who pissed him off. Such a shame.

Cameron would like nothing more than to show Evan some tough love, but Megan was right. That was easier said than done. And as much as Cameron loathed the man, he *was* Megan's brother and she loved him.

"I'll come back when we can talk in private," Evan said, looking back to Megan.

"My answer won't change," she informed him. "But you're always welcome in my house."

Evan merely grunted and started to turn.

"I love you," Megan said, her voice shaky.

Evan froze, didn't look back, didn't comment, just paused before he disappeared around the corner. Moments later, the back door opened and closed again.

Megan turned, a fake smile pasted across her face, and started down the hall toward her room, skirting around him. "Well, let me change and then maybe we can do dinner. You want to go out? I'm not sure I have a lot here—"

Cameron followed her into the bedroom and watched as she jerked off her robe and tossed it onto the mound of clothes on her bed. As she glanced into the mirror and sighed, Cameron came up behind her, resting his hands on her shoulders and meeting her gaze in the reflection.

"You don't have to pretend with me."

Her bright green eyes held his. "I'm not pretending," she assured him. "I'm ignoring the fact that for years I've been an enabler to someone who really doesn't care about me, and I'm done. I'm also starving, so while I change, figure out what you want to eat."

Cameron knew there was so much more in her, but he wasn't pressing the matter...not when she was staring back at him with such vulnerability and was half-naked. They were back to that damn body-hugging dress again, and Cameron didn't know if he wanted to keep looking or if he wanted her to cover up.

Megan's entire body relaxed against his. Her bottom nestled against his groin, and Cameron tried to ignore the innocent gesture as he wrapped his arms around her shoulders and held her securely. She needed comfort, needed to lean on someone even though it was against everything she stood for. She'd never admit she needed to draw from his strength, but Cameron was freely giving it.

Unfortunately, his fingertips barely brushed across the tops of her breasts before he could complete his hold. A shiver racked her body and vibrated through his.

"I'm glad you're here," she whispered, her eyes still locked on his in the mirror.

Looking at her reflection was quite different from being face-to-face. He didn't know why, but in the mirror he saw so much, too much. Her vulnerability stared back at him at the same time that her killer body mocked him. He was her friend, damn it. He shouldn't be having these thoughts of how perfect she felt against him, how sexy she was.

"I wouldn't be anywhere else." Even though his libido was taking a hard hit, it was the truth.

With a deep breath, Megan straightened and turned, all but brushing those breasts against his chest. Okay, really. He was a guy already on the brink of snapping the stretched line of control, and there was only so much more of this he could take.

"Are you working tonight?" she asked, oblivious to his inner turmoil.

"No." He dropped his arms to his side and took a slight step back, away from that chest, the killer body that was slowly unraveling him. "Why don't I run to the store and grab something while you change?"

"A night in?" She beamed. "Only if I get to pick the movie."

Cameron groaned. "If I have to watch *The Godfather* again…"

With an evil laugh and a shrug, Megan stepped around him and started digging through clothes. "You choose the meal—I choose the movie. You know that's how we work."

Yeah, that's how they worked. They'd been working like this for years, before his deployment and since. But in all the years they'd had this routine of spontaneous date nights with each other, never once had the urge to peel her out of her clothes been this strong.

Of course now that he'd seen her, held her and visually enjoyed her in this dress, he could think of little else. So in a moot attempt at holding on to his sanity, and their friendship, Cameron conceded.

"You win," he told her. "I'll be back."

Even if he removed himself from the situation, Cameron knew he was screwed. Now that he'd seen her lush, curvy body, and felt it so intimately against his, he couldn't *not* see it. The image, the feel of her, was permanently ingrained into him.

Penance for his sins of lying to her.

Every single time they settled in for a movie, Megan fell asleep within the first hour without fail. Tonight was no exception.

She'd curled her feet beneath her, rested her head on his shoulder and before the mobsters could leave the gun and take the cannoli, Megan was out.

Cameron propped his feet up on her coffee table and slid farther down on the sofa. Carefully, he adjusted Megan so she lay down, her head on his lap. Resting his own head against the back cushion, Cameron shut his eyes and attempted to relax. Her delicate hand settled right over his thigh as she let out a soft sigh.

With his hand curled over her shoulder, feeling the steady rise and fall, Cameron realized he actually preferred resting just like this to his bed at home. At least here he had company. At home he had thoughts that kept him awake and staring at the ceiling fan. Work never fully left him—occupational hazard.

But here, with Megan, he could let work shuffle to

the back of his mind. He didn't want to burden her with his stress, so he purposely tried to be a friend first and a cop second whenever he was with her. Added to that, he reveled in the fact she was comfortable and sleeping soundly. He wanted to be her protector, her stable force. Somehow knowing he was all of that allowed him to let down his guard just a bit.

Crossing his ankles, Cameron rested an elbow on the arm of the couch. He'd muted the movie once Megan had fallen asleep, but the flicker of the screen lit up the room. As always, when they had movie night, all lights were off.

A shrill ring pierced the silence, and Cameron jerked awake. The TV had gone black, indicating he'd dozed off for a good bit, but he didn't really recall how long ago that had been. The ring sounded again. He grabbed his side, but Megan's phone on the table was the one lit up. Normally his phone was the one that rang at all hours.

She was still out with her head on his lap. He didn't recognize the number on the screen. Shocked the caller wasn't her brother, Cameron nudged Megan's shoulder.

"Meg."

She groaned and rolled to her back, blinking as she looked up at him. The sight of her utterly exhausted and rumpled from sleeping on his lap shouldn't have his body stirring. Damn that red dress from the christening and the skimpy number she'd had on earlier.

The third ring ripped through the silence, and Megan was on instant alert. She jerked up, grabbed the phone and answered.

Cameron shifted his legs to the floor, immediately getting some blood flow back. They'd obviously been asleep for a while, which was what they had both needed.

Megan came to her feet and spoke in hushed tones as she walked into the other room. He assumed it was a client. Megan often counseled long after regular office hours were over. She was so good at her job because of how caring she was, how much she sacrificed to make sure her clients' needs came first.

Cameron got to his feet, then twisted at the waist until his back popped in all the right places. He was getting too old to sleep on a couch, a car, his office. Unfortunately, he didn't see an end to his bad habits anytime soon.

He turned off the TV, sending the living room into utter darkness. Megan rounded the corner from the kitchen just as he started to reach over and click on the lamp, but his hand bumped the stand and sent the light to the hardwood floor. He cringed at the racket.

"Don't move." Megan turned on the kitchen light, sending an instant glow shining into the living room. "Let me grab my broom."

"You're barefoot," he told her. "Let me clean it up."

"You don't have shoes on, either." She disappeared down the hall and came back with broom and dustpan in hand. "Sit on the couch, and I'll get this."

Like hell. Ignoring her, he reached down to pick up the cockeyed lampshade and the remains of the lamp. The bulb and base had completely shattered.

"I'll bring you a new one later." He set the awkward

shade and lamp guts on the coffee table and reached to take the broom.

Stepping around him, she handed him the dustpan and started sweeping. *Stubborn woman.* No wonder they were best friends. Nobody else would put up with how hardheaded they both were.

He squatted down and held the pan while she scooped in the shards. "At least this wasn't a family heirloom," he joked.

Shoving her hair from her eyes, she threw him a glance. "Funny."

Cameron headed into the kitchen to toss the debris. As he was tying the bag, the vacuum kicked on in the living room, the occasional cracking noise indicating she was removing the rest of the slivers from the floor.

He tugged the liner from the trash can and tied it, wanting to get it out so she didn't cut herself later. As Cameron jerked the knot in place, a hunk of glass he hadn't seen poking from the small hole sliced through the edge of his hand.

Damn. That hurt.

He opened her back door, tossed the bag into the larger can on her patio and closed and locked the door. The vacuum shut off in the other room as Cameron headed to the sink. Running his hand beneath the cool water eased the burning sensation and washed away the mess, allowing him to see just how deep the cut was. Megan didn't need to know he'd hurt himself. She'd make a bigger deal of it than need be.

After rinsing his hand, he examined the area fur-

ther. Instantly he started bleeding again. Apparently
it was deeper than he thought.

"Hiding something?"

Cringing, Cameron ripped off a paper towel, pressed
it against the side of his hand and turned toward his
accuser. Megan rested one shoulder against the door
frame, arms crossed over her chest, and merely lifted
a brow.

"Just a scratch." That hurt like hell. Apparently he
was old and wimpy. Great combo for the police chief.

Cameron's eyes locked on to her shapely legs as she
crossed the room. *Damn it.*

Carefully, she took his hand and pulled the paper
towel away. "Oh, Cam. This needs stitches."

She examined his hand, then brought her gaze up
to meet his. In the middle of the night, with everything so quiet and intimate, Cameron knew for a fact
he was starting to delve into a territory he had no business being in.

Her eyes held his, dropped to his mouth, then traveled back up. That gesture said more than any words
could. But this was Megan, his best friend, the girl
who'd been his senior prom date and the girl who'd
sneaked out with him and his brothers that same night
and got absolutely plastered near the lake.

She was pretty much family. So why was she looking at him beneath those heavy lids? Why was he enjoying this rush of new sensations, wondering if she
had deeper feelings? He shouldn't want her to have
stronger emotions for him. That added complication
was the last thing either of them needed.

"Come with me."

Cameron blinked. "Excuse me?"

Megan smiled. "To the bathroom. You're too stubborn to go get stitches, so I'll fix you up with my first-aid kit."

When she turned and headed back down the hall, Cameron released a breath he hadn't been aware he'd bottled up. Had he been the only one thinking about what would happen if they kissed? The way she'd looked at him, his mouth, as though she wanted more, wasn't something he'd made up. But the desire flashing in her eyes was gone in a second.

What was going on in that head of hers? More to the point, what the hell was he going to do if her feelings did match his?

"Cam?"

Pushing off the edge of the counter, Cameron moved through the kitchen. They were both sleep deprived; that was all. He'd been without a woman for so long, was so wrapped up in work, and Megan had quite a bit on her plate, as well.

Once daylight came, once reality settled back in and the ambience was gone, this intense moment would be forgotten. Wouldn't it?

Chapter Four

Megan squeezed her eyes shut and willed her hands to stop shaking. That was a close call. She'd nearly ignored every single red flag waving around in her mind and kissed Cameron.

She'd been examining his hand one second and the next she'd found herself lost in those St. John signature blue eyes. After just coming off a phone call with one of her teen clients, Megan had wanted to lose herself in Cameron, even if only for a moment. Bad idea, bad timing.

Heavy footsteps sounded down the hall. Megan stepped aside to give Cameron room. Her guest bath was the smallest in her house, but it was where she kept her first-aid kit.

Without a word he came in and sat down on the

edge of the garden tub. If she thought the bathroom was tiny before, having a man of Cameron's size there only solidified the fact.

"I can take care of this at home," he informed her. "It's the middle of the night."

Ignoring him, Megan cleaned the area, concentrating on her task and not the enclosed space or the warmth radiating from Cameron's body...or the fact she stood directly between his spread legs and only had on a tank and a pair of old boxers.

You'd think she'd at least take a bit more pride in her appearance when he came over, but this was Cameron. He knew her better than anybody so if she donned something halfway dressy, he'd wonder what was wrong.

Megan feared she'd doomed herself into the friend category for life where Cameron was concerned. She'd had feelings for him for years, yet the man was utterly oblivious.

Once the area was clean and dry, Megan quickly placed butterfly bandages over the cut. The strips weren't nearly as effective as stitches, but she wasn't fighting with the stubborn man. Men were like children—you had to pick your battles.

Megan turned to throw away the used supplies and wrappers, only her body and her mind weren't in sync and she swayed slightly. Strong arms circled her waist, holding her steady in an instant.

"You okay?"

Nodding, Megan closed her eyes as his caring words

and warm breath washed over her. "Yeah. The room started spinning for a second. I'm just tired, I guess."

With a gentle power she'd come to appreciate, he eased her down onto his leg. Megan twisted to face him, wondering if this would turn awkward. She didn't want awkward anywhere near their perfectly built relationship. They'd been friends too long to allow anything negative or evil to slip in.

When Cameron's uninjured hand covered her bare thigh, Megan's first thought was how she was glad she'd shaved that day…or the day before, considering it was after midnight.

Her second thought was that she hoped he didn't feel her body trembling beneath his touch. Unfortunately, keeping her body controlled around Cameron was impossible.

"Was that call earlier from a client?" he asked, his thumb tracing an invisible pattern over her thigh.

Staring into those eyes, Megan could only nod.

"You're working yourself too hard, Meg." His bandaged hand slid up, pushing her hair off her shoulder and down her back. "I know you want to be there for your patients, be there for your brother, but when will you do something for yourself?"

Actually, being on his lap right now fell nicely into the "doing something for yourself" category.

"Are you the pot or the kettle?" she asked with a smile.

A corner of his mouth tipped up into a tired grin, causing the corners of his eyes to crease. "Whichever one you aren't."

Megan yawned. "Sorry. You want to crash in the guest room tonight?"

"I'll just walk home."

As Megan came to her feet, Cameron stood with her and kept a hand on her waist.

"Dizzy?" he asked.

Shaking her head, Megan started putting the first-aid kit back. "I'm fine. I've just not been sleeping lately and with the call and then your injury, I think my body was trying to crash before I was ready."

Without even looking at the man, she knew his eyes were on her. She could feel them, feel him.

"Is your client all right?"

Megan thought back to the call. No matter how many years she'd been counseling, certain topics never got easier to deal with, and there were those special cases that truly touched her heart. Megan wished more than anything she could wave a magic wand and heal all the hurt she dealt with on a daily basis.

"Honestly, no." Megan put the kit back under the vanity. She leaned back against the counter and crossed her arms over her chest. "She's unstable, scared and can't live a normal teenage life. It's not fair and I want to go get her and bring her here. She needs love and guidance and to be able to sleep without worrying about her family."

After taking one step, Cameron stood in front of her. His good hand came down and rested on the edge of the sink beside her hip.

"You can't make up for the past, Megan."

How easily this man could see through her. He

knew how she equated every teen to her brother when he'd been an out-of-control hellion after their parents' deaths. Still, the day Megan quit caring about her clients would be the day she quit her job.

"I can't," she agreed, trying not to think about how close he was, how his breath tickled her face or how his body was nearly covering hers. "But I can help one person. I can help steer them toward a better future."

Cameron wrapped his other arm around her shoulders and pulled her against his hard chest. Tilting her head to rest her cheek against him, Megan inhaled the familiar masculine scent. What she wouldn't give to be able to wrap her arms around him and have the embrace mean so much more than friendship. An embrace that led to something intimate, something that would take them to the next level.

"Why don't you concentrate on getting sleep for what's left of the night?"

Megan eased back and smiled. "You sure you don't want the spare room?"

Cameron shook his head and took a step back. "I need to be back at the station early. I'll just head home."

A sliver of disappointment slid through her, but Megan kept smiling. Seriously, if he stayed it wasn't like she'd make a move, even though she'd thought she was ready to admit her feelings. Why couldn't she be more forward about what she wanted? She admired women who targeted a man and went after him.

Megan walked him to the door, rubbing her tired, burning eyes. "If that hand still looks bad by afternoon I want you to think about getting stitches. I'm not a nurse, you know."

Cameron glanced down to the bandage and shrugged. "It's not my shooting hand. I'll be fine."

Rolling her eyes, Megan reached around him and opened the front door. The living room and foyer were still only illuminated by the light spilling in from the kitchen.

"I have a crazy schedule the next couple of days, but I swear I'll get that lamp replaced."

"Don't worry about it." Megan covered her mouth as another yawn slipped out. "I'll just take one from the spare room until I get to a store. No big deal."

The screen door creaked open as Cameron stepped onto her porch. A cool breeze drifted through as he turned and studied her once more. He opened his mouth as if to say something, but he ended up tightening his lips. Megan wanted to know what he was thinking after they'd shared those intense moments.

Finally he swallowed and nodded. "Lock up behind me."

Megan reached for the screen door to prevent it from slamming. "Always."

"You've got to be kidding me."

Cameron crossed his arms over his chest and stood back, admiring the gaudy gold dragon lamp he'd found on his lunch break at one of the antiques stores in town.

"What?" he asked, pretending to be offended. "It puts out more light than the one you had—plus it was only eight bucks."

Megan laughed. "You got screwed if you paid more than a dime for that hideous thing."

"So you'd rather pay more for something that does the exact same thing?"

Megan stepped closer, bending down to inspect the new piece. She wrinkled her nose, squinted her eyes and her mouth contorted into an expression that looked as if she'd just inhaled the sickening aroma of a sewer plant.

This was the exact reaction he'd expected…which was why he'd bought the ugly thing.

"You did this on purpose," she accused, turning her scrunched face to him. "You know how I am about gifts, and you know I'll keep it just because you got it for me."

Cameron shrugged. "Maybe. Do you still have that unicorn salt-and-pepper-shaker set?"

Her eyes narrowed as she crossed her arms and mirrored his stance. "You know I do. I just don't get it out of the cabinet."

For years he'd randomly bought her tacky things from time to time just for a laugh. He knew how she treasured every present because she hadn't had much growing up and gifts were few and far between. Megan had a loving heart, and she'd never give away something someone bought her.

And now this tacky dragon lamp, with the light shooting out of the open mouth directed toward the ceiling, adorned her neutral-toned living room. A dragon that projectile vomited light? This was a new level of tacky. Cameron had to really bite the inside of his cheek to keep from bursting out laughing.

"I thought you were too busy to see me today."

The list of things Cameron needed to do flooded his mind. Tonight he'd be staking out another parking lot, waiting for the familiar crew of drug runners to pass through. Cameron only hoped Evan wasn't with them this time. He truly hoped Megan's brother would get away from that crowd. This case would not have a positive ending, and Cameron didn't want to arrest Evan and help convict him of a felony. That crushing blow would kill Megan.

"I'm on my way back in," he told her. "But when I saw this, I just knew you had to have it. I couldn't wait to see your face."

"There will be retaliation," she promised with a gleam in her eyes.

"I can't wait," he retorted, laughing.

Rain started splattering the windows as the gray clouds moved over the sun, blocking out the natural light.

"Got this lamp in just in time," he said, not even trying to hold back his grin. "It's supposed to storm all night. It'll be good for you to sit in here and read."

"I'd hate for the power to go out and my lamp to have some malfunction due to the storm."

Cameron patted the top of the beastly thing. "This is an antique. I'd say she's been around through many storms. Don't worry."

"She? You're giving that thing a gender?"

Cameron may have initially been drawn to the lamp

because of the shock factor and the entertainment value of presenting it to Megan, but there was more. After he'd gotten over the amusement, he realized in some weird way, this dragon reminded him of Megan. Sturdy and fierce. Of course, if he mentioned any of that to her she'd probably launch the heavy atrocity right at his head.

"You can give her a name," he added, just wanting to get under her skin. The unladylike growl was perfect. "Think about it. No need to call her anything right now. You'll want to acquaint yourself."

"I'm thinking of a few names," Megan said through gritted teeth. "None of them are for her, though."

Cameron swatted her arm. "See? You're already thinking of the lamp as her. You'll have her named by the end of the day."

Another unladylike growl escaped Megan as her eyes narrowed to slits. "Don't you have a city to protect?"

More so now than ever, yet he found himself not wanting to leave. This was the first time in a while he actually smiled for good reason. Added to that, he felt they needed this ridiculous moment after way too many close calls. His control was about to snap.

Even if he had wanted to risk their friendship and delve into a more intimate relationship, he couldn't ignore the flashes of his old partner that ripped through him. The man had been married to his job and he'd had a beautiful young wife at home. Now she was a widow. Cameron tried to check in on her from time to time, and he would never forget her face when she'd learned her husband had been killed in the line of duty. Killed by a bullet meant for Cameron. The guilt used to eat at him, but now he realized he would've done the same thing. Jumping into the line of fire wasn't something you thought about, you just did it.

"Cam?"

Megan's hand on his arm and her soft tone pulled him from his thoughts. "Yeah. Sorry."

"You left me for a minute." Her arched brows drew in. "You can talk to me. I know you can't discuss open cases, but you can at least get out some frustration."

No, he couldn't because the second those words left her lips, he found himself studying her mouth. The very thought of kissing her should have made awkwardness rise to the surface, but he found himself curious how she would taste, how she would respond. There was only one way to get her out of his system.

"I'm fine," he assured her. Well, as fine as he could be considering he was now fantasizing about kissing his best friend and keeping the fact that her brother was in way over his head with drug runners a secret. "I need to get going."

Megan reached out, wrapping her arms around him. She held on tighter than usual and damn if that didn't send a shot of arousal straight through him. Cameron slid his arms around her waist, loving how she just knew when he needed a connection most.

"Be careful," she whispered just before she stepped back. "I know you're working on a big case, but promise me you're cautious."

Cameron swallowed, hating the worry that settled

in her bright eyes. This was the reason he wouldn't subject her or any other woman to his line of work.

"I promise," he told her. "Text me and tell me what you name her."

Megan's eyes darted to the dragon lamp and back to him. "Distracting me from worry won't work."

Cameron gave her shoulder a squeeze and headed to the door. "No need to worry. Call me if you need anything."

"You know I won't call you." She smiled and tipped that adorable defiant chin up a notch. "I'm perfectly capable of taking care of myself."

Yes, but she didn't know what she was up against if her loser brother opted to somehow use her in his latest dealings. Cameron had to be on full alert because the likelihood of Evan trying to get something from Megan or bringing the rest of the cronies into her life was viable. Cameron might be watching the entire city, but his focus was zeroed in on keeping Megan safe and oblivious to the activity hitting way too close to home.

Granted, this was a small town, but that didn't mean evils wouldn't try to reach their arms in and infiltrate anyone who proved to be an easy target. Cameron wouldn't allow his town to be overrun by corrupt, illegal activities as long as he was chief.

Cameron headed back to the station, where he would be meeting up with an FBI agent to discuss the case. Too often cops developed inflated egos and didn't want outside assistance. Cameron wasn't that stupid. When the FBI had come in, he had welcomed the extra help. He'd do anything to keep his town safe, to keep drugs from filtering into the schools and homes of innocent, unsuspecting kids.

He wasn't naive enough to believe he could stop all drug trafficking, but he was damn sure going to stop this group from bringing shipments into Stonerock. Every bust, every seller taken off the streets, could possibly be saving someone's life.

Cameron couldn't wait for this case to wrap up. They had a good amount of evidence so far, but they needed a bit more. An undercover FBI agent had been placed deep in the runners' inner circle months ago. Another reason Cameron was elated to have them all on board.

All they had to do was wait on his signal, and then the group would be taken down.

Glancing back at Megan's one-story cottage, complete with cheery colorful flowers and a yellow front door, Cameron only hoped he could save her from the pain of seeing her own brother in prison. Unfortunately, Cameron didn't think that was possible.

Chapter Five

The storm had ripped through the night, putting off the surveillance. Cameron and a few other officers and FBI agents had waited around the station, hoping the storm would pass. Unfortunately, with lightning bolting across the sky and claps of thunder raging at the same time, even the dealers weren't stupid enough to be outdoors.

At around three in the morning, Cameron headed home, ready to get a few hours of sleep before coming back. Their informant had told them another meet was scheduled to happen in three days. Cameron honestly thought of taking a day off to do absolutely nothing. He was running on fumes. All he wanted to do was fall face-first into his bed and sleep for a good solid eight hours. Was that too much to ask?

He and the other agents and officers were convinced

it would only take one or two more meets before they could bring the group down. The day wouldn't come soon enough.

His headlights cut through the darkness as he pulled into his drive. He needed a shower and a bed. He actually needed food, but that would have to wait. He was too exhausted to even pry open a package of toaster pastries at this point.

After letting himself in the back door, he removed his shoulder holster and gun. After carrying it through the darkened hall, he stepped into his bedroom and placed the gun on the dresser just inside the door. Turning around, he went into the bathroom directly across the hall from his room.

The shower was quick, hot and enough to loosen his sore muscles and have him one step closer to falling into oblivion as soon as he slid between his sheets.

Wrapping the towel around his waist and tucking the edge in to secure it in place, Cameron padded back across the hall. He kept his blackout shades pulled at all times, seeing as how he never knew when he'd get shut-eye and he wanted to keep the room nice and dark. Of course tonight, with the storm, the moon wasn't even out to offer a glow.

Cameron jerked off the towel and hung it on the closet doorknob. Shuffling toward the king-size bed, Cameron nearly wept at the thought of falling asleep. Now, if he could stay asleep that would be a miracle.

Jerking back the covers quickly revealed two things: there was a woman in his bed, and there would be no sleep tonight.

* * *

His hands glided over her bare skin, sending ripples of satisfaction coursing through her. Finally, after all these years, she would finally know what making love to her best friend was like.

A soft groan escaped her lips; her body arched in eager anticipation.

"Megan."

Even his voice aroused her. That low, throaty tone. She'd imagined him growling her name while looking into her eyes as his body leaned over hers.

"Meg."

The firm grip on her shoulder had her lifting her lids, blinking. Darkness surrounded her, but the shape before her was so familiar, so close. She reached up, slid her hands over his stubbled jaw and pulled him down. Her mouth covered his and for a second she wondered why he wasn't responding.

The thought was fleeting as Cameron's hesitant state snapped; his hold on her shoulders tightened. His mouth opened, his tongue plunging in to tangle with hers. Yes, this is what she needed, what she craved.

The weight of his body pressing hers back into the bed, the sheer strength of this man, consumed her in every single way and made all her fantasies seem so minor in comparison.

The euphoria of coming from a dream into reality—

Megan froze. Dream into reality? *Oh, no.* She had been dreaming earlier…now she wasn't.

As if sensing her detachment, Cameron stilled and lifted his head. She lay on the bed, the top half of his body covering hers, the tingling sensations still rippling through her as she focused back on the cold, harsh reality.

"Cam?"

"Yeah." His husky voice did nothing to rid her body's ache. "Um…sorry. That was…I don't…why did you kiss me?"

With her palms plastered to his bare chest—his bare, damp chest—Megan closed her eyes and battled with telling the truth or saving her pride.

"I was dreaming."

Pride won out. How could she tell her best friend she'd been dreaming of seducing him and fully succeeding? How could she tell him that for years she'd dreamed of taking control and making him see just how amazing they'd be together?

"That was one hell of a dream." He eased himself off her, and as her eyes fully adjusted to the darkened room, she realized he wore… *Oh, mercy.* He wore absolutely nothing.

Embarrassed, yet incredibly still aroused, Megan shoved her hair away from her face. "I didn't want to bother you at work and I thought I'd be gone by morning since I figured you'd be out all night." She realized she was rambling, but nerves had taken over and she'd lost all control. As she rambled, though, it gave him time to retrieve a towel from the closet knob and secure it around his waist. "I couldn't sleep at my house and had you been home I would've taken the couch, but since you were out…"

Cameron smiled as she trailed off, and she figured

she sounded as nervous as she felt. Silence settled between them, and he crossed his arms over his chest, as if wearing only a towel was the most comfortable thing in the world.

Was he not affected at all by that kiss? She knew for a fact he'd been somewhat aroused when he'd been on top of her, but now he merely looked at her with that lopsided grin she'd come to love.

"I don't mind a bit that you came here," he informed her. "But what was wrong with your house?"

Restless on so many levels, Megan came to her feet and started smoothing out the covers. "My back door had been tampered with and the lock was broken. I wasn't comfortable sleeping there. I didn't figure you'd mind."

"What the hell, Meg?" Reaching around her, he clicked on the bedside lamp. "Someone broke in and you were afraid to call my cell?"

"I wasn't afraid," she defended herself, testing every bit of her self-control as she kept her eyes on his and not on the stark white towel riding low on his hips or the sprinkling of dark hair across his bare torso. "I knew you were busy and…can you put some pants on? I can't talk like this."

A corner of his mouth kicked up into a grin. "You've seen me in swim trunks, Meg."

Yes, but in those instances he hadn't just been lying on top of her, kissing her back as if she were his next breath of air. Would her lips ever stop tingling from all that heat? His body's imprint was permanently ingrained onto hers.

Her eyes darted to the bed, re-creating an image of how close she'd been to attaining her greatest fantasy. When she glanced back up, Cameron's jaw was clenched, his eyes holding hers as if he knew exactly where her thoughts had traveled and he was having a hard time keeping his own from going there.

"It's not the same," she whispered.

With a nod, he turned, pulled a pair of shorts from his drawer and slid them on beneath the towel. With a flick of his wrist, the towel came off and he hung it back on the doorknob before he crossed the intimate room to stand within a breath of her.

"Now, tell me what the hell is going on. What happened at your house?"

Megan pulled in a deep breath, giving herself an extra minute to figure out how to control her emotions and get back on track to where their conversation needed to be.

"My back door had been kicked in or something. It was open and the lock was busted."

Cameron raked a hand over his still-damp hair and muttered a curse. "You'll call me next time anything happens. Me, not the department, not another officer. You'll call my cell."

A little surprised at his demanding tone, Megan propped her hands on her hips. "What would you have done? Left whatever you've been working undercover on for months?"

His narrowed eyes held hers as he eased forward just enough for his bare chest to brush against her. "Yes."

He'd put work second? That was a first. Work never

came after anything for Cameron. He took pride in keeping his town's reputation favorable and the crime rate low. To know he would've dropped everything for her caused a new warmth to spread through her, overlaying the previous heat from their intimate encounter moments ago.

"I didn't need to call you for a busted door," she said. "I knew you'd look at it sometime in the morning. I just wanted to sleep. Like I said, had I known you'd be home, I'd have taken the couch."

While his small cottage had two bedrooms, the second bedroom was full of workout equipment that aided in bulking up his already magnificent physic.

"I'll take the couch," he told her. "Go on back to sleep."

Oh, sure. As if she could crawl back into that bed after what had just happened. She'd had a hard enough time getting to sleep in the first place because she'd nearly suffocated herself by burying her face into his pillow and inhaling that familiar masculine scent. She really needed to get a grip before she made a complete fool of herself.

"I'll take the couch." She smiled up at him, hoping the friendly gesture would ease the tension. Granted, the tension was most likely all one-sided. "You've been up long enough and there's no way you'll fit."

"What kind of gentleman and friend would I be if I booted my best friend to the couch?"

Best friend. Had he thrown those two words at her to remind her of their status? Had she completely freaked him out when she'd attacked him, rubbed herself all over him and claimed his mouth? Part of her was mortified; the other part of her was a bit relieved she'd finally kissed him. She'd not only kissed him, she'd full-out devoured him. But now she knew how he tasted, how he felt. That knowledge was both a blessing and a curse.

"I either take the couch or I head home where it may not be safe."

True, she wasn't fighting fair because no way would he let her go if he thought for a second she wasn't well protected. He studied her for a moment, and Megan tried not to look away or fidget beneath that hypnotic gaze. Would she ever stop tingling? Would she ever forget how perfectly his body felt pressed against hers? She hoped not. Those were memories she'd want to relive over and over for as long as possible.

"You're stubborn."

Megan shrugged. "One of my many talents," she told him, patting his bare shoulder because she was having a hard time resisting all that glorious skin mere inches away. "Sleep tight."

Inching around him, inhaling that fresh-from-the-shower scent, Megan made her way out of his room and headed to the couch. She may as well just head on home because there was no way she could sleep now, not after that kiss. But she would stay. If Cameron knew she was home, he wouldn't rest, either, and he desperately needed to before he worked himself to death.

Megan pulled a blanket from the back of the couch, fluffed the throw pillow and lay on her side, facing the hallway. The darkened space offered nothing of comfort or peace. The silence was equally as empty.

Was Cameron already lying in bed? Had he already slid between the sheets she'd just come from? Had that kiss even made an impact on him, or was he completely repulsed at the fact his best friend had tried to consume him?

More than likely the man's head had barely hit the pillow before he was out. At least one of them would get some sleep tonight.

Chapter Six

How the hell could a man rest after finding a woman in his bed, being kissed in such an arousing way by said woman and now smelling her fruity scent on his sheets?

Cameron laced his fingers over his abdomen and stared up at the ceiling fan. Whoever Megan had been dreaming about was one lucky man. The way she'd all but plastered her curvy body against his had him instantly responding. Hence the problem with sleeping. How the hell did he react to this? For a few brief moments, he'd found something with Megan he'd never experienced with any other woman. Ever.

What was the protocol for discovering your best friend kissed like every man's fantasy? He knew he'd wanted her on a primal level, but to actually have evidence of the fact only added to his confusion.

This was Megan, the woman who knew all his secrets, all his annoying quirks. They'd been through everything together from riding their first rollercoaster to her brother's ups and downs.

She was like family, only he was feeling close to her in a way that had nothing to do with family. He'd secretly hoped if he ever got his hands or lips on her, he'd get her out of his system because he'd feel nothing. Unfortunately, that was completely the opposite of what had just happened. He felt too much, too fast.

Cameron's body still hadn't settled back down, and it wouldn't anytime soon. Who the hell had Megan been dreaming about? She wasn't dating anyone, unless she was keeping it a secret.

Damn it. Jealousy was an ugly, unwelcome trait.

Swiping a hand down his face, Cameron cursed himself. Here he was, dead on his feet, unable to sleep for fantasizing about his best friend dreaming about a mysterious man. How messed up had his life become in the past hour?

Licking his lips, he still tasted her. He couldn't want more. Wanting anything more from Megan was out of the question. Their friendship was solid—why mess that up just because she kissed like every dream he'd ever had?

Movement in the house made him focus on the darkness instead of his wayward thoughts. Bare feet slid over the hardwood. The refrigerator door opened, closed, followed by the sound of a cabinet being shut softly. She was trying to be so quiet, but he wasn't sleeping and he was trained to hear even the slightest disturbances.

This new tension that had settled between them wasn't going anywhere. She may have tried to act calm after what they'd shared, but he knew her well enough to know she was anything but. Her nerves and emotions were just as jumbled, just as buzzing, as his were.

With a sigh, he sat up and swung his legs over the side of the bed. Might as well face this head-on. He didn't want uneasiness to become an uninvited third party in their relationship. Maybe she really was just dreaming, but the way his body responded, the way she'd been jittery afterward, told him there was more.

He padded his way down the hall, his eyes adjusting to the darkness in his familiar surroundings. The living room was empty, so he turned toward the kitchen, where he saw her. Leaning against the counter, looking out onto the backyard, Megan held a glass in her hand. Cameron studied her in a new light. He couldn't deny her beauty, with her perfectly shaped curves and hair that tumbled down her back. Those green eyes could pierce you in an instant, and now he knew that mouth could render a man speechless.

Still clutching the glass and staring, Megan hadn't moved one bit since he'd stood here. Something, or someone, consumed her mind.

"Who is he?"

Megan jumped, turned and the glass she'd been clutching dropped to the floor with a crackling shatter.

"Damn it." He started to move forward but stopped. He reached around the doorjamb and flicked on the light, blinking against the bright glare. "Don't move. Neither of us have shoes on."

First the lamp at her house and now this. They hadn't even delved into relationship territory, and already things were breaking all around them. A metaphor for things to come?

He ran back to his room and shoved his feet into a pair of tennis shoes at the foot of the bed. When he got back to the kitchen, Megan was bending over, picking up pieces of glass.

"I told you not to move," he growled, not knowing which situation he was angrier at.

"I didn't take a step. I'm just picking up the large pieces."

He jerked open the small built-in utility closet and grabbed the broom and dustpan. After sweeping up the majority of the glass, Megan set the shards she'd held into the dustpan, too.

After dumping the mess into the trash, he went back and scooped her up into his arms without a word.

With a squeak of surprise, Megan landed against his chest and he had no idea how to react to the fact his body warmed and responded with her against him once again.

"This is overkill—don't you think?" she asked, sliding one arm around his neck.

"I need you out of the way so I can get the rest and you're not wearing shoes. So no, I don't think it's overkill."

He deposited her on the couch in the living room and made his way back to clean up the water and make sure all the fragments were swept up. Several minutes later, he headed back into the living room to find Megan gone.

Heading down the hall, he heard water running from the bathroom. She'd left the door open, allowing the light to spill into the hallway. When he peeked into the room, Megan was at the sink, holding one hand under the water. Blood seeped to the surface of her palm as soon as water could wash it away.

"Why didn't you tell me you'd cut yourself?" he asked.

"Like you told me the other day?" Throwing him a glance over her shoulder, Megan shrugged. "You were cleaning up the mess. Seriously, it's very minor. I could use a bandage, though."

Stepping forward, Cameron reached around, shut the water off and held on to her wrist to examine her hand. Her hair tickled the side of his face, and the pulse beneath his fingertips sped up. Gritting his teeth to shove aside any emotions outside the friend zone, Cameron inspected the injury.

"It is small," he agreed, still inspecting the area.

She glanced up, catching his eyes in the mirror. "It just needs to be cleaned up and a bandage. I wasn't lying."

When he continued to stare at her, she merely quirked a brow. Damn woman would make a nun curse like a sailor.

"Sit," he said, pointing to the toilet lid. "It's my turn to take care of you."

Grabbing the first-aid kit from beneath the sink, he

shuffled the supplies around and found what he needed to fix her up.

He took a seat on the edge of the tub and balanced the supplies on his thigh. With careful movements, he uncurled her fingers and examined the cut again. It was bleeding pretty good, but it wasn't deep at all.

"I'm thinking you and I need only plastic, child-safe things in our homes," she joked.

"At the very least, we should stop handling glass in the middle of the night."

Cameron appreciated her attempt to lighten the mood, but he'd come out of his room for a reason and he needed to get this off his chest.

"Why couldn't you sleep?" he asked, keeping his eyes locked on his task as he swiped her palm with gauze.

"Insomnia has become a close friend of mine lately."

That was something he definitely understood. Still, she'd been sleeping just fine earlier in his bed.

"I'll make sure your door is fixed so you can sleep in your bed." Confident the bleeding had slowed enough not to come through the bandage, Cameron held a fresh gauze pad over the cut and applied pressure. "I'm sorry I startled you earlier."

Her hand tensed beneath his touch. "What were you asking me when you came into the kitchen, anyway?"

Keeping his thumb over the pad, he lifted his gaze to hers. Those bright green eyes outlined by dark lashes held him captivated and speechless for a second. "Nothing. Forget it."

"You asked who he was," she went on. "What *he* are you referring to?"

Knowing she wouldn't back down, Cameron opted to face this head-on as he'd originally intended. He was chief of police, for crying out loud, yet the thought of discussing another man with Megan had him trembling and nearly breaking out into a sweat…not to mention ready to punch someone in the face.

"I wanted to know who you were dreaming about."

Megan lowered her lids, took a deep breath and let it out. "I'm not sure you're ready for that answer."

Not ready for the answer? What was she about to tell him? Was she fantasizing about someone he didn't care for? Cameron got along with nearly everybody on the right side of the law.

"It's none of my business," he repeated, not sure he was ready for the answer, either. "The way you kissed me…"

Megan stared at him as his words died in the crackling air between them. "I was dreaming of you."

Nerves and fear settled deep in her stomach as if weighted by an anchor. She kept her gaze on his, refusing to back down or show weakness. He wanted the truth—he got it. Now they would both have to deal with the consequences because she'd just opened a door and shoved him right on through into the black abyss. Neither of them had a clue what waited for them.

Cameron's warm hand continued to hold hers, protecting her injury. He clenched the muscle in his jaw

as if he was holding back his response. Not knowing what was going on in his head was only adding
to her worry.

"Say something." She tried for a smile but swallowed instead, blinking as her eyes began to burn with
the threat of tears. *Oh, no.* She wouldn't break down.
Not here, not now. "It was a kiss, Cam. No big deal."

Okay, so she'd tried to be strong and not back down,
but right now, in the wake of his silence, she figured
backpedaling was the only approach.

"Don't lie to me," he commanded. "I was on the
receiving end of that kiss, and it was definitely a big
deal."

Megan pulled her hand away and got to her feet,
causing him to scoot back and try to catch all the supplies from his lap before they scattered to the floor.

"I was still asleep, Cameron. I was in your bed, surrounded by your scent. I can't help what I was dreaming."

Lifting the pad from her hand, she studied her palm.
The cut only stung a little, not enough to keep her focus
off the fact she was in this minuscule bathroom with
Cameron and she'd just told him she'd been fantasizing
about him. There wasn't enough air or space because
he came up right behind her, practically caging her in
between his hard, broad body and the vanity.

"So you're saying if I kissed you now that you're
fully awake, you wouldn't respond like earlier?"

His bold, challenging question had her jerking her
gaze up to meet his in the mirror. Slowly turning to
face him, brushing against every plane of his torso in

the process, Megan clutched her injured hand against her chest. Though the cut was insignificant in the grand scheme of things, holding on to it gave her a prop she needed to calm her shaky hands.

"It's late…or early," she told him. "Let's forget any of this happened and try to salvage what's left of the night. We both need sleep."

He braced his hands on the sink, officially trapping her in between his arms. "You're not a coward."

"No, I'm not. But this little exercise is ridiculous."

Lowering his lids, he stared at her mouth. "Then this won't be a problem."

His mouth slid over hers, and Megan pulled up every ounce of self-control to keep from moaning. Earlier she'd been half dreaming when she'd kissed him, but now she was fully awake and able to truly enjoy how amazing her best friend was in the kissing department.

Even though he was demanding and controlling, Cameron somehow managed to also be gentle with his touch. One strong hand splayed across her back, urging her closer. Her injured hand remained trapped between their bodies, and she fisted the other at her side because she didn't want to show emotion, not now. As much as she yearned to wrap herself around him and give in to anything he was willing to offer, she wasn't ready.

Cameron nipped at her lips, easing his way out of the kiss. But he didn't stop. No, the man merely angled his head the other way and dived back in for more.

The way he had her partially bent back over the vanity, Megan had to bring up her good hand to clutch his bare shoulder. She couldn't recall the last time she'd been so thoroughly kissed. No matter the time, she'd certainly never been kissed as passionately, as intensely, as now. Even those kisses that led straight to the bedroom had never gotten her this hot, this turned on.

Cameron fisted her T-shirt in his hand, pulling it tighter against her back as he lifted his head slightly. His forehead rested against hers.

"You're awake now," he muttered. "Feeling anything?"

Because she needed to think, and she knew *he* needed to think, Megan patted his shoulder and smiled. "You're a good kisser, Cam. No denying that. But I'm not dreaming anymore."

Cameron stepped back, hands on his narrowed hips where his shorts were riding low. "Tell me that didn't make your body respond."

She knew for a fact his body had responded, but she wouldn't be so tacky as to drop her gaze to the front of his shorts. They both knew she was fully aware.

Cameron had never even hinted he wanted to kiss her before. And even though she knew she should take this chance to tell him how she felt, she found herself lying to his face to save hers.

"Like I said, you're a great kisser," she told him. "But I've had better."

With that bold-faced lie, she marched from the bathroom and straight to the sofa, where she lay down facing the back cushions and covered up with the throw.

Megan wasn't quite sure if she'd put this experiment to rest or if she'd awakened the beast inside Cameron.

She had a feeling she'd find out soon enough. Thrills of anticipation coursed through her at the prospect.

Chapter Seven

Cameron needed this break. Between work and keeping track of Evan at various late-night meetings and that semierotic evening spent with Megan, he was about to lose it.

Drinking a beer on Eli's new patio with his brothers while their wives sat in the house discussing babies or shoes or some other frightening topic was exactly what he needed to relax.

Of course the incident with Megan had happened only two days ago and he still hadn't been able to get a grasp on how much that kiss, both kisses, had affected him.

"We've lost him again," Eli mocked, pulling Cameron from his daze.

"He's still working in his head." Drake took a pull of

his beer, then let the bottle dangle between his knees. "You're off the clock right now. Enjoy it."

Cameron rested his forearms on the edge of the deck railing and glanced out into the wooded backyard. Eli had built an addition on his home and then added the deck. He and his wife of nearly a year, and their baby, lived in their own little corner on the edge of town.

Drake, with his new bride and adorable stepdaughter, was embracing family life, as well. Drake had even mentioned how he and Marly wanted to try for a baby of their own.

Cameron couldn't be happier for his brothers, but they could keep their minivans, grocery lists and scheduled bedtimes. That wasn't a lifestyle he saw himself settling into anytime soon...if ever.

"I'm not working in my head," he defended himself. "I'm just enjoying listening to you two go on about recipes and paint swatches like a bunch of old ladies at a hair salon."

"Someone's grouchy," Eli muttered.

"Maybe he doesn't have a recipe worth sharing and he's embarrassed," Drake added with a low chuckle.

Cameron turned, flipping his brothers the one-finger salute. He missed getting together with them. They used to try to have a cookout or something once a week, especially since Eli's deployments were over and he was officially a civilian now, but Cameron's schedule was anything but regular. He hated putting work ahead of his family, but sometimes he couldn't help the matter. The criminals didn't seem to keep nine-to-five hours.

"Oh, hell," Drake whispered as he sat straight up in his deck chair. "You've finally got woman issues."

Eli's head whipped around, his gaze narrowing on Cameron. "Seriously? Because if you have woman issues, that means you have a woman, which is a damn miracle."

Finishing off his beer, knowing full well he needed something stronger to get into this discussion, Cameron tossed his empty bottle into the bin.

"I don't have a woman," he ground out, dropping onto the settee. "I have a headache over one."

Why did he have to go and issue Megan that challenge? Why did he have to push her into proving she was lying? Because all he'd gotten out of the deal was a hell of a great kiss, sleepless nights full of fantasies fueled by his best friend and a whole lot of anger with himself for crossing the line.

His own issues aside, how could he actually move to another level with Megan knowing her brother was well on his way to prison? Hell, Cameron was having a hard time keeping that bottled up now, and they were just friends. How could he keep secrets if he allowed intimacy to slip into the picture?

"Who is she?" Eli asked. "Oh, is it the new lady in town that lives out behind the grocery store? I hear she's single and if those tight-fitting clothes and spike heels aren't an invitation—"

"An invitation to what?" Nora asked from the patio door with her arms crossed over her chest, a quirked brow and a knowing grin on her face.

Eli cleared his throat. "Hey, babe," he said, crossing the wide area to wrap an arm around her waist. "I was just thinking about you."

She swatted him in the stomach. "If you think I'll ever dress like I work a pole every night, you're insane."

Eli groaned. "Please, don't mention a pole."

Cameron and Drake exchanged a conspiratorial look before they busted out laughing. "Still scarred from the image of Maddie Mays?"

Squeezing his eyes shut, Eli shook his head. "I'm trying to forget, but she was in again yesterday. Why does she always bring up her workout regime with me?"

"Because you're her doctor," Cameron smirked, enjoying the idea of his brother in such an awkward position. "Aren't you sworn to secrecy? I don't think you should share such things with us."

Eli blinked, narrowing his gaze. "If I have to suffer at the image, then so do you two."

"Mad" Maddie Mays had seemed to be a hundred years old when they were kids. At this point she may have been the same age as Noah and survived by hiding out on the ark. She'd never been a fan of the St. John boys and found their shenanigans less than amusing. More often than not, she'd chased them out of her yard wielding a rolling pin, baseball bat or sometimes both to really get her point across.

Now with Eli taking over their father's clinic, Maddie had no choice but to associate with at least one of the St. John boys, unless she wanted to find a doctor in a neighboring town. Apparently she'd warmed up to Eli. Perhaps sharing her unorthodox exercise routine was just her way of getting back at him for being a menace as a kid.

"If you guys are done discussing that poor woman, I wanted to know if you all had mentioned date night to Cameron." Nora took the bottle from Eli's hands and took a drink.

"What date night?" Cameron eyed his brothers. "You two aren't my type."

Nora smiled. "Actually we were wondering if you'd like to play the cool uncle while we went out. I was hesitant to ask you, but Eli and Drake assured me you wouldn't mind if you weren't busy."

Stunned, Cameron considered the idea, then shrugged. "Sure, I can do it." He'd just schedule the diaper changing and mac-and-cheese dinner around watching for drug smugglers. "How hard can watching a baby and a six-year-old be?"

His brothers exchanged a look and nearly turned red trying to hold back a comment or laughter. *Oh, they think I'm not capable? Challenge accepted.*

"Seriously?" Cameron went on. "You're already thinking I'm going to blow this? I run a town, for pity's sake. Surely I can handle two kids."

Nora stepped forward, patted his arm and offered a smile that was a bit on the patronizing side. Did nobody have faith in him?

"Just tell us when you're free," she told him.

Running his crazy schedule through his mind, Cameron knew there wouldn't be a great night, but he could surely spare a few hours. "I could do it Sunday evening."

"I work until four, but we could go after that," Drake chimed in.

"Great." Nora beamed. She leaned down, kissed Cameron on the cheek and patted his shoulder. "I'll go tell Marly."

She raced back into the house and Cameron leaned his head back against the cushion on the settee. Both brothers stared down at him.

"What?"

"You're not getting off the hook about this woman that has you tied in knots just because you're babysitting," Eli insisted. "We'll get the truth out of you one way or another."

Cameron didn't even know what there was to tell. Megan had kissed him, he'd kissed her and since then they hadn't spoken. What a mess, and most of it was his fault. If he hadn't insisted on challenging her, if he'd let her lie her way out of the first kiss, they would've moved on and ignored that pivotal turn they'd taken.

No way would he reveal Megan's name to his brothers. She was like a sister to them, and he wasn't sure they'd be on board with how Cameron had treated her.

But damn it, she'd tied him up in knots the second she'd slid her body against his.

"Come on—you can't sit there brooding and not fill us in." Drake leaned an elbow against the railing. "It has to be someone you know since you work every waking second. You don't have time to meet women unless it's someone you're arresting. Please, tell me you don't have some prisoner-guard romance going because if you do we're staging an intervention."

"Do you ever shut up?" Cameron asked, without heat. "Can't a guy keep some things to himself?"

"No," Eli and Drake replied in unison.

Raking a hand down his face, Cameron came to his feet. He couldn't stay any longer. If he did, they'd figure out who had him in knots and he couldn't afford to let that out right now, not when he was so confused. And he had no clue what was going through Megan's head, either.

"Now he's leaving." Eli laughed. "This must be bad if you're running from your own brothers."

"It's a small town," Drake added with a smile that stated he'd get to the bottom of it. "Secrets don't stay hidden long. The truth will come out eventually."

Cameron glared at his brothers before heading into the house to say goodbye to his sisters-in-law and his nieces.

The truth coming out was precisely what he couldn't have happen. But he knew he wasn't telling anybody about the incident and he doubted Megan would tell anyone, so that left the secret bottled up good and tight.

The question now was: When would it explode?

Megan hadn't even made it home from work when her cell rang. She'd just pulled onto her road when she answered without looking.

"Hello."

"I'm sorry to bother you."

Instantly Megan recognized the voice of one of her clients…a girl who'd just been in earlier that afternoon and the same one who'd called in the middle of the night days ago. Farrah wasn't the most stable person, and Megan made a point to really work with her. Megan cared for all her clients' well-being, but Farrah was extremely unstable and truly had no one else to turn to.

"Don't apologize," Megan insisted as she neared her driveway. "I'm here for you anytime."

"Earlier you told me that moving forward was the only way to start over."

Megan eased her car into the detached garage. "That's right."

Farrah sniffed. "I'm going to look for a job tomorrow. It's time I move out and try to make my life my own."

Megan had been waiting for Farrah to see that she needed to stand on her own two feet, to get away from the controlling man who held so much power over her. Megan had tried to stress how control can often quickly turn to abuse.

"I just wanted to thank you for today, and maybe… Could I put you down as a reference?"

Megan smiled as she killed the engine. "That would be fine. I'm really proud of you, Farrah."

Farrah thanked her, then ended the call. By the time Megan gathered her things and headed across the stone walkway to her back door, her phone was ringing again. She glanced at the screen and saw Evan's number. She hated how her first instinct was to groan.

How was it she could counsel total strangers, yet her own flesh and blood refused to take her advice or even consider for a moment that she wasn't trying to control him?

With a sigh, she answered as she shoved her key in her new doorknob. "Hi, Evan."

"Can I stay with you for a few nights?"

Stunned, Megan froze with her hand on the knob. She wasn't shocked at his abrupt question without so much as a greeting, but at the request. It was unusual for him not to ask for money first.

"Are you all right?"

"Yeah, yeah. I just…I need a place to crash. You going to help me or not?"

Closing her eyes, Megan leaned her head against the glass on the door. Even though his tone was put out and angry, he was at least coming to her for support.

"I'll always help you, Evan. But are you asking because you're ready to make changes in your life or because you're hiding?"

"Forget it," he grunted. "You're always judging me."

"No, Evan. I'm not judging—I'm worried."

Silence filled the line. Megan straightened and strained to hear.

"Evan?"

"If I wanted to change, could you help me?"

Now his voice came out in a near whisper, reminding her of the young boy he'd once been. At one time he'd looked up to her. When did all of that change?

"I'd do anything for you," she assured him. "Do you need help? I can come get you right now."

Again silence filled the line. She waited, not wanting to push further. This was the first time he actually sounded as if he may want to let her in. Megan prayed he would take the olive branch she'd been holding out for so long.

Commotion from the other end of the line, muffled voices and Evan's swearing told her the conversation was dead.

"I'll, uh, I'll call you later," he whispered as if he didn't want to be heard.

Gripping her phone, Megan pushed her way into the house. She didn't know why she'd let herself get her hopes up for those few seconds. She didn't know why she was constantly beating herself up over a man who might just continue to use her for the rest of their lives. But he was her brother and she would never give up. She may be frustrated and oftentimes deflated, but she wasn't a quitter and she would make damn sure he wasn't, either.

He'd called; that was a major step.

After hanging her purse on the peg by the back door, Megan slid her keys and phone inside. Her stomach growled, reminding her that she'd skipped lunch again in order to squeeze in one more client. Her supervisor kept telling her she needed to take breaks, but how could Megan justify them when someone's life could very well be in her hands? What if it was the patient who was contemplating suicide or leaving a spouse and they needed to talk right then? Megan couldn't turn them away.

Her eyes landed on the letter she'd tacked to the side

of her refrigerator. The letter outlining every detail for the new position she'd been offered in Memphis. The job was almost too good to be true, but it meant leaving Cameron, leaving the chance for something she'd wanted her whole life.

The directors had certainly pulled out all the stops to get her to take the position. The opportunity to help launch a free clinic in an area of town where people had been forgotten, left to their own devices. Megan wasn't married, didn't have kids and had been recommended for this job by her boss. How could she say no?

Two very valid reasons kept her from jumping at this chance of a lifetime: Evan and Cameron. Both men were fixtures in her life, and both men needed her whether either of them admitted it or not.

She hadn't spoken to Cameron in a few days, and emptiness had long since settled into that pit in her stomach, joining the fear and worry there. This was precisely why she hadn't made a move before, why she'd kept her feelings to herself. If a few kisses had already wedged an awkward wall between them, what would've happened had she told him she wanted to try a real relationship with him?

Megan glanced at the letter again and sighed. Maybe she should go. Maybe she needed to get away from the man who was a constant in her life but would never fill the slot she needed him to. And perhaps her new start would be the perfect opportunity for Evan to make a clean break, as well.

Chapter Eight

"I need you." Cameron surveyed the chaos around him and cringed. "How soon can you be at my house?"

Shrill cries pierced his eardrums for at least the fifteenth time in as many minutes. Every single parent in the world officially had his respect and deserved some type of recognized award for their patience.

"Where are you?" Megan asked. "What's all that noise?"

Cameron raked a hand over his hair and realized he needed to get a cut. He'd add that to the many things he'd slacked on lately. Right now, though, he was groveling to his best friend to come save him even though he'd been a jerk and hadn't spoken to her since.

His house was a complete war zone thanks to a spunky six-year-old and an infant.

Willow was dancing her stuffed horse in front of Amber's reddened, angry, tear-soaked face in an attempt to calm the baby, but Cameron figured that was only making it worse. Not to mention the fact that Willow had a slight goose egg on her head after tripping over the baby and falling into the corner of the coffee table.

Why had he insisted on watching the kids at his house? A house that was as far from baby proof as possible. He was a bachelor. Unfortunately, his bachelor pad had now tragically converted into a failing day-care center.

"Please," he begged. He never begged. "I'm home, and you can't get here fast enough. I'm...babysitting."

Okay, so he muttered that last word because he knew Megan well enough to know she'd burst out laughing and he wasn't in the mood.

"I'm sorry. Did you say *babysitting*?"

Cameron bent over and pulled Amber into his arms. "Front door's unlocked," he said right before disconnecting the call and sliding his cell back into his pocket. He had no time for mockery; this was crisis mode. Code red.

Megan would most likely dash down here within minutes, if nothing else to see firsthand how out of his comfort zone he was. The humiliation he was about to suffer would be long lasting, but at this point he didn't care. He needed reinforcements in the worst possible way.

This was not how he'd intended to apologize to Megan or how he'd planned on contacting her for the first time since he'd all but consumed her in his bathroom. Cameron hadn't mapped out a plan, exactly, but he knew he needed to be the one to take the next step. But the step he wanted to take and the step he needed to take were on opposite ends of the spectrum.

Cameron patted Amber on her back and tried to console her. How could someone so tiny be so filled with rage? Fatherhood was not his area of expertise. He wished there was some how-to manual he could read. Did Eli have this much trouble with his little girl? Cameron had never seen this side of his infant niece.

"Maybe you should sing her a song," Willow said, smiling up at him with a grin that lacked the front two teeth. "Do you know any songs?"

AC/DC's "Back in Black" sprang to mind, but he didn't figure an infant would find that particular tune as appealing as a nearly forty-year-old man did.

"I bet you know some," he countered. "What songs have you learned in school so far?"

Brows drawn, Willow looked lost in thought. Apparently, something brilliant came to her because she jumped up and down, her lopsided ponytails bouncing off her shoulders.

"'Wheels on the Bus'! That's my favorite."

After taking a seat on the sofa, Cameron adjusted Amber on his lap so the infant could see Willow and hopefully hear the song.

What else could he do? He'd fed her. Then she'd played on the floor with her toys, and now she was angrier than any woman he'd ever encountered on either side of the law.

Willow started singing, extremely off-key and loud, but hey, the extra noise caught Amber's attention and for a blessed moment she stopped screaming.

Then she started again, burying her face against his chest. Unfazed, Willow continued to sing.

The front door flew open, and Megan stepped in, instantly surveying the room. A smirk threatened to take over, but Cameron narrowed his gaze across the room, silently daring her to laugh.

He'd never been so happy to see another person in his entire life.

Willow stopped singing the second the door closed. "Hey, Megan. I didn't know you were coming over."

Megan smiled and crossed the room. "I didn't, either, but here I am."

Cameron tried to focus on the reason he'd called her here, but his eyes drank in the sight of Megan wearing a pair of body-hugging jeans and a plain white T-shirt with her signature off-duty cowgirl boots. With her hair pulled back in a ponytail, she looked about twenty years old.

Megan reached for Amber and held the infant against her body. Without giving Cameron another glance, she turned and started walking around the room, patting Amber's back and singing softly.

Well, what did he expect? He'd called her to help with the situation he obviously had lost control over, not to take up where they'd left off the other night.

Still, the fact she didn't say a word to him made him wonder if he'd hurt her more than he realized. He was botching up their relationship in every way, and he didn't blame her for being upset or angry.

Almost instantly the crying ceased. "Seriously? You hold her and she stops?"

Megan laughed, easing back to look Amber in the face. "I don't think it was me at all," she corrected him. "I think her stomach was upset. I just felt rumbling on my hand."

Cameron glanced to Megan's hand resting on Amber's bottom. Realization hit him hard. "Oh, no."

Willow giggled. "She feels better now."

Megan lifted Amber around to face Cameron. "She doesn't smell better," Megan said, scrunching up her nose.

Oh, please, please, please. There were few things that truly left him crippled, but the top of that list was changing a diaper...a dirty, smelly diaper.

Slowly rising to his feet, Cameron locked eyes with Megan. "I'll give you a hundred bucks to change that diaper."

Megan quirked a brow, her eyes glazed over with something much more devious than humor. "Keep your hundred bucks. I'll decide payment later."

Oh, mercy. Was she flirting with him? No, she was upset...wasn't she? Chalk this up to reason number 947 as to why he didn't do relationships. He'd never understand women. Ever.

"Where's the diapers and wipes?" she asked.

"Oh, I know," Willow raised her hand as if she were in school. "Follow me."

Mcgan trailed after Drake's stepdaughter and went down the hall to his bedroom. His bedroom.

"Don't change that diaper on my bed," he yelled. Laughter answered him, and he knew he was in for it. This was all part of his punishment.

The reeking smell in his bedroom was the least of his worries, because in just over an hour his brothers would be back to retrieve their kids—leaving him and Megan alone once again.

She should've left when everyone else did, but she'd put her pride and her emotions aside because she and Cameron needed to talk. He also needed help picking up his living room. Between the fort with couch cushions and blankets and the towels Willow had used as capes, making sure Cameron and Megan were superheroes, too, the place was anything but organized. The furniture had been pushed aside to allow room for "flying," and Megan hadn't even walked into the kitchen yet. She'd started making marshmallow treats with Willow just before she left and the mess was epic. She had to get in there before Cameron, with all his straight, orderly ways, had a heart attack.

Another thing she and Cameron saw eye to eye on. They both had a knack for cleanliness and keeping everything in its place…except for these emotions. They were all over, and nothing was orderly about them.

Best to start in the kitchen. Not only could she get that back in order, she could think of how best to approach being back in his house and all alone together…

Especially after that giant gauntlet she'd thrown down when he'd offered her a hundred bucks.

What had she been thinking? The flirty comment had literally slid out of her mouth. Clearly she needed a filter.

She'd been so amused by him babysitting, at the chaos his normally perfectly polished house was in. Then she'd seen him holding Amber and something very female, very biological-clock-ticking, snapped in her. She'd always known Cameron was a strong man who could handle anything. Yet the sight of those big tanned hands cradling an infant, of Cameron trying to console her with fear and vulnerability in his eyes, had sent her attraction to a whole new level. As if she needed yet another reason to be drawn to every facet of her best friend.

Surveying the cereal on the floor, Megan tiptoed carefully through to the other side of the kitchen to get the broom from the utility closet. In the midst of sweeping, a tingle slid up her spine and she knew she wasn't alone.

"Sorry." She went back to her chore, keeping her back to him. "Willow wanted to do everything on her own, so I let her. She's too cute to deny. I'll get this cleaned up and be gone."

When a warm, firm hand gripped her arm, Megan froze. Her heart kicked up, and she hated how she'd become this weak woman around her best friend. A part of her regretted sneaking into his bed. She'd cursed herself over and over for dreaming of him. The timing of the all-too-real dream at the same time he'd tricd to wake her had thrown her control completely out the window.

But she couldn't wish away those kisses. No matter how she wanted things to be different between them right now, she would cherish those moments when his mouth had been on hers, his body flush against her own.

"Stop avoiding me." His low tone washed over her, and Megan closed her eyes, comforted in that familiar richness of his voice. "We haven't talked in days, and when the kids were here you barely said a word to me."

So she'd been using two innocent children as a buffer. What was a girl to do when she was so far out of her comfort zone she couldn't even see the zone anymore?

"You called me to help, so I helped." She started sweeping the dry cereal again, her swift movements causing Cameron's hand to fall away. "Let me get this cleaned up before you step on it and make it worse."

"Damn it, would you turn around and look at me? Stop being a coward."

That commanding tone had her gripping the broom, straightening her shoulders and pivoting, cereal crunching beneath her boots.

"Coward?" she repeated, ready to use her broom to knock some sense into him. "You could've contacted me, too, you know. How dare you call me a coward after that stunt you pulled? Did you think I'd wither at your feet or declare my undying love? What did you want me to say or do when you all but challenged me?"

She hated how anger was her instant reaction, but damn it, the man was dead-on. She had been a coward. She'd purposely not contacted him. Still, in her defense, he could've texted her or something.

"I'm not trying to start a fight." That calm, controlled cop tone remained in place, grating on her nerves even more because now she was fired up and he wasn't proving to be a worthy opponent. "I just wanted to talk."

"Fine," she spat. "You talk while I clean."

Angrier at herself for letting her emotions take control, Megan went back to focusing on the floor. With jerky movements, she had a rather large pile in no time. When she glanced out the corner of her eye and saw Cameron with his arms crossed over his chest, she had to grit her teeth to keep from saying something even more childish. The last thing she wanted was to be the reason this relationship plummeted, and if she didn't rein in her irritability about the fact he'd called her out, that's exactly what would happen.

Once she'd scooped up the mess and dumped everything into the trash, she put the broom and dustpan back in the closet. The counters weren't as bad, but the big brute was blocking them.

Propping her hands on her hips, Megan stared across the room. "You're going to have to move."

He moved—leaning back against the counter, crossing one ankle over the other. "You can't seriously be mad at me. Let's put the kissing aside, which I know for a fact you enjoyed. An hour ago you flirted with me and now you're ready to fight. What has gotten into you?"

The way he studied her, as if she were a stranger,

madc hcr want that proverbial hole to open and swallow her. To be honest, she didn't know what had gotten into her, either. One minute she was ready to tell him her true feelings; the next minute she was angry at him for not reading her mind and at herself for being afraid to risk dignity.

Yeah, she was all woman when it came to moods and indecisiveness.

"We've already established the kisses were good," she agreed. "I didn't want your hundred bucks, and now I have leverage over you when I actually need something."

"I think you know I'd do anything for you," he told her. "You don't need to hold anything over me."

With a shrug, Megan went to the sink to wet the rag. "Fine, then get out of my way so I can clean and get home. I've had a long day, and I'm pretty tired."

She wrung out the water and turned, colliding with a hard, wide chest. Megan tipped her head slightly to look into Cameron's blue eyes. Those signature St. John baby blues could mesmerize any woman… She was no exception.

"Thank you for coming." He slid his hand up her arm, pushing a wayward strand of hair behind her ear and resting his hand on her shoulder. "I'm sorry for how I treated you the other night. Sorry I made you uncomfortable. But I'm not sorry I kissed you."

Megan heard the words, even processed what he was saying; she just couldn't believe Cameron was confessing this to her.

"Cam—"

The way his eyes locked on to hers cut off whatever she was about to say. The always-controlled cop she'd known most of her life looked as if he was barely hanging on. The level of hunger staring back at her was new. Had she misread him? Had he responded to that kiss in a way that mirrored her own need? Physically he'd responded, but what about emotionally?

"I won't lie and say I haven't thought of you as more than a friend before," he started. "I can't deny you're stunning, and you know more about me than anyone outside of my family."

Why did this sound like a stepping-stone to a gentle letdown?

"You don't have to defend your feelings," she told him, offering a smile. "I'm not asking for anything. I feel the same way."

Those strong hands came up to frame her face. "I liked kissing you, loved it, if I'm being honest."

Between that firm hold he had on her and his raw words, Megan wanted to let that hope blossom, but she wasn't ready to start celebrating just yet. The worry lines between Cameron's brows, the thin lips and the way he gritted his teeth between sentences were all red flags that he was in a battle with himself. Nothing spoke volumes like that raw passion staring back at her.

"Then why do you look so angry?" she asked.

His hands dropped to her shoulders, his fingertips curling into her skin. "Because this is such a bad idea on so many levels, Meg."

Heart beating fast, nerves swirling around in her

stomach, Megan forced all the courage she could muster to rise and take center stage.

"Why is that?" she countered with a defiant tip of her chin. "You're afraid of what it would do to our relationship? You think this is just some random emotion and it will pass?"

"Yes to both of those." His clutch on her shoulders lessened as he leaned in so close, his warm breath tickled her face. "And because if I start kissing you again, I won't stop."

Every nerve ending in her entire body instantly went on alert at his declaration. How could he drop a bomb like that and not expect her to react? Did he think he was helping matters? Did he truly believe with this knowledge she now possessed that she would give up?

"What if I don't want you to stop?"

By his swift intake of breath, she knew she'd shocked him with her bold question.

"You don't mean that," Cameron muttered.

Megan flattened her palms against his chest, slid them up to his shoulders and on up to frame his face. Touching him intimately like this was just the first step of many she hoped they'd take together. She wanted him to see she wasn't blowing this off anymore, wasn't pretending whatever was happening between them wasn't real.

"I mean every word. If you want something, why not take it?"

The way he continued to stare at her, as if listening to both the devil and the angel on his shoulders, made her take action into her own hands.

Rising to her toes, she pulled his head down and captured his lips with her own. She knew she'd made a good judgment call when Cameron instantly melted against her.

Chapter Nine

Every single valid reason for keeping his distance from Megan flew out the window with her lips on his. He'd always admired her take-charge attitude, but she'd never fully executed that power with him before.

He didn't know if he should be terrified or turned on.

Wrapping his arms around her, pulling her flush against his body, just seemed to happen without him even thinking. One second he was talking himself out of kissing her ever again. Then he'd touched her, and the next thing he knew she was on him…which wasn't a bad thing.

Cameron held one arm against her lower back, forcing her hips against his, and slid one hand up to the nape of her neck to hold her right where he wanted her.

Soft moans escaped Megan, and he couldn't stop the dam of need from bursting.

Bending her back, Cameron eased his fingertips beneath the hem of her shirt. Smooth, silky skin slid beneath his touch. The ache he had burning inside completely blindsided him. He'd known he'd wanted her, but the all-consuming passion that completely took hold of him was new.

Megan's hands traveled down to the edge of his shirt and the second her petite hands roamed up his abdomen, Cameron nearly lost it. It wasn't as if he hadn't been touched by a woman before, but never by the one woman he'd craved for years. Her touch was so much more hypnotizing than he'd ever imagined…and he'd imagined plenty.

Megan tore her mouth from his, tipping her head back and arching against him. "Cam," she panted.

Hearing his name on her lips in such an intimate way was the equivalent of throwing cold water on him. This was Megan. Evan's sister. A guy he was within days of arresting.

Cameron jerked back, his hands falling from beneath her shirt. Megan got tangled in his until he lifted the hem and took another step back.

Her moist, swollen lips seemed to mock him, showcasing what he'd just had and what he was turning down. He clenched his fists at his side, trying to grasp on to some form of control. Lately, where Megan was concerned, he was losing every bit of it.

"This can't happen."

Why did it sound as if his vocal chords were rubbing

against sandpaper? He couldn't put up a strong front if he didn't have control over his own voice.

Her eyes searched his, and Cameron hated the confusion laced with arousal staring back at him. Of course she was confused. He'd all but taken over the second she'd touched him and nearly devoured her; then he told her no and backed away as if she had some contagious disease.

Megan pushed off the counter. "What is the problem?"

Swallowing the truth, Cameron gave her another reason that was just as valid. "Sex would take us into a whole new territory. Who's to say that once we give in to this lust, that we won't resent each other or regret what happened?"

She crossed her arms over her breasts and shrugged. "Judging from that kiss, I can't imagine either of us would have regrets. So maybe we would actually enjoy ourselves and find that we may want to keep moving and building on our relationship."

That right there was the biggest worry of all. No way would he go through with this knowing he would have to tear her and her brother apart. Megan would hate Cameron when that time came, and if he slept with her now, she would hate him even more. He couldn't handle it. He only hoped their friendship would carry them over this hurdle once Evan went to jail and Megan understood that Cameron had no choice but to do his job.

Besides, if they went beyond the lust, beyond the sex, Cameron refused to let Megan lead a life married to a cop.

Married? Yes, he loved Megan more than any other woman, but marriage was not in his future.

"There's a reason I don't have relationships, Megan. You know that."

After staring at him for another minute, she laughed and threw her arms out. "So, what, you're just giving up before anything can get started? You're denying yourself, denying me what we both want because you already know the outcome?"

Pretty much.

"We can't come back to this after we have sex," he retorted.

"Come back to what?" she asked, taking a step closer, fire blazing in her eyes. "Friendship? We already crossed that threshold when your mouth was on mine and your hand was up my shirt."

Her angry, frustrated tone matched the turmoil raging inside him. What could he counter with when she was absolutely right? The second they'd crossed that line, an invisible wall had been erected, preventing them from turning back.

Why had he allowed this to happen? Why hadn't he let it go after she'd kissed him when she'd been dreaming? Even though she'd been dreaming of him, he could've moved on to save their friendship. But Megan's kiss had turned something inside him; something had clicked into place…something he couldn't identify because he was too scared to even try.

Megan threw her arms in the air and let out a low groan. "Forget it. Clearly you don't even know what you want. Or, if you do, you're afraid to face it. I don't have time for games."

"Games?" Cameron all but yelled, and he never yelled at anyone, let alone his best friend. "You think I'm playing a game here?"

When she started to walk by him, he reached out and snagged her arm until their shoulders were touching, her face tipping up toward his. The fury in her eyes wasn't something he'd seen too often and never before directed at him. Her chest rose and fell as her heavy breathing filled the silence. He didn't release his grip on her arm, apparently because he wanted to torture himself further by feeling that silky skin beneath his fingertips once more.

"Let me go," she whispered, her chin quivering.

Even with her eyes starting to fill, the anger penetrated through the hurt. As he watched her struggle with holding her emotions together, Cameron's heart jumped as he reluctantly slid his hand down her arm, stopping at her wrist and finally releasing her.

"I'm not trying to hurt you." That pitiful statement sounded flat and cold even to his own ears. "You're the last person I want to make cry."

A watery laugh escaped her. "You think I'm crying over you? These tears are over my own foolishness."

One lone tear slid down her cheek. Just as she reached up to swat it away, he caught her hand in his and used the pad of his thumb to swipe at the moisture.

He turned toward her and tugged her until she fell against him. Wrapping his arms around her, ignoring

her protest, Cameron waited until she stopped struggling before he spoke.

"I don't want this between us, Meg. I can't lose you."

Her head dropped to his chest as she sniffed, her
palms flattened against his shoulders. "This is just a
really bad time, and my emotions are getting the best
of me. Don't worry."

Cameron stroked her back, trying to ease all the
tension, knowing he'd never fully get her relaxed and
calm. But that wouldn't stop him from trying.

"You don't have to defend yourself," he muttered
against her ear. "We've both had pressure on us lately.
Finding you in my bed the other night and then kissing
you, it was all unexpected and it takes a lot to catch
me off guard."

Megan eased back, lifted her eyes to his and
blinked. Wet lashes framed her green eyes as a wide
smile spread across her face. "The fact that I manage
to keep you on your toes after all these years makes
me happier than it should."

The way she worded that, *after all these years*,
sounded so personal. More personal than friendship.
Married couples said such things to each other.

"I'm not blaming those kisses on pressure or the
chaos in my life," she told him. "I realized soon after
your lips touched mine that I wasn't dreaming anymore. I could've stopped, but it just felt so good and
you were responding."

Hell yeah, he'd responded. He hadn't been with a
woman for so long, but even he couldn't make that his
excuse. Cameron had to at least be honest with him-

self. The second her lips had touched his, her arms encircled his neck, he'd been pulled under. All control had slid from him to her in the span of a second, and he hadn't minded one bit.

Then reality had come crashing back and he'd known what a mistake he'd made. Unfortunately, he'd gotten her in his system and now he was paying the price.

Damn it.

"I need to get going." She pulled completely away, eased around him and headed toward the living room. "The kitchen is done. Can you handle the living room?"

Why did his eyes have to zero in on the sway of her hips? Why was his body still humming from the way she'd been leaning against him?

Years ago he'd wondered, but he'd never made a move because either she or he had been dating someone. Then they got to a point where they were just perfectly happy being friends and not expecting anything more. He'd been deployed and hoped when he'd returned the feelings would've lessened. They hadn't. And then he'd become a cop, lost a partner and hardened his heart toward anything permanent.

So here they were, still best friends who each knew just how well the other one kissed. Cameron was also extremely aware of exactly how Megan liked to be touched and how hard and demanding she wanted those kisses. Her sighs, her moans, the way she arched her body against his were all images he'd live with forever.

He had to endure his own personal hell because he couldn't have her, wouldn't put her through coming in second to his job. And he damn well wouldn't expect her to want more once she learned he'd spent months bringing down a drug ring that now involved her brother.

Megan grabbed her keys off the small table just inside the entryway. "I'll be out of town Thursday and Friday," she told him without turning to look at him as she pulled open the door. "I should be home late Friday night."

"Where are you going?"

With her hand on the knob, she tossed her hair over her shoulder and stared back at him. "Just something for work."

Cameron curled his fingers around the edge of the wood door. "Is it a conference?"

"You might say that."

She was lying. Whatever she was doing, she didn't want to tell him.

"I don't expect you to share every aspect of your life," he told her. "But don't lie to my face."

Megan reached up, patted his cheek. "Kind of like you lying about not wanting more with me? That goes both ways, Cam."

Before he could respond, the cell in his pocket vibrated. *Damn it.* Now was not the time to deal with work unless it was to bring this ring down once and for all.

He pulled the phone out, saw his brother's number and didn't know if he was disappointed or relieved that work wasn't calling him in.

"Hang on," he told Megan. "It's just Eli. I'm not done with you."

Her eyes flared, and he realized how that sounded considering all that had transpired between them within the past week.

"What?" he growled into the phone.

"Mom fell." Eli didn't bother with any pleasantries. "I'm pretty sure her ankle is broken."

"Oh, hell." Cameron ran a hand down his face and sighed, meeting the concerned look in Megan's eyes. "Want me to meet you at the hospital?"

"I've already got her here," Eli answered. "You don't have to come, but I wanted to let you know what was up. Dad is home, and he's watching Amber for me. Nora came with me to sit with mom. Drake got called into work when one of his guys reported in sick."

"I'll be right there."

Cameron shoved the phone back in his pocket and yanked his keys from the peg by the door.

"Mom fell," he said, answering Megan's worried look. "Eli thinks her ankle is broken. I'm heading to the ER now. Dad is babysitting for Eli."

Megan stepped out onto the porch, holding the screen door open for him. "I'll go by your parents' house and sit with Mac and Amber. I'm sure he's worried. Keep me posted."

Before she walked away, Cameron reached out, wrapped his hand around the nape of her neck and looked her straight in the eyes. "I meant what I said. We're not done talking."

Megan's eyes locked on to his, her shoulders

straightened and that defiant chin lifted. "I'm pretty sure we're done discussing just how much you're denying both of us something that could be amazing. Until you're ready to face the fact you enjoyed kissing me, rubbing your hands on me, and admit you're just running scared, don't bring it up again."

She pulled away and bounded down the porch steps. "Just text with an update on your mom. No need to call."

And with that she headed toward her house, leaving Cameron to stare at those mocking hips.

Yes, he'd liked kissing her, thoroughly appreciated the feel of her curves beneath his hands. He was a man and she was a sensual woman whom he'd wanted for years. So what if he was running scared? Better to stop the disaster before it completely ruined their friendship.

As Cameron headed to his truck, he had a sinking feeling their friendship had already rounded a curve and was speeding out of control, and there wasn't a damn thing he could do about it.

Chapter Ten

"This fuss isn't necessary." Bev tried to maneuver her new crutches as Eli and Cameron flanked her sides, assisting her into the house. "I'll be fine. There's no need for everyone to hover."

"You will be fine," Eli agreed. "But for now we're going to hover. Just be glad Drake had to go in or you'd have all of us."

Megan held the door open with one hand and propped Amber on her hip with the other. "You know it's useless to argue with these guys, Bev," Megan said, catching the woman's grin. "Just let them think what they want to boost their egos."

Cameron's gaze swung to hers, and Megan merely lifted a brow. If he wanted to apply those words to the turmoil they had going on, so be it. Wasn't her fault if he had a guilty conscience.

Megan closed the door and pulled Amber around to settle against her chest as the baby continued chewing on her cloth rattle.

"I've already brought your pillows and pajamas down to the guest room," Mac stated, moving forward to take the place of his sons. "We'll be sleeping down here until you're healed and can do the stairs."

"And I'll be stopping by in the mornings," Nora stated, coming in through the door, holding Bev's purse. "I can do your grocery shopping after work so Mac doesn't have to worry about anything."

"One of my patients has volunteered to babysit Amber until you're feeling better," Eli added.

"Oh, for pity's sake." Bev stopped in the foyer and sighed, shooting glares at all those around her. "I can get through these next six weeks without rearranging everyone's lives."

Mac placed a hand over her shoulder. "Complain all you want, but when I had bypass surgery, you all steamrolled me and took care of me. Now it's our turn to cater to you."

A lump formed in Megan's throat at the sincere, loving way Mac looked to Bev. They'd always been such a dynamic couple, always strong even when dealing with hellion teen boys and all their shenanigans.

Megan knew that Mac's bypass surgery last year had rocked them all because the pillar of the family wasn't as indestructible as they'd all thought him to be.

Megan's eyes traveled to Cameron. Her breath caught in her throat when she found herself under the scrutiny of his bright blue eyes. Amber started fussing, pulling Megan's focus back to the infant in her arms.

"It's okay, sweetheart." Megan patted her back. "You're just getting sleepy, aren't you?"

Nora smiled, set the purse down on the accent table and reached out. "I can take her. She's not used to being awake this late."

"I'll run Eli home," Cameron chimed in. "Go on ahead and take her."

Nora said her goodbyes in a frantic attempt to get her unhappy child out the door. Once she was gone, Mac assisted Bev down the hall and into the spare room.

"I'll get her meds from the car," Eli volunteered. "She won't need any more tonight, but I'll put them in the kitchen where Dad can see them."

Eli headed out the front door, leaving Cameron and Megan alone. Why did they always somehow gravitate toward these situations? Before last week she wouldn't think twice about being alone with Cameron, but with all this tension crackling between them, she truly didn't know what step to take next. And she'd made it clear that the ball was in his court.

"I'm heading out," she told him. "Let your mom know I'm here if she needs anything. I'm free all weekend once I get back."

Cameron nodded. "Thanks for your help."

She waited for him to say something else, but he continued to stare in silence. Eli came back inside, carrying a small white pharmacy bag. He glanced between Megan and Cameron.

"Everything okay?" he asked, his brows drawn together.

"Fine," Megan and Cameron replied in unison, still eyeing each other.

"O-kay," Eli whispered as he moved on through to the kitchen.

Shoving her hair away from her face, Megan gritted her teeth as she reached into her pocket and pulled out her keys. Without another word, she headed out the front door and into the cool evening. She'd just hit the bottom step when she heard the screen door slam.

"Is this how it's going to be?" Cameron yelled. "This awkward, sometimes-polite chitchat like we're virtual strangers?"

Megan took in a deep breath before turning to face the man on the porch illuminated by the soft glow of outdoor lights. With his hands on his narrow hips, black T-shirt stretched tightly over toned shoulders and that perfectly cropped hair, Cameron gave off the impression of someone in control and pulled together.

Megan knew better. She'd experienced just how much he relinquished that power when she'd touched him, kissed him, pressed her body to his. And that interesting tidbit of information was something worth hanging on to.

The chill in the air slid through her. A shiver racked her body as she wrapped her arms around her midsection.

"If you feel awkward around me, then it sounds like you have some issues to work out," she threw back. She wasn't going to make this easy on him, not when he was being so infuriating. "I've always heard intimacy helps people relax."

Maybe she shouldn't poke the bear, but they'd already gone past the point of no return. She may as well toss it all out there.

Cameron took a step forward, his eyes still locked on hers. "Why are you acting like this?"

Megan shrugged. "Maybe that kiss was a wake-up for both of us, and I'm willing to face it instead of run from it."

Cameron bounded down the steps, coming to stand right in front of her. So close, she could feel his warm breath, but he didn't touch her.

"You keep coming to me," she added, looking up into those eyes filled with torment. "You keep provoking me, too, but then you back off. You can't have it both ways, Cam."

He gripped her arms in an almost bruising manner as he leaned over her, giving her no choice but to lean back to keep her gaze locked on to his.

Without a word, his mouth crushed hers. The instant demand had her clutching his shoulders and cursing herself for giving in to his impulses so easily. But damn it, she was human. She'd wanted this man for as long as she could remember, and she was going to take what she could get...for now. She wasn't settling for seconds; she was biding her time until Cameron realized this was right. Everything about them coming together was perfectly, wonderfully right.

Reluctant, Megan tore her mouth away. "If you're

only kissing me because you're angry with yourself or you're trying to prove a point, then stop."

His forehead rested against her temple, those lips barely touching her jawline. "I don't know, Meg. You make me crazy. I can't do relationships, and I won't do a fling—not with you. But part of me can't seem to stop now that we've started."

Not quite the victory she'd hoped for, but one she would definitely take. She had him torn, had him thinking. Still, she wanted, *deserved*, more.

"I won't be someone you figure things out with along the way," she told him, sliding her hands away from his taut shoulders. "If you want more, you say so."

She stepped back, waited until he looked at her before she continued. "Be damn sure if you come to me that you want what I've offered because there's no going back."

Megan waited, giving him an opportunity to respond. When silence greeted her and the muscle in Cameron's jaw moved, Megan swallowed, turned on her heel and headed to her car.

Maybe her going out of town would give them the space they both needed to regroup. Maybe the time away would give her the insight she needed on whether to stay or go.

That reminded her—she still needed to inform Evan that she'd be gone. Hopefully he wouldn't tell his questionable friends that her house sat empty. She wanted to be honest with him, wanted him to know that she trusted him, but in all honesty, she didn't. She knew the group he was with was only making his attitude worse, hence his phone call. She had no clue what he truly did with his free time, but she had a feeling it wasn't legal.

Evan had obviously felt himself sinking deeper into a place he didn't want to be when he'd reached out to her. Megan could only pray while she was gone for these two days that the most important men in her life came to some decisions…and she hoped the outcomes would be what she wanted.

"Care to explain what I just saw?"

Cameron winced as he stepped back into his parents' house. Eli stood in the foyer near the sidelight like some Peeping Tom.

"Yeah, I care," Cameron mumbled. The last thing he wanted was to discuss what had just happened because each time he lost his damn mind and kissed Megan, he always felt worse afterward. He was using her to feed his desires, knowing he couldn't go any further.

"Then would you like to tell me why you and Megan look like you're ready to fight one minute and the next thing I know I look out and see you all but devouring her?"

Cameron clenched his fists at his side. Eli's arms crossed over his chest as his eyes narrowed. Eli had married his high school sweetheart, but Megan had been around for so long. And they'd all been friends. *Damn it.* Cameron hadn't even thought of how his brothers would react if they knew…

Hell. Cameron couldn't even put a label on the debacle he'd made of his life in the past month.

"Leave it," Cameron warned as he started down the hall to check on his mom.

"She's resting and Dad's in there." Eli moved quickly, coming to block the entrance to the hall. "I told them we'd lock up and turn off all the lights."

"Fine. You get the lights. I'll check the back door."

Eli made no attempt to move. Raising his gaze to the ceiling, Cameron sighed. He should've known this wasn't going to be easy.

"I have no idea what's going on," he conceded, looking back to his brother. "We've kissed. I know on every level it's a bad idea, but I can't stop myself."

A little of the anger in Eli's eyes dimmed as his shoulders relaxed. "How does she feel?"

Cameron couldn't help but laugh. "Oh, she's made it clear she's ready to step from the friend zone to something more."

Eli tipped his head and shrugged. "And you're angry about this?"

"You know I've made it clear for years I don't want a commitment. Megan's heard me say it over and over." Damn her for making him so confused. "I won't use her, Eli. She's the type of woman who deserves stability and a family. I can't give her either."

"Can't or won't?"

No, he wasn't getting into this. Cameron maneuvered around Eli and went to make sure the back door was locked. When he came back to the front, Eli had turned off the lights except the small lamp on the accent table.

Eli opened the door and gestured for Cameron to

go on ahead. Once they were on the porch, Cameron started to head down the steps, but Eli had to open his mouth again. Ridiculous to think he'd be able to make a break for it.

"You can't be married to your job forever," Eli called out. "At some point you're going to be lonely. Megan's a great girl. You two would be good together."

Cameron spun around. "I'm not looking for advice on my love life. There are complications that you don't know about and I can't get into. So just drop it, and don't mention what you saw to anybody."

Eli stared back, not saying a word.

"Promise me," Cameron demanded. "Not Drake, not Mom or Dad."

After a minute, Eli nodded. "Fine. But you better not mess around and hurt Megan. She's the only woman in your life other than your mother who puts up with your moodiness and your unruly schedule."

Cameron turned back, heading toward his truck parked last in the driveway. He wasn't even entertaining thoughts of how much Megan had put up with. Because then he'd have to admit how much she truly did care for him.

Cameron knew he wasn't going to get any sleep at all tonight, so he headed to the station. Might as well check in with his guys and see if there were any new developments. Of course, if there had been anything, he would've been called. Still, he couldn't go home because Megan's presence was in every single room... especially his bedroom.

His office was practically Megan-free, and he always had work he could do. But Eli was right. Cameron was afraid to go deeper with Megan. How could he be anything else? Too much rested on his shoulders, and no matter what weight he relieved himself of, he'd have more taking its place.

Everything in his life, both personal and professional, all pointed back to Megan somehow. There wasn't a damn thing he could do to save her from his choices, regardless of the path he took.

Chapter Eleven

Megan thought for sure that after visiting the new facility and meeting the staff she'd potentially be working with, she'd have a clearer insight on a decision.

As she maneuvered her car onto the exit ramp that would take her back into Stonerock, she was more confused than ever.

Yes, the facility was beautiful. But the nicest computer equipment or fancy waiting areas, complete with a waterfall wall for a calming atmosphere, weren't going to sway her into making a life-altering decision.

What Megan cared about was the people she'd be able to reach, to help, the difference she could make in their lives. Megan's potential supervisor had gone into great detail about the areas the clinic planned to target. Topping the list were poverty-stricken neighborhoods where alcoholism and drug abuse had spiked in the past few years.

Just the mention of that area had pulled Megan's mind back home with Evan. She knew he had a problem, and she'd give anything to fix him. That's what she did; she had a degree to fix people. But if he didn't want to change completely, she could use all the fancy words and textbook cures in the world and he'd still remain in the pit he'd dug for himself. Though she didn't think he was using drugs—she hadn't seen the telltale signs—she did believe he was mixed up with a group who wasn't immune to the industry. Why else did he always need money? Why else would he always be worried about his safety?

So did she truly want to leave, risking Evan choosing to stay behind? Or did she want to stay in Stonerock where she'd already developed relationships with clients? Those clients trusted her, counted on her. Would they feel as if they were being abandoned if she accepted the new position?

Megan's cell rang, cutting off the radio. Pressing the button on her steering wheel, Megan answered.

"Hello?"

"Hey, Megan." Marly's chipper voice came through the car speakers. "Are you busy?"

"Just driving. What's up?"

"Nora and I were wondering if you were free tonight. I know it's last minute, but Eli said he didn't mind keeping the girls for us."

As exhausted as she was from her whirlwind trip, a girls' night out sounded like the reward she needed.

Megan couldn't remember the last time she'd been out with a group of friends. Going out with Cameron didn't count, not that they went out. They tended to grill at his house or watch movies, and then she'd go back to her house.

"Count me in," Megan said, turning onto her road. "I'm almost home. I need to change, but I can meet you all somewhere."

"We're heading to Dolly's Bar and Grill."

They arranged the time and Megan suddenly found herself getting another burst of energy. She wouldn't think about Evan, Cameron or her work situation. She'd have a beer, chat with the girls and have a good time. A simple, relaxing evening.

With the days losing light earlier and earlier, she too often found herself in pajamas by six o'clock. When had she gotten to that stage in life that the best part of her day was spent in pj's? Mercy, she was getting old.

As soon as Megan examined her closet, she knew she wanted to dress a little sassier than usual tonight. Even if she was just going out with Nora and Marly, Megan had that female urge to step up her game a notch.

When had she let herself get so dowdy and boring? Lately she'd only donned the barest of makeup for work, and she couldn't remember the last time she'd pulled out her curling iron or straightener. If she looked under her bathroom sink, she'd probably find them overtaken by dust.

Glancing at the clock, Megan decided she had time to put some effort into her appearance tonight. After a quick shower, she opted for the big iron and put large, bouncy waves into her hair. A little more shadow than usual made her green eyes pop. Why didn't she do this more often? Just what she'd done so far had boosted both her energy level and confidence.

After pulling on a simple yellow tank-style dress, Megan wrapped a thick belt around her waist, threw on a fitted navy cardigan and pulled on her favorite cowgirl boots. Surely she had earrings that went with this outfit. Digging through her meager stash of jewelry, she managed to find some dangly hoops and a chunky silver bracelet.

Megan grabbed her purse and headed out the door. She hadn't heard from Evan in a couple of days, and, surprisingly, her house hadn't been bothered while she'd been gone.

The guilt of expecting him or his friends to steal something weighed heavily in her gut.

Megan shook off all negative thoughts as she pulled into Dolly's. It being a Friday night, the place was bustling with cars filling the parking lot and people piling in through the front doors.

Music blasted out of the bar as a group of guys held the door open and gestured for her to enter. Smiling her thanks, Megan stepped inside, quickly scanned the room and found Nora and Marly in a booth along the wall.

With a wave, Megan wove her way through the crowd as a slow country song filled the room. Hand in hand, couples made their way to the scarred wooden dance floor. Megan refused to allow the image of her and Cameron dancing to occupy her mind. She was here for fun and for a girls' night. Nothing more.

Nora slid over, giving Megan room to ease onto the leather seat.

"You look beautiful," Nora said with a huge smile. "I was just happy to shower and actually attempt to fix my hair."

Marly laughed. "You're always gorgeous, Nora. But, seriously, Megan, you look great."

"Thanks." Megan sat her purse between her and Nora and thanked God she'd taken some extra time to get ready. "I was going for the fun Megan instead of therapist Megan."

"Well, honey, you nailed it." Nora waved her hand at a waitress. "First round's on me."

"I need a drink," Marly stated. "I've been sewing on Willow's Halloween costume for a week and it still looks like a hot mess. Why the hell did I think I could be supermom instead of just buying one?"

Nora patted Marly's arm. "Because you're an awesome mom and Willow doesn't care what it looks like. She's just excited her mom is making the Darth Vader-cowgirl-princess getup."

Marly moaned. "I suppose. I think letting her pick her favorite themes was a bad idea. I meant one character, not three combined."

Once they ordered their drinks plus a basket of chips and salsa, Megan turned to Nora.

"How's Bev? She getting used to those crutches?" Megan asked.

"Eli said she's still complaining about using them,

but he told her she'd get used to it." Nora rested an elbow on the dull wooden tabletop and smiled. "As long as Mac is there, though, she doesn't have to get up for anything except to use the bathroom. He's right at her side making sure she doesn't even have to ask."

Marly laughed, pushing back a wayward curl from her forehead. "The St. John males have a tendency to go overboard with protecting and assisting their ladies."

Megan thought about how Cameron had wanted her to show Evan some tough love. Cameron was ready to step in and be her human shield, but she had held him back. She remembered a time in high school when a guy was insistent she leave a party with him and all but dragged her toward his car. Cameron had stepped in then, as well, and punched the guy in the face.

The waitress came back with the drinks and each woman took a long, sigh-worthy sip. Megan licked the frothy, fruity foam off her top lip and glanced up to see the other two staring at her.

"What?"

"You were daydreaming." Nora quirked a brow while sliding her fingertip over the condensation on her tall, slender glass. "I know this is absolutely none of my business, but we've known each other a really long time."

Megan braced herself for whatever Nora was about to ask.

"Any chance you and Cameron…" Nora let the silent question settle between them as she pulled the toothpick full of pineapple out of her drink and plucked a piece off.

Marly eased her forearms onto the table and leaned forward, obviously eager to hear the answer, as well.

Megan shrugged. "We're best friends." That was the truth. "I'm not sure we would know how to be anything else."

"Have you tried?" Marly asked.

The waitress returned, setting a giant basket of tortilla chips and three small bowls of salsa on the table.

Megan pretended to look for the perfect chip while she contemplated the answer she should give over the answer she wanted to give.

"I believe the silence speaks for itself," Nora proudly stated as she dipped her chip. "There's no way a man like Cameron can ignore you for years."

Yeah, well, he had. At least in any form beyond friendship. But when his mouth had been on hers, his hands up her shirt, he'd certainly given off the vibe he was staking a claim.

"How long have you guys been a secret?" Nora asked, leaning in just a bit more, a wide, knowing smile spread across her face.

Megan sighed. "There's no secret. To be honest, we only kissed for the first time last week and that was because I was sleeping, he startled me from a dream and I..."

"Please, please don't stop there." Marly reached across and squeezed her arm. "I may not have known you that long, but I'm wrapped up in this and I know it's not my business. So, tell Nora and just let me listen in."

Megan laughed and took a drink, welcoming the chill of the strawberry-flavored, alcohol-enriched slush. "I yanked him down and kissed him," she muttered.

Both women's eyes widened as their grins spread even wider. Megan couldn't help but smile back because she so had to get this off her chest. And there wasn't a doubt in her mind these two ladies would offer her some much-needed advice.

"Then he cornered me in his kitchen the other night after we watched your kids during your date." Megan found herself moving forward with the story without being prompted. She wanted to blame the alcohol, but after only two sips, that defense fell flat. "He was angry at the kiss we'd shared."

"If he cornered you and was angry, sounds to me like he's turned on and is mad at himself," Nora supplied. "Probably for just now taking notice, if you ask me."

"Yeah, well, we argued. That led to another kiss and his hand up my shirt."

Nora and Marly high-fived each other across the table, and Megan felt her face flush. "This is silly." She laughed. "I feel like I'm in high school."

"Better than high school," Marly chimed in. "Way better. So what happened next? This is the best girls' night ever."

Megan reached for another chip. "Sorry to disappoint, but hc pulled back and wc argued again. I just don't know what to do."

Nora shifted in her seat and all smiling vanished as she looked Megan straight in the eyes. "Take my advice. Don't wait to tell him how you feel, what you truly want. I did that with Eli the first time. We let a lot of years and hurt build between us, and then we had to overcome so much to be together. You're not guaranteed a tomorrow."

Megan felt the quick sting in her nose as her eyes started to fill. Nora had been in love with Eli in school, and then he had gone into the military. After a few years, Nora married Eli's friend, who had ultimately died while deployed. Nora had taken the long, hard road to find love, and Megan could only nod as the lump formed in her throat.

"Damn it." Marly yanked her napkin from under her drink and dabbed beneath her eyes. "I had my makeup so nice, too, thanks to that pin I saw on Pinterest."

"I didn't mean to cause tears," Nora defended herself, passing another napkin over to Marly. "I'm just trying to help."

Megan blinked back her own unshed tears and gripped her icy-cold glass. "You did help. I know I need to tell him how I feel, but I guess I just needed encouragement. I'm a bit of a coward. What if we mess up? He's the most stable person in my life, and I can't lose him as a best friend."

Nora nodded. "I understand the fear, but if he loves you beyond friends, isn't that worth the risk? Is he worth it?"

Without a doubt. Cameron was worth risking everything for.

Her phone chimed from her purse. She thought it was rude to be on the phone when out with a group of people, but it could be a patient in need.

"Sorry," she said, digging out the phone. "Give me one second."

The caller ID flashed her brother's name. Megan swiped the screen and answered.

"Evan?"

"I'm ready."

Those two words held so much meaning. "You want me to come and get you?"

"Yeah, um, I was dropped off at the parking lot beside the old gas station that closed. You know where that's at?"

Megan nodded, even though he couldn't see her. "Yes. I'll be there in five minutes."

She hung up, quickly pulled money from her purse and tossed it on the table before explaining to the girls that she had to get her brother. There was no time to go into further details because Evan changed his mind so often, she wanted to jump through this window of opportunity.

Besides, he might be in danger if he was in a parking lot at night all alone.

Megan raced for her SUV. As she pulled into the lot, at first she didn't see anybody. As soon as she got out, she felt the presence of someone behind her. Spinning around, her heart leaped into her throat. The hulking figure wasn't Evan.

Pulling all her experience and courage to the surface, Megan lifted her chin and squared her shoulders. "Where's my brother?" she asked.

The sneer on the stranger's face sent a cold chill down her spine. He stepped closer, all the while raking his eyes over her. Curse this dress she'd felt beautiful in earlier. Why was she now feeling as if she was being punished for wanting to look nice?

"I'm right here."

Megan jerked around to see Evan, hands in his pockets, staring across the open space. She could barely see him for the glow from the streetlight that was at the other end of the block. But the tone of his voice worried her. He sounded sad, nervous, almost desperate.

"What's going on?" she asked Evan as she started to take a step forward.

The man behind her gripped her arm. Megan had taken a self-defense course, a requirement for her job. Instantly the lessons came flooding to her mind. She whirled around and shoved the palm of her free hand straight up into the man's nose.

With a howl, he dropped her arm and covered his face. She shook out her wrist and glanced over her shoulder to Evan.

"Get in my car," she ordered, her gaze volleying back and forth between her brother and the man who would no doubt be angry. She didn't want to be there when he decided to retaliate. "Now, Evan."

"I can't."

Another man seemed to materialize behind Evan. This man held a gun...pointed at her. The hulk behind her gripped her arm once again, this time tighter as he yanked her back against his chest.

"They'll kill us if we don't do what they want," Evan told her. "I had no clue they were setting me up, Meg. I'm sorry."

Apologies could wait. Right now she needed to figure out how to get them out of here without getting shot. "What do you want?" she asked, still trying to keep her voice calm though she was anything but.

"Your brother here owes us twenty thousand dollars," the man behind her stated, his hot breath against her cheek making her gag. "And after that stunt you just pulled on me, I'm adding another five K."

Why hadn't she paid more attention to her brother? Whatever mess he'd gotten wrapped up in had apparently been going on awhile if he owed that kind of money. Still, all that could be dealt with later. Right now she needed to figure out a way to survive the night. She wanted Cameron. He wouldn't be afraid; he would arrest these guys and save her and Evan. But Cameron wasn't here, and she'd have to fend for herself.

"I'm sure you know I don't have that much money on me," she told them, her eyes darting to the gun still aimed at her.

Sirens filled the night, and Megan nearly wept with relief. She forced herself to keep in mind her surroundings and the men who were threatening her. She may not be a cop like Cameron, but she'd counseled enough addicts to know that if they were high, they didn't care who they hurt. They had nothing to lose. Which meant she was expendable.

•

Before she knew it, the man behind her let go, causing her to stumble back from the force of his departure. The man with the gun patted Evan on the shoulder as if they were the best of friends.

"Come on, man." The guy shoved his gun in his waistband. "You ain't waiting to talk to no cops. You're with us till you pay up."

Evan threw her one last pained look and mouthed "sorry" before turning and running off into the night with the men who'd just threatened their lives. With shaky knees and tremors overtaking her body, Megan sank to the cool concrete. Moments later, a cruiser pulled in, too late to save her brother.

Chapter Twelve

Never in his life had fear crippled him to the point of losing control and being ready to throw it all away.

But the sight of Megan in the clutches of notorious gang leader "The Shark" was an image that would haunt him forever.

Then the gun had appeared, and Cameron had to get a patrol car sounding that second. He knew those guys. He knew they wouldn't shoot Megan unless provoked. The siren did its job and the criminals fled— including her lowlife brother. Cameron wanted to get ahold of that man and punch him in the face for not protecting his sister.

What the hell had Megan been doing there, anyway? His heart had nearly exploded in his chest when he saw her black SUV pull into the lot. He'd gotten a good look at her sexy little dress and cowgirl boots, showcasing those shapely legs. But even that punch of lust had vanished the second those dangerous thugs had surrounded her.

Now, an hour later, Cameron stood on her porch. He knew she was inside because his officer had told him he'd driven Megan's car home while another officer drove her in his cruiser. She was too shaken up, too scared to drive.

Cameron slid his key into her lock and let himself in. The second he stepped over the threshold, he called her name, not wanting to alarm her because he'd come in the front door and not the back as he normally did.

He heard the sound of her boots clicking over the wooden floor from the rear of the house. Megan came down the hallway, her arms wrapped around her midsection, her face pale.

For her fear alone he vowed to get enough evidence on these guys to put them away for a long, long time. Right now, though, he wished he wasn't on the right side of the law. He wished more than anything he could track them down and beat them within an inch of their lives, forgetting about the justice system altogether and saving the taxpayers' dollars.

"I knew they'd call you." She pasted on a smile that fell short of convincing. "Did they find Evan? I've texted and called him, but…"

Fury threatened to take over. She was worried about Evan? After a man had held her at gunpoint while another practically held her captive?

"My officers were more concerned with you." Only

because the FBI was still out there right now keeping an eye on the traffickers...and because Cameron had told his two officers to make sure Megan was watched until he arrived. "Evan is a big boy."

Anything else he said would be out of anger, and the last thing he wanted to do was fight. Between the way her vulnerability had settled between them like a third party and the way that dress hugged her body, Cameron was having a really difficult time prioritizing his emotions.

"Are you okay?" he asked, taking a step forward, then another, until he was within reaching distance. But he fisted his hands at his side. "My officers told me you weren't hurt, but I needed to hear it from you. I needed to see you."

Those bright green eyes seemed even more vibrant than usual. Cameron didn't know if he was just now noticing or if she'd done something tricky with her makeup. Regardless, the way she watched him, the way she seemed to be holding herself back, had him nearing the breaking point. He'd been holding on by the proverbial thread for so long now; it was only a matter of time before he fell.

Megan reached up, shoved her hair back from her face. "I'm fine."

Her action drew his gaze to her arm, to the fingerprint-size bruises dotting her perfect skin. Cameron clenched his teeth, reining in his anger because none of this was her fault and he wouldn't make her the target simply because she was the only one here once the rage fully surfaced. The only thing he could fault Megan with was having a kind heart and wanting to help people who would continue to stomp on her and use her.

Cameron gripped her wrist in one hand and slid a fingertip from his other over around the marred skin. "You're not fine. This never should've happened."

He'd cursed himself for standing by and watching as events unfolded, but had he gone charging for her as he'd wanted to, as his heart told him to, his cover would've been blown and she would have known the cops were watching Evan. *Cameron* was watching Evan.

That heavy ball of guilt was something he'd have to live with. If there had ever been any doubt before, tonight just proved that he would choose his job first every single time. He hated himself for it, but that's how he was made up.

"They're just bruises," she whispered, her eyes still on his.

Goose bumps raised beneath his fingertips as he continued to stroke her skin. "I don't like them."

Megan placed a hand over his, halting his movement. Her lids closed as she whispered, "Please, Cam. I just…"

Bowing her head, Megan sighed.

"You what, baby?"

"I wanted you to come," she muttered beneath the curtain of her hair that had cascaded around her face. "I wanted you here because I knew I'd feel safe. But now that you're here, I can't let you touch me." Slowly lifting her head, she brought her eyes up to lock on to his. "It makes me want things. Want you."

Damn it. There went that last thread he'd been holding on to.

Cameron stepped into her, trapping their hands between their bodies. The tip of his nose brushed against hers, leaving their mouths barely a whisper apart.

"You are always safe with me," he told her, slowly moving his lips across hers with the lightest of touches. "And tonight you're mine."

"Just tonight," she agreed. "We don't need to put a label on it, and I don't want to think beyond now."

Cameron captured her mouth, completely ignoring all the warnings pounding through his head. Totally shoving aside all the reasons this was a terrible idea: the investigation, the risk of losing his best friend and the fact he'd just admitted to himself that his job would always come first. All that mattered was Megan and this ache he'd had for her for years. It wasn't going away no matter how noble he tried to be. His hormones didn't give a damn about his morals or standards.

Megan's mouth opened beneath his as she tried to pull her hands free. Cameron was quicker, holding them firm as he broke from the kiss.

"You're mine," he repeated, nipping her lips, her chin, trailing a line down to her collarbone. "I don't know why you have on this dress with these boots, but it's driving me crazy. Tell me you weren't on a date earlier."

Tipping her head back, arching into him, Megan let out one of those sweet moans he was starting to love. "No, no date," she panted. "I was out with Nora and Marly."

The fact she was out with his sisters-in-law thrilled him because if she'd been out with a guy, Cameron would've had to admit jealousy.

Cameron released her hands and slid his palms over her curvy hips. He gripped her and pulled her pelvis flush with his as he continued to rain kisses along her exposed skin just above the dip in her dress. Just above the perfect swell of her breasts.

Megan wrapped her delicate fingers around his biceps and squeezed as he yanked down the top of her dress. Material tore, but he didn't care. He'd buy her a new one.

"Cam."

He froze at her plea. "Meg, I'm sorry. After what you went through tonight, I wasn't thinking."

Her lips curved into a smile. "I wasn't complaining. I know you'd never hurt me."

Seeing her lips swollen from his kisses, her neck and the tops of her breasts pink from arousal, an instant flood of possessiveness filled him. The only mark he ever wanted on her was from him, from passion.

"If you keep this up, I don't know how much longer I can stand." Her arms slid around his neck as she rubbed her body against his. "You make my knees weak and we're still fully clothed."

"I'm about to fix that problem."

He unbuckled her belt and let it drop with a clatter to the wood floor. He gripped the hem of her dress, yanked it up and over her head, then tossed the unwanted garment aside.

The sight of her standing before him wearing a pale pink bra and matching panties along with those cowgirl boots was enough to make his own knees weak.

Megan reached for his shirt, but he pulled it off before she could touch him. In record time their clothes were mere puddles on the floor. From the way her eyes kept sampling him, Cameron knew if he didn't try to keep some sort of control, this night would be over before he could truly enjoy it.

"I've waited to see you look at me like that," Megan told him, rising up on her toes to kiss his jawline. "Like you really want me."

She was killing him. With the way the lace from her bra pressed against his bare skin, her raw, honest words and the delicate way her mouth cruised over him, Megan was gradually overpowering him.

Gliding his hands around her curves, Cameron lifted her until her legs went around his waist. The leather from her cowgirl boots rubbed his back, but the fact he finally had this woman wrapped all over him overrode his discomfort.

"I'm too heavy for you," she argued, nipping at his ear.

Palming her backside, his thumb teased the edge of her lacy panty line. "Baby, you're the perfect weight for me," he growled as he headed toward the living room and the L-shaped sofa. "Absolutely perfect."

Without easing his hold, Cameron settled her onto

the corner of the couch as his lips took hold of hers once again. He could kiss her forever.

Too bad he couldn't do forever. Selfishly, he was doing now, tonight, and he'd hate himself later for taking advantage even if she had given him the green light.

Megan's legs fell away from his waist, her boots landing on either side of his feet. Cameron eased back, picked up one leg at a time and pried off her cowgirl boots. She watched him beneath heavy lids, her chest rising and falling as she licked her lips in anticipation.

Coming to his full height, Cameron stared down at this magnificent woman practically laid out for him. His throat grew tight with emotions…emotions he could certainly identify but he couldn't allow to take over.

"You're stunning," he told her, completely taking in the display.

Without a word, Megan sat up, reached behind and unfastened her bra. After sliding it down her arms and tossing it to the side, she hooked her thumbs beneath her panties and slid them down, never once taking her eyes off his. The minor striptease was the most erotic moment of his life, and it had lasted all of ten seconds. Megan had a power over him that no other woman could match.

"Tell me you have protection," she whispered as she reached for him. Flat palms slid up over his chest and around his neck.

Cameron allowed her to pull him down, and he loved the feel of her beneath him. He had to remind himself not to get used to this, not to want this ever again.

"I don't have anything." One fingertip slid up and over her breast. "But I'm clean. I have regular physicals for work and I've always used protection. It's your call."

"I'm clean, too, and I've always been protected." Megan smiled, wrapping her legs around Cameron's narrow waist once again. "So what are we waiting for?"

The darkness that had settled into Cameron's blue eyes revealed so much. Who knew her best friend had a possessive streak when it came to intimacy? The way he held her, spoke to her, dominated her, thrilled Megan in a way she'd never before experienced and she knew without a doubt that this was it for her... *He* was it for her. No other man would compare with Cameron St. John.

She wanted to lose herself in him, wanted to forget all the ugliness and worries in her life. She wanted him to show her how beautiful they could be together because her fantasy had already paled in comparison.

"Tell me what you want," he murmured against her lips.

She trembled beneath his touch. No, that wasn't her. Cameron's hands were shaking as he slid them over her breasts.

Framing his face with her hands, she held his gaze. "You're nervous." She didn't ask and she wasn't making fun of him.

Cameron closed his eyes, resting his forehead against hers. "Nobody else has ever mattered this much."

Megan didn't know what to say to that revealing piece of information, so she tucked it in the back of her mind. Stroking his bottom lip with her thumb, she kept her eyes on his.

"I want anything you're willing to give," she said, answering his earlier question. "Anything you want to do."

A low groan escaped him. Then, as if some invisible barrier broke, Cameron consumed her. His hands took journeys all over her body, leaving goose bumps in their wake. That talented mouth demanded kisses, demanded passion.

Cameron settled himself between her legs, gliding one hand down her quivering abdomen to cup her most aching area. Megan tilted her hips, ready to burst for just one simple touch. She was officially at his mercy.

Easing his hand away, he held on to her waist. "Look at me," he demanded. "Only me."

"Only you."

As he slid into her, Megan gasped. Every dream, every waking fantasy she'd ever had about her best friend, didn't prepare her for the onslaught of emotions, waves of pleasure and such an awakening. They moved together as if they'd been made for each other, as if their bodies automatically knew how to respond to each other.

Cameron's arms wrapped around her as he lifted her off the couch. Still connected, he turned and sat, leaving her to straddle him…surrendering all power and control to Megan.

In that moment, she knew he loved her. He may not say it, he may not want to face the fact, but there was no way this man could look at her, make love to her, as if she were the only woman in the world and not love her.

Ripples of pleasure began to build, each one stronger than the last. Megan wanted to be fully fused with him when her body flew apart. Gripping his shoulders, she leaned down and claimed his mouth. Seconds later spasms took hold. With one hand firmly against the small of her back and the other cupping the nape of her neck, Cameron held her tight against his body as he stilled and trembled right along with her.

Moments after they fell over the edge together, Cameron still held on to her, still commanded her lips. The man wasn't done just because his body had hit the finish line.

His tongue slid along her bottom lip, his kisses softer, shorter...as if he didn't want this moment to end. At least, that's how she hoped he felt.

"Stay with me," she muttered around his kisses. "In my bed. Just for tonight."

His darkened, heavy-lidded gaze met hers. She thought for sure he'd deny her—they'd only agreed on this one time—but she had to ask. She wasn't ready to let him go.

Circling his arms tighter around her waist, Cameron came to his feet. Megan's legs instinctively wrapped around him.

"You seem to like my legs here," she joked, hoping to break the tension because he still hadn't answered her.

He headed out into the hall and toward her bedroom. "I intend to keep them here."

Chapter Thirteen

He'd guaranteed nothing beyond that night. Hadn't promised pretty words or a happily-ever-after. Megan had known exactly what she was getting into with him. He'd made his intentions perfectly clear before he'd peeled her out of her clothes.

So why did he feel like a jerk for leaving her before she woke?

Because he was.

Cameron sat on his deck, looking out over the pond as the morning sun reflected off the water. He didn't take time out here anymore, didn't just relax and enjoy life.

Last night he'd enjoyed life to the absolute fullest, which only made him want more. But his career didn't mesh well with a personal life. He couldn't compartmentalize and keep things separated, neat and orderly anymore. But he wanted Megan in one area, the friend area. He wanted her far away from anything that could harm her, like her useless brother who hadn't been able to protect her last night.

Cameron cursed, propping his bare feet up on the rail. He hadn't been able to protect her, either. Apparently he was no better than Evan at this point.

Opting to beat himself up over how everything went down last night was better than rehashing all that could have gone wrong in those few seconds. It also kept his mind off what had happened afterward.

Okay, so that was a lie. Even Cameron couldn't pretend to be unfazed by what had happened at Megan's house. How could he forget how perfectly they'd come together? How she'd clung to him? He could practically still feel her breath on his cheek, feel her curvy body beneath his hands. Those sighs of pleasure tickling his ear and the way she called his name on a groan were locked so deep in to his soul, he knew forgetting the intimacy they'd shared was impossible.

Closing his eyes, Cameron clenched his fists on the arms of his Adirondack chair. He hadn't given a thought to what would happen after he'd made love to Megan. Hadn't cared about feelings or excuses after the fact. All Cameron had wanted was to feel her, consume her. The fantasy come to life had been his only focus, and now here he sat with a sated body and a guilty conscience.

Between his ever-evolving feelings and the worry he'd seen in her eyes when he'd arrived at her house,

Cameron had told himself he was there to console her. That was a flat-out lie. He'd needed to comfort himself because he'd been a trembling mess.

Now his priority was to check in with the station, where some of the FBI agents had set up temporary headquarters until this case was over. He knew if something major had happened, he would have been notified. Still, as the chief, he needed to check in and get an update.

His cell vibrated in his pocket. Dropping his feet to the deck floor, he slid the phone out and read the screen.

I didn't take you for a coward

The harsh words hit right where Megan intended... his heart. Her text couldn't have been more accurate. He was a coward, and she'd called him out. One of the things he loved about her was her ability to never back down.

He honestly had no clue how to reply, and this wasn't a conversation to be had via text. He wouldn't be that guy and he sure as hell would treat Megan with more respect. The thought was laughable, considering he'd done the walk of shame out her back door, but he would make it up to her. Somehow.

Ignoring the text wasn't an option, either. Cameron quickly replied.

Be at my place at noon

That would give him time to check in with the station, figure out where the hell Evan was and grab a quick shower. Cameron planned to have a little talk with Evan. Cameron had to play every scenario out in his head because he couldn't tip off the guy. But he had every intention of making it clear that dragging Megan into his illegal mess was unacceptable and intolerable.

The phone vibrated in his hand.

If I have time

Smiling, Cameron came to his feet. She'd be there. He was sure of it. If she wasn't, then he'd find her. They weren't done. Not by a long shot.

Now he just had to figure out what the hell to do with his feelings and how to eliminate the possibility of hurting hers. Because, damn it, he still wanted her. Wanted Megan with a passion that went beyond all they'd shared last night. How could he tell her that and still try to keep her at a distance? How could he even try to take a chance with her but keep her safe and away from his job?

Granted, he worked in a small town and the crime rate, for the most part, was low. But there were instances that crept up, and he was the man to take control. He couldn't have his life both ways, and the decision ate at him because he knew he'd have to give up something—or someone—he loved.

Cameron headed inside to make a few calls. First things first. Right now he needed to find Evan and have a man-to-man talk. Then he'd deal with Megan.

If Cameron St. John thought he could turn her world inside out with a few orgasms, leave without a word and then have the nerve to summon her to his house, he truly didn't know her.

Megan took a deep breath, counted backward from ten and mounted the steps to Mac and Bev's house. She hadn't seen Cameron's truck in the drive or along the street, so she figured now would be a good time to stop and check on Bev. No doubt the woman was fed up with St. John testosterone ordering her to stay put while they did everything for her.

Megan didn't want to go in all angry and frustrated because then she'd have to explain. There was absolutely no way she'd be revealing to Cameron's parents why she was a bit irritable this morning.

After ringing the doorbell, Megan stepped back and waited. Mac pulled the door open, sending the fall floral wreath swaying against the glass.

"Megan." Mac extended his hand, taking hers and pulling her into the foyer. "I'm so glad to see you."

Laughing, Megan allowed herself to be ushered in. "Wow, I've never had such a lovely greeting before."

"I think Bev hates me," he whispered. "She just threatened to bash me with her crutch if I asked her one more time if she needed anything."

Megan patted Mac's arm and smiled. "I'm sure the threat was out of love."

Glancing toward the living room, Mac shook his head. "I doubt it," he said, turning back to her. "If you're going to be a few minutes, would you mind if I ran out to the hardware store? I hate to leave her even though she's told me to go."

Megan nodded. "You go on. We'll be just fine."

Mac seemed to breathe a sigh of relief as his shoulders relaxed. "Thanks, Megan. I'll only be twenty minutes, at the most."

"Take your time."

Mac eased around her, grabbed his keys from the table and headed out the door. Still amused at the fear in Mac's eyes, Megan headed to the living room, where Bev had her feet propped up on the footrest of the recliner. Some cooking channel was muted on the TV.

"Thank God he's gone," Bev said as soon as Megan stepped into the room. "That man needs to stop hovering."

Megan sank onto the edge of the old sofa, angling her body to face Bev. "He just loves you."

Bev dropped the remote into her lap. "I know. I keep telling myself that, but it's a broken ankle. I'm not dying."

Megan glanced around the walls at all the years of memories, family vacations and military medals adorning the space. This family was full of love, full of life and always so supportive.

She couldn't help but wonder what her life would've been like had her parents survived. What would her brother's life have been like? Would he still have felt that urge to rebel at every single thing? "You okay, honey?"

Glancing back to Bev, Megan nodded, swallowing the lump of emotions threatening to clog her throat. "I've been better," Megan answered honestly. "But I came to check on you, not discuss me."

Bev waved a hand. "Oh, please. Everyone has checked on me. I'm fine. What's got you so worried?"

There was no way Megan would get into all the issues that swirled around in her mind. Whatever she and Cameron had going on—or not going on—would remain between them. She had no label for it, had no way of knowing where the next step would take them.

Bev knew enough about Evan, though, that Megan found herself opening up about him. She explained what happened the night before, stopping at the point where Cameron ended up staying the night. Megan had been around this family for so long, Bev had seen Evan's downfall, witnessed Megan's frustration.

"As a woman who raised three hellions, let me tell you that you can only do so much." Bev shifted in her chair until she could reach out and take Megan's hand in hers. "You guide them the best way you can, but in the end they have to make their own decisions."

These were all facts Megan knew, but she still ached for a peace she may never find with her only living relative.

"Those were your kids. It's a bit different with Evan because he's always quick to throw in my face how I'm not his mother." Megan smiled and shrugged. "Besides, your boys all turned out perfect."

Bev's laughter filled the cozy living room. "Oh, honey. They're far from perfect. I had a full head of gray hair by the time I was thirty-five. I swore I wouldn't make it through their teen years without getting a call from the cops about one or all three. They seemed to travel in a pack."

Megan couldn't help but laugh herself. "Yeah, they got me drunk during my senior prom."

"Oh, mercy," Bev whispered, shaking her head. "I think I'm better off not knowing some of the things they did. I cringe just thinking of the stuff I know about."

Megan took comfort in Bev's gentle hand. So many times she'd wanted motherly advice and she'd always known she could turn to Bev at any time. Unfortunately, with the Cameron situation, Megan wasn't about to seek support. She'd have to figure out that one all on her own.

"Evan wouldn't keep in contact with you if he didn't love you," Bev went on. "He may take some time, but you're the only stable person in his life. He'll come back to you."

Megan squeezed Bev's hand. "I hope so."

Because even though she didn't have concrete evidence of his extracurricular activities, she wasn't stupid. If he didn't change his ways, the end result would be either jail or death. Megan didn't know if she had the strength to get through either of those.

Cameron kept his voice low, his back to the brick building, so he could keep an eye on the open end of the alley. He'd found out Evan was in the shady part of a neighboring town, just outside Cameron's jurisdiction.

After throwing on a ball cap and sunglasses, Cameron had gone into the pool hall and firmly told Evan to meet him out back.

Now the coward had the nerve to look worried.

"Maybe you should've been a little more concerned last night for your sister." It took every ounce of Cameron's self-control to keep him from pummeling Megan's brother. "Do you have any idea how scared she was? You may run with these guys, but she doesn't, and she has a heart of gold. You realize that afterward she was more worried about you than what could've happened to her?"

Evan glanced away, but Cameron wasn't having it. Cameron smacked his cheek. "Look at me. Megan said one of your so-called friends had a gun on her. Do you want to see your sister wrapped up in this mess you're in? Do you want to see her hurt or worse?"

Something flared in Evan's eyes. Anger, hatred, who knew what, but at least there was some sign that he actually cared about Megan.

"You have no idea what's going on in my life," Evan spat.

Cameron didn't react, didn't say a word. No sense in giving away that he in fact knew nearly everything that was going on. Knew so much that warrants were about to be processed for the arrest of two major players in the drug-running ring and for Evan, though Evan's charges weren't as harsh. Still, Cameron wanted the charges to stick. He wanted Evan to hit rock bottom so he'd get the help he needed and maybe eventually be the brother Megan deserved.

Disgusted that he was getting nowhere, Cameron started to turn away. "Keep her safe." Evan's low, pleading words froze Cameron in his tracks.

Glancing over his shoulder, Cameron met Evan's

eyes and for the first time he actually saw a man who showed genuine concern and fear for someone other than himself. "She doesn't have anybody else," Evan stated, still holding Cameron's gaze.

Cameron nodded. "Whose fault is that?"

When Evan continued to stare, as if waiting for affirmation, Cameron replied, "I won't let anything happen to her."

As he walked away and headed back toward his truck, he wondered if he'd just lied. Could he honestly keep Megan from getting hurt? Oh, he could prevent her from physical harm, but what about her heart?

The mental scars from this entire scenario would live with her forever. She'd blame herself; she'd question every decision she ever made where her brother was concerned. And she'd hate Cameron.

He slid behind the wheel and brought the engine to life. The clock on his dash showed only thirty minutes until she was due at his house. Knowing Megan, she'd keep him waiting out of spite—which was fine. He needed the extra time to calm down from seeing Evan, from realizing that so much was about to come to a head. All Cameron could do was sit back and proceed with his job...just like always.

Chapter Fourteen

So what if it was nearly two o'clock? Megan wished she could chalk up her tardiness to stubbornness or even the fact she'd been visiting with Bev and Mac. In reality, she'd stuck around with Bev out of nerves.

What would she and Cameron discuss? How did they jump from best friends to the most intimate experience of her life to her waking up alone? Did he really think they would just pal up, watch a movie, grill a steak and hang like they always did on their days off?

Only one way to find out.

Megan mounted the steps and raised her hand to knock. She'd never knocked before. Letting out a sigh, she opened the screen door and twisted the knob on the old oak door. She wouldn't put it past Cameron to lock it since she was late, but the knob turned beneath her palm.

She stepped over the threshold, nerves swirling in her stomach as the familiar scent of Cameron's masculine aroma surrounded her. She'd inhaled that woodsy scent when her face had been pressed into his neck as he'd lowered her into her bed. Never again could she breathe in Cameron's signature scent and not instantly be taken to the time when he'd fulfilled her every desire, her every wish.

Closing the door at her back, Megan sat her purse and keys on the built-in bookshelf to the left of the doorway. The same place she always sat her things when she came in, as if this were her home, too.

Silly thought, really. They'd slept together, not exchanged rings or vows.

A part of Megan wouldn't mind doing just that, but she wouldn't beg any man to love her. Either Cameron would want the same things she did or he wouldn't. No matter how this next phase played out, Megan was a big girl and she'd survive.

But even knowing they'd taken another step deeper into their relationship, Megan still didn't know what to do about the job in Memphis. Being with Cameron was more important than any position she could ever have. She'd give up her dream job in order to have a life with him, but was that something she could convince him of?

She didn't want to have to convince him, though. Megan wanted Cam to come to the realization they belonged together.

And if he didn't, Megan knew she'd have to make

the move because she couldn't live here, see him every day and act as if her heart wasn't shattered.

Heavy footsteps sounded from overhead. Megan glanced toward the stairs just as Cameron came down the first set, then stopped on the landing. His piercing blue eyes held hers as she remained by the door.

"Contemplating whether to stay or go?" he asked.

Shoving her hands in the pockets of her favorite pair of faded jeans, Megan tipped her head. "I don't run away."

Cameron rested his hand on the newel post as he continued to stare down at her. What was he thinking? And why did he look even sexier today now that they'd been intimate?

Keeping his eyes on hers, Cameron slid his hand down the banister as he descended the steps. Megan didn't move, didn't glance away even though her heart was pounding so hard. Cameron came to stand directly in front of her. The way he towered over her had Megan tipping her head back to hold his gaze. Nowhere did he touch her, yet his demanding presence commanded her body to react.

Cameron leaned forward, his lips by her ear. "Don't call me a coward again," he growled.

Pleased he was just as affected by their predicament as she was, Megan forced herself to remain still, to not reach for him and cling as she desperately wanted to. And that was the problem wrapped in the proverbial nutshell. She was desperate for this man's touch, his passion.

When Cameron eased back, just enough for a sliver

of sunlight from the windows to pass through, Megan smiled.

"Hit a nerve, did I?"

"You knew you would."

"Maybe."

Was he just going to stand within a breath of her and not touch her? Maybe he wasn't as affected by their connection as she'd thought. Or perhaps he was into torturing her.

"What's the protocol here, Cam?" she asked, unable to stand the tension for another second. Someone had to step up and start this conversation. "What happens now?"

"What do you want to happen?" he countered.

Megan pulled in a deep breath, knowing full well she walked on a tightrope. "I think I've made things pretty clear. It's you who seems to be torn about what you want."

The muscle in his jaw jumped. He gripped her wrists with one hand, tugging them over her head, causing her to lean back against the door. He trailed his other hand down her arm until she trembled, all the while keeping his eyes locked on hers. She held her breath, unable to fully comprehend the power he had over her and the helpless state she was currently in.

"I'm not torn," he corrected as he brought his palm up to cup her cheek, his thumb stroking her lips. "I know exactly what I want."

That low, sultry tone of his made her body hum with anticipation. Or maybe she was still shaking from the simple touch of his fingertips. Perhaps every single thing about the man made her tingle now that she had let her guard down.

His eyes held hers. "What I want and what is possible are two different things."

It took a moment for the words to register. Megan made to pull his hands away, shaking her head. "That makes no sense," she all but shouted. "You're an adult. You pretty much decide what you want. Do you not want me? I can handle it if that's the case."

Okay, she might not handle it very well, but she would move on. She wasn't playing around anymore.

"I'd say after last night it's obvious I want you."

"Nothing is obvious," she hissed, hating how she still was held captive by him. "I have no clue what's going on with you, Cam. What are you fighting against?"

Cameron opened his mouth as if to say something, but then he shut it. Glancing toward the ground, he muttered a curse as he rubbed the back of his neck and released his hold on her.

He was battling some inner turmoil. Whatever it was, he wasn't opening up about it. The fact he was keeping something that obviously involved her locked inside had Megan hurting in a way she hadn't known possible.

"You know what, forget it." She sighed, throwing her hands in the air. "We'll go back to being friends. We'll chalk last night up to a—"

His eyes narrowed in on her. "Don't say mistake."

"An amazing experience," she finished slowly. "I

won't call it a mistake. What we shared can't be labeled as a mistake. But it won't happen again."

When he merely nodded, a portion of the hope she'd been clinging to died. He offered nothing but that simple gesture of agreement, as if his entire life hadn't changed after the intimacy they'd shared.

Seeing as how he was not much into conversation today, Megan turned toward the built-in and grabbed her keys and purse. In an instant, Cameron's hands covered hers, his body was plastered to her back, his arms stretched out with hers.

"Don't go," he whispered in her ear.

Closing her eyes, Megan dropped her head between her shoulders. "Why did you tell me to come?"

"I wanted to see you." He nuzzled his way through her hair, his lips barely brushing against the side of her neck. "I had no clue what I'd do once you got here. I told myself to keep the friendship above my desire for you. But I can't."

His fingers laced through hers as he placed openmouthed kisses over the side of her neck and down onto her shoulder. Megan didn't want to respond, wanted to make him work for it, but her head tipped to the side before she could even think.

"I don't know what the hell to do here, Meg."

So much tension radiated from him. She wanted to turn, to hold him and comfort him. Whatever war he waged with himself was something he felt he needed to face alone.

"I've fought this for so long," he went on as his lips continued to travel over her heated skin. "I never wanted to cross this line with you because I knew once I had you, it wouldn't be nearly enough."

Well, that certainly sounded promising.

"Then why do you sound so upset?" she asked, trying to focus on his unspoken problem and not the way he was setting her body on fire with each simple touch of those talented lips.

"I've always said I won't get involved." His fingers tightened around hers, balling their joined hands into fists. "I'm married to this job. The stress, the worry, I wouldn't put that on anybody, least of all you."

Everything always came down his job. She loved how noble he was, but, damn it, he was a man, too. A man with needs, desires. And he was ready to shove it all aside for the sake of his badge?

"I don't mind," she answered honestly. "Maybe you wouldn't feel so stressed if you had someone to share the burden with."

"I can't," he muttered, resting his forehead on her shoulder. "You don't understand."

She started to turn, but he held her away. "Damn it, let me look at you," she cried.

Finally he eased back, releasing her hands. When Megan fully turned to face him, angst and torment stared back at her. She'd never thought she'd see a day when Cameron St. John seemed anything but strong and resilient.

They needed to get off this emotional roller coaster. They needed to return to familiar territory where they weren't so wrapped up in what the next step should be. If that step happened to be in opposite directions, then so be it. But they couldn't lose sight of what was important.

Megan slid a fingertip along the worry lines between Cameron's indrawn brows. "We need a break. *You* need a break." Smiling, she dropped her hand. "I have the perfect idea. Don't go anywhere. I'll be back in thirty minutes to pick you up."

His eyes narrowed. "What do you have in mind?"

"Oh, please." She laughed. "After the shenanigans you and your brothers got into, you're afraid of me?"

His gaze darted to her lips, then back up. "More than you know," he whispered.

How could her body continually respond to his words, his tone and those heated looks? How much did she have to endure before she was put out of her misery and he either moved forward or stepped away? In all honesty, she was done playing. So she was going after all she wanted…and she wanted him.

"I'll be back," she told him. "Just be ready."

"I'm not sure that's possible," he said.

So Cameron didn't miss the meaning in her final warning. *Good.*

Chapter Fifteen

How the hell did he go from telling himself he'd keep the intimacy and sexual tension out of his mind to sitting in Megan's SUV heading toward an unknown destination, fantasizing about peeling that dress up and over her head?

Cameron gritted his teeth and watched out the side window as his familiar town flew by. Megan may be teetering on the edge of speeding, but he wasn't about to say anything. In all honesty, he could use the distraction. He needed to focus on something other than the way she'd shown back up at his door with a wide smile, a little white dress that shifted against her thighs when she turned and those beat-up brown cowgirl boots. She'd done this on purpose. He wasn't a fool, and he knew Megan better than he knew any other woman. When she set her mind to something, she got it. Which meant he was not only fighting himself; now he'd be battling her.

He didn't stand a chance.

"Where are we going?" he asked, still not turning to look back at those tanned thighs peeking beneath the lacy edge of her dress.

"You're like a little kid." Megan turned onto a dirt road just outside the city limits. "This property is for sale and there's a cute little pond. We're having a picnic. Nobody is around, and I doubt there's even cell service here because it's nestled in the woods. It's too nice of a day to waste inside. The temperature is perfect."

Private. Woods. No cell service. Yeah, she'd definitely be the end of him. They were officially going to be alone, and Cameron knew without a doubt he wouldn't be able to keep his hands off her no matter how good his intentions may be. He was human, and every part of him wanted Megan for himself.

She pulled her SUV under a canopy of trees and killed the engine. Before he could pull on his door handle, Megan reached over the console and gripped his hand.

"No pressure, Cam." Her eyes held his; her unpainted lips called to him. "I just wanted to get away and relax. You've been tense the whole way here."

"I wouldn't say tense," he defended himself.

Megan laughed, smacked a brief kiss on his lips and patted his arm. "You're right. Not tense. Terrified. Now help me get the stuff out of the back."

Cameron had no choice but to follow her around to

the back and pull out the basket she'd hidden beneath a large red blanket. Allowing her to lead the way, Cameron had a hard time keeping his eyes off the sway of the hem of her skirt as the lace edge shifted against her skin. He knew firsthand how silky she felt, how perfectly his fingertips slid over her.

Those damn cowgirl boots were only adding to his arousal. She was so modest, so small-town girl, yet everything about her called to him on a level so primal and carnal she'd probably be terrified if she discovered just how much he craved her.

Beyond the physical pull he had toward her, Megan was the only woman who made him want more for his personal life. She was the only woman who inspired him to want to make the impossible actually work.

"I can practically hear you thinking," she called without looking back. "You're not relaxing."

Megan stopped near the edge of the pond. After giving the folded blanket a jerk, she sent it floating down over the grass. Cameron set the basket down and took a seat. She was right. The weather was rather warm for this time of year and he doubted they'd have many days like this left. Taking advantage of the time was a great idea. Now he just had to figure out how to remain in control here.

"For your information, I'm more relaxed now than I have been in weeks," he told her as he flipped the lid on the basket.

Easing down onto the blanket, Megan shifted her legs to her side and smoothed her skirt around her knees. "Liar. You've barely said a word. That tells me you're analyzing something." She pulled out two bottles of water. "Most likely you're overthinking us."

Us. They were an *us* at this point whether he wanted to admit it or not.

Megan continued to pull out items from the basket, as if discussing their confusing relationship with the surmounting tension was an everyday occurrence. Grapes, slices of bread, peanut butter, chips and cookies were all scattered around the blanket before he felt confident enough to speak.

Damn it. He was police chief, for pity's sake. He'd put up with quite a bit in his years on the force, dealt with even more before that when he'd been in the army. Yet here he was, trying to find the right words, the courage to talk to Megan as if nothing had changed.

Everything mattered where she was concerned. That's why he was so nervous about hurting her.

"Can I be honest?" he asked.

Her hand froze in the middle of smearing a generous amount of peanut butter onto a slice of bread. Her eyes lifted to his as a slow smile spread across her face.

"You must really be torn up about something. You've never asked permission to do anything and I've never known you to lie to me." She quirked an arched brow. "Have you lied to me?"

That smile held in place, and he knew she was joking. Little did she know how close she was to the truth. He had lied to her—by omission. He'd kept a secret that would most definitely crush her. And that was just the one about her brother, never mind the truth behind his feelings toward her.

"Okay," she muttered as she went back to making a sandwich. "Apparently your lack of smile or response tells me all I need to know. I never thought you'd actually lie to my face."

Cameron reached out, wrapping his hand around her slender wrist until she looked at him again. "There are things I can't tell you, Megan. You know that. Right now I wanted to talk about what's going on with us. I know you wanted me to relax, but I can't when there's so much between us that we're both trying to ignore."

"Oh, I'm not ignoring anything," she countered. "I'm giving you space to come to grips with the fact we slept together."

A soft breeze filtered through, picking up the curled ends of her hair and sending them dancing. Those silky strands had slid all over his body, he'd threaded his fingers through them, and right now he itched to touch her intimately once again.

"I handled that entire situation wrong," he told her, releasing her wrist.

She reached for another slice of bread and put it on top of the peanut butter. When she offered him the sandwich, he shook his head and started making his own.

"You were so vulnerable," he started, still recalling exactly how she'd trembled. "I was, too, for that matter. I'd hit a breaking point, though. I couldn't hold back anymore."

Megan swallowed a bite of her sandwich, reached for a bottle of water and took a drink before responding. "I don't understand why you denied either of us for so long when we wanted the same thing."

"Because in the end we *don't* want the same thing," he corrected her. "You know my stance on serious relationships, and I know you want a family. We're better off as friends, and I never meant to cross the line because now we're having a damn hard time finding our way back."

Megan plucked off a grape and popped it into her mouth. "There's no reason to turn back. Unless you think sleeping with me was a mistake."

The way her green eyes held his, the way so many questions stared back at him, Cameron found himself shaking his head. "No. That wasn't a mistake. I didn't plan on it, but no way could I call what happened a mistake."

"But you don't want it to happen again."

She couldn't be more wrong. "It can't happen again. Big difference."

With a cocky smile, she went back to her sandwich. He had no clue what that smile meant; more than likely he'd find out because he had no doubt she was plotting something. Cameron finished his sandwich and dived right into the BBQ chips, his favorite. She always kept them on hand for him at her house.

And it was all those little things that added up to make a giant impact on his life.

"So how did you know this property is for sale?" Cameron stretched his legs out in front of him, resting his hands behind his back.

Megan started putting the leftover food back into the

baskct. "I have a coworker whose sister is the Realtor. She told me I could come anytime and fish or swim until the property sold. I guess the land was their parents' and now the sisters don't want it, so they're selling it and splitting the profit."

Cameron looked around at all the old oak trees, the perfectly shaped pond, complete with a small dock for fishing or jumping off. He could practically picture a large, two-story cabin-like home off in the distance on the flat stretch of land.

"Beautiful, isn't it?" she asked.

Cameron glanced back to her. "It is."

He watched as her eyes surveyed the land, saw a soft smile settle on her face. Such a look of happiness and contentment.

"You want this land, don't you?"

Blinking, she met his gaze and shrugged. "Who wouldn't? It's just another daydream, though."

He wanted her to have this, wanted her to achieve all those dreams because her entire life she'd put everyone ahead of her own needs. He knew she'd already fantasized about having a family here, kids running through the field and jumping off a dock into the pond. "Buy it," he told her. "Nothing is holding you back. Buy this land and it will be here when you're ready to build."

Megan lay on her back, her head on his thigh and her booted ankles crossed. She laced her fingers over her abdomen and stared up at the sky.

"There's so much holding me back." Her reply came on a soft sigh as she smiled. "I just want to lie here and pretend for a bit longer. I love the sound of absolute nothing. There's something so peaceful, so perfect about it. Like the world is one big happy place."

Her eyes drifted closed, and Cameron's heart broke for her. All she'd ever wanted was for everyone around her to be happy and have a peaceful life. She wasn't naive by any means, but Cameron wondered if she truly believed she could make that happen. The woman was relentless; she'd try to help everyone she knew or she'd go down swinging.

Unable to keep his hands from her another moment, he smoothed her hair away from her face, trailing his fingertip down along her shoulder. "What's holding you back from buying?" he asked.

He knew she was extremely frugal with her finances and she rarely bought anything for herself. Her house and SUV were both paid off. She wasn't a shopper like some women he knew.

Those bright green eyes focused on his. Sometimes looking at her physically hurt him, because he knew one day she'd find the one. She'd settle down and marry, probably have children. And all that happiness was exactly what he wanted for her. He just couldn't be the one to supply her needs.

"I may be moving."

Cameron's hand stilled, and the fine strands of her hair slid right out of his fingers. "You're moving?"

"I haven't decided yet."

All Cameron could do was stare. The air seemed a bit thicker as the severity of her words hit him like a punch to the stomach. He hadn't seen this coming, and it took a lot to send his shock factor gauge soaring.

"Where would you be moving?" he asked.

"Memphis."

Almost two hours away. Not terribly far, but not down the street, either, as he'd grown used to. He'd already told himself he couldn't have his job and her. Something had to give. He just hadn't been prepared to let her go so far. Damn it, he didn't want this, but she had to make her own choices.

"I was offered a position at a new facility," she told him, her tone soft as if she was afraid to go into details. "That's where I was when I went out of town."

Nodding, Cameron rested his hand at his side. "Did you like the place?"

Why did the selfish part of him want her to say she hated it? Why did he hope she would turn this opportunity down? Hadn't he just told himself he wanted to see her happy, to see all her wishes and dreams come true for once?

Yet here he was, craving her, knowing he wouldn't give in to his own desires all because he wanted her to live the life she deserved and not be tied to the stress and obligations of being with a cop.

"I did." Megan focused back on the sky as the sun took cover behind a large white cloud. "There's just so many pros and cons no matter what decision I make."

"You need to do what's best for you, not what's best for everyone else."

There, that was the right thing to say. Still, the thought of her leaving was like a vise on his heart. He didn't want her to go, but he wouldn't sway her decision unless she asked his opinion. Even then, he wouldn't tell her to stay because he selfishly couldn't stand the thought of going days or even weeks without seeing her.

She was obviously just as torn or she would've told him her decision sooner. "Have you talked to Evan about the move?"

Megan sighed. "No. On one hand, I think leaving and having him come with me would be the fresh start he needs. On the other hand, I don't know that he would come."

Cameron really wished he could tell her that most likely Evan would be in jail before long.

"Don't let Evan factor into this," he commanded, a little harsher than he'd meant to.

Megan's eyes snapped to his. "How can I not?" she asked, jerking up into a sitting position. The way she twisted to confront him had their faces within inches of each other. "He's my only family, and he needs me."

"He needs to help himself for once."

Anger flashed through her eyes. "I won't fight with you about this again. You love Eli and Drake no matter what they do, and I love Evan no matter how much he screws up. He's still my brother."

Cameron wasn't about to state the obvious, that Evan wasn't near the men Eli and Drake were. Megan knew exactly how those three men lived their lives.

Tamping down his worry and frustration, Cameron lifted his hand to her cheek. Stroking his thumb along her soft skin, he held her gaze.

"I want you to make a decision that is strictly self-ish," he told her. "I want you to do whatever you want without thinking of the consequences, without thinking of who will be hurt or angry. What does Megan want?"

Without a word, she shifted away and came to her feet. Toeing off her cowgirl boots, she kept her eyes locked on to his. In a move he hadn't seen coming, she lifted the hem of her skirt and pulled the dress over her head, tossing the garment to the side. Seeing her standing before him in a simple white cotton bra and panties shouldn't have turned him on as much as it did, but every single thing about Megan had his body responding.

"What are you doing?" he asked, cursing his raspy voice.

Reaching around to unfasten her bra, Megan let the straps slide down her arms. "I'm making a selfish decision. Right now, I want to go lay at the edge of the pond and get lost in a fantasy." She met his gaze as she hooked her thumbs in her panties and pulled them down. "With you."

He'd never been one to turn away from a challenge. No matter how many warnings blared through his head, there wasn't a man alive who would turn Megan Richards away.

Even with the high, full trees, sunlight filtered through and seemed to land right on the perfect body she'd placed on display for him.

"What if someone sees us?" he asked.

Megan laughed. "Well, we're pretty secluded and nobody is around. We'll hear a car if it comes up the road. Plus I'm the only one naked, so I guess I'm the only one who should worry about being seen. Am I right?"

She quirked a brow and turned away, heading toward the deck. Cameron came to his feet and began to strip, all the while watching that soft sway of those rounded hips.

There would be no good outcome to this story. Not one. He figured he might as well enjoy every moment with her that he could, because once those warrants came through, Megan would not be throwing those sassy, sultry smiles his way any longer. She'd look at him with disdain, and the thought crushed him.

Right now, he wanted to feel her in his arms, wanted to show her he truly did love her...even if he could never say the words aloud and mean them the way she needed him to.

Chapter Sixteen

Out of all the spontaneous things she'd done in her life, not that there had been many, making love with Cameron out in the open without a care in the world had to top the list.

Come to think of it, making love with Cameron had topped any and all lists she'd ever made or ever would make.

As Megan pulled into her drive after dropping Cameron off, she realized they'd been out much later than she'd meant and she hadn't left a porch light on. The street lamp was enough for her to see, but she still hated coming home to a dark, empty house.

She didn't regret one moment of today, though. Spending the day with Cameron, not worrying about Evan or how this change in her and Cam's dynamic would affect their friendship was quite refreshing.

Speaking of refreshing, her body still tingled as she recalled how Cameron had lifted her naked body against his and walked into the water. The water had been surprisingly warm. When Cameron had knelt down, with her wrapped all around him, and made love to her as the water lapped at their waistlines, she'd fallen completely in love with him. The moment had been perfect, the man even more perfect. And she knew she'd loved him all along, but that moment, that beautiful, special moment, had opened her eyes to what was truly happening between them.

Megan pulled into the garage, grabbed the basket from the trunk and headed to the back door. Holding up her keys toward the glow from streetlights, Megan squealed when a shadow of a man stood on her back steps.

"It's just me."

Heart pounding nearly through her chest, Megan gripped her keys and the basket. "Evan, you scared me to death. Why are you out here in the dark?"

"Can I stay here? At least for tonight?"

Megan stepped forward, still unable to see him very well. "Of course you can. You're my brother."

He shrugged. "I just…I didn't know after the other night."

"Let's get inside and then we'll talk."

She opened the back door and ushered him in ahead of her. After flicking on the kitchen light and setting the basket on the dinette table, she turned to Evan.

"What happened?" she asked, examining his swollen eye and cut lip. This looked far worse than the injury from the other day. And this was the other eye because the other one still sported a fading purple bruise.

Evan sank into a wooden chair at the table. "Wrong place, wrong time. Story of my life."

She wanted to tell him he'd written his own story and it was never too late to start a new chapter, but she figured all that psychoanalyzing would only irritate him even more. It would be the equivalent of teaching a drowning person to swim. Not the time.

So, for now, she'd tend to his wounds and listen. He was here because he felt safe, and she wasn't about to run him off with all the questions swirling around in her mind or by scolding him like a warden.

"Let me get my first-aid kit."

By the time she came back, Evan had flipped the lid off the basket and was making a sandwich.

"I can make you real food if you're hungry." She sat in the chair at the head of the table and checked the supplies in the kit. "I know I have some spaghetti and a quesadilla I could heat up."

Evan shook his head. "This will be fine."

After pulling out the things she needed to fix Evan up, she turned toward him. "I only have one question."

His eyes came up to meet hers. Eyes so like hers, but they'd dimmed somewhere along the way. Perhaps the process had been slow, and that's why she hadn't noticed. Most likely the light started fading when he'd been kicked out of two schools in two years, before junior high. They'd had to move, but eventually Megan came back to her school in Stonerock because she'd missed Cameron and his brothers.

Evan's eyes definitely lost some shine on the night their parents died. Since then he'd been at a rapid decline and spiraling into a territory she feared she'd never rescue him from.

"Are you ready to get out?" she asked.

Evan reached across the space between them and gripped her hand. "Yes."

Relief flooded through her. "Are you on something now?"

She didn't need to go into details; he knew exactly what she was asking.

"No. I don't use. I only supply."

As if that made his position any better? Megan sandwiched his hand in her grip so he'd understand how much she wanted him here, how much she loved him and would support him on all levels.

"We'll get through this, Evan," she promised. "But first we need to go to the police."

"No." He jerked back, shaking his head. "I can't do that. You don't know what those guys are capable of."

Megan repressed a shudder as the memory of being held at gunpoint flashed through her mind. "I've got a pretty good idea," she told him. Easing forward, she pleaded, "Cameron can help, but you have to tell him everything."

Evan closed his eyes and sighed. "I can't right now."

Megan started to say something, but Evan opened his eyes and offered a weak smile. "Just let me get some rest tonight. Okay? Can we discuss this tomorrow?"

He was exhausted and broken. Megan's heart ached for him. But he was making progress, and she wasn't about to upset him further and risk driving him away.

The job opportunity in Memphis was weighing heavily on her mind, especially after being with Cameron again. He'd seemed stunned and speechless about her offer, but she desperately needed to know how he felt about her moving, how that would impact anything they had. At some point he was going to have to be honest with her about what he wanted.

Megan dabbed at the cut on Evan's swollen eye with a cotton ball. After applying some antibiotic ointment, she placed a small butterfly bandage on the wound and turned her attention toward his mouth.

"If we could move away, would you go?" she asked.

"Where would we go?"

Shrugging, Megan didn't want to give too much away about the job offer. "I've thought about Memphis, but I wouldn't do anything without discussing it with you."

"I like it here."

Megan nodded. "If you want to escape the mess you're in, you need to get away, and not just in theory."

A frustrated sigh escaped him. "I don't want to fight. I just want to rest."

"Fine." She wasn't going to get anywhere right now. She had to be patient. "You're more than welcome to stay. Will they come here looking for you?"

"I don't think so."

Megan finished up and started putting supplies

away. "If they come, I am calling Cameron. No arguments. Got it?"

Evan straightened in his seat. "Meg—"

She held up her hand. "No. Arguments." This was her turf, and no way in hell was it going to be penetrated by guys who were only out to cause harm.

"Fine."

He scooted away from the table, rising to his feet as he grabbed his side.

"What's wrong?" She started to reach for him, but he stepped back. "Are you hurt there, too?"

"It's nothing but some bruised ribs. I'm gonna go crash."

With that, Evan turned and headed toward the spare bedroom. Megan stared at the empty doorway, wondering how the conversation would go in the morning. Would Evan still be ready to talk about a new life or would his current fear disappear?

For now, he was safe and she wouldn't go to Cameron unless someone from Evan's circle showed up. She would do anything to keep her brother safe, and now that he was in her home, nobody would get through. She kept a gun for security in her closet. She'd never had to use it before, but she wouldn't hesitate to defend her family. No matter what.

Megan was thankful today was Sunday and she could relax. She tended to work a few hours on Saturday, so Sunday was her only full day off.

Halloween was tomorrow night. She enjoyed seeing the kids in her neighborhood all dressed up in adorable costumes. She couldn't wait until the day she got to parade her own little gremlin or witch around.

Megan had finished making breakfast an hour ago, and when Evan continued to sleep, she covered his plate and set it in the microwave. She wanted him to have a nice home-cooked meal because she doubted anyone else truly cared for him.

Her phone vibrated on the kitchen table. Glancing at the screen, she read Cameron's message.

Still coming to the cookout at my parents'?

Megan hesitated. She'd forgotten all about the cookout and bonfire, complete with s'mores, at Mac and Bev's. But she couldn't leave her brother behind to go to the St. Johns' house, and she couldn't very well take him.

Until she knew how the day unfolded, she wasn't going to respond.

By the time Evan woke, Megan had already cleaned the entire kitchen and dusted her living room. Wearing only his jeans, Evan shuffled in and sank onto the couch. His dark hair stood on end, the bruises over his face and along his right side more prominent this morning. He hadn't let her look last night and she wasn't going to coddle him today. He was a grown man, and he was here for security, not lecturing.

"Morning," he mumbled, raking a hand over his face, the stubble along his jaw and chin bristling beneath his palm. "Thought you'd be at work."

Megan leaned a hip against the back of her oversize chair and crossed her arms. "I don't work on Sunday."

"It's Sunday? I've lost track of the days." He eyed her, drawing his dark brows in. "You have plans?"

"Not really," she replied with a shrug. "You have anything you want to do?"

Evan scratched his bare chest. "I need to get my stuff sometime."

"Where is it?"

"All over. My clothes are at Spider's place. He's cool, though, so I can go there alone. I have a few things at this girl Mary's house, but she's probably sold it all by now."

As Megan listened to her brother go through his list of minute belongings scattered all around, another layer of how different their lives were slid into place. He had no stability, while she thrived on a solid foundation. He had no real friends, and she'd had Cameron and his family since grade school. Evan worried about day-to-day life, whereas Megan worried about advancing in her already successful career.

Where had she gone wrong? At some point along the way she'd missed something.

"If you have plans, go on and do them," Evan told her. "I'm going to go get my clothes and just chill here. I don't expect you to put your life on hold for me."

"I'm not putting my life on hold," she corrected him, easing around the chair. Taking a seat on the edge, she angled her body to face him fully. "Do you have a plan beyond today?"

"Not really." Wincing and grabbing his side, he

started to sit up. "I know you like details and schedules, but that's not me, Meg. I'm not sure about moving, but I wouldn't mind staying here for a while if you don't mind."

Reaching out to pat his leg, she offered a smile. "You're always welcome here, Evan. I just can't have the group you hang around with. I've worked hard to get where I am and I'll do anything to help you. Consider this your home, but if anyone jeopardizes my little world, I won't back down. I'm not afraid of them."

Covering her hand with his, Evan's eyes held hers. "You should be afraid. They're ruthless, Megan. They don't care who they hurt, so long as they have money and drugs. Maybe I should stay somewhere else."

"No," she answered without thinking. "I worry when I don't see you or hear from you. You're staying here, where I can help you."

The muscle moved in his jaw, and his eyes darted down, then back up. "I don't even know if getting out is possible."

"We'll make it possible," she promised.

The back door opened at the same time Cameron's voice called out for her. "Megan?"

"Living room."

Evan's face went from worry for her to instant stone. "You didn't respond earlier so—"

Cameron's words died as he stepped around the corner and froze in the entryway. "Evan."

The tension between these two was so thick it was like a concrete block had been dropped into the room.

Still, she loved them both, and if they loved her, they'd just have to grow up.

"Evan needed a place to crash," she explained.

Cameron didn't take his eyes off Evan. "Looks like he was already in a crash."

"Something like that," Evan muttered.

They'd never made it a secret they weren't buddies, but still, couldn't they at least try to be civil while she was around?

Megan twisted in her seat, letting go of Evan's hand. "What's up?"

Cameron stared at Evan another few seconds before turning his attention to Megan. "I didn't hear from you earlier, so I thought I'd see if you were coming tonight."

"Actually, I probably won't."

"Megan, go," Evan told her. "Don't stay here because of me."

She glanced back to her brother, knowing he expected her to just leave him in pain. He'd just have to get used to the fact that not everyone abandoned him. Damn it, she wanted him to see that she was here no matter what and his needs came before her own.

"I really don't want to leave you alone."

"Because you don't trust me?" he asked, masking his hurt with a rough tone.

"No," she told him, purposely softening her voice. "Because I worry about you, especially after last night."

"You can come, too."

Both Evan and Megan turned to Cameron as his invitation settled in the air between them.

"You're inviting me to your family dinner?" Evan asked.

With a shrug, Cameron leaned a shoulder against the door frame. "Sure. It's no big deal, and you have to eat, too."

Megan held her breath, her eyes darting between the two men. She was beyond shocked that Cameron had invited Evan. That was the type of noble man he was. Cameron was reaching out all because he cared for her and—dare she hope—loved her.

"I don't think your family would want me there," Evan said as he came to his feet.

"They won't mind. Come with Megan if you want or don't come. No big deal. Just extending the offer."

Megan caught Cameron's gaze and mouthed "thank you" when Evan wasn't looking. Cameron's eyes held hers, a small smirk formed on his lips and Megan knew he was only doing this for her.

If she hadn't already loved him, this would've sealed the deal. He was trying. Did that mean he wanted to try more with her, as well?

"I was just heading out for a run and thought I'd swing in," Cameron stated, pushing off the frame. "Megan, I'll see you tonight."

So, he wanted to see her whether Evan came or not. When the front door closed again, Evan glanced down to where she remained seated.

"He's in love with you."

Jerking her eyes up to him, Megan laughed. "Don't be ridiculous, Evan. We've been best friends since grade school."

"The guy has always been territorial with you, but he was looking at you like… Oh, great." Evan shook his head and laughed. "Tell me you didn't fall in love with him. Come on, Meg. He's a cop."

Yeah, he was a cop. He was also perfect for her little world, amazing in bed and irreplaceable.

"Who I love or don't love is really none of your concern," she told him. "I'm not being rude, but you have your own issues to work out. Now, if you want to come with me later, that's fine. If you don't, that's fine, too. I'll be leaving at six."

Megan turned and left Evan alone. She didn't want to hear anything else about why she should or shouldn't fall in love with Cameron. The reasons were moot at this point because she'd already fallen so deep, she'd never find her way back out.

Chapter Seventeen

Keep your friends close and your enemies closer.

Cameron had always hated that saying. Having enemies so close made him twitchy and irritable.

As he glanced across the field toward Evan, who sat in a folding chair all by himself, Cameron figured if Evan was here, he wasn't getting into anything illegal. Megan could rest easy tonight.

Speaking of Megan, she'd gotten cold earlier when the sun had gone down and he'd grabbed a hoodie sweatshirt from the back of his truck. The fact she was wrapped in his shirt made him feel even more territorial. The way she all but disappeared inside the fleecy material made her seem even more adorable. How could a woman be so many things at once? Sexy, cute, intriguing, strong… Megan was all of that and much more.

She laughed at something Eli said before turning her gaze and meeting his. Instantly the air crackled. Nothing else mattered but Megan. The case should be wrapped up by tomorrow evening when the next "trade" took place. He knew all key players were supposed to be in attendance, according to their inside source.

Maybe once all of this was tied up, maybe once Evan was out of the picture and not weighing so heavily on Megan's mind and conscience, she would figure out how to seek that happiness she deserved.

Drake came to stand beside Megan, and she turned, breaking the moment. Only Eli knew of the tension between them, and Cameron doubted anyone else was picking up on the vibes he and Megan were sending out.

Cameron's gaze darted back to Evan…who was shooting death glares across the distance. Okay, maybe one more person knew something was happening between him and Megan, but Cameron didn't care what Evan's opinion was.

"You seem quiet tonight."

Cameron merely nodded as his father came up beside him. "Been a stressful time at work," Cameron replied.

"Looks to me like you have something else on your mind."

Cameron glanced to his father, who was looking straight at Megan. She excused herself, picked up a roasting stick and took it over to her brother. Cameron watched as they talked, and finally Evan came to his feet, took the stick, and he and Megan went over to the fire to roast marshmallows.

"I figured you two would figure this out eventually," his father went on.

Cameron groaned inwardly. "There's nothing to figure out, Dad. We're friends."

"Friends is a good start," Mac agreed. "Building on that only makes a stronger relationship."

Frustration slid through him. He really didn't want to get into this right now with his dad...or anybody else for that matter.

"Look, Dad—"

"Hear me out." Mac turned to face Cameron. The wrinkles around his father's eyes were more prominent as he drew his brows together. "You are overthinking things, son. Megan isn't going to wait around for you to come to your senses."

Clenching his fists at his side, Cameron nodded. "I don't expect her to. Things would be easier if she met someone and moved on."

"Easier for you?" he asked. "Because from where I'm standing, Megan only has eyes for one person. I figured you'd be smart enough to make your friendship more permanent."

"You don't get it," Cameron began, absently noting that Evan had taken a phone call.

"Get what?" Licking marshmallow off his thumb, Drake came up beside their dad.

"Nothing," Cameron stated.

"Your brother is having women problems."

Still focused on his gooey thumb, Drake laughed. "Megan giving you fits?"

What the hell? Is nothing sacred around here?

"I'm going to kill Eli," Cameron muttered.

Drake's smile widened. "He didn't tell me. Marly

did. Women just seem to be in tune with each other, but I think something happened when they all went out to Dolly's the other night."

Had Megan mentioned him to Marly and Nora? Surely she hadn't.

When he sought her out again, she was helping Willow roast a marshmallow. She fit in perfectly with his family. What would happen if he decided to take a chance? What would happen if he gave in to both of their needs and took this friendship beyond the bedroom?

"For what it's worth," Drake went on, "I think Megan is great. I always figured you guys would end up together."

Apparently every single person in his family had some creepy psychic ability because Cameron had fought the urge for years to ever make Megan more than a buddy or a pal. Unfortunately he knew firsthand just how sexy and feisty his "pal" was.

Evan rushed to Megan's side as he slid his phone back into his pocket. Just as Evan said something to her and hurried toward the front of the house, Cameron's cell vibrated in his pocket.

"Excuse me," he told his father and Drake.

Stepping away from the crowd, he pulled out the phone and read the text.

Moving day changed. 30 min.

Damn it. That's why Evan rushed out?

Cameron caught Drake's eye. "Something came up. Tell everyone—"

Drake waved him away. "Go—we know."

This family was more than used to Cameron getting called away. All three St. John brothers were in high demand in Stonerock, so it wasn't unusual for at least one of them to get called away from a family gathering.

Cameron rushed to his house to grab his work gun and Kevlar vest. Thankfully, the designated parking lot was less than ten minutes away. By the time he pulled in, he still had ten minutes to spare.

The outcome tonight was not going to be good, but right now all Cameron could focus on was doing his job. Just when he'd been about to open himself up to the possibility of a relationship with Megan, this call had come through. Was it a sign that keeping his distance was the right thing to do?

Cameron settled in with his fellow officers and FBI agents. Now all they had to do was watch and wait, and hopefully this entire ordeal would be wrapped up tonight.

He had no idea if he should be elated or terrified.

Megan had no clue where Evan had run off to and then Cameron had gotten called into work. She'd stayed behind and chatted with Nora and Marly, roasted more marshmallows than her stomach appreciated and now lay curled up in the corner of her sofa trying to read a book by the vomited light of the evil dragon.

Megan couldn't help but look at that tacky piece and laugh. Because if she didn't laugh, she'd surely cry. Some people had a beautiful art sculpture or painting as the focal point in their living rooms. Nope, Megan had this monstrosity.

Flipping through the pages of her book, Megan wanted to see when the good scenes were coming up because the current chapter was nearly putting her to sleep.

Before she could decide whether or not to give up, her cell rang. Dropping the book on the end table, she picked up her phone, not recognizing the number. Most likely a client.

"Hello?"

"Meg. I've been arrested."

Jumping to her feet, Megan started toward her bedroom to put clothes on. "What happened, Evan?"

Dread flooded her. Whatever he'd hightailed it out of the St. Johns' party for had obviously not been a good idea.

"Your boyfriend brought me in." Evan's tone was filled with disgust. "I wasn't doing anything, Meg. I need you to come get me."

Cameron arrested Evan? How the hell had the night gone from roasting marshmallows to her brother being thrown in jail?

"How much is bail?" she asked, shoving her feet into her cowgirl boots.

"I don't think they're allowing it to be set."

Megan froze. "What did you do?"

"Listen, I need you to fix this, Meg," he pleaded, near hysterics. "I don't want to be here. Call your attorney and get me out of this place."

Megan sank onto the edge of her bed. "If bail isn't an option, there's nothing I can do right now. I'll call my lawyer, but I doubt he can do anything tonight, either."

"Maybe you should tell Cameron I'm innocent," he spat, seconds before hanging up.

Defeated, angry and cold, Megan stared at the cell in her hand. In her heart she'd known this day was coming. Evan had reached out to her for help only twenty-four hours ago...obviously too late to make a difference.

Before she could allow her mind to travel into what Cameron knew about this situation, she had to call her attorney. Evan's fear had been apparent through the line. She knew from a few of her clients just how terrifying being arrested for the first time could be. No matter what the attorney's fee would be, she'd pay it and do every single thing in her power to get him away from this city where he was only staying in trouble. If he wanted to truly get away, he needed a fresh start away from the thugs he'd been with.

Hours later, Megan was still wound tight. She'd discovered there was nothing to do for Evan right now. There would be a hearing on Monday morning to decide the next step.

Megan had hung up with her attorney thirty minutes ago and couldn't go in to bed if she tried. She glanced at the book on the end table and knew that wouldn't hold her interest, either.

Heading to the hall closet, she was just about to sink to a whole new level of desperate and pull out her vacuum when her back door opened and closed.

The late hour didn't stop Cameron from letting himself in. *Great.* She wasn't sure she was ready to deal with this, with him. She was still shaking from the fact that her brother was behind bars with criminals and her best friend had arrested him.

Moving down the hall, she met Cameron just as he stepped out of the kitchen. The dark bruise beneath his eye, the cut across his other brow and his disheveled clothes stopped her in her tracks.

"What the hell happened tonight?" she cried. "Evan's arrested and you've been in a fight."

Cameron's tired eyes closed as he shook his head. "I wanted to be the one to tell you about Evan, but I knew there was no way I could finish everything up and get here before he called you."

Anger coursed through her. "You knew my brother was in trouble. Enough trouble to get arrested, didn't you?"

Slowly, his lids opened, those signature baby blues locked on her. "Yes. I've been watching him for some time now. Him and several others."

Megan felt as if someone had taken a pointy-toed shoe and kicked her straight in the stomach.

"Evan wasn't a key player," Cameron went on. "He just fell in with the wrong crowd and ended up deeper than I think he intended."

Bursts of cold shot through her system. Megan wrapped her arms around her waist and pushed past Cameron.

"So you just arrest him anyway?" she asked, moving to the living room to sink onto the sofa. "You know he's trying to break away and you still arrest him like some hardened criminal?"

Cameron rested his hands on his hips, remaining across the room. "He is a criminal, Meg. He was with the group we've been tracking for months. Evan has been running drugs."

No. This was her brother, her baby brother. She didn't want this to be his life even though he'd admitted as much to her just yesterday. He'd said he wanted to get out. She'd give anything if he would have come to her sooner; maybe they wouldn't be in this position now.

Bending forward, her arms still tight around her midsection, she wanted to just curl up and cry or scream. "You should go," she whispered, already feeling the burn of tears in her throat.

"I'm not leaving until we talk."

Of course he wasn't.

"I know you aren't happy with me right now," he started. "But you have to know I was doing my job. I can't let our relationship prevent me from keeping Stonerock safe."

A laugh erupted from her before she could prevent it. Megan sat back up and rested her elbows on her knees.

"I don't expect you to not do your job, Chief. But I never thought you'd be spying on my brother one minute and sleeping with me the next."

Okay, he deserved that. Megan needed to get all her anger out because he'd had months to deal with the fact that Evan was into illegal activities. While Megan had suspected her brother's involvement, tonight she'd been dealt some cold, hard facts—and then learned her best friend was the arresting officer.

"How could you do this to me?" she asked, her voice husky from emotion. "How could you use me like that? We've been friends so long, Cam. I trusted you with everything in my life and you just…"

Her words died in the air as she covered her face with her hands. Sobs tore through her, filling the room and slicing his heart. Cameron knew full well that right at this moment she felt she hated him, but that didn't stop him from stepping forward and squatting down in front of her.

"I didn't use you," he said, realizing how pathetic he sounded. "I couldn't tell you, Meg. I wanted to. I wanted you to know what you were in the midst of. I wanted to somehow soften the blow, but my hands were tied."

Her hands dropped to her lap as she focused her watery stare on him. Tear tracks marred her creamy skin, and Cameron knew if he attempted to reach out to wipe away the physical evidence of her pain, she would push him away.

"You mean you chose your job again over everything else. Over me."

Cameron eased up enough to sit on the edge of the coffee table, his elbows on his knees, as he fought the urge to take her hands in his. She had to get all this anger out, and he had to absorb it. There was no other way to move beyond this mess…if they even could move on.

"Wait." Megan sat up straighter, her gaze darting to the floor, then back up to his. "You were there, weren't you? The night I was with Evan and those guys showed up?"

Regret filled him, cutting off any pathetic defense he could've come up with. As if the entire lying-by-omission thing weren't enough, now he had to face the ugly truth that he'd not done a damn thing to help her.

She continued to stare at him, continued to study him as if she didn't even recognize him anymore. "Tell me you weren't there," she whispered.

Swallowing a lump of rage and remorse all rolled into one, he replied, "I can't."

He expected her to slap him, to stand up and charge from the room or start yelling and throwing things. He expected pure anger. Anger he could've dealt with.

But when she closed her eyes, unleashing a fresh set of tears as she fell back against the couch, defeated, Cameron knew he'd broken something between them. He'd broken something in her, and he had no idea how to fix it or even if their relationship was repairable.

"I want to hate you right now."

Those harsh words from such a tiny voice was the equivalent of salt to the wound…a self-inflicted wound. He had absolutely nobody to blame but himself.

Megan eased up, just enough to look him in the eye. "I want to hate you so you'll be out of my life, so I never have to see you again," she told him through tears. "But I can't because no matter how deeply you hurt me, I still love you. Damn it, Cameron, I love you more than I've ever loved anybody. I was prepared to turn down this job in Memphis for you. I was ready to fight for you, for us."

Her voice shook as she went on, swiping at the tears streaking down her cheeks. "I was ready to live with your dedication to your job. I foolishly thought you could love me just as much, but now I know I'll never be equal, never be enough."

Cameron had no clue he'd shed his own tears until he felt the trickle down his cheek. He'd never cried over a woman. Hell, he couldn't recall the last time he'd cried at all. But Megan was worth the emotion; she was worth absolutely everything.

"Stay," he pleaded. "Don't take the job. We can get through this."

"Can we?" she tossed back. "And how would we do that? You spied on my brother for who knows how long. You watched me from a distance during one of my scariest moments. I think that is enough to prove you'd never put me first, so don't preach to me about staying to make this work. I've been here for years, Cam. Years. I can't help it if you're just now ready."

Megan came to her feet, anger fueling her now if the way she swatted at the tears on her face was any indication. Cameron eased back on the table but didn't rise. He knew she needed the control, the upper hand here.

"You always said you wouldn't ever make a woman compete with your job," she went on. "But what do you think I've been doing all this time? I was with you during deployments, during the police academy and your entire law enforcement career. You think I worried less because we were friends and not married? You think I didn't play the 'what-if' game while you were overseas or if a day or two went by that I didn't hear from you?"

Reality hit him square in the gut.

"You're right." Slowly, he got to his feet. Considering she didn't back away, he reached for her hands. "You were there for me every step of the way. I didn't see your angle until now, or maybe I was afraid to."

Megan fisted her hands beneath his. "You need to go. I'm exhausted. I've got to figure out what I can do for Evan, and I need to make arrangements for Memphis."

The last bit of hope he'd had died as he released her fists. "You're leaving."

Megan's gaze slid to the floor as she nodded, not saying a word. Conversation over.

There had never been such an emptiness, such a hollow feeling in his soul. The bond they'd honed and strengthened for years had just been severed in the span of minutes. He'd known how this would hurt her, but he hadn't expected her to erect this steel wall between them, completely shutting him out.

Cameron turned, headed toward the back door.

"Did you ever love me?" Megan's question tore through the thick tension.

Stopping, Cameron leaned a hand on the door frame to steady himself. Not only was he starting to tear up again but his knees were shaking.

"I've always loved you," he told her. "More than you could ever know."

When she said nothing in reply, Cameron headed straight out the back door. He had to keep going or he'd drop to his knees and beg her forgiveness. But Megan wasn't in the frame of mind to forgive.

He had a feeling after all he'd done to destroy their friendship and the intimacy they'd discovered, she never would be.

Chapter Eighteen

Two weeks later, Evan was still in jail. She'd been able to see him several times and each time she went her heart broke even more. He'd hinted that maybe he'd be getting out soon, but she couldn't get details from him.

After taking another picture from the wall, Megan wrapped it in bubble wrap and placed it in the box with the other fragile items. Her new job was to start in two weeks and she was moving in to her new rental within days.

The thought of leaving this house that she'd loved for so long had her reminiscing with each room she walked through, each item she boxed up. She'd yet to pack the dragon lamp because each time she passed by the hideous thing, she started tearing up once again.

In the two weeks since she'd last seen Cameron, her

emotions had been all over the place. She'd gone from angry to depressed, from crying to yelling at the empty space. Other than during his deployments, she'd never gone this long without seeing or talking to him. How could her best friend since childhood be out of her life so fast? How did she move on without the stability and support he'd always offered?

By sticking to her plans. She would move towns, make new friends and start a new life. And if Evan somehow miraculously got out, he could join her.

Of course, all of that would be in a perfect world, and she knew she lived in anything but.

Tomorrow she'd have the difficult task of telling her clients that she was leaving. She'd really formed some wonderful friendships during her time at the counseling center. Her supervisor was sorry to see her go, but understood, considering she'd been the one to recommend Megan for the position.

Before she could pull another piece of artwork from the wall, the doorbell rang. Glancing around the boxes, bubble wrap and her own state of haphazardness, Megan shrugged. She wasn't expecting company, though she'd been surprised Cameron hadn't attempted to contact her again. A piece of her was disappointed and a little more than hurt at the fact, but she'd told him to go and he was honoring her wishes. Noble until the end, that man was.

Adjusting her ratty old T-shirt and smoothing back the wayward strands that had escaped her ponytail, Megan flicked the lock and tugged on the door.

Speak of the devil.

Only he didn't look like the devil at all. He didn't even look worn and haggard as she did. Damn the man for standing on her porch looking all polished and tempting. The fall breeze kicked up, bringing his familiar scent straight to her and teasing her further.

His eyes darted behind her, no doubt taking in the chaos.

"When do you leave?" he asked, returning those baby blues to her.

Gripping the door frame, she prayed for strength, prayed to be able to hold it together while she figured out the reason for his visit.

"Next week."

He glanced down, then back up and sighed. "Can I come in? Just for a minute?"

Said the lion to its prey.

Megan stepped back, opening the old oak door even more to accommodate his broad frame. As soon as he entered, she closed the door, leaned back against it and waited while he continued to survey the room.

"I came to fill you in on Evan."

He turned to face her, and now that he was closer, she could see the worry lines etched between his brows, more prominent than ever. The dark circles beneath his eyes were evidence he'd been sleeping about as much as she had.

"What about him?" she asked, crossing her arms over her chest, resisting the urge to touch Cameron just one more time.

"I'm not supposed to tell you this, so please don't say anything. This could cost me my badge."

Megan stood up straighter. He was here as her friend, putting her above his job for once. A piece of the hard shell around her heart crumbled.

"Is he in more trouble?" she asked, fearful for the unknown.

"No." Cameron toyed with the open flap of a box on the coffee table. "He's actually going to take a plea bargain. He was offered immunity in exchange for every bit of information he knows."

Elation filled her. Megan clutched the scoop neck of her T-shirt and sucked in a deep breath. "Thank you," she whispered, unable to say anything else.

"There's more."

She tensed up at Cameron's hard stare. Whatever the "more" was apparently wasn't good news.

"He's going to go into Witness Protection first thing in the morning."

Witness Protection. The words registered but not fully at first. Then she realized what Cameron was truly telling her.

"I won't see him again?"

Shaking his head, Cameron held her gaze for a moment, then looked away as if he couldn't bear to see her. "I tried to get you in, but that power is above me. I had to fight to get the immunity. He had some stiff charges against him, but since he was a latecomer to the group, we needed the big names he could provide."

Megan nodded, hating what he was saying but knowing this was for the best. This was the only option for her brother to make a fresh start and stay safe.

"Could I write him a letter or something?" she asked. "Maybe you could get it to him?"

The muscle in Cameron's jaw jumped. "I can't."

Megan pulled in a shaky breath and pushed away from the door. Heading back to her task, something she had control over and something she could concentrate on, she pulled a picture off the wall and tore off more bubble wrap.

Methodically, she wrapped the frame, all the while coming to grips with the new level of pain that had settled deep into her chest.

"If you happen to have something that needs to be said, I could perhaps stop by and tell him before they take him away."

Cameron's generous offer hovered between them. After placing the package in the box, she closed the flaps and held her hand over the opening as she focused on Cameron.

"Tell him...just tell him I'm proud of him and I love him." Megan couldn't believe she'd never be able to tell him in person again, but if this was all she had, she was going to take it. Cameron nodded and turned to go. Megan stared at his back. Had he only come to deliver the message? Weren't they going to talk about anything or even pretend to be...what? What could they discuss at this point? She'd thrown him out weeks ago, and she hadn't extended a branch to him since.

"Cam," she called just as his hand fell to her door-knob. "Wait."

Glancing over his shoulder, he raised a brow as his eyes locked on to hers.

Gathering her strength and courage, she stepped around the coffee table and crossed the room to stand in front of him. He turned to face her, but the minuscule space between them may as well have been an ocean for all the tension that settled in the slot.

"Thank you."

Megan looked up at him, at the man she'd fallen so deeply in love with, and seriously had no clue how she would go on without Evan or Cameron in her life.

"I know Evan and I had our issues," Cameron started. "But we have one thing in common. We both love you."

Megan swallowed the tears that threatened. The last time Cameron had been here she'd cried enough to last a lifetime.

"We both want to see you happy," he went on. "Unfortunately we both had a terrible way of showing it."

Cameron started to reach out, then stopped. She glanced at his hand, hovering so close, and slid her fingers through his.

"They always say the ones you love the most can hurt you the most." The feel of his hand in hers sent a warmth spreading through her—a warmth she'd missed for two weeks. "I didn't know that to be true until recently."

Cameron's free hand slid along the side of her face. Megan tilted her head just enough to take the comfort he was offering.

"To know that you did this for Evan means everything to me," she added. "The thought of not seeing him again hurts, but it's far better than seeing him through glass. He'll have freedom and he'll be able to start over. That's all I've ever wanted for him."

"What about you?" Cameron's thumb stroked her cheek, the simple touch sending chills all over her body. "Are you going to start over?"

"That's my plan," she muttered. "It's my only option at this point."

Cameron's mouth covered hers without warning. The hungry kiss started so demandingly, Megan had no choice but to clutch at his wide shoulders. Just as she was getting used to being overtaken, Cam lightened his touch, turning the kiss into something less forceful but every bit as potent and primal.

By the time he eased away and rested his head against hers, they were both panting.

"I'm begging you, Meg. Don't leave." Both his hands framed her face; the strength of his body covered hers, and the raw words hit her straight in her heart. "I don't care if I look weak or pathetic. I'll beg you to stay. I need you so much more than you need me. You're so strong, and I know you would be just fine in Memphis. But I would not be okay here without you."

Wrapping her arms around his waist, Megan couldn't hold back any longer. The dam completely burst and tears she'd sworn never to shed in front of him again came flooding out. Cameron enveloped her, pulling her tighter against his chest as she let out all her fear, worry and uncertainty.

"I know I broke something in you with the choices I made." His hand smoothed up and down her back, comforting her. "I'll spend the rest of my life making all of that up to you. Please, please give me a chance."

"I'm scared, Cam," she murmured into his chest. "What happens when another big case comes along? What happens the next time you shut me out? What will I do when you decide the job is more important than I am or we are?"

Pulling back, Cameron looked her in the eye. "Nothing is more important than you are. Nothing. I came here expecting nothing from you, Megan. I came here to tell you about Evan, knowing full well that I could lose my job if anyone found out. I don't care. You are worth every risk, every chance I'll ever take."

Megan hiccupped as the next onslaught of tears took over. "I'm a mess," she told him, wiping the backs of her hands over her cheeks. "Look what you do to me."

His eyes focused on her. "I'm looking, and I've never seen a more beautiful woman in my life. You're it for me, Megan. I want to marry you and start a family with you. I know that's a lot to absorb right now, but just stay so we can work this out."

Megan couldn't believe what he was saying. He wanted to marry her?

"If you can't stay, if you're already committed and cannot get out of the Memphis job, or if that's really where your heart is, we can buy a place between here and there and we'll commute." Cameron kissed her lightly once more. "Just say you'll give us a chance."

"How could I refuse you?" she told him, raining kisses over his face. "How could I ever let you go?"

Cameron picked her up and started toward the hallway. "You'll never have to find out."

By the time they hit the bedroom, Megan knew she wasn't going anywhere for a long, long time.

Epilogue

"How much farther?"

Cameron squeezed Megan's hand and laughed. "Just don't move that blindfold. We're almost there."

"I think you're just driving in circles," she mumbled. "If you keep going too much farther, I'm going to get carsick. We're supposed to be on our way to our honeymoon."

They'd been married for three hours. He'd promised her a memorable wedding night, and he intended to deliver, but they weren't going far. He'd requested she keep her wedding dress on, told her it was important to him.

He glanced over, still a little choked up at the vision in white lace beside him. Her strapless gown fitted her body beautifully from her breasts to her waist with such a delicate fabric, he was afraid to touch her. In just a few short minutes she'd see why he wanted to keep her in her wedding gown. The airport could wait until tomorrow.

Tonight, he had a special surprise.

Cameron turned onto the dirt road and brought his truck to a stop just in front of the clearing. "Don't move. I'll come around to get you."

By the time he'd gotten Megan out of the truck and stood her beside him, she was looking a bit pale.

"You feeling okay?" he asked. "I thought you were joking about the carsick thing."

Megan whipped off her blindfold. "I'm not carsick— I'm pregnant," she cried.

Shock slid over him at the same time she gasped as she took in her surroundings. "What are we doing back here?" she asked.

Cameron couldn't think, couldn't speak. His gaze darted to her flat stomach beneath her vintage gown and all he could think was he was going to be a father. He and Megan were going to be parents.

With a shout, he wrapped his arms around her, picked her up and spun her in a circle, the train of her dress wrapping around his feet.

"Sickness, remember?" she yelled.

Easing her down, Cameron kissed her thoroughly. "How long have you known?" he asked when he pulled back.

"I just took a test at home this morning. I wanted to wait until after the reception to tell you, when we were alone, but then you said you had a surprise for me so I waited."

The flash of her coming down the aisle, smiling with tears in her eyes took on a whole new meaning now. She'd been radiant, beaming, a bright light coming toward him to make his life complete. She'd been there all along, and he was so thankful she hadn't given up on them.

Their ceremony had been perfect, planned by his sisters-in-law, his mother and Megan. The church had been covered in a variety of flowers, vibrant colors splashed all around. No doubt all of it was gorgeous, but he'd only had eyes for Megan. There was nothing more beautiful than seeing your best friend walk toward you, knowing you were going to start down a path that would forever bind you in love. And when she'd kissed him, he'd felt every bit of her love. And he wanted to spend the rest of his life showing her how precious she was to him.

Cameron choked back his own tears because this was the happiest day of his life. He didn't deserve all of this, but he was going to embrace every bit of it and build a family with the only woman he'd ever wanted.

"You've picked the perfect time to tell me." Laughing, Cameron held out his arms and eased the train aside with his foot. "This is it. I bought this for us to build our house on."

A wide smile spread across her face. "You're serious? You mean it?"

Seeing how happy she was made draining his entire savings completely worth it. A baby on the way, a new house and a wedding just around the holidays was a whole lot to be thankful for.

"I wanted to see you here, on our land in that dress." He reached out and stroked her cheek. "I wanted to capture this moment, this memory with you because I know it's only going to get better."

"I'm so glad I decided not to take that job in Memphis," she told him, still smiling. "How did you keep this a secret from me?"

Cameron shrugged. "It wasn't easy and I know I promised not to lie to you ever again, but I really wanted this to be a surprise."

"Oh, Cameron." Megan plastered herself against his side, wrapping her arms around his waist. "This is going to be perfect for our family. And maybe by this time next year we'll have our house done, and we can have all of your family over for the holidays. We'll have our little baby for everyone to fuss over."

Kissing the top of her head, Cameron smiled as he surveyed the land. "I think that sounds like a plan. First thing we'll move into the house will be—"

"Don't say it," she warned.

"Come on," he joked. "The lamp has to come with us."

Megan tipped her face up to his. "The only place that lamp needs to go is the Dumpster."

Squeezing her tight, Cameron rubbed her back. "Well, we can negotiate that later, but I think it would be a great piece for the nursery."

Smacking his abdomen, Megan groaned. "I will not give our child nightmares."

"You're right. It should stay in the living room. It has made quite a conversation starter."

Megan laughed, easing up on her toes to kiss his cheek. "You know I love you, but it's either me or the dragon lamp."

Turning to fully engulf her in his arms, Cameron smiled and slid his lips across hers. "You. It's always been you."

* * * * *

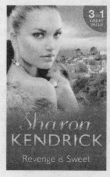

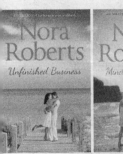
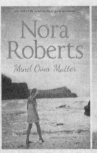
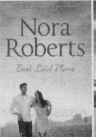
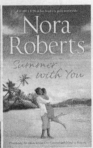

MILLS & BOON®

The Thirty List

* cover in development

At thirty, Rachel has slid down every ladder she has ever climbed. Jobless, broke and ditched by her husband, she has to move in with grumpy Patrick and his four-year-old son.

Patrick is also getting divorced, so to cheer themselves up the two decide to draw up bucket lists. Soon they are learning to tango, abseiling, trying stand-up comedy and more. But, as she gets closer to Patrick, Rachel wonders if their relationship is too good to be true...

Order yours today at
www.millsandboon.co.uk/Thethirtylist

The World of
MILLS & BOON®

HISTORICAL

*Awaken the romance
of the past*
6 new stories every month

*The ultimate in romantic
medical drama*
6 new stories every month

MODERN™

*Power, passion and
irresistible temptation*
8 new stories every month

By Request

*Relive the romance with the
best of the best*
12 stories every month

WORLD_ M&B2b

MILLS & BOON®

Cherish™

EXPERIENCE THE ULTIMATE RUSH OF FALLING IN LOVE

A sneak peek at next month's titles…

In stores from 15th May 2015:

- **His Unexpected Baby Bombshell** – Soraya Lane *and* **The Instant Family Man** – Shirley Jump

- **Falling for the Bridesmaid** – Sophie Pembroke *and* **Fortune's June Bride** – Allison Leigh

In stores from 5th June 2015:

- **Her Red-Carpet Romance** – Marie Ferrarella *and* **A Millionaire for Cinderella** – Barbara Wallace

- **Falling for the Mum-to-Be** – Lynne Marshall *and* **From Paradise…to Pregnant!** – Kandy Shepherd

Available at WHSmith, Tesco, Asda, Eason, Amazon and Apple

Just can't wait?
Buy our books online a month before they hit the shops!
visit www.millsandboon.co.uk

These books are also available in eBook format!